On the Beach

He leaned towards her. 'The thing is this, dear. There's no recovery. But you don't have to die in a mess. You can die decently, when things begin to get too bad.' He drew the smaller of the two red boxes from his pocket.

She stared at it, fascinated. 'What's that?' she whispered.

He undid the little carton and took out the vial. 'This is a dummy,' he said. 'These aren't real. Goldie gave it me to show you what to do. You just take one of them with a drink – any kind of drink. Whatever you like best. And then you just lie back, and that's the end.'

'You mean, you die?' The cigarette was dead between her fingers.

He nodded. 'When it gets too bad – it's the way out.'

'What's the other pill for?' she whispered.

'That's a spare,' he said. 'I suppose they give it you in case you lose one of them, or funk it.'

Nevil Shute

On the Beach

Mandarin

A Mandarin Paperback

ON THE BEACH

First published 1957 by William Heinemann Ltd
This edition published 1990 by Mandarin Paperbacks
Michelin House, 81 Fulham Road, London SW3 6RB

Mandarin is an imprint of the Octopus Publishing Group

Copyright © by the Trustees of
the Estate of the late Nevil Shute Norway
© 1957

A CIP catalogue record for this book
is available from the British Library
ISBN 0 7493 0408 1

Printed in Great Britain
by Cox & Wyman Ltd, Reading

In this last of meeting places
We grope together
And avoid speech
Gathered on this beach of the tumid river . . .

This is the way the world ends
This is the way the world ends
This is the way the world ends
Not with a bang but a whimper.

T. S. Eliot

ACKNOWLEDGEMENT

The lines from 'The Hollow Men' in *Collected Poems* 1909-1935 by T. S. Eliot are printed by permission of Faber & Faber Ltd.

I

Lieutenant-Commander Peter Holmes of the Royal Australian Navy woke soon after dawn. He lay drowsily for a while, lulled by the warm comfort of Mary sleeping beside him, watching the first light of the Australian sun upon the cretonne curtains of their room. He knew from the sun's rays that it was about five o'clock: very soon the light would wake his baby daughter Jennifer in her cot, and then they would have to get up and start doing things. No need to start before that happened; he could lie a little longer.

He woke happy, and it was some time before his conscious senses realized and pinned down the origin of this happiness. It was not Christmas, because that was over. He had illuminated the little fir tree in their garden with a string of coloured lights with a long lead to the plug beside the fireplace in the lounge, a small replica of the great illuminated tree a mile away outside the Town Hall of Falmouth. They had had a barbecue in the garden on the evening of Christmas Day, with a few friends. Christmas was over, and this – his mind turned over slowly – this must be Thursday the 27th. As he lay in bed the sunburn on his back was still a little sore from their day on the beach yesterday, and from sailing in the race. He would do well to keep his shirt on today. And then, as consciousness came fully to him, he realized that of course he would keep his shirt on today. He had a date at eleven o'clock in the Second Naval Member's office, in the Navy Department up in Melbourne. It meant a new appointment, his first work for five months. It could even mean a seagoing job if he were very lucky, and he ached for a ship again.

It meant work, anyway. The thought of it had made him happy when he went to sleep, and his happiness had lasted through the night. He had had no appointment since he had been promoted lieutenant-commander in August and in the circumstances of the time he had almost given up hope of ever working again. The Navy Department, however, had maintained him on full pay throughout these months, and he was grateful to them.

The baby stirred, and started chuntering and making little whimpering noises. The naval officer reached out and turned the switch of the electric kettle on the tray of tea things and baby food beside the bed, and Mary stirred beside him. She asked the time, and he told her. Then he kissed her, and said, 'It's a lovely morning again.'

She sat up, brushing back her hair. 'I got so burned yesterday. I put some calamine stuff on Jennifer last night, but I really don't think she ought to go down to the beach again today.' Then she, too, recollected. 'Oh – Peter, it's today you're going up to Melbourne, isn't it?'

He nodded. 'I should stay at home, have a day in the shade.'

'I think I will.'

He got up and went to the bathroom. When he came back Mary was up, too; the baby was sitting on her pot and Mary was drawing a comb through her hair before the glass. He sat down on the edge of the bed in a horizontal beam of sunlight, and made the tea.

She said, 'It's going to be very hot in Melbourne today, Peter. I thought we might go down to the club about four, and you join us there for a swim. I could take the trailer and your bathers.'

They had a small car in the garage, but since the short war had ended a year previously it remained unused. However, Peter Holmes was an ingenious man and good with tools, and he had contrived a tolerable substitute. Both Mary and he had bicycles. He had built a small two-wheeled trailer using the front wheels of two motor bicycles, and he had contrived a trailer hitch on both Mary's bicycle and his own so that either could pull this thing, which served them as a perambulator and a general goods carrier. Their chief trouble was the long hill up from Falmouth.

He nodded. 'That's not a bad idea. I'll take my bike and leave it at the station.'

'What train have you got to catch?'

'The nine-five.' He sipped his tea and glanced at his watch. 'I'll go and get the milk as soon as I've drunk this.'

He put on a pair of shorts and a singlet and went out. He lived in the ground floor flat of an old house upon the hill above the town that had been divided into apartments; he had the garage and a good part of the garden in his share of the property. There was a veranda, and here he kept the bicycles and the trailer. It would have been logical to park the car under the trees and use the garage, but he could not bring himself to do that. The little Morris was the first car he had ever owned, and he had courted Mary in it. They had been married in 1961 six months before the war, before he sailed in HMAS *Anzac* for what they thought would be indefinite separation. The short, bewildering war had followed, the war of which no history had been written or ever would be written now, that had flared all round the northern hemisphere and had died away with the last seismic record of explosion on the thirty-seventh day. At the end of the third month he had returned to Williamstown in *Anzac* on the last of her fuel oil while the statesmen of the southern hemisphere gathered in conference at Wellington in New Zealand to compare notes and assess the new conditions; had returned to Falmouth to his Mary and his Morris Minor car. The car had three gallons in the tank; he used that unheeding, and another five that he bought at a pump, before it dawned upon Australians that all oil came from the northern hemisphere.

He pulled the trailer and his bicycle down from the veranda on to the lawn and fitted the trailer hitch; then he mounted and rode off. He had four miles to go to fetch the milk and cream, for the transport shortage now prevented all collections from the farms in his district and they had learned to make their own butter in the Mixmaster. He rode off down the road in the warm morning sunlight, the empty billies rattling in the trailer at his back, happy in the thought of work before him.

There was very little traffic on the road. He passed one vehicle that once had been a car, the engine removed and the windscreen knocked out, drawn by an Angus bullock. He passed two riders upon horses, going carefully upon the gravel verge to the road beside the bitumen surface. He did not want one; they were scarce and delicate creatures that changed hands for a thousand pounds or more, but he had sometimes thought about a bullock for Mary. He could convert the Morris easily enough, though it would break his heart to do so.

He reached the farm in half an hour, and went straight to the milking shed. He knew the farmer well, a slow speaking, tall, lean man who walked with a limp from the

Second World War. He found him in the separator room, where the milk flowed into one churn and the cream into another in a low murmur of sound from the electric motor that drove the machine. 'Morning, Mr Paul,' said the naval officer. 'How are you today?'

'Good, Mr Holmes.' The farmer took the milk billy from him and filled it at the vat. 'Everything all right with you?'

'Fine. I've got to go up to Melbourne, to the Navy Department. I think they've got a job for me at last.'

'Ah,' said the farmer, 'that'll be good. Kind of wearisome, waiting around, I'd say.'

Peter nodded. 'It's going to complicate things a bit if it's a seagoing job. Mary'll be coming for the milk, though, twice a week. She'll bring the money, just the same.'

The farmer said, 'You don't have to worry about the money till you come back, anyway. I've got more milk than the pigs will take even now, dry as it is. Put twenty gallons in the creek last night – can't get it away. Suppose I ought to raise more pigs, but then it doesn't seem worth while. It's hard to say what to do . . .' He stood in silence for a minute, and then he said, 'Going to be kind of awkward for the wife, coming over here. What's she going to do with Jennifer?'

'She'll probably bring her over with her, in the trailer.'

'Kind of awkward for her, that.' The farmer walked to the alley of the milking shed and stood in the warm sunlight, looking the bicycle and trailer over. 'That's a good trailer,' he said. 'As good a little trailer as I ever saw. Made it yourself, didn't you?'

'That's right.'

'Where did you get the wheels, if I may ask?'

'They're motor bike wheels. I got them in Elizabeth Street.'

'Think you could get a pair for me?'

'I could try,' Peter said. 'I think there may be some of them about still. They're better than the little wheels – they tow more easily.' The farmer nodded. 'They may be a bit scarce now. People seem to be hanging on to motor bikes.'

'I was saying to the wife,' the farmer remarked slowly, 'if I had a little trailer like that I could make it like a chair for her, put on behind the push bike and take her into Falmouth, shopping. It's mighty lonely for a woman in a place like this, these days,' he explained. 'Not like it was before the war, when she could take the car and get into town in twenty minutes. The bullock cart takes three and a half hours, and three and a half hours back; that's seven hours for travelling alone. She did try to learn to ride a bike but she'll never make a go of it, not at her age and another baby on the way. I wouldn't want her to try. But if I had a little trailer like you've got I could take her into Falmouth twice a week, and take the milk and cream along to Mrs Holmes at the same time.' He paused. 'I'd like to be able to do that for the wife,' he remarked. 'After all, from what they say on the wireless, there's not so long to go.'

The naval officer nodded. 'I'll scout around a bit today and see what I can find. You don't mind what they cost?'

The farmer shook his head. 'So long as they're good wheels, to give no trouble. Good tyres, that's the main thing – last the time out. Like those you've got.'

The officer nodded. 'I'll have a look for some today.'

'Taking you a good bit out of your way.'

'I can slip up there by tram. It won't be any trouble. Thank God for the brown coal.'

The farmer turned to where the separator was still

running. 'That's right. We'd be in a pretty mess but for the electricity.' He slipped an empty churn into the stream of skim milk deftly and pulled the full churn away. 'Tell me, Mr Holmes,' he said. 'Don't they use big digging machines to get the coal? Like bulldozers, and things like that?' The officer nodded. 'Well, where do they get the oil to run those things?'

'I asked about that once,' Peter said. 'They distil it on the spot, out of the brown coal. It costs about two pounds a gallon.'

'You don't say!' The farmer stood in thought. 'I was thinking may be if they could do that for themselves, they might do some for us. But at that price, it wouldn't hardly be practical . . .'

Peter took the milk and cream billies, put them in the trailer, and set off for home. It was six-thirty when he got back. He had a shower and dressed in the uniform he had so seldom worn since his promotion, accelerated his breakfast, and rode his bicycle down the hill to catch the 8.15 in order that he might explore the motor dealers for the wheels before his appointment.

He left his bicycle at the garage that had serviced his small car in bygone days. It serviced no cars now. Horses stood stabled where the cars had been, the horses of the business men who lived outside the town, who now rode in in jodhpurs and plastic coats to stable their horses while they commuted up to town in the electric train. The petrol pumps served them as hitching posts. In the evening they would come down on the train, saddle their horses, strap the attaché case to the saddle, and ride home again. The tempo of business life was slowing down and this was a help to them; the 5.3 express train from the city had been cancelled and a 4.17 put on to replace it.

Peter Holmes travelled to the city immersed in speculations about his new appointment, for the paper famine had closed down all the daily newspapers and news now came by radio alone. The Royal Australian Navy was a very small fleet now. Seven small ships had been converted from oil burners to most unsatisfactory coal burners at great cost and effort; an attempt to convert the aircraft carrier *Melbourne* had been suspended when it proved that she would be too slow to allow the aircraft to land on with safety except in the strongest wind. Moreover, stocks of aviation fuel had to be husbanded so carefully that training programmes had been reduced to virtually nil, so that it now seemed inexpedient to carry on the Fleet Air Arm at all. He had not heard of any changes in the officers of the seven minesweepers and frigates that remained in commission. It might be that somebody was sick and had to be replaced, or it might be that they had decided to rotate employed officers with the unemployed to keep up seagoing experience. More probably it meant a posting to some dreary job on shore, an office job in the Barracks or doing something with the stores at some disconsolate, deserted place like Flinders Naval Depot. He would be deeply disappointed if he did not get to sea, and yet he knew it would be better for him so. On shore he could look after Mary and the baby as he had been doing, and there was now not so long to go.

He got to the city in about an hour and went out of the station to get upon the tram. It rattled unobstructed through streets innocent of other vehicles and took him quickly to the motor dealing district. Most of the shops here were closed or taken over by the few that remained open, the windows still encumbered with the useless stock. He shopped around here for a time, searching for two light wheels in good condition that would make a pair, and finally bought wheels of the same size from two makes of motor cycle, which would make complications with the axle that could be got over by the one mechanic still left in his garage.

He took the tram back to the Navy Department, carrying the wheels tied together with a bit of rope. In the Second Naval Member's offices he reported to the secretary, a paymaster lieutenant who was known to him. The young man said, 'Good morning, sir. The Admiral's got your posting on his desk. He wants to see you personally. I'll tell him that you're here.'

The Lieutenant-Commander raised his eyebrows. It seemed unusual, but then in this reduced navy everything was apt to be a bit unusual. He put the wheels down by the paymaster's desk, looked over his uniform with some concern, picked a bit of thread off the lapel of his jacket, and tucked his cap under his arm.

'The Admiral will see you now, sir.'

He marched into the office and came to attention. The Admiral, seated at his desk, inclined his head. 'Good morning, Lieutenant-Commander. You can stand easy. Sit down.'

Peter sat down in the chair beside the desk. The Admiral leaned over and offered him a cigarette out of his case, and lit it for him with a lighter. 'You've been unemployed for some time.'

'Yes, sir.'

The Admiral lit a cigarette himself. 'Well, I've got a seagoing appointment for you. I can't give you a command, I'm afraid, and I can't even put you in one of our own ships. I'm posting you as liaison officer in USS *Scorpion*.'

He glanced at the younger man. 'I understand you've met Commander Towers.'

'Yes, sir.' He had met the captain of *Scorpion* two or three times in the last few months, a quiet, soft spoken man of thirty-five or so with a slight New England accent. He had read the American's report upon his ship's war service. Towers had been at sea in his atomic powered submarine on patrol between Kiska and Midway when the war began, and opening his sealed orders at the appropriate signal he submerged and set course for Manila at full cruising speed. On the fourth day, somewhere north of Iwojima, he came to periscope depth for an inspection of the empty sea, as was his routine in each watch of the daylight hours, and found the visibility to be extremely low, apparently with some sort of dust; at the same time the detector on his periscope head indicated a high level of radioactivity. He attempted to report this to Pearl Harbor in a signal, but got no reply; he carried on, the radioactivity increasing as he neared the Philippines. Next night he made contact with Dutch Harbor and passed a signal in code to his admiral, but was told that all communications were now irregular, and he got no reply. On the next night he failed to raise Dutch Harbor. He carried on upon his mission, setting course around the north of Luzon. In the Balintang Channel he found much dust and the radioactivity far above the lethal level, the wind being westerly, Force Four to Five. On the seventh day of the war he was in Manila Bay looking at the city through his periscope, still without orders. The atmospheric radioactivity was rather less here, though still above the danger level; he did not care to surface or go up on to the bridge. Visibility was moderate; through the periscope he saw a pall of smoke drifting up above the city and formed the opinion that at least one nuclear explosion had taken place there within the last few days. He saw no activity on shore from five miles out in the bay. Proceeding to close the land, he grounded his ship unexpectedly at periscope depth, being then in the main channel where the chart showed twelve fathoms; this reinforced his previous opinion. He blew his tanks and got off without difficulty, turned round, and went out to the open sea again.

That night he failed again to raise any American station, or any ship that could relay his signals. Blowing his tanks had used up much of his compressed air, and he did not care to take in the contaminated air in that vicinity. He had been submerged by that time for eight days; his crew were still fairly fit, though various neuroses were beginning to appear, born of anxiety about conditions in their homes. He established radio contact with an Australian station at Port Moresby in New Guinea; conditions there appeared to be normal, but they could not relay any of his signals.

It seemed to him that the best thing he could do would be to go south. He went back round the north of Luzon and set course for Yap Island, a cable station under the control of the United States. He got there three days later. Here the radioactive level was so low as to be practically normal; he surfaced in a moderate sea, blew out the ship with clean air, charged his tanks, and let the crew up on the bridge in batches. On entering the roads he was relieved to find an American cruiser there. She directed him to an anchorage and sent a boat; he moored ship, let the whole crew up on deck, and went off in the boat to put himself under the command of the captain of the cruiser, a Captain Shaw. Here he learned for the first time of the Russo-Chinese war that had flared up out of the Russo-NATO war, that had in turn been born of the Israeli-Arab war, initiated by Albania. He learned of the use of cobalt bombs by both the Russians and the Chinese; that news came deviously from Australia, relayed from Kenya. The cruiser was waiting at Yap to rendezvous

17

with a Fleet tanker; she had been there for a week and in the last five days she had been out of communication with the United States. The captain had sufficient bunker fuel to get his ship to Brisbane at her most economical speed, but no further.

Commander Towers stayed at Yap for six days while the news, such as it was, grew steadily worse. They did not succeed in making contact with any station in the United States or Europe, but for the first two days or so they were able to pick up news broadcasts from Mexico City, and that news was just about as bad as it could be. Then that station went off the air, and they could only get Panama, Bogota, and Valparaiso, who knew practically nothing about what was going on up in the northern continent. They made contact with a few ships of the US Navy in the South Pacific, most of them as short of fuel as they were themselves. The captain of the cruiser at Yap proved to be the senior officer of all these ships; he made the decision to sail all US ships into Australian waters and to place his forces under Australian command. He made signals to all ships to rendezvous with him at Brisbane. They congregated there a fortnight later, eleven ships of the US Navy, all out of bunker fuel and with very little hope of getting any more. That was a year ago; they were there still.

The nuclear fuel required for USS *Scorpion* was not available in Australia at the time of her arrival, but it could be prepared. She proved to be the only naval vessel in Australian waters with any worthwhile radius of action, so she was sailed to Williamstown, the naval dockyard of Melbourne, being the nearest port to the headquarters of the Navy Department. She was in fact, the only warship in Australia worth bothering about. She stayed idle for some time while her nuclear fuel was prepared till, six months previously, she had been restored to operational mobility. She then made a cruise to Rio de Janeiro carrying supplies of fuel for another American nuclear submarine that had taken refuge there, and returned to Melbourne to undergo a fairly extensive refit in the dockyard.

All this was known to Peter Holmes as the background of Commander Towers, USN, and it passed quickly through his mind as he sat before the Admiral's desk. The appointment that he had been offered was a new one; there had been no Australian liaison officer in *Scorpion* when she had made her South American cruise. The thought of Mary and his little daughter troubled him now and prompted him to ask, 'How long is this appointment for, sir?'

The Admiral shrugged his shoulders slightly. 'We could say a year. I imagine it will be your last posting, Holmes.'

The younger man said, 'I know, sir. I'm very grateful for the opportunity.' He hesitated, and then he asked, 'Will the ship be at sea for much of that time, sir? I'm married, and we've got a baby. Things aren't too easy now, compared with what they used to be, and it's a bit difficult at home. And anyway, there's not so long to go.'

The Admiral nodded. 'We're all in the same boat, of course. That's why I wanted to see you before offering this posting. I shan't hold it against you if you ask to be excused, but in that case I can't hold out much prospect of any further employment. As regards sea time, at the conclusion of the refit on the fourth' – he glanced at the calendar – 'that's in a little over a week from now – the ship is to proceed to Cairns, Port Moresby, and Port Darwin to report upon conditions in those places, returning to Williamstown. Commander Towers estimates eleven days for that cruise. After that we have in mind a longer cruise for her, lasting perhaps two months.'

'Would there be an interval between those cruises, sir?'

'I should think the ship might be in the dockyard for about a fortnight.'

'And nothing on the programme after that?'

'Nothing at present.'

The young officer sat in thought for a moment, revolving in his mind the shopping, the ailments of the baby, the milk supply. It was summer weather; there would be no firewood to be cut. If the second cruise began about the middle of February he would be home by the middle of April, before the weather got cold enough for fires. Perhaps the farmer would see Mary right for firewood if he was away longer than that, now that he had got him the wheels for his trailer. It should be all right for him to go, so long as nothing further went wrong. But if the electricity supply failed, or the radioactivity spread south more quickly than the wise men estimated . . . Put away that thought.

Mary would be furious if he turned down this job and sacrificed his career. She was a naval officer's daughter born and brought up at Southsea in the south of England; he had first met her at a dance in *Indefatigable* when he was doing his sea time in England with the Royal Navy. She would want him to take this appointment . . .

He raised his head. 'I should be all right for those two cruises, sir,' he said. 'Would it be possible to review the situation after that? I mean, it's not so easy to make plans ahead – at home – with all this going on.'

The Admiral thought for a moment. In the circumstances it was a reasonable request for a man to make, especially a newly married man with a young baby. The case was a new one, for postings were now so few, but he could hardly expect this officer to accept sea duty outside Australian waters in the last few months. He nodded. 'I can do that, Holmes,' he said. 'I'll make this posting for five months, till the thirty-first of May. Report to me again when you get back from the second cruise.'

'Very good, sir.'

'You'll report in *Scorpion* on Tuesday, New Year's Day. If you wait outside a quarter of an hour you can have your letter to the captain. The vessel is at Williamstown, lying alongside *Sydney* as her mother ship.'

'I know, sir.'

The Admiral rose to his feet. 'All right, Lieutenant-Commander.' He held out his hand. 'Good luck in the appointment.'

Peter Holmes shook hands. 'Thank you for considering me, sir.' He paused before leaving the room. 'Do you happen to know if Commander Towers is on board today?' he asked. 'As I'm here, I might slip down and make my number with him, and perhaps see the ship. I'd rather like to do that before joining.'

'So far as I know he is on board,' the Admiral said. 'You can put a call through to *Sydney* – ask my secretary.' He glanced at his watch. 'There's a transport leaving from the main gate at eleven-thirty. You'll be able to catch that.'

Twenty minutes later Peter Holmes was seated by the driver in the electric truck that ran the ferry service down to Williamstown, bowling along in silence through the deserted streets. In former days the truck had been a delivery van for a great Melbourne store; it had been requisitioned at the conclusion of the war and painted naval grey. It moved along at a steady twenty miles an hour unimpeded by any other traffic on the roads. It got to the dockyard at noon, and Peter Holmes walked down

21

to the berth occupied by HMAS *Sydney*, an aircraft carrier immobilized at the quay side. He went on board, and went down to the wardroom.

There were only about a dozen officers in the great wardroom, six of them in the khaki gabardine working uniform of the US Navy. The captain of *Scorpion* was among them; he came forward smiling to meet Peter. 'Say, Lieutenant-Commander, I'm glad you could come down.'

Peter Holmes said, 'I hoped you wouldn't mind, sir. I'm not due to join till Tuesday. But as I was at the Navy Department I hoped you wouldn't mind if I came down for lunch, and perhaps had a look through the ship.'

'Why, sure,' said the captain. 'I was glad when Admiral Grimwade told me he was posting you to join us. I'd like you to meet some of my officers.' He turned to the others. 'This is my executive officer, Mr Farrell, and my engineering officer, Mr Lundgren.' He smiled. 'It takes a pretty high-grade engineering staff to run our motors. This is Mr Benson, Mr O'Doherty, and Mr Hirsch.' The young men bowed, a little awkwardly. The captain turned to Peter. 'How about a drink before lunch, Commander?'

The Australian said, 'Well – thank you very much. I'll have a pink gin.' The captain pressed the bell upon the bulkhead. 'How many officers have you in *Scorpion*, sir?'

'Eleven, all told. She's quite a submarine, of course, and we carry four engineer officers.'

'You must have a big wardroom.'

'It's a bit cramped when we're all sitting down together, but that doesn't happen very often in a submarine. But we've got a cot for you, Commander.'

Peter smiled. 'All to myself, or is it Box and Cox?'

The captain was a little shocked at the suggestion. 'Why, no. Every officer and every enlisted man has an individual berth in *Scorpion*.'

The wardroom steward came in answer to the bell. The captain said, 'Will you bring one pink gin and six orangeades.'

Peter was embarrassed, and could have kicked himself for his indiscretion. He checked the steward. 'Don't you drink in port, sir?'

The captain smiled. 'Why, no. Uncle Sam doesn't like it. But you go right ahead. This is a British ship.'

'I'd rather have it your way, if you don't mind,' Peter replied. 'Seven orangeades.'

'Seven it is,' said the captain nonchalantly. The steward went away. 'Some navies have it one way and some another,' he remarked. 'I never noticed that it made much difference in the end result.'

They lunched in *Sydney*, a dozen officers at one end of one of the long, empty tables. Then they went down into *Scorpion*, moored alongside. She was the biggest submarine that Peter Holmes had ever seen; she displaced about six thousand tons and her atomic powered turbines developed well over ten thousand horsepower. Besides her eleven officers she carried a crew of about seventy petty officers and enlisted men. All these men messed and slept among a maze of pipes and wiring as is common in all submarines, but she was well equipped for the tropics with good air conditioning and a very large cold store. Peter Holmes was no submariner and could not judge her from a technical point of view, but the captain told him that she was easy on controls and quite manoeuvrable in spite of her great length.

Most of her armament and warlike stores had been taken off her during her refit, and all but two of her torpedo tubes had been removed. This made more room for messdecks and amenities than is usual in a submarine, and the removal of the aft tubes and torpedo stowage made conditions in the engine-room a good deal easier for the engineers. Peter spent an hour in this part of the ship with the engineering officer, Lieutenant-Commander Lundgren. He had never served in an atomic powered ship, and as much of the equipment was classified for security a great deal of it was novel to him. He spent some time absorbing the general layout of the liquid sodium circuit to take heat from the reactor, the various heat exchangers, and the closed-cycle helium circuits for the twin high-speed turbines that drove the ship through the enormous reduction gears, so much larger and more sensitive than the other units of the power plant.

He came back to the captain's tiny cabin in the end. Commander Towers rang for the coloured steward, ordered coffee for two, and let down the folding seat for Peter. 'Have a good look at the engines?' he asked.

The Australian nodded. 'I'm not an engineer,' he said. 'Much of it is just a bit over my head, but it was very interesting. Do they give you much trouble?'

The captain shook his head. 'They never have so far. There's nothing much that you can do with them at sea if they do. Just keep your fingers crossed and hope they'll keep on spinning around.'

The coffee came and they sipped it in silence. 'My orders are to report to you on Tuesday,' Peter said. 'What time would you like me here, sir?'

'We sail on Tuesday on sea trials,' the captain said. 'It might be Wednesday, but I don't think we'll be so late as that. We're taking on stores Monday and the crew come aboard.'

'I'd better report to you on Monday, then,' said the Australian. 'Some time in the forenoon?'

'That might be a good thing,' said the captain. 'I think we'll get away by Tuesday noon. I told the Admiral I'd

24

like to take a little cruise in Bass Strait as a shakedown, and come back maybe on Friday and report operational readiness. I'd say if you're on board any time Monday forenoon that would be okay.'

'Is there anything that I can do for you in the meantime? I'd come aboard on Saturday if I could help at all.'

'I appreciate that, Commander, but there's not a thing. Half the crew are off on leave right now, and I'm letting the other half go off on weekend pass tomorrow noon. There'll be nobody here Saturday and Sunday barring one officer and six men on watch. No, Monday forenoon will be time enough for you.'

He glanced at Peter. 'Anybody tell you what they want us to do?'

The Australian was surprised. 'Haven't they told you, sir?'

The American laughed. 'Not a thing. I'd say the last person to hear the sailing orders is the captain.'

'The Second Naval Member sent for me about this posting,' Peter said. 'He told me that you were making a cruise to Cairns, Port Moresby, and Darwin, and that it was going to take eleven days.'

'Your Captain Nixon in the Operations Division, he asked me how long that would take,' the captain remarked. 'I haven't had it as an order yet.'

'The Admiral said, this morning, that after that was over there'd be a much longer cruise, that would take about two months.'

Commander Towers paused, motionless, his cup suspended in mid air. 'That's news to me,' he remarked. 'Did he say where we were going?'

Peter shook his head. 'He just said it would take about two months.'

There was a short silence. Then the American roused

himself and smiled. 'I guess if you look in around midnight you'll find me drawing radiuses on the chart,' he said quietly. 'And tomorrow night, and the night after that.'

It seemed better to the Australian to turn the conversation to a lighter tone. 'Aren't you going away for the weekend?' he asked.

The captain shook his head. 'I'll stick around. Maybe go up to the city one day and take in a movie.'

It seemed a dreary sort of programme for his weekend, a stranger far from home in a strange land. On the impulse Peter said, 'Would you care to come down to Falmouth for a couple of nights, sir? We've got a spare bedroom. We've been spending most of our time at the sailing club this weather, swimming and sailing. My wife would like it if you could come.'

'That's mighty nice of you,' the captain said thoughtfully. He took another drink of coffee while he considered the proposal. Northern hemisphere people seldom mixed well, now, with people of the southern hemisphere. Too much lay between them, too great a difference of experience. The intolerable sympathy made a barrier. He knew that very well and, more, he knew that this Australian officer must know it in spite of his invitation. In the line of duty, however, he felt that he would like to know more about the liaison officer. If he had to communicate through him with the Australian Naval Command he would like to know what sort of man he was; that was a point in favour of this visit to his home. The change would certainly be some relief from the vile inactivity that had tormented him in the last months; however great the awkwardness, it might be better than a weekend in the echoing, empty aircraft carrier with only his own thoughts and memories for company.

He smiled faintly as he put his cup down. It might be

awkward if he went down there, but it could be even more awkward if he churlishly refused an invitation kindly meant from his new officer. 'You sure it wouldn't be too much for your wife?' he asked. 'With a young baby?'

Peter shook his head. 'She'd like it,' he said. 'Make a bit of a change for her. She doesn't see many new faces, with things as they are. Of course, the baby makes a tie as well.'

'I certainly would like to come down for one night,' the American said. 'I'll have to stick around here tomorrow, but I could use a swim on Saturday. It's a long time since I had a swim. How would it be if I came down to Falmouth on the train Saturday morning? I'll have to be back here on Sunday.'

'I'll meet you at the station.' They discussed trains for a little. Then Peter asked, 'Can you ride a push bike?' The other nodded. 'I'll bring another bike down with me to the station. We live about two miles out.'

Commander Towers said, 'That'll be fine.' The red Oldsmobile was fading to a dream. It was only fifteen months since he had driven it to the airport, but now he could hardly remember what the fascia panel looked like or on which side the seat adjustment lever lay. It must be still in the garage of his Connecticut home, untouched perhaps, with all the other things that he had schooled himself not to think about. One had to live in the new world and do one's best, forgetting about the old; now it was push bikes at the railway station in Australia.

Peter left to catch the ferry truck back to the Navy Department; he picked up his letter of appointment and his wheels, and took the tram to the station. He got back to Falmouth at about six o'clock, hung the wheels awkwardly on the handlebars of his bicycle, took off his jacket, and trudged the pedals heavily up the hill to his home. He got

27

there half an hour later, sweating profusely in the heat of the evening, to find Mary cool in a summer frock in the refreshing murmur of a sprinkler on the lawn.

She came to meet him. 'Oh Peter, you're so hot!' she said. 'I see you got the wheels.'

He nodded. 'Sorry I couldn't get down to the beach.'

'I guessed you'd been held up. We came home about half past five. What happened about the appointment?'

'It's a long story,' he said. He parked the bicycle and the wheels on the veranda. 'I'd like to have a shower first, and tell you then.'

'Good or bad?' she asked.

'Good,' he replied. 'Seagoing until April. Nothing after that.'

'Oh, Peter,' she cried, 'that's just perfect! Go on and have your shower and tell me about it when you're cool. I'll bring out the deck chairs and there's a bottle of beer in the fridge.'

A quarter of an hour later, cool in an open necked shirt and light drill trousers, sitting in the shade with the cold beer, he told her all about it. In the end he asked, 'Have you ever met Commander Towers?'

She shook her head. 'Jane Freeman met them all at the party in *Sydney*. She said he was rather nice. What's he going to be like to serve under?'

'All right, I think,' he replied. 'He's very competent. It's going to be a bit strange at first, in an American ship. But I liked them all, I must say.' He laughed. 'I put up a blue right away by ordering a pink gin.' He told her.

She nodded. 'That's what Jane said. They drink on shore but not in a ship. I don't believe they drink in uniform at all. They had some kind of a fruit cocktail, rather dismal. Everybody else was drinking like a fish.'

'I asked him down for the weekend,' he told her. 'He's coming down on Saturday morning.'

She stared at him in consternation. 'Not Commander Towers?'

He nodded. 'I felt I had to ask him. He'll be all right.'

'Oh . . . Peter, he won't be. They're never all right. It's much too painful for them, coming into people's homes.'

He tried to reassure her. 'He's different. He's a good bit older, for one thing. Honestly, he'll be quite all right.'

'That's what you thought about that RAF squadron leader,' she retorted. 'You know – I forget his name. The one who cried.'

He did not care to be reminded of that evening. 'I know it's difficult for them,' he said. 'Coming into someone's home, with the baby and everything. But honestly, this chap won't be like that.'

She resigned herself to the inevitable. 'How long is he staying for?'

'Only the one night,' he told her. 'He says he's got to be back in *Scorpion* on Sunday.'

'If it's only for one night it shouldn't be too bad . . .' She sat in thought for a minute, frowning a little. 'The thing is, we'll have to find him plenty to do. Keep him occupied all the time. Never a dull moment. That's the mistake we made with that RAF bloke. What does he like doing?'

'Swimming,' he told her. 'He wants to have a swim.'

'Sailing? There's a race on Saturday.'

'I didn't ask him. I should think he sails. He's the sort of man who would.'

She took a drink of beer. 'We could take him to the movies,' she said thoughtfully.

'What's on?'

'I don't know. It doesn't really matter, so long as we keep him occupied.'

'It might not be so good if it was about America,' he pointed out. 'We might just hit on one that was shot in his home town.'

She stared at him in consternation. 'Wouldn't that be *awful!* Where is his home town, Peter? What part of America?'

'I haven't a clue,' he said. 'I didn't ask him.'

'Oh dear. We'll have to do *something* with him in the evening, Peter. I should think a British picture would be safest, but there may not be one on.'

'We could have a party,' he suggested.

'We'll have to, if there's not a British picture. It might be better, anyway.' She sat in thought, and then she asked, 'Was he married, do you know?'

'I don't. I should think he must have been.'

'I believe Moira Davidson would come and help us out,' she said thoughtfully. 'If she isn't doing anything else.'

'If she isn't drunk,' he observed.

'She's not like that all the time,' his wife replied. 'She'd keep the party lively, anyway.'

He considered the proposal. 'That's not a bad idea,' he said. 'I should tell her right out what she's got to do. Never a dull moment.' He paused, thoughtful. 'In bed or out of it.'

'She doesn't, you know. It's all on the surface.'

He grinned. 'Have it your own way.'

They rang Moira Davidson that evening and put the proposition to her. 'Peter felt he had to ask him,' Mary told her. 'I mean, he's his new captain. But you know how they are and how they feel when they come into someone's home, with children and a smell of nappies and a feeding bottle in a saucepan of warm water and all that sort of thing. So we thought we'd clean the house up a bit and put all that away, and try and give him a gay time – all the time, you know. The trouble is, I can't do much myself with Jennifer. Could you come and help us out, dear? I'm afraid it means a camp bed in the lounge or out on the veranda, if you'd rather. It's just for Saturday and Sunday. Keep him occupied, all the time – that's what we thought. Never a dull moment. I thought we'd have a party on Saturday night, and get some people in.'

'Sounds a bit dreary,' said Miss Davidson. 'Tell me, is he a fearful stick? Will he start weeping in my arms and telling me I'm just like his late wife? Some of them do that.'

'I suppose he might,' said Mary uncertainly. 'I've never met him. Half a minute while I ask Peter.' She came back to the telephone. 'Moira? Peter says he'll probably start knocking you about when he gets a skinful.'

'That's better,' said Miss Davidson. 'All right, I'll come over on Saturday morning. By the way, I've given up gin.'

'Given up gin?'

'Rots your insides. Perforates the intestine and gives you ulcers. I've been having them each morning, so I've given it away. It's brandy now. About six bottles, I should think – for the weekend. You can drink a lot of brandy.'

On Saturday morning Peter Holmes rode down to Falmouth station on his push bike. He met Moira Davidson there. She was a slightly built girl with straight blonde hair and a white face, the daughter of a grazier with a small property at a place called Harkaway near Berwick. She arrived at the station in a very smart four-wheeled trap, snatched from some junk yard and reconditioned at considerable expense a year before, with a good-looking, high spirited grey mare between the shafts. She was wearing slacks of the brightest red and a shirt of the same colour, with lips, fingernails, and toenails to match. She waved to Peter, who went to the horse's head, got down from her outfit, and tied the reins loosely to a rail where once the passengers had stood in line before boarding the bus. 'Morning, Peter,' she said. 'Boy friend not turned up?'

'He'll be on this train coming now,' he said. 'What time did you leave home?' She had driven twenty miles to Falmouth.

'Eight o'clock. Ghastly.'

'You've had breakfast?'

She nodded. 'Brandy. I'm going to have another one before I get up in that jinker again.'

He was concerned for her. 'Haven't you had anything to eat?'

'Eat? Bacon and eggs and all that muck? My dear child, the Symes had a party last night. I'd have sicked it up.'

They turned to walk together to meet the train. 'What time did you get to bed?' he asked.

'About half past two.'

'I don't know how you can keep it up. I couldn't.'

'I can. I can keep it up as long as I've got to, and that's not so long now. I mean, why waste time in sleeping?' She laughed, a little shrilly. 'Just doesn't make sense.'

He did not reply because she was quite right, only it wasn't his own way. They stood and waited till the train came in, and met Commander Towers on the platform. He came in civilian clothes, a light grey jacket and fawn drill trousers, slightly American in cut, so that he stood out as a stranger in the crowd.

Peter Holmes made the introductions. As they walked down the ramp from the platforms the American said,

'I haven't ridden a bicycle in years. I'll probably fall off.'

'We're doing better for you than that,' Peter said. 'Moira's got her jinker here.'

The other wrinkled his brows. 'I didn't get that?'

'Sports car,' the girl said. 'Jaguar XK 140. Thunderbird to you, I suppose. New model, only one horsepower, but she does a good eight miles an hour on the flat. Christ, I want a drink!'

They came to the jinker with the grey standing in the shafts; she went to untie the reins. The American stood back and looked it over, gleaming in the sun and very smart. 'Say,' he exclaimed, 'this is quite a buggy you've got!'

Moira stood back and laughed. 'A buggy! That's the word for it. It's a buggy, isn't it? All right, Peter – that's not dirty. And anyway, it is. We've got a Customline sitting in the garage, Commander Towers, but I didn't bring that. It's a buggy. Come on and get up into it, and I'll step on it and show you how she goes.'

'I've got my bike here, sir,' Peter said. 'I'll ride that up and meet you at the house.'

Commander Towers climbed up into the buggy and the girl got up beside him; she took the whip and turned the grey and trotted up the road behind the bicycle. 'One thing I'm going to do before we leave town,' she told her companion, 'and that's have a drink. Peter's a dear, and Mary too, but they don't drink enough. Mary says it gives the baby colic. I hope you don't mind. You can have a Coke or something if you'd rather.'

Commander Towers felt a little dazed, but refreshed. It was a long time since he had had to deal with this sort of a young woman. 'I'll go along with you,' he said. 'I've

33

swallowed enough Cokes in the last year to float my ship, periscope depth. I could use a drink.'

'Then there's two of us,' she remarked. She steered her outfit into the main street, not unskilfully. A few cars stood abandoned, parked diagonally by the kerb; they had been there for over a year. So little traffic used the streets that they were not in the way, and there had been no petrol to tow them away. She drew up outside the Pier Hotel and got down; she tied the reins to the bumper of one of these cars and went with her companion into the Ladies' Lounge.

He asked, 'What can I order for you?'

'Double brandy.'

'Water?'

'Just a little, and a lot of ice.'

He gave the order to the barman and stood considering for a moment while the girl watched him. There never had been any rye, and there had been no Scotch for many months. He was unreasonably suspicious of Australian whisky. 'I never drank brandy like that,' he remarked. 'What's it like?'

'No kick,' the girl said, 'but it creeps up on you. Good for the guts. That's the reason why I drink it.'

'I guess I'll stick to whisky.' He ordered, and then turned to her, amused. 'You drink quite a lot, don't you?'

'That's what they tell me.' She took the drink he handed to her and produced a pack of cigarettes from her bag, blended South African and Australian tobacco. 'Have one of these things? They're horrible, but they're all that I could get.'

He offered one of his own, equally horrible, and lit it for her. She blew a long cloud of smoke from her nostrils. 'It's a change, anyway. What's your name?'

34

'Dwight,' he told her. 'Dwight Lionel.'

'Dwight Lionel Towers,' she repeated. 'I'm Moira Davidson. We've got a grazing property about twenty miles from here. You're the captain of the submarine, aren't you?'

'That's right.'

'Happy in your job?' she asked cynically.

'It was quite an honour to be given the command,' he said quietly. 'I reckon it's quite an honour still.'

She dropped her eyes. 'Sorry I said that. I'm a bit of a pig when I'm sober.' She tossed off her drink. 'Buy me another, Dwight.'

He bought her another, but stood himself upon his whisky. 'Tell me,' the girl asked, 'what do you do when you're on leave? Play golf? Sail a boat? Go fishing?'

'Fishing, mostly,' he said. A far-off holiday with Sharon in the Gaspé Peninsula floated through his mind, but he put the thought away. One must concentrate upon the present and forget the past. 'It's kind of hot for golf,' he said. 'Commander Holmes said something about a swim.'

'That's easy,' she said. 'There's a sailing race this afternoon, down at the club. Is that in your line?'

'It certainly is,' he said, with pleasure in his voice. 'What kind of a boat does he have?'

'A thing called a Gwen Twelve,' she said. 'It's a sort of watertight box with sails on it. I don't know if he wants to sail it himself. I'll crew for you if he doesn't.'

'If we're going sailing,' he said firmly, 'we'd better stop drinking.'

'I'm not going to crew for you if you're going to be all US Navy,' she retorted. 'Our ships aren't dry, like yours.'

'Okay,' he said equably. 'Then I'll crew for you.'

35

She stared at him. 'Has anyone ever bashed you over the head with a bottle?'

He smiled. 'Lots of times.'

She drained her glass. 'Well, have another drink.'

'No, thank you. The Holmeses will be wondering what's become of us.'

'They'll know,' the girl said.

'Come on. I want to see the world from up in that jinker.' He steered her towards the door.

She went with him unresisting. 'It's a buggy,' she said.

'No it's not. We're in Australia now. It's a jinker.'

'That's where you're wrong,' she said. 'It's a buggy – an Abbott buggy. It's over seventy years old. Daddy says it was built in America.'

He looked at it with new interest. 'Say,' he exclaimed, 'I was wondering where I'd seen it before. My grandpa had one just like it in the woodshed, up in Maine, when I was a boy.'

She mustn't let him think about the past. 'Just stand by her head as I back out of this,' she said. 'She's not so good in reverse.' She swung herself up into the driving seat and tweaked the mare's mouth cruelly, so that he had plenty to do. The mare stood up and pawed at him with her fore feet; he managed to get her headed round towards the street and swung up beside the girl as they dashed off in a canter. Moira said, 'She's a bit fresh. The hill'll stop her in a minute. These bloody bitumen roads . . .' The American sat clinging to his seat as they careered out of town, the mare slithering and sliding on the smooth surfaces, wondering that any girl could drive a horse so badly.

They came to the Holmeses' house a few minutes later with the grey in a lather of sweat. The Lieutenant-Commander and his wife came out to meet them. 'Sorry we're late, Mary,' the girl said coolly. 'I couldn't get Commander Towers past the pub.'

Peter remarked, 'Looks like you've been making up lost time.'

'We had quite a ride,' the submarine commander observed. He got down and was introduced to Mary. Then he turned to the girl. 'How would it be if I walk her up and down a little, till she cools off?'

'Fine,' said the girl. 'I should unharness her and put her in the paddock – Peter'll show you. I'll give Mary a hand with the lunch. Peter, Dwight wants to sail your boat this afternoon.'

'I never said that,' the American protested.

'But you do.' She eyed the horse, glad that her father wasn't there to see. 'Give her a rub down with something – there's a cloth in the back underneath the oats. I'll give her a drink later on, after we've had one ourselves.'

That afternoon Mary stayed at home with the baby, quietly preparing for the evening party; Dwight Towers rode unsteadily with Peter and Moira to the sailing club on bicycles. They went with towels round their necks and swimming trunks tucked into pockets; they changed at the club in anticipation of a wet sail. The boat was a sealed plywood box with a small cockpit and an efficient spread of sail. They rigged and launched her and got to the starting line with five minutes to spare, the American sailing the boat, Moira crewing for him, and Peter watching the race from the shore.

They sailed in bathing costumes, Dwight Towers in an old pair of fawn trunks and the girl in a two-piece costume mainly white; they had shirts with them in the boat in case of sunburn. For a few minutes they manoeuvred about in the warm sun behind the starting line, milling around among a dozen others of mixed classes in the race. The

Commander had not sailed a boat for some years and he had never handled a boat of that particular type before; she handled well, however, and he quickly learned that she was very fast. He had confidence in her by the time the gun went, and they were fifth over the line at the start of a race three times round a triangular course.

As is the case on Port Phillip Bay, the wind blew up very quickly. By the time they had been round once it was blowing quite hard and they were sailing gunwale under; Commander Towers was too busy with the sheet and tiller keeping the boat upright and on her course to have much attention for anything else. They started on the second round and beat up to the farther turning point in brilliant sunshine and clouds of spray like diamonds; so occupied was he that he failed to notice the girl's toe as she kicked a coil of mainsheet round the cleat and laid a tangle of jib sheet down on top of it. They came to the buoy and he bore away smartly, putting up the tiller and letting out the sheet, which ran two feet and fouled. A gust came down on them and laid the vessel over, the girl played dumb and pulled the jib sheet in, and the boat gave up and laid her sails down flat upon the water. In a moment they were swimming by her side.

She said accusingly, 'You held on to the mainsheet!' And then she said, 'Oh hell, my bra's coming off!'

Indeed, she had contrived to give the knot between her shoulder blades a tweak as she went into the water, and it now floated by her side. She grabbed it with one hand and said, 'Swim round to the other side and sit on the centre-board. She'll come up all right.' She swam with him.

In the distance they saw the white motor boat on safety patrol turn and head towards them. She said to her companion, 'Here's the crash boat coming now. Just one thing after another. Help me get this on before they come, Dwight.' She could have done it perfectly well herself, lying face down in the water. 'That's right – a good hard knot. Not quite so tight as that; I'm not a Japanese. That's right. Now let's get this boat up and go on with the race.'

She climbed on to the centreboard that stuck out horizontally from the hull at water level and stood on it holding on to the gunwale while he swam below, marvelling at the slim lines of her figure and at her effrontery. He bore his weight down on the plate with her and the boat lifted sodden sails out of the water, hesitated, and then came upright with a rush. The girl tumbled over the topsides into the cockpit and fell in a heap as she cast off the mainsheet, and Dwight clambered in beside her. In a minute they were under way again, the vessel tender with the weight of water on her sails, before the crash boat reached them. 'Don't you do that again,' she said severely. 'This is my sun-bathing suit. It's not meant for swimming in.'

'I don't know how I came to do it,' he apologized. 'We were doing all right up till then.'

They completed the course without further incident, finishing last but one. They sailed in to the beach, and Peter met them waist deep in the water. He caught the boat and turned her into wind. 'Have a good sail?' he asked. 'I saw you bottle her.'

'It's been a lovely sail,' the girl replied. 'Dwight bottled her and then my bra came off, so one way and another we've had a thrilling time. Never a dull moment. She goes beautifully, Peter.'

They jumped over into the water and pulled the boat ashore, let down the sails, and put her on the trolley on the slipway to park her up on the beach. Then they bathed off the end of the jetty and sat smoking in the

39

warm evening sun, sheltered from the offshore wind by the cliff behind them.

The American looked at the blue water, the red cliffs, the moored motor boats rocking on the water. 'This is quite a place you've got here,' he said reflectively. 'For its size it's as nice a little club as any that I've seen.'

'They don't take sailing too seriously,' Peter remarked. 'That's the secret.'

The girl said, 'That's the secret of everything. When do we start drinking again, Peter?'

'The crowd are coming in at about eight o'clock,' he told her. He turned to his guest. 'We've got a few people coming in this evening,' he said. 'I thought we'd go down and have dinner at the hotel first. Eases the strain on the domestic side.'

'Sure. That'll be fine.'

The girl said, 'You're not taking Commander Towers to the Pier Hotel again?'

'That's where we thought of going for dinner.'

She said darkly, 'It seems to me to be very unwise.'

The American laughed. 'You're building up quite a reputation for me in these parts.'

'You're doing that for yourself,' she retorted. 'I'm doing all I can to whitewash you. I'm not going to say a word about you tearing off my bra.'

Dwight Towers glanced at her uncertainly, and then he laughed. He laughed as he had not laughed for a year, unrestrained by thoughts of what had gone before. 'Okay,' he said at last. 'We'll keep that a secret, just between you and me.'

'It will be on my side,' she said primly. 'You'll probably be telling everyone about it later on this evening when you're a bit full.'

Peter said, 'Maybe we'd better think about changing. I told Mary we'd be back up at the house by six.'

They walked down the jetty towards the dressing-rooms, changed, and rode back on their bicycles. At the house they found Mary on the lawn watering the garden. They discussed ways and means of getting down to the hotel, and decided to harness up the grey and take the buggy down. 'We'd better do that for Commander Towers,' the girl said. 'He'd never make it back up the hill after another session in the Pier Hotel.'

She went off with Peter to the paddock to catch the grey and harness her. As she slipped the bit between the teeth and pulled the ears through the bridle she said, 'How am I doing, Peter?'

He grinned. 'You're doing all right. Never a dull moment.'

'Well, that's what Mary said she wanted. He's not burst into tears yet, anyway.'

'More likely to burst a blood-vessel if you keep going on at him.'

'I don't know that I'll be able to. I've worked through most of my repertoire.' She laid the saddle over the mare's back.

'You'll get a bit more inspiration as the night goes on,' he remarked.

'Maybe.'

The night went on. They dined at the hotel and drove back up the hill more moderately than before, unharnessed the horse and put her in the paddock for the night, and were ready to meet the guests at eight o'clock. Four couples came to the modest little party; a young doctor and his wife, another naval officer, a cheerful young man described as a chook farmer whose way of life was a mystery to the American, and the young owner of a tiny engineering works. For three hours they danced and drank together, sedulously avoiding any serious topic of conversation. In the warm night the room grew hotter and hotter, coats and ties were jettisoned at an early stage, and the gramophone went on working through an enormous pile of records, half of which Peter had borrowed for the evening. In spite of the wide open windows behind the fly wire the room grew full of cigarette smoke. From time to time Peter would throw the contents of the ash trays into the waste paper bin; from time to time Mary would collect the empty glasses, take them out to the kitchen to wash them, and bring them back again. Finally at about half past eleven she brought in a tray of tea and buttered scones and cakes, the universal signal in Australia that the party was coming to an end. Presently the guests began to take their leave, wobbling away on their bicycles.

Moira and Dwight walked down the little drive to see the doctor and his wife safely off the premises. They turned back towards the house. 'Nice party,' said the submarine commander. 'Really nice people, all of them.'

It was cool and pleasant in the garden after the hot stuffiness of the house. The night was very still. Between the trees they could see the shore line of Port Phillip running up from Falmouth towards Nelson in the bright light of the stars. 'It was awfully hot in there,' the girl remarked. 'I'm going to stay out here a bit before going to bed, and cool off.'

'I'd better get you a wrap.'

'You'd better get me a drink, Dwight.'

'A soft one?' he suggested.

She shook her head. 'About an inch and a half of brandy and a lot of ice, if there's any left.'

He left her and went in to get her drink. When he came out again, a glass in each hand, he found her sitting on the edge of the veranda in the darkness. She took the glass from him with a word of thanks and he sat down beside her. After the noise and turmoil of the evening the peace of the garden in the night was a relief to him. 'It certainly is nice to sit quiet for a little while,' he said.

'Till the mosquitoes start biting,' she said. A little warm breeze blew around them. 'They may not, with this wind. I shouldn't sleep now if I went to bed, full as I am. I'd just lie and toss about all night.'

'You were up late last night?' he asked.

She nodded. 'And the night before.'

'I'd say you might try going to bed early, once in a while.'

'What's the use?' she demanded. 'What's the use of anything now?' He did not try to answer that, and presently she asked, 'Why is Peter joining you in *Scorpion*, Dwight?'

'He's our new liaison officer,' he told her.

'Did you have one before him?'

He shook his head. 'We never had one before.'

'Why have they given you one now?'

'I wouldn't know,' he replied. 'Maybe we'll be going for a cruise in Australian waters. I've had no orders, but that's what people tell me. The captain seems to be about the last person they tell in this navy.'

'Where do they say you're going to, Dwight?'

He hesitated for a moment. Security was now a thing of the past though it took a conscious effort to remember it; with no enemy in all the world there was little but the force of habit in it. 'People are saying we're to make a little cruise up to Port Moresby,' he told her. 'It may be just a rumour, but that's all I know.'

'But Port Moresby's out, isn't it?'

'I believe it is. They haven't had any radio from there for quite a while.'

'But you can't go on shore there if it's out, can you?'

'Somebody has to go and see, some time,' he said. 'We wouldn't go outside the hull unless the radiation level's near to normal. If it's high I wouldn't even surface. But someone has to go and see, some time.' He paused and there was silence in the starlight, in the garden. 'There's a lot of places someone ought to go and see,' he said at last. 'There's radio transmission still coming through from some place near Seattle. It doesn't make any sense, just now and then, a kind of jumble of dots and dashes. Sometimes a fortnight goes by, and then it comes again. It could be somebody's alive up there, doesn't know how to handle the set. There's a lot of funny things up in the northern hemisphere that someone ought to go and see.'

'*Could* anybody be alive up there?'

'I wouldn't think so. It's not quite impossible. He'd have to be living in a hermetically sealed room with all air filtered as it comes in and all food and water stored in with him some way. I wouldn't think it's practical.'

She nodded. 'Is it true that Cairns is out, Dwight?'

'I think it is – Cairns and Darwin. Maybe we'll have to go and see those, too. Maybe that's why Peter has been drafted in to *Scorpion*. He knows those waters.'

'Somebody was telling Daddy that they've got radiation sickness in Townsville now. Do you think that's right?'

'I don't really know – I hadn't heard it. But I'd say it might be right. It's south of Cairns.'

'It's going to go on spreading down here, southwards, till it gets to us?'

'That's what they say.'

'There never was a bomb dropped in the southern

44

hemisphere,' she said angrily. 'Why must it come to us? Can't anything be done to stop it?'

He shook his head. 'Not a thing. It's the winds. It's mighty difficult to dodge what's carried on the wind. You just can't do it. You've got to take what's coming to you, and make the best of it.'

'I don't understand it,' she said stubbornly. 'People were saying once that no wind blows across the equator, so we'd be all right. And now it seems we aren't all right at all . . .'

'We'd never have been all right,' he said quietly. 'Even if they'd been correct about the heavy particles – the radioactive dust – which they weren't, we'd still have got the lightest particles carried by diffusion. We've got them now. The background level of the radiation here, today, is eight or nine times what it was before the war.'

'That doesn't seem to hurt us,' she retorted. 'But this dust they talk about. That's blown about on the wind, isn't it?'

'That's so,' he replied. 'But no wind does blow right into the southern hemisphere from the northern hemisphere. If it did we'd all be dead right now.'

'I wish we were,' she said bitterly. 'It's like waiting to be hung.'

'Maybe it is. Or maybe it's a period of grace.'

There was a little silence after he said that. 'Why *is* it taking so long, Dwight?' she asked at last. 'Why can't the wind blow straight and get it over?'

'It's not so difficult to understand, really,' he said. 'In each hemisphere the winds go around in great whorls, thousands of miles across, between the pole and the equator. There's a circulatory system of winds in the northern hemisphere and another in the southern hemisphere. But what divides them isn't the equator that you see on a globe. It's a thing called the Pressure Equator, and that shifts north and south with the season. In January the whole of Borneo and Indonesia is in the northern system, but in July the division has shifted away up north, so that all of India and Siam, and everything that's to the south of that, is in the southern system. So in January the northern winds carry the radioactive dust from the fall-out down into Malaya, say. Then in July that's in the southern system, and our own winds pick it up and carry it down here. That's the reason why it's coming to us slowly.'

'And they can't do anything about it?'

'Not a thing. It's just too big a matter for mankind to tackle. We've just got to take it.'

'I won't take it,' she said vehemently. 'It's not fair. No one in the southern hemisphere ever dropped a bomb, a hydrogen bomb or a cobalt bomb or any other sort of bomb. We had nothing to do with it. Why should we have to die because other countries nine or ten thousand miles away from us wanted to have a war? It's so bloody unfair.'

'It's that all right,' he said. 'But that's the way it is.'

There was a pause, and then she said angrily, 'It's not that I'm afraid of dying, Dwight. We've all got to do that some time. It's all the things I'm going to have to miss . . .' She turned to him in the starlight. 'I'm never going to get outside Australia. All my life I've wanted to see the Rue de Rivoli. I suppose it's the romantic name. It's silly, because I suppose it's just a street like any other street. But that's what I've wanted, and I'm never going to see it. Because there isn't any Paris now, or London, or New York.'

He smiled at her gently. 'The Rue de Rivoli may still be there, with things in the shop windows and everything. I wouldn't know if Paris got a bomb or not. Maybe it's all there still just as it was, with the sun shining down the street the way you'd want to see it. That's the way I like to think about that sort of place. It's just that folks don't live there any more.'

She got restlessly to her feet. 'That's not the way I wanted to see it. A city of dead people . . . Get me another drink, Dwight.'

Still seated, he smiled up at her. 'Not on your life. It's time you went to bed.'

'Then I'll get it for myself.' She marched angrily into the house. He heard the tinkle of glass and she came out almost immediately, a tumbler more than half full in hand with a lump of ice floating in it. 'I was going home in March,' she exclaimed. 'To London. It's been arranged for years. I was to have six months in England and on the Continent, and then I was coming back through America. I'd have seen Madison Avenue. It's so bloody unfair.'

She took a long gulp at her glass, and held it away from her in disgust. 'Christ, what's this muck I'm drinking?'

He got up and took the glass from her and smelt it. 'That's whisky,' he told her.

She took it back from him and smelt it herself. 'So it is,' she said vaguely. 'It'll probably kill me, on top of brandy.' She lifted the glass of neat liquor and tossed it down, and threw the ice cube out upon the grass.

She faced him, unsteady in the starlight. 'I'll never have a family like Mary,' she muttered. 'It's so unfair. Even if you took me to bed tonight I'd never have a family, because there wouldn't be time.' She laughed hysterically. 'It's really damn funny. Mary was afraid that you'd start bursting into tears when you saw the baby and the nappies hanging on the line. Like the squadron leader in the RAF they had before.' Her words began to slur. 'Keep him occ . . . occupied.' She swayed, and caught a post of the

47

veranda. 'That's what she said. Never a dull moment. Don't let him see the baby or perhaps . . . perhaps he'll start crying.' The tears began to trickle down her cheeks. 'She never thought it might be me who'd do the crying, and not you.'

She collapsed by the veranda, head down in a torrent of tears. The submarine commander hesitated for a moment, went to touch her on the shoulder and then drew back, uncertain what to do. Finally he turned away and went into the house. He found Mary in the kitchen tidying up the mess left by the party.

'Mrs Holmes,' he said a little diffidently. 'Maybe you could step outside and take a look at Miss Davidson. She just drank a full glass of neat whisky on top of brandy. I think she might want somebody to put her to bed.'

2

Infants take no account of Sundays or of midnight parties; by six o'clock next morning the Holmeses were up and doing and Peter was on the road pedalling his bicycle with the trailer attached to fetch the milk and cream. He stayed with the farmer for a while discussing the axle for the new trailer, and the towbar, and making a few sketches for the mechanic to work from. 'I've got to report for duty tomorrow,' he said. 'This is the last time that I'll be coming over for the milk.'

'That'll be all right,' said Mr Paul. 'Leave it to me. Tuesdays and Saturdays. I'll see Mrs Holmes gets the milk and cream.'

He got back to his house at about eight o'clock; he shaved and had a shower, dressed, and began to help Mary with the breakfast. Commander Towers put in an appearance at about a quarter to nine with a fresh, scrubbed look about him. 'That was a nice party that you had last night,' he said. 'I don't know when I enjoyed one so much.'

His host said, 'There are some very pleasant people living just round here.' He glanced at his captain and grinned. 'Sorry about Moira. She doesn't usually pass out like that.'

'It was the whisky. She isn't up yet?'

'I wouldn't expect to see her just yet. I heard someone being sick at about two in the morning. I take it that it wasn't you?'

The American laughed. 'No *sir*.'

The breakfast came upon the table, and the three of them sat down. 'Like another swim this morning?' Peter asked his guest. 'It looks like being another hot day.'

The American hesitated. 'I rather like to go to church on Sunday morning. It's what we do at home. Would there be a Church of England church around here any place?'

Mary said, 'It's just down the hill. Only about three quarters of a mile away. The service is at eleven o'clock.'

'I might take a walk down there. Would that fit in with what you're doing, though?'

Peter said, 'Of course, sir. I don't think I'll come with you. I've got a good bit to sort out here before I join in *Scorpion*.'

The captain nodded. 'Sure. I'll be back here in time for lunch, and then I'll have to get back to the ship. I'd like to take a train around three o'clock.'

He walked down to the church in the warm sunlight. He left plenty of time, so that he was a quarter of an hour early for the service, but he went in. The sidesman gave him a prayer book and a hymn book, and he chose a seat towards the back, because the order of the service was still strange to him and from there he could see when other people knelt, and when they stood. He said the conventional prayer that he had been taught in childhood and then he sat back, looking around. The little church was very like the church in his own town, in Mystic, Connecticut. It even smelt the same.

That girl Moira Davidson certainly was all mixed up. She drank too much, but some people never could accept things as they were. She was a nice kid, though. He thought Sharon would like her.

In the tranquillity of the church he set himself to think about his family, and to visualize them. He was, essentially, a very simple man. He would be going back to them in September, home from his travels. He would see them all again in less than nine months' time. They must not feel, when he rejoined them, that he was out of touch, or that he had forgotten things that were important in their lives. Junior must have grown quite a bit; kids did at that age. He had probably outgrown the coonskin cap and outfit, mentally and physically. It was time he had a fishing rod, a little Fiberglas spinning rod, and learned to use it. It would be fun teaching Junior to fish. His birthday was July 10th. Dwight couldn't send the rod for his birthday, and probably he couldn't take it with him, though that would be worth trying. Perhaps he could get one over there.

Helen's birthday was April 17th; she would be six then. Again, he'd miss her birthday unless something happened to *Scorpion*. He must remember to tell her he was sorry, and he must think of something to take her between now and September. Sharon would explain to her on the day, would tell her that Daddy was away at sea, but he'd be coming home before the winter and he'd bring his present then. Sharon would make it all right with Helen.

He sat there thinking of his family throughout the service, kneeling when other people knelt and standing when they stood. From time to time he roused himself to take part in the simple and uncomplicated words of a hymn, but for the rest of the time he was lost in a daydream of his family and of his home. He walked out of the church at the end of the service mentally refreshed. Outside the church he knew nobody and nobody knew him; the vicar smiled

51

at him uncertainly in the porch and he smiled back, and then he was strolling back uphill in the warm sunlight, his head now full of *Scorpion*, the supplies, and the many chores he had to do, the many checks he had to make, before he took her to sea.

At the house he found Mary and Moira Davidson sitting in deck chairs on the veranda, the baby in its pram beside them. Mary got up from her chair as he walked up to them. 'You look hot,' she said. 'Take off your coat and come and sit down in the shade. You found the church all right?'

'Why, yes,' he said. He took his coat off and sat down on the edge of the veranda. 'You've got a mighty fine congregation,' he observed. 'There wasn't a seat vacant.'

'It wasn't always like that,' she said drily. 'Let me get you a drink.'

'I'd like something soft,' he said. He eyed their glasses. 'What's that you're drinking?'

Miss Davidson replied, 'Lime juice and water. All right, don't say it.'

He laughed. 'I'd like one of those, too.' Mary went off to get it for him, and he turned to the girl. 'Did you get any breakfast this morning?'

'Half a banana and a small brandy,' she said equably. 'I wasn't very well.'

'It was the whisky,' he said. 'That was the mistake you made.'

'One of them,' she replied. 'I don't remember anything after talking to you on the lawn, after the party. Did you put me to bed?'

He shook his head. 'I thought that was Mrs Holmes' job.'

She smiled faintly. 'You missed an opportunity. I must remember to thank Mary.'

52

'I should do that. She's a mighty nice person, Mrs Holmes.'

'She says you're going back to Williamstown this afternoon. Can't you stay and have another bathe?'

He shook his head. 'I've got a lot to do on board before tomorrow. We go to sea this week. There's probably a flock of messages on my desk.'

'I suppose you're the sort of person who works very hard, all the time, whether you've got to or not.'

He laughed. 'I suppose I must be.' He glanced at her. 'Do you do any work?'

'Of course. I'm a very busy woman.'

'What do you work at?'

She lifted her glass. 'This. What I've been doing ever since I met you yesterday.'

He grinned. 'You find that the routine gets tedious, sometimes?'

'Life gets tedious,' she quoted. 'Not sometimes. All the time.'

He nodded. 'I'm lucky, having plenty to do.'

She glanced at him. 'Can I come and see your submarine next week?'

He laughed, thinking of the mass of work there was to do on board. 'No, you can't. We go to sea next week.' And then, because that seemed ungracious, he said, 'You interested in submarines?'

'Not really,' she said a little listlessly. 'I kind of thought I'd like to see it, but not if it's a bother.'

'I'd be glad to show it to you,' he told her. 'But not next week. I'd like it if you'd come down and have lunch with me one day when things are quiet and we're not dashing round like scalded cats. A quiet day, when I could show you everything. And then maybe we could go up to the city and have dinner some place.'

'That sounds good,' she said. 'When will that be, so that I can look forward to it?'

He thought for a moment. 'I couldn't say right now. I'll be reporting a state of operational readiness around the end of this coming week, and I'd think they'd send us off on the first cruise within a day or so. After that we ought to have a spell in the dockyard before going off again.'

'This first cruise – that's the one up to Port Moresby?'

'That's right. I'll try to fit it in before we go away on that, but I couldn't guarantee it. If you'll give me your telephone I'll call you around Friday and let you know.'

'Berwick 8641,' she said. He wrote it down. 'Before ten o'clock is the best time to ring. I'm almost always out in the evening.'

He nodded. 'That'll be fine. It's possible we'll still be at sea on Friday. It might be Saturday before I call. But I *will* call, Miss Davidson.'

She smiled. 'Moira's the name, Dwight.'

He laughed. 'Okay.'

She drove him to the station in the buggy after lunch, being herself on her way home to Berwick. As he got down in the station yard she said, 'Goodbye, Dwight. Don't work too hard.' And then she said, 'Sorry I made such a fool of myself last night.'

He grinned. 'Mixing drinks, that's what does it. Let that be a lesson to you.'

She laughed harshly. 'Nothing's a lesson to me, ever. I'll probably do that again tomorrow night, and the night after.'

'It's your body,' he said equably.

'That's the trouble,' she replied. 'Mine, and nobody else's. If anybody else became involved it might be different, but there's no time for that. Too bad.'

He nodded. 'I'll be seeing you.'

'You really will?'

'Why, sure,' he said. 'I'll call you like I said.'

He travelled back to Williamstown in the electric train, while she drove twenty miles to her country home. She got there about six o'clock, unharnessed the mare and put her in the stable. Her father came to help her, and together they pushed the buggy into the garage shed beside the unused Customline, gave the mare a bucket of water and a feed of oats, and went into the house. Her mother was sitting in the screened veranda, sewing.

'Hullo, dear,' she said. 'Did you have a nice time?'

'All right,' the girl replied. 'Peter and Mary threw a party last night. Quite good fun. Knocked me back a bit, though.'

Her mother sighed a little, but she had learned that it was no use to protest. 'You must go to bed early tonight,' she said. 'You've had so many late nights recently.'

'I think I will.'

'What was the American like?'

'He's nice. Very quiet and navy.'

'Was he married?'

'I didn't ask him. I should think he must have been.'

'What did you do?'

The girl repressed her irritation at the catechism; Ma was like that, and there was now too little time to spend it in quarrelling. 'We went sailing in the afternoon.' She settled down to tell her mother most of what had happened during the week-end, repressing the bit about her bra and much of what had happened at the party.

At Williamstown Commander Towers walked into the dockyard and made his way to *Sydney*. He occupied two adjoining cabins with a communicating door in the bulkhead, one of which was used for office purposes. He sent a messenger for the officer of the deck in *Scorpion*

55

and Lieutenant Hirsch appeared with a sheaf of signals in his hand. He took these from the young man and read them through. Mostly they dealt with routine matters of the fuelling and victualling, but one from the Third Naval Member's office was unexpected. It told him that a civilian scientific officer of the Commonwealth Scientific and Industrial Research Organization had been ordered to report in *Scorpion* for scientific duties. This officer would be under the command of the Australian liaison officer in *Scorpion*. His name was Mr J.S. Osborne.

Commander Towers held this signal in his hand, and glanced at the Lieutenant. 'Say, do you know anything about this guy?'

'He's here right now, sir. He arrived this morning. I put him in the wardroom and got the duty officer to allocate a cabin for him for tonight.'

The captain raised his eyebrows. 'Well, what do you know! What does he look like?'

'Very tall and thin. Mousey sort of hair. Wears spectacles.'

'How old?'

'A little older than me, I'd say. Under thirty, though.'

The captain thought for a minute. 'Going to make things kind of crowded in the wardroom. I think we'll berth him with Commander Holmes. You got three men aboard?'

'That's right. Isaacs, Holman, and de Vries. Chief of the Boat Mortimer is on board, too.'

'Tell the Chief I want another cot rigged on the forward side of Bulkhead F, transverse to the ship, head to starboard. He can take one out of the forward torpedo flat.'

'Okay, sir.'

Commander Towers ran through the routine matters in the other signals with his officer, and then sent the Lieutenant to ask Mr Osborne to come to the office.

When the civilian appeared he motioned him to a chair, gave him a cigarette, and dismissed his officer. 'Well, Mr Osborne,' he said, 'this is quite a surprise. I just read the order posting you to join us. I'm glad to know you.'

'I'm afraid it was rather a quick decision,' the scientist said. 'I only heard about it the day before yesterday.'

'That's very often the way it is in service matters,' said the captain. 'Well, first things first. What's your full name?'

'John Seymour Osborne.'

'Married?'

'No.'

'Okay. Aboard *Scorpion*, or aboard any naval vessel, you address me as Captain Towers, and every now and then you call me "sir". On shore, off duty, my name is Dwight to you – not to the junior officers.'

The scientist smiled. 'Very good, sir.'

'Ever been to sea in a submarine before?'

'No.'

'You'll find things just a little cramped till you get used to it. I'm fixing you a berth in Officer's Country, and you'll mess with the officers in the wardroom.' He glanced at the neat grey suit upon the scientist. 'You'll probably need clothing. See Lieutenant-Commander Holmes about that when he comes aboard tomorrow morning, and get him to draw clothing for you from the store. You'll get that suit messed up if you go down in *Scorpion* in that.'

'Thank you, sir.'

The captain leaned back in his chair and glanced at the scientist, noting the lean, intelligent face, the loose, ungainly figure. 'Tell me, what are you supposed to be doing in this outfit?'

'I'm to make observations and keep records of the radioactive levels, atmospheric and marine, with special reference to the sub-surface levels and radioactive intensity within the hull. I understand you're making a cruise northwards.'

'That's what everybody understands but me. It must be right, and I'll be told one day.' He frowned slightly. 'Are you anticipating a rise in the radioactive level inside the hull?'

'I don't think so. I very much hope not. I doubt if it could happen when you are submerged, except under very extreme conditions. But it's just as well to keep an eye on it. I take it that you'd want to know at once of any significant rise.'

'Sure I would.'

They proceeded to discuss the various techniques involved. Most of the gear that Osborne had brought with him was portable and involved no installation in the ship. In the evening light he put on an overall suit lent him by the captain and went down with Dwight into *Scorpion* to inspect the radiation detector mounted on the aft periscope, and formulate a programme for its calibration against a standard instrument as they went down the Bay. A similar check was to be made upon the detector installed in the engine-room, and a small amount of engineering was required at one of the two remaining torpedo tubes for the sampling of sea water. It was practically dark when they climbed back into *Sydney*, to take supper in the great, echoing, empty wardroom.

Next day was a turmoil of activity. When Peter came aboard in the forenoon his first job was to telephone a friend in the Operations Division and point out that it would be courteous, to say the least, to tell the captain what was common knowledge to the Australian officers under his command, and to make a signal requesting his comments on a draft operation order. By evening this signal had come in and had been dealt with, John Osborne was suitably clothed for life in a submarine, the work on the aft door of the torpedo tube was finished, and the two Australians were packing their gear into the little space that had been allocated to them for personal effects. They slept that night in *Sydney*, and moved into *Scorpion* on Tuesday morning. A few more chores were finished in a couple of hours, and Dwight reported readiness to proceed upon sea trials. They were cleared for sea, had lunch at noon beside the *Sydney*, and cast off. Dwight turned his ship and set a course at slow speed down the Bay towards the Heads.

All afternoon they carried out their radioactive trials, cruising around a barge with a mildly radioactive element on board anchored in the middle of the Bay, while John Osborne ran around noting the readings on his various instruments, barking his long shins upon steel manholes as he clambered up and down the conning tower to the bridge, cracking his tall head painfully on bulkheads and control wheels as he moved quickly in the control room. By five o'clock the trials were over; they left the barge to be disposed of by the shore party of scientists who had put it there, and set course for the open sea.

They stayed on the surface all night, settling into the sea routine as they proceeded westward. At dawn they were off Cape Banks in South Australia, in a fresh south-westerly breeze and a moderate sea. Here they submerged and went down to about fifty feet, returning to periscope depth for a look round once an hour. In the late afternoon they were off Cape Borda on Kangaroo Island, and set course up the strait at periscope depth towards Port Adelaide. By about ten o'clock on Wednesday night they were looking at the town through the periscope; after ten minutes the captain turned around without surfacing and made for the open sea again. At sunset on Thursday they were off the north of King Island and setting course for home. They surfaced as they neared the Heads and passed into Port Phillip Bay at the first light of dawn, and berthed alongside the aircraft carrier at Williamstown in time for breakfast on Friday, with nothing but minor defects to be rectified.

That morning the First Naval Member, Vice-Admiral Sir David Hartman, came down to inspect the only ship in his command that was worth bothering about. That took about an hour, and he spent a quarter of an hour with Dwight and Peter Holmes in the office cabin, discussing with them the modifications that they had proposed to the draft operation order. He left then for a conference with the Prime Minister, at that time in Melbourne; with no aircraft flying on the airlines, Federal Government from Canberra was growing difficult, and parliamentary sessions there were growing shorter and less frequent.

That evening Dwight rang Moira Davidson, as he had promised. 'Well,' he said, 'we got back in one piece. There's just a little being done on board the ship, but nothing very much.'

She asked, 'Does that mean I can see her?'

'I'd be glad to show her to you. We shan't be going off again before Monday.'

'I'd like to see her, Dwight. Would tomorrow or Sunday be the best?'

He thought for a moment. If they were to sail on Monday, Sunday might be busy. 'I'd say tomorrow would be best.'

In turn, she thought rapidly. She would have to run out on Anne Sutherland's party, but it looked like a dreary sort of party anyway. 'I'd love to come tomorrow,' she said. 'Do I come to Williamstown station?'

'That's the best way. I'll meet you there. What train will you be coming on?'

'I don't know the times. Let's say the first one after eleven thirty.'

'Okay. If I should be all tied up, I'll get Peter Holmes or else John Osborne to go down and meet you.'

'Did you say John Osborne?'

'That's right. Do you know him?'

'An Australian – with CSIRO?'

'That's the one. A tall guy with spectacles.'

'He's a sort of relation – his aunt married one of my uncles. Is he in your party?'

'Definitely. He joined us as scientific officer.'

'He's dippy,' she informed him. 'Absolutely mad. He'll wreck your ship for you.'

He laughed. 'Okay. Come down and see it before he pulls the bung out.'

'I'd love to do that, Dwight. See you on Saturday morning.'

He met her at the station the next morning, having nothing particular to do in the ship. She came in a white outfit, white pleated skirt, white blouse with coloured thread embroidery vaguely Norwegian in style, white shoes. She was pleasant to look at, but there was concern in him as he greeted her; how in hell he was going to get her through the cramped maze of greasy machinery that was *Scorpion* with her clothes unsullied was a problem, and he was to take her out in the evening.

'Morning, Dwight,' she said. 'Have you been waiting long?'

'Just a few minutes,' he replied. 'Did you have to start very early?'

'Not as early as last time,' she informed him. 'Daddy drove me to the station, and I got a train soon after nine.

Early enough, though. You'll give me a drink before lunch, won't you?'

He hesitated. 'Uncle Sam doesn't like it aboard ship,' he said. 'It'll have to be Coke or orangeade.'

'Even in *Sydney*?'

'Even in *Sydney*,' he said firmly. 'You wouldn't want to drink hard liquor with my officers when they were drinking Cokes.'

She said restlessly, 'I want to drink hard liquor, as you call it, before lunch. I've got a mouth like the bottom of the parrot's cage. You wouldn't want me to throw a screaming fit in front of all your officers.' She glanced around. 'There must be a hotel here somewhere. Buy me a drink before we go on board, and then I'd just breathe brandy at them while I'm drinking Coke.'

'Okay,' he said equably. 'There's a hotel on the corner. We'll go in there.'

They walked together to the hotel; he entered and looked around, unsure of his surroundings. He led her into the Ladies' Lounge. 'I think this must be it.'

'Don't you know? Haven't you ever been in here before?'

He shook his head. 'Brandy?'

'Double,' she said. 'With ice, and just a little water. Don't you come in here?'

'I've never been in here,' he told her.

'Don't you ever want to go out on a bender?' she inquired. 'In the evenings, when you've got nothing to do?'

'I used to just at first,' he admitted. 'But then I went up to the city for it. Don't mess on your own doorstep. I gave it up after a week or two. It wasn't very satisfactory.'

'What do you do in the evenings, when the ship's not at sea?' she asked.

'Read a magazine, or else maybe a book. Sometimes we go out and take in a movie.' The barman came, and he ordered her brandy, with a small whisky for himself.

'It all sounds very unhealthy,' she observed. 'I'm going to the Ladies. Look after my bag.'

He managed to detach her from the hotel after her second double brandy and took her into the dockyard and to *Sydney*, hoping that she would behave herself in front of his officers. But he need have had no fears; she was demure and courteous to all the Americans. Only to Osborne did she reveal her real self.

'Hullo, John,' she said. 'What on earth are you doing here?'

'I'm part of the ship's company,' he told her. 'Scientific observation. Making a nuisance of myself generally.'

'That's what Commander Towers told me,' she observed. 'You're really going to live with them in the submarine? For days on end?'

'So it seems.'

'Do they know your habits?'

'I beg your pardon?'

'All right, I won't tell them. It's nothing to do with me.' She turned away to talk to Commander Lundgren.

When he offered her a drink she chose an orangeade; she made an attractive picture in the wardroom of *Sydney* that morning, drinking with the Americans, standing beneath the portrait of the Queen. While she was occupied the captain drew his liaison officer to one side. 'Say,' he observed in a low tone, 'she can't go down in *Scorpion* in those clothes. Can you rustle up an overall for her?'

Peter nodded. 'I'll draw a boiler suit. About size one, I should think. Where's she going to change?'

The captain rubbed his chin. 'Do you know any place?'

'Nothing better than your sleeping cabin, sir. She wouldn't be disturbed there.'

'I'll never hear the last of it – from her.'

'I'm sure you won't,' said Peter.

She lunched with the Americans at the end of one of the long tables, and took coffee with them in the ante-room. Then the junior officers dispersed to go about their business, and she was left with Dwight and Peter. Peter laid a clean, laundered boiler suit upon the table. 'There's the overall,' he said.

Dwight cleared his throat. 'It's liable to be greasy in a submarine, Miss Davidson,' he said.

'Moira,' she interrupted.

'Okay, Moira. I was thinking maybe you should go down in an overall. I'm afraid you might get that dress pretty dirty down in *Scorpion*.'

She took the boiler suit and unfolded it. 'It's a comprehensive change,' she observed. 'Where can I put it on?'

'I was thinking you might use my sleeping cabin,' he suggested. 'You wouldn't be disturbed there.'

'I hope not, but I wouldn't be too sure,' she said. 'Not after what happened in the boat.' He laughed. 'All right, Dwight, lead me to it. I'll try everything once.'

He took her to the cabin and went back to the ante-room himself to wait for her. In the little sleeping cabin she looked about her curiously. There were photographs there, four of them. All showed a dark haired young woman with two children, a boy eight or nine years old and a girl a couple of years younger. One was a studio portrait of a mother with two children. The others were enlargements of snapshots, one at a bathing place with the family seated on a spring-board, perhaps at a lake shore. Another was apparently taken on a lawn, perhaps the lawn before his home, for a long car showed in the background and a portion of a white wooden house. She stood examining them with interest; they looked nice people. It was hard, but so was everything these days. No good agonizing about it.

She changed, leaving her outer clothes and her bag on the bunk, scowled at her appearance in the little mirror, and went out and down the corridor to find her host. He came forward to meet her. 'Well, here I am,' she said. 'Looking like hell. Your submarine will have to be good, Dwight, to make up for this.'

He laughed, and took her arm to guide her. 'Sure, it's good,' he said. 'Best in the US Navy. This way.' She repressed the comment that it was probably the only one in the US Navy; no sense in hurting him.

He took her down the gangplank to the narrow deck and up on to the bridge, and began explaining his ship to her. She knew little of ships and nothing about submarines, but she was attentive and once or twice surprised him with the quick intelligence of her questions. 'When you go down, why doesn't the water go down the voice pipe?' she asked.

'You turn off this cock.'

'What happens if you forget?'

He grinned. 'There's another one down below.'

He took her down through the narrow hatchways into the control-room. She spent some time at the periscope looking around the harbour and got the hang of that, but the ballasting and trim controls were beyond her and she was not much interested. She stared uncomprehending at the engines, but the sleeping and messing quarters intrigued her, so did the galley. 'What happens about smells?' she asked. 'What happens when you're cooking cabbage under water?'

'You try not to have to do it,' he told her. 'Not fresh

cabbage. The smell hangs around for quite a while. Finally
the deodoriser deals with it, as the air gets changed and
re-oxygenated. There wouldn't be much left after an hour
or two.'

He gave her a cup of tea in the tiny cubicle that was
his cabin. Sipping it, she asked him, 'Have you got your
orders yet, Dwight?'

He nodded. 'Cairns, Port Moresby, and Darwin. Then
we come back here.'

'There isn't anybody left alive in any of those places,
is there?'

'I wouldn't know. That's what we've got to find out.'

'Will you go ashore?'

He shook his head. 'I don't think so. It all depends
upon the radiation levels, but I wouldn't think we'd land.
Maybe we won't even go outside the hull. We might stay
at periscope depth if the conditions are really bad. But
that's why we're taking John Osborne along with us, so
we'll have somebody who really understands what the
risks are.'

She wrinkled her brows. 'But if you can't go out on
deck, how can you know if there's anyone still living in
those places?'

'We can call through the loud hailer,' he said. 'Get as
close inshore as we can manage, and call through the
loud hailer.'

'Could you hear them if they answer?'

'Not so well as we can talk. We've got a microphone
hooked up beside the hailer, but you'd have to be
very close to hear a person calling in reply. Still, it's
something.'

She glanced at him. 'Has anybody been into the radioactive area before, Dwight?'

'Why, yes,' he said. 'It's okay if you're sensible, and

don't take risks. We were in it quite a while, while the war was on, from Iwojima to the Philippines and then down south to Yap. You stay submerged, and carry on as usual. Of course, you don't want to go out on deck.'

'I mean – recently. Has anyone been up into the radio-active areas since the war stopped?'

He nodded. 'The *Swordfish* – that's our sister ship – she made a cruise up in the North Atlantic. She got back to Rio de Janeiro about a month ago. I've been waiting for a copy of Johnny Dismore's report – he's her captain – but I haven't seen it yet. There hasn't been a ship across to South America for quite a while. I asked for a copy to be sent by teleprinter, but it's low priority upon the radio.'

'How far did she get?'

'She got all over, I believe,' he said. 'She did the Eastern States from Florida to Maine and went right in to New York Harbor, right on up the Hudson till she tangled with the wreck of the George Washington Bridge. She went to New London and to Halifax and to St John's, and then she crossed the Atlantic and went up the English Channel and into the London River, but she couldn't get far up that. Then she took a look at Brest and at Lisbon, and by that time she was running out of stores and her crew were in pretty bad shape, so she went back to Rio.' He paused. 'I haven't heard yet how many days she was submerged – I'd like to know. She certainly set a new record, anyway.'

'Did she find anyone alive, Dwight?'

'I don't think so. We'd certainly have heard about it if she did.'

She stared down the narrow alleyway outside the curtain forming the cabin wall, the running maze of pipes and electric cables. 'Can you visualize it, Dwight?'

'Visualize what?'

'All those cities, all those fields and farms, with nobody,

67

and nothing left alive. Just nothing there. I simply can't take it in.'

'I can't, either,' he said. 'I don't know that I want to try. I'd rather think of them the way they were.'

'I never saw them, of course,' she observed. 'I've never been outside Australia, and now I'll never go. Not that I want to, now. I only know all those places from the movies and the books – that's as they were. I don't suppose there'll ever be a movie made of them as they are now.'

He shook his head. 'It wouldn't be possible. A cameraman couldn't live, as far as I can see. I guess nobody will ever know what the northern hemisphere looks like now, excepting God.' He paused. 'I think that's a good thing. You don't want to remember how a person looked when he was dead – you want to remember how he was when he was alive. That's the way I like to think about New York.'

'It's too big,' she repeated. 'I can't take it in.'

'It's too big for me, too,' he replied. 'I can't really believe in it, just can't get used to the idea. I suppose it's lack of imagination. I don't want to have any more imagination. They're all alive to me, those places in the States, just like they were. I'd like them to stay that way till next September.'

She said softly, 'Of course.'

He stirred. 'Have another cup of tea?'

'No thanks.'

He took her out on deck again; she paused on the bridge, rubbing a bruised shin, breathing the sea air gratefully. 'It must be the hell of a thing to be submerged in her for any length of time,' she said. 'How long will you be under water for this cruise?'

'Not long,' he said. 'Six or seven days, maybe.'

'It must be terribly unhealthy.'

'Not physically,' he said. 'You do suffer from a lack of

sunlight. We've got a couple of sunray lamps, but they're not the same as being out on deck. It's the psychological effect that's worst. Some men – good men in every other way – they just can't take it. Everybody gets kind of on edge after a while. You need a steady kind of temperament. Kind of placid, I'd say.'

She nodded, thinking that it fitted in with his own character. 'Are all of you like that?'

'I'd say we might be. Most of us.'

'Keep an eye on John Osborne,' she remarked. 'I don't believe he is.'

He glanced at her in surprise. He had not thought of that, and the scientist had survived the trial trip quite well. But now that she had mentioned it, he wondered. 'Why – I'll do that,' he said. 'Thanks for the suggestion.'

They went up the gangway into *Sydney*. In the hangar of the aircraft carrier there were still aircraft parked with folded wings; the ship seemed dead and silent. She paused for a moment. 'None of these will ever fly again, will they?'

'I wouldn't think so.'

'Do any aeroplanes fly now, at all?'

'I haven't heard one in the air for quite a while,' he said. 'I know they're short of aviation gas.'

She walked quietly with him to the cabin, unusually subdued. As she got out of the boiler suit and into her own clothes her spirits revived. These morbid bloody ships, these morbid bloody realities! She was urgent to get away from them, to drink, hear music, and to dance. Before the mirror, before the pictures of his wife and children, she made her lips redder, her cheeks brighter, her eyes sparkling. Snap out of it! Get right outside these riveted steel walls, and get out quick! This was no place for her. Into the world of romance, of make-believe and double brandies! Snap out of it, and get back to the world where she belonged!

From the photograph frames Sharon looked at her with understanding and approval.

In the wardroom he came forward to meet her. 'Say,' he exclaimed in admiration, 'you look swell!'

She smiled quickly. 'I'm feeling lousy,' she said. 'Let's get out of it and into the fresh air. Let's go to that hotel and have a drink, and then go up and find somewhere to dance.'

'Anything you say.'

He left her with John Osborne while he went to change into civilian clothes. 'Take me up on to the flight deck, John,' she said. 'I'll throw a screaming fit if I stay in these ships one minute longer.'

'I'm not sure that I know the way up to the roof,' he remarked. 'I'm a new boy here.' They found a steep ladder that led up to a gun turret, came down again, wandered along a steel corridor, asked a rating, and finally got up into the island and out on to the deck. On the wide, unencumbered flight deck the sun was warm, the sea blue, and the wind fresh. 'Thank God I'm out of that,' she said.

'I take it that you aren't enamoured of the navy,' he observed.

'Well, are you having fun?'

He considered the matter. 'Yes, I think I am. It's going to be rather interesting.'

'Looking at dead people through a periscope. I can think of funnier sorts of fun.'

They walked a step or two in silence. 'It's all knowledge,' he said at last. 'One has to try and find out what has happened. It could be that it's all quite different from what we think. The radioactive elements may be getting absorbed by something. Something may have happened to the half-life that we don't know about. Even if we don't discover anything that's good, it's still discovering things. I don't think we *shall* discover anything that's good, or very hopeful. But even so, it's fun just finding out.'

'You call finding out the bad things fun?'

'Yes, I do,' he said firmly. 'Some games are fun even when you lose. Even when you know you're going to lose before you start. It's fun just playing them.'

'You've got a pretty queer idea of fun and games.'

'Your trouble is you won't face up to things,' he told her. 'All this has happened, and is happening, but you won't accept it. You've got to face the facts of life some day.'

'All right,' she said angrily, 'I've got to face them. Next September, if what all you people say is right. That's time enough for me.'

'Have it your own way.' He glanced at her, grinning. 'I wouldn't bank too much upon September,' he remarked. 'It's September plus or minus about three months. We may be going to cop it in June, for all that anybody knows. Or, then again, I might be buying you a Christmas present.'

She said furiously, 'Don't you *know*?'

'No, I don't,' he replied. 'Nothing like this has ever happened in the history of the world before.' He paused, and then he added whimsically, 'If it had, we wouldn't be here talking about it.'

'If you say one word more I'm going to push you over the edge of that deck.'

Commander Towers came out of the island and walked across to them, neat in a double-breasted blue suit. 'I wondered where you'd got to,' he remarked.

The girl said, 'Sorry, Dwight. We should have left a message. I wanted some fresh air.'

John Osborne said, 'You'd better watch out, sir. She's

in a pretty bad temper. I'd stand away from her head, if I were you, in case she bites.'

'He's been teasing me,' she said. 'Like Albert and the lion. Let's go, Dwight.'

'See you tomorrow, sir,' the scientist said. 'I'll be staying on board over the weekend.'

The captain turned away with the girl, and they went down the stairs within the island. As they passed down the steel corridor towards the gangway he asked her, 'What was he teasing you about, honey?'

'Everything,' she said vaguely. 'Took his stick and poked it in my ear. Let's have a drink before we start looking for a train, Dwight. I'll feel better then.'

He took her to the same hotel in the main street. Over the drinks he asked her. 'How long have we got, this evening?'

'The last train leaves Flinders Street at eleven-fifteen. I'd better get on that, Dwight. Mummy would never forgive me if I spent the night with you.'

'I'll say she wouldn't. What happens when you get to Berwick? Is anybody meeting you?'

She shook her head. 'We left a bicycle at the station this morning. If you do the right thing by me I won't be able to ride it, but it's there, anyway.' She finished her first double brandy. 'Buy me another, Dwight.'

'I'll buy you one more,' he said. 'After that we're getting on the train. You promised me that we'd be going dancing.'

'So we are,' she said. 'I booked a table at Mario's. But I shuffle beautifully when I'm tight.'

'I don't want to shuffle,' he said. 'I want to dance.'

She took the drink he handed her. 'You're very exacting,' she said. 'Don't go poking any more sticks in my

72

ear – I just can't bear it. Most men don't know how to dance, anyway.'

'You'll find me one of them,' he said. 'We used to dance a lot back in the States. But I've not danced since the war began.'

She said, 'I think you live a very restricted life.'

He managed to detach her from the hotel after her second drink, and they walked to the station in the evening light. They arrived at the city half an hour later, and walked out into the street. 'It's a bit early,' she said. 'Let's walk.'

He took her arm to guide her through the Saturday evening crowds. Most of the shops had plenty of good stock still in the windows but few were open. The restaurants and cafés were all full, doing a roaring trade; the bars were shut, but the streets were full of drunks. The general effect was one of boisterous and uninhibited lightheartedness, more in the style of 1890 than of 1963. There was no traffic in the wide streets but for the trams, and people swarmed all over the road. At the corner of Swanston and Collins Streets an Italian was playing a very large and garish accordion, and playing it very well indeed. Around him, people were dancing to it. As they passed the Regal Cinema a man, staggering along in front of them, fell down, paused for a moment upon hands and knees, and rolled dead drunk into the gutter. Nobody paid much attention to him. A policeman, strolling down the pavement, turned him over, examined him casually, and strolled on.

'They have quite a time here in the evenings,' Dwight remarked.

'It's nothing like so bad as it used to be,' the girl replied. 'It was much worse than this just after the war.'

'I know it. I'd say they're getting tired of it.' He paused, and then he said, 'Like I did.'

She nodded. 'This is Saturday, of course. It's very quiet here on an ordinary night. Almost like it was before the war.'

They walked on to the restaurant. The proprietor welcomed them because he knew her well; she was in his establishment at least once a week and frequently more often. Dwight Towers had been there half a dozen times, perhaps, preferring his club, but he was known to the head waiter as the captain of the American submarine. They were well received and given a good table in a corner away from the band; they ordered drinks and dinner.

'They're pretty nice people here,' Dwight said appreciatively. 'I don't come in so often, and I don't spend much when I do come.'

'I come here pretty frequently,' the girl said. She sat in reflection for a moment. 'You know, you're a very lucky man.'

'Why do you say that?'

'You've got a full time job to do.'

It had not occurred to him before that he was fortunate. 'That's so,' he said slowly. 'I certainly don't seem to get a lot of time to go kicking around on the loose.'

'I do,' she said. 'It's all I've got to do.'

'Don't you work at anything? No job at all?'

'Nothing at all,' she said. 'Sometimes I drive a bullock round the farm at home, harrowing the muck. That's all I ever do.'

'I'd have thought you'd have been working in the city some place,' he remarked.

'So would I,' she said a little cynically. 'But it's not so easy as that. I took honours in history up at the Shop, just before the war.'

'The Shop?'

'The University. I was going to do a course of shorthand and typing. But what's the sense in working for a year at that? I wouldn't have time to finish it. And if I did, there aren't any jobs.'

'You mean, business is slowing down?'

She nodded. 'Lots of my friends are out of a job now. People aren't working like they used to, and they don't want secretaries. Half of Daddy's friends – people who used to go to the office – they just don't go now. They live at home, as if they were retired. An awful lot of offices have closed, you know.'

'I suppose that makes sense,' he remarked. 'A man has a right to do the things he wants to do in the last months, if he can get by with the money.'

'A girl has a right to, too' she said. 'Even if the things she wants to do are something different to driving a bullock round the farm to spread the dung.'

'There's just no work at all?' he asked.

'Nothing that I could find,' she said. 'And I've tried hard enough. You see, I can't even type.'

'You could learn,' he said. 'You could go and take that course that you were going to take.'

'What's the sense of that, if there's no time to finish it, or use it afterwards?'

'Something to work at,' he remarked. 'Just as an alternative to all the double brandies.'

'Work just for the sake of working?' she inquired. 'It sounds simply foul.' Her fingers drummed restlessly upon the table.

'Better than drinking just for the sake of drinking,' he observed. 'Doesn't give you a hangover.'

She said irritably, 'Order me a double brandy, Dwight, and then let's see if you can dance.'

He took her out upon the dance floor, feeling vaguely sorry for her. She was in a prickly kind of mood. Immersed in his own troubles and occupations, it had never occurred to him that young, unmarried people had their own frustrations in these times. He set himself to make the evening pleasant for her, talking about the films and musicals they both had seen, the mutual friends they had. 'Peter and Mary Holmes are funny,' she told him once. 'She's absolutely nuts on gardening. They've got that flat upon a three years' lease. She's planning to plant things this autumn that'll come up next year.'

He smiled. 'I'd say she's got the right idea. You never know.' He steered the conversation back to safer subjects. 'Did you see the Danny Kaye movie at the Plaza?'

Yachting and sailing were safe topics, and they talked around those for some time. The floor show came on as they finished dinner, and amused them for a while, and then they danced again. Finally the girl said, 'Cinderella. I'll have to start and think about that train, Dwight.'

He paid the bill while she was in the cloak-room, and met her by the door. In the streets of the city it was quiet now; the music was stilled, the restaurants and cafés were now closed. Only the drunks remained, reeling down the pavements aimlessly or lying down to sleep. The girl wrinkled her nose. 'They ought to do something about all this,' she said. 'It never was like this before the war.'

'It's quite a problem,' he said thoughtfully. 'It comes up all the time in the ship. I reckon a man has a right to do the things he wants to when he goes ashore, so long as he doesn't go bothering other people. Some folks just have to have the liquor, times like these.' He eyed a policeman on the corner. 'That's what the cops here seem to think, in this city, at any rate. I've never seen a drunk arrested yet, not just for being drunk.'

At the station she paused to thank him and to wish him goodnight. 'It's been a beaut evening,' she said. 'The day, too. Thanks for everything, Dwight.'

'I've enjoyed it, Moira,' he said. 'It's years since I danced.'

'You're not too bad,' she told him. And then she asked, 'Do you know when you go off up north?'

He shook his head. 'Not yet. A message came in just before we left, telling me to report Monday morning in the First Naval Member's offices, with Lieutenant-Commander Holmes. I imagine we'll get our final briefing then, and maybe get away on Monday afternoon.'

She said, 'Good luck. Will you give me a ring when you come back to Williamstown?'

'Why, sure,' he said. 'I'd like to do that. Maybe we could go sailing again some place, or else do this again.'

She said, 'That'd be fun. I'll have to go now, or I'll miss this train. Goodnight again, and thanks for everything.'

'It's been a lot of fun,' he said. 'Goodnight.' He stood and watched her go till she was lost in the crowd. From the back view, in that light summer dress, she was not unlike Sharon – or could it be that he was forgetting, muddling them up? No, she really was a bit like Sharon in the way she walked. Not in any other way. Perhaps that was why he liked her, that she was just a little like his wife.

He turned away, and went to catch his train to Williamstown.

He went to church next morning in Williamstown, as was his habit on a Sunday when circumstances made it possible. At ten o'clock on Monday morning he was with Peter Holmes in the Navy Department, waiting in the outer office to see the First Naval Member, Sir David Hartman. The secretary said, 'He won't be a minute, sir.

I understand he's taking you both over to the Commonwealth Government Offices.'

'He is?'

The Lieutenant nodded. 'He ordered a car.' A buzzer sounded and the young man went into the inner office. He reappeared in a moment. 'Will you both go in now.'

They went into the inner office. The Vice-Admiral got up to meet them. 'Morning, Commander Towers. Morning, Holmes. The Prime Minister wants to have a word with you before you go, so we'll go over to his office in a minute. Before we do that, I want to give you this.' He turned, and lifted a fairly bulky typescript from his desk. 'This is the report of the commanding officer of USS *Swordfish* on his cruise from Rio de Janeiro up into the North Atlantic.' He handed it to Dwight. 'I'm sorry that it's been so long in coming, but the pressure on the radio to South America is very great, and there's a good deal of it. You can take it with you and look it over at your leisure.'

The American took it, and turned it over with interest. 'It's going to be very valuable to us, sir. Is there anything in it to affect this operation?'

'I don't think there is. He found a high level of radioactivity – atmospheric radioactivity – over the whole area, greater in the north than in the south, as you'd expect. He submerged – let's see' – he took the typescript back and turned the pages quickly – 'he submerged in Latitude Two South, off Parnaiba, and stayed submerged for the whole cruise, surfacing again in Latitude Five South off Cape Sao Roque.'

'How long was he submerged, sir?'

'Thirty-two days.'

'That might be a record.'

The Admiral nodded. 'I think it is. I think he says

so, somewhere.' He handed back the typescript. 'Well, take it with you and study it. It gives an indication of conditions in the north. By the way, if you should want to get in touch with him, he's moved his ship down into Uruguay. He's at Montevideo now.'

Peter asked, 'Are things getting hot in Rio, sir?'

'It's getting a bit close.'

They left the office in the Navy Department, went down into the yard, and got into an electric truck. It took them silently through the empty streets of the city, up tree-lined Collins Street to the Commonwealth Offices. In a few minutes they found themselves seated with Mr Donald Ritchie, the Prime Minister, around a table.

He said, 'I wanted to see you before you sailed, Captain, to tell you a little bit about the purpose of this cruise, and to wish you luck. I've read your operation order, and I have very little to add to that. You are to proceed to Cairns, to Port Moresby, and to Darwin for the purpose of reporting on conditions in those places. Any signs of life would be particularly interesting, of course, whether human or animal. Vegetation, too. And seabirds, if you can gather any information about those.'

'I think that's going to be difficult, sir,' Dwight said.

'Yes, I suppose so. Anyway, I understand you're taking a member of the CSIRO with you.'

'Yes, sir. Mr Osborne.'

The Prime Minister passed his hand across his face, a habitual gesture. 'Well. I don't expect you to take risks. In fact, I forbid it. We want you back here with your ship intact and your crew in good health. You will use your own discretion whether you expose yourself on deck, whether you expose your ship upon the surface, guided by your scientific officer. Within the limits of that instruction, we want all the information we can get. If the radiation level makes it possible, you should land and inspect the towns. But I don't think it will.'

The First Naval Member shook his head. 'I very much doubt it. I think you may find it necessary to submerge by the time you get to Twenty-two South.'

The American thought rapidly. 'That's south of Townsville.'

The Prime Minister said heavily, 'Yes. There are still people alive in Townsville. You are expressly forbidden to go there, unless your operation order should be modified by a signal from the Navy Department.' He raised his head, and looked at the American. 'That may seem hard to you, Commander. But you can't help them, and it's better not to raise false hopes by showing them your ship. And after all, we know what the conditions are in Townsville. We still have telegraphic contact with them there.'

'I understand that, sir.'

'That leads me to the last point that I have to make,' the Prime Minister said. 'You are expressly forbidden to take anybody on board your ship during this cruise, except with the prior permission of the Navy Department obtained by radio. I know that you will understand the obvious necessity that neither you or any member of your crew should be exposed to contact with a radioactive person. Is that quite clear?'

'Quite clear, sir.'

The Prime Minister rose to his feet. 'Well, good luck to all of you. I shall look forward to talking to you again, Commander Towers, in a fortnight's time.'

3

Nine days later USS *Scorpion* surfaced at dawn. In the grey light, as the stars faded, the periscopes emerged from a calm sea off Sandy Cape near Bundaberg in Queensland, in Latitude Twenty-four degrees South. She stayed below the surface for a quarter of an hour while the captain checked his position by the lighthouse on the distant shore and by echo soundings, and while John Osborne checked the atmospheric and sea radiation levels, with fingers fumbling irritably upon his instruments. Then she slid up out of the depths, a long grey hull, low in the water, heading south at twenty knots. On the bridge deck a hatch clanged open and the officer of the deck emerged, followed by the captain and by many others. In the calm weather the forward and aft torpedo hatches were opened and clean air began to circulate throughout the boat. A life line was rigged from the bow to the bridge structure and another to the stern, and all the men off duty clambered up on deck into the fresh morning air, white faced, rejoicing to be out of it, to see the rising sun. They had been submerged for over a week.

Half an hour later they were hungry, hungrier than they had been for several days. When breakfast was sounded they tumbled below quickly; the cooks in turn came up for a spell on deck. When the watch was relieved more men came quickly up into the bright sunlight. The officers appeared upon the bridge, smoking, and the ship settled into the normal routine of surface operation, heading southwards on a blue sea down the Queensland coast. The radio mast was rigged, and they reported their position in a signal. Then they began to receive the broadcasting for entertainment, and light music filled the hull, mingling with the murmur of the turbines and the rushing noise of water alongside.

On the bridge the captain said to his liaison officer, 'This report's going to be just a little difficult to write.'

Peter nodded. 'There's the tanker, sir.'

Dwight said, 'Sure, there's the tanker.' Between Cairns and Port Moresby, in the Coral Sea, they had come upon a ship. She was a tanker, empty and in ballast, drifting with her engines stopped. She was registered in Amsterdam. They cruised around her, hailing through the loud hailer, and getting no response, looking at her through the periscope as they checked her details with Lloyds Register. All her boats were in place at the davits, but there seemed to be nobody alive on board her. She was rusty, very rusty indeed. They came to the conclusion finally that she was a derelict that had been drifting about the oceans since the war; she did not seem to have suffered any damage, other than the weather. There was nothing to be done about her, and the atmospheric radiation level was too high for them to go on deck or make any attempt to board her, even if it had been possible for them to get up her sheer sides. So, after an hour, they left her where they found her, photographing her through the periscope and noting the position. This was the only ship that they had met throughout the cruise.

The liaison officer said, 'It's going to boil down to a report on Honest John's radioactive readings.'

'That's about the size of it,' the captain agreed. 'We did see that dog.'

Indeed, the report was not going to be an easy one to write, for they had seen and learned very little in the course of their cruise. They had approached Cairns upon the surface but within the hull, the radiation level being too great to allow exposure on the bridge. They had threaded their way cautiously through the Barrier Reef to get to it, spending one night hove-to because Dwight judged it dangerous to navigate in darkness in such waters, where the lighthouses and leading lights were unreliable. When finally they picked up Green Island and approached the land, the town looked absolutely normal to them. It stood bathed in sunshine on the shore, with the mountain range of the Atherton tableland behind. Through the periscope they could see streets of shops shaded with palm trees, a hospital, and trim villas of one storey raised on posts above the ground; there were cars parked in the streets and one or two flags flying. They went on up the river to the docks. Here there was little to be seen except a few fishing boats at anchor up the river, completely normal; there were no ships at the wharves. The cranes were trimmed fore and aft along the wharves and properly secured. Although they were close in to shore they could see little here, for the periscope reached barely higher than the wharf decking, and the warehouses then blocked the view. All that they could see was a silent water-front, exactly as it would have looked upon a Sunday or a holiday, though then there would have been activity among the smaller craft. A large black dog appeared and barked at them from a wharf.

They had stayed in the river off the wharves for a couple of hours, hailing through the loud hailer at its maximum volume in tones that must have sounded all

83

over the town. Nothing happened, for the whole town was asleep.

They turned the ship around, and went out a little way till they could see the Strand Hotel and part of the shopping centre again. They stayed there for a time, still calling and still getting no response. Then they gave up, and headed out to sea again to get clear of the Barrier Reef before the darkness fell. Apart from the radioactive information gathered by John Osborne they had learned nothing, unless it was the purely negative information that Cairns looked exactly as it always had before. The sun shone in the streets, the flame trees brightened the far hills, the deep verandas shaded the shop windows of the town. A pleasant little place to live in in the tropics, though nobody lived there except, apparently, one dog.

Port Moresby had been the same. From the sea they could see nothing the matter with the town, viewed through the periscope. A merchant ship registered in Liverpool lay at anchor in the roads, a Jacob's ladder up her side. Two more ships lay on the beach, probably having dragged their anchors in some storm. They stayed there for some hours, cruising the roads and going in to the dock, calling through the loud hailer. There was no response, but there seemed to be nothing the matter with the town. They left after a time, for there was nothing there to stay for.

Two days later they reached Port Darwin and lay in the harbour beneath the town. Here they could see nothing but the wharf, the roof of Government House, and a bit of the Darwin Hotel. Fishing boats lay at anchor and they cruised around these, hailing, and examining them through the periscope. They learned nothing, save for the inference that when the end had come the people had died tidily. 'It's what animals do,' John Osborne said. 'Creep away into holes to die. They're probably all in bed.'

'That's enough about that,' the captain said.

'It's true,' the scientist remarked.

'Okay, it's true. Now let's not talk about it any more.'

The report certainly was going to be a difficult one to write.

They had left Port Darwin as they had left Cairns and Port Moresby; they had gone back through the Torres Strait and headed southwards down the Queensland coast, submerged. By that time the strain of the cruise was telling on them; they talked little among themselves till they surfaced three days after leaving Darwin. Refreshed by a spell on deck, they now had time to think about what story they could tell about their cruise when they got back to Melbourne.

They talked of it after lunch, smoking at the wardroom table. 'It's what *Swordfish* found, of course,' Dwight said. 'She saw practically nothing either in the States or in Europe.'

Peter reached out for the well-thumbed report that lay behind him on the cupboard top. He leafed it through again, though it had been his constant reading on the cruise. 'I never thought of that,' he said slowly. 'I missed that angle on it, but now that you mention it, it's true. There's practically nothing here about conditions on shore.'

'They couldn't look on shore, any more than we could,' the captain said. 'Nobody will ever really know what a hot place looks like. And that goes for the whole of the northern hemisphere.'

Peter said, 'That's probably as well.'

'I think that's right,' said the Commander. 'There's some things that a person shouldn't want to go and see.'

John Osborne said, 'I was thinking about that last night. Did it ever strike you that nobody will ever – *ever* – see Cairns again? Or Moresby, or Darwin?'

They stared at him while they turned over the new idea. 'Nobody could see more than we've seen,' the captain said.

'Who else can go there, except us? And we shan't go again. Not in the time.'

'That's so,' Dwight said thoughtfully. 'I wouldn't think they'd send us back there again. I never thought of it that way, but I'd say you're right. We're the last living people that will ever see those places.' He paused. 'And we saw practically nothing. Well, I think that's right.'

Peter stirred uneasily. 'That's historical,' he said. 'It ought to go on record somewhere, oughtn't it? Is anybody writing any kind of history about these times?'

John Osborne said, 'I haven't heard of one. I'll find out about that. After all, there doesn't seem to be much point in writing stuff that nobody will read.'

'There should be something written, all the same,' said the American. 'Even if it's only going to be read in the next few months.' He paused. 'I'd like to read a history of this last war,' he said. 'I was in it for a little while, but I don't know a thing about it. Hasn't anybody written anything?'

'Not as a history,' John Osborne said. 'Not that I know of, anyway. The information that we've got is all available, of course, but not as a coherent story. I think there'd be too many gaps – the things we just don't know.'

'I'd settle for the things we *do* know,' the captain remarked.

'What sort of things, sir?'

'Well, as a start, how many bombs were dropped? Nuclear bombs, I mean.'

86

'The seismic records show about four thousand seven hundred. Some of the records were pretty weak, so there were probably more than that.'

'How many of those were big ones – fusion bombs, hydrogen bombs, or whatever you call them?'

'I couldn't tell you. Probably most of them. All the bombs dropped in the Russo-Chinese war were hydrogen bombs, I think – most of them with a cobalt element.'

'Why did they do that? Use cobalt, I mean?' Peter asked.

The scientist shrugged his shoulders. 'Radiological warfare. I can't tell you any more than that.'

'I think I can,' said the American. 'I attended a commanding officers' course at Yerba Buena, San Francisco, the month before the war. They told us what they thought might happen between Russia and China. Whether they told us what *did* happen six weeks later – well, your guess is as good as mine.'

John Osborne asked quietly, 'What did they tell you?'

The captain considered for a minute. Then he said, 'It was all tied up with the warm water ports. Russia hasn't got a port that doesn't freeze up in the winter except Odessa, and that's on the Black Sea. To get out of Odessa on to the high seas the traffic has to pass two narrow straits both commanded by NATO in time of war – the Bosporus and Gibraltar. Murmansk and Vladivostok can be kept open by icebreakers in the winter, but they're a mighty long way from any place in Russia that makes things to export.' He paused. 'This guy from Intelligence said that what Russia really wanted was Shanghai.'

The scientist asked, 'Is that handy for their Siberian industries?'

The captain nodded. 'That's exactly it. During the Second War they moved a great many industries way

87

back along the Trans-Siberian railway east of the Urals, back as far as Lake Baikal. They built new towns and everything. Well, it's a long, long way from those places to a port like Odessa. It's only about half the distance to Shanghai.'

He paused. 'There was another thing he told us,' he said thoughtfully. 'China had three times the population of Russia, all desperately overcrowded in their country. Russia, next door to the north of them, had millions and millions of square miles of land she didn't use at all because she didn't have the people to populate it. This guy said that as the Chinese industries increased over the last twenty years, Russia got to be afraid of an attack by China. She'd have been a great deal happier if there had been two hundred million fewer Chinese, and she wanted Shanghai. And that adds up to radiological warfare . . .'

Peter said, 'But using cobalt, she couldn't follow up and take Shanghai.'

'That's true. But she could make North China uninhabitable for quite a number of years by spacing the bombs right. If they put them down in the right places the fall-out would cover China to the sea. Any left over would go round the world eastwards across the Pacific; if a little got to the United States I don't suppose the Russians would have wept salt tears. If they planned it right there would be very little left when it got round the world again to Europe and to western Russia. Certainly she couldn't follow up and take Shanghai for quite a number of years, but she'd get it in the end.'

Peter turned to the scientist. 'How long would it be before people could work in Shanghai?'

'With cobalt fall-out? I wouldn't even guess. It depends on so many things. You'd have to send in exploratory teams. More than five years, I should think —

that's the half-life. Less than twenty. But you just can't say.'

Dwight nodded. 'By the time anyone could get there, Chinese or anyone else, they'd find the Russians there already.'

John Osborne turned to him. 'What did the Chinese think about all this?'

'Oh, they had another angle altogether. They didn't specially want to kill Russians. What they wanted to do was to turn the Russians back into an agricultural people that wouldn't want Shanghai or any other port. The Chinese aimed to blanket the Russian industrial regions with a cobalt fall-out, city by city, put there with their inter-continental rockets. What they wanted was to stop any Russian from using a machine tool for the next ten years or so. They planned a limited fall-out of heavy particles, not going very far around the world. They probably didn't plan to hit the city, even – just to burst maybe ten miles west of it, and let the wind do the rest.' He paused. 'With no Russian industry left, the Chinese could have walked in any time they liked and occupied the safe parts of the country, any that they fancied. Then, as the radiation eased, they'd occupy the towns.'

'Find the lathes a bit rusty,' Peter said.

'I'd say they might be. But they'd have had an easy war.'

John Osborne asked, 'Do you think that's what happened?'

'I wouldn't know,' said the American. 'Maybe no one knows. That's just what this officer from the Pentagon told us at the commanding officers' course.' He paused. 'One thing was in Russia's favour,' he said thoughtfully. 'China hadn't any friends or allies, except Russia. When Russia went for China, nobody else would make much trouble – start war on another front, or anything like that.'

They sat smoking in silence for a few minutes. 'You think that's what flared up finally?' Peter said at last. 'I mean, after the original attacks the Russians made on Washington and London?'

John Osborne and the captain stared at him. 'The Russians never bombed Washington,' Dwight said. 'They proved that in the end.'

He stared back at them. 'I mean, the very first attack of all.'

'That's right. The very first attack. They were Russian long range bombers, II 626s, but they were Egyptian manned. They flew from Cairo.'

'Are you sure that's true?'

'It's true enough. They got the one that landed at Porto Rico on the way home. They only found out it was Egyptian after we'd bombed Leningrad and Odessa and the nuclear establishments at Kharkov, Kuibyshev, and Molotov. Things must have happened kind of quick that day.'

'Do you mean to say we bombed Russia by mistake?' It was so horrible a thought as to be incredible.

John Osborne said, 'That's true, Peter. It's never been admitted publicly, but it's quite true. The first one was the bomb on Naples. That was the Albanians, of course. Then there was the bomb on Tel Aviv. Nobody knows who dropped that one, not that I've heard, anyway. Then the British and Americans intervened and made that demonstration flight over Cairo. Next day the Egyptians sent out all the serviceable bombers that they'd got, six to Washington and seven to London. One got through to Washington, and two to London. After that there weren't many American or British statesmen left alive.'

Dwight nodded. 'The bombers were Russian, and I've heard it said that they had Russian markings. It's quite possible.'

'Good God!' said the Australian. 'So we bombed Russia?'

'That's what happened,' said the captain heavily.

John Osborne said, 'It's understandable. London and Washington were out – right out. Decisions had to be made by the military commanders at dispersal in the field, and they had to be made quick before another lot of bombs arrived. Things were very strained with Russia, after the Albanian bomb, and these aircraft were identified as Russian.' He paused. 'Somebody had to make a decision, of course, and make it in a matter of minutes. Up at Canberra they think now that he made it wrong.'

'But if it was a mistake, why didn't they get together and stop it? Why did they go on?'

The captain said, 'It's mighty difficult to stop a war when all the statesmen have been killed.'

The scientist said, 'The trouble is, the damn things got too cheap. The original uranium bomb only cost about fifty thousand quid towards the end. Every little pip-squeak country like Albania could have a stockpile of them, and every little country that had that thought it could defeat the major countries in a surprise attack. That was the real trouble.'

'Another was the aeroplanes,' the captain said. 'The Russians had been giving the Egyptians aeroplanes for years. So had Britain for that matter, and to Israel, and to Jordan. The big mistake was ever to have given them a long range aeroplane.'

Peter said quietly, 'Well, after that the war was on between Russia and the Western Powers. When did China come in?'

The captain said, 'I don't think anybody knows exactly. But I'd say that probably China came in right there with her rockets and her radiological warfare against Russia, taking advantage of the opportunity. Probably they didn't know how ready Russia was with radiological warfare against China.' He paused. 'But that's all surmise,' he said. 'Most of the communications went out pretty soon, and what were left didn't have much time to talk to us down here, or to South Africa. All we know is that the command came down to quite junior officers, in most countries.'

John Osborne smiled wryly. 'Major Chan Sze Lin.'

Peter asked, 'Who *was* Chan Sze Lin, anyway?'

The scientist said, 'I don't think anybody really knows, except that he was an officer in the Chinese Air Force, and towards the end he seems to have been in command. The Prime Minister was in touch with him, trying to intervene to stop it all. He seems to have had a lot of rockets in various parts of China, and a lot of bombs to drop. His opposite number in Russia may have been someone equally insignificant. But I don't think the Prime Minister ever succeeded in making contact with the Russians. I never heard a name, anyway.'

There was a pause. 'It must have been a difficult situation,' Dwight said at last. 'I mean, what could the guy do? He had a war upon his hands and plenty of weapons left to fight it with. I'd say it was the same in all the countries, after the statesmen got killed. It makes a war very difficult to stop.'

'It certainly made this one. It just didn't stop, till all the bombs were gone and all the aircraft were unserviceable. And by that time, of course, they'd gone too far.'

'Christ,' said the American softly, 'I don't know what I'd have done in their shoes. I'm glad I wasn't.'

The scientist said, 'I should think you'd have tried to negotiate.'

'With an enemy knocking hell out of the United States and killing all our people? When I still had weapons in my hands? Just stop fighting and give in? I'd like to think that I was so high-minded but – well, I don't know.' He raised his head. 'I was never trained for diplomacy,' he said. 'If that situation had devolved on me, I wouldn't have known how to handle it.'

'They didn't, either,' said the scientist. He stretched himself, and yawned. 'Just too bad. But don't go blaming the Russians. It wasn't the big countries that set off this thing. It was the little ones, the Irresponsibles.'

Peter Holmes grinned, and said, 'It's a bit hard on all the rest of us.'

'You've got six months more,' remarked John Osborne. 'Plus or minus something. Be satisfied with that. You've always known that you were going to die some time. Well, now you know when. That's all.' He laughed. 'Just make the most of what you've got left.'

'I know that,' said Peter. 'The trouble is I can't think of anything that I want to do more than what I'm doing now.'

'Cooped up in bloody *Scorpion*?'

'Well – yes. It's our job. I really meant, at home.'

'No imagination. You want to turn Mohammedan and start a harem.'

The submarine commander laughed. 'Maybe he's got something there.'

The liaison officer shook his head. 'It's a nice idea, but it wouldn't be practical. Mary wouldn't like it.' He stopped smiling. 'The trouble is, I can't really believe it's going to happen. Can you?'

'Not after what you've seen?'

Peter shook his head. 'No. If we'd seen any *damage* . . .'

'No imagination whatsoever,' remarked the scientist. 'It's the same with all you service people. "That can't happen to *me*".' He paused. 'But it can. And it certainly will.'

'I suppose I haven't got any imagination,' said Peter thoughtfully. 'It's – it's the end of the world. I've never had to imagine anything like that before.'

John Osborne laughed. 'It's not the end of the world at all,' he said. 'It's only the end of us. The world will go on just the same, only we shan't be in it. I dare say it will get along all right without us.'

Dwight Towers raised his head. 'I suppose that's right. There didn't seem to be much wrong with Cairns, or Port Moresby either.' He paused, thinking of the flowering trees that he had seen on shore through the periscope, cascaras and flame trees, the palms standing in the sunlight. 'Maybe we've been too silly to deserve a world like this,' he said.

The scientist said, 'That's absolutely and precisely right.'

There didn't seem to be much more to say upon that subject, so they went up on to the bridge for a smoke, in the sunlight and fresh air.

They passed the Heads at the entrance to Sydney harbour soon after dawn next day and went on southwards into the Bass Strait. Next morning they were in Port Phillip Bay, and they berthed alongside the aircraft carrier at Williamstown at about noon. The First Naval Member was there to meet them and he was piped aboard *Scorpion* as soon as the gangway was run out.

Dwight Towers met him on the narrow deck. The Admiral returned his salute. 'Well, Captain, what sort of a cruise did you have?'

'We had no troubles, sir. The operation went through in accordance with the orders. But I'm afraid you may find the results are disappointing.'

'You didn't get very much information?'

'We got plenty of radiation data, sir. North of Twenty Latitude we couldn't go on deck.'

The Admiral nodded. 'Have you had any sickness?'

'One case that the surgeon says is measles. Nothing of a radioactive nature.'

They went below into the tiny captain's cabin. Dwight displayed the draft of his report, written in pencil upon sheets of foolscap with an appendix of the radiation levels at each watch of the cruise, long columns of small figures in John Osborne's neat handwriting. 'I'll get this typed in *Sydney* right away,' he said. 'But what it comes to is just this – we found out very little.'

'No signs of life in any of those places?'

'Nothing at all. Of course, you can't see very much, at periscope height from the waterfront. I never realized before we went how little we'd be able to see. I should have, perhaps. You're quite a ways from Cairns out in the main channel, and the same at Moresby. We never saw the town of Darwin at all, up on the cliff. Just the waterfront.' He paused. 'There didn't seem to be much wrong with that.'

The Admiral turned over the pencilled pages, stopping now and then to read a paragraph. 'You stayed some time at each place?'

'About five hours. We were calling all the time through the loud hailer.'

'Getting no answer?'

'No, sir. We thought we did at Darwin just at first, but it was only a crane shackle squeaking on the wharf. We moved right up to it and tracked it down.'

95

'Seabirds?'

'None at all. We never saw a bird north of Latitude Twenty. We saw a dog at Cairns.'

The Admiral stayed twenty minutes. Finally he said, 'Well, get in this report as soon as you can, marking one copy by messenger direct to me. It's a bit disappointing, but you probably did all that anybody could have done.'

The American said, 'I was reading that report of *Swordfish*, sir. There's very little information about things on shore in that, either in the States or in Europe. I guess they didn't see much more than we did, from the waterfront.' He hesitated for a moment. 'There's one suggestion that I'd like to put forward.'

'What's that, Captain?'

'The radiation levels aren't very high, anywhere along the line. The scientific officer tells me that a man could work safely in an insulating suit – helmet, gloves, and all, of course. We could put an officer on shore in any of those places, rowing in a dinghy, working with an oxygen pack on his back.'

'Decontamination when he comes on board again,' said the Admiral. 'That makes a problem. Probably not insuperable. I'll suggest it to the Prime Minister and see if he wants information upon any specific point. He may not think it worth while. But it's an idea.'

He turned to the control-room to go up the ladder to the bridge. 'Will we be able to give shore leave, sir?'

'Any defects?'

'Nothing of importance.'

'Ten days,' said the Admiral. 'I'll make a signal about that this afternoon.'

Peter Holmes rang up Mary after lunch. 'Home again, all in one piece,' he said. 'Look, darling, I'll be home some time tonight – I don't know when. I've got a report to get off first, and I'll drop it in myself at the Navy Department on my way through – I've got to go there, anyway. I don't know when I'll be back. Don't bother about meeting me – I'll walk up from the station.'

'It's lovely to hear you again,' she said. 'You won't have had supper, will you?'

'I shouldn't think so. I'll do myself some eggs or something when I get in.'

She thought rapidly. 'I'll make a casserole, and we can have that any time.'

'Fine. Look, there's just one thing. We had a case of measles on board, so I'm in a kind of quarantine.'

'Oh, Peter! You've had it before, though, haven't you?'

'Not since I was about four years old. The surgeon says I can get it again. The incubation time is three weeks. Have you had it – recently?'

'I had it when I was about thirteen.'

'I think that makes you pretty safe.'

She thought quickly. 'What about Jennifer, though?'

'I know. I've been thinking about her. I'll have to keep out of her way.'

'Oh dear . . . *Can* anyone get measles when she's as young as Jennifer?'

'I don't know, darling. I could ask the surgeon commander.'

'Would he know about babies?'

He thought for a moment. 'I don't suppose he's had a great deal of experience with them.'

'Ask him, Peter, and I'll ring up Dr Halloran. We'll fix up something, anyway. It's lovely that you're back.'

He rang off and went on with his work, while Mary settled down to her besetting sin, the telephone. She rang up Mrs Foster down the road, who was going into town to a meeting of the Countrywomen's Association, and asked her to bring out a pound of steak and a couple of onions. She rang the doctor, who told her that a baby could get measles and that she must be very careful. And then she thought of Moira Davidson, who had rung her up the night before to ask if she had any news of *Scorpion*. She got her at tea time at the farm near Berwick.

'My dear,' she said. 'They're back. Peter rang me from the ship just now. They've all got measles.'

'They've got *what*?'

'Measles – like you have when you're at school.'

There was a burst of laughter on the line, a little hysterical and shrill. 'It's nothing to laugh about,' Mary said. 'I'm thinking about Jennifer. She might catch it from Peter. He's had it once, but he can get it again. It's all so worrying . . .'

The laughter subsided. 'Sorry, darling, but it seems so funny. It's nothing to do with radioactivity, is it?'

'Oh, I don't think so. Peter said it was just measles.' She paused. 'Isn't it awful?'

Miss Davidson laughed again. 'It's just the sort of thing they *would* do. Here they go cruising for a fortnight up in parts where everyone is dead of radiation, and all that they can catch is measles! I'll have to speak to Dwight about it, very sharply. Did they find anyone alive up there?'

'I don't know, darling. Peter didn't say anything about it. But anyway, that's not important. What *am* I going to do about Jennifer? Dr Halloran says she can catch it, and Peter's going to be contagious for three weeks.'

'He'll have to sleep and have his meals out on the veranda.'

'Don't be silly, darling.'

'Well, let Jennifer sleep and have *her* meals out on the veranda.'

'Flies,' said her mother. 'Mosquitoes. A cat might come and lie on her face and smother her. They do, you know.'

'Put a mosquito net over the pram.'

'I haven't got a mosquito net.'

'I think we've got some somewhere, that Daddy used to use in Queensland. They're probably full of holes.'

'I do wish you'd have a look, darling. It's the cat I'm worried about.'

'I'll go and have a look now. If I can find one I'll put it in the post tonight. Or I might bring it over. Are you going to have Commander Towers down again, now that they're home?'

'I really hadn't thought. I don't know if Peter wants to have him. They may be hating the sight of each other after a fortnight in that submarine. Would you like us to have him over?'

'It's nothing to me,' said the girl carelessly. 'I don't care if you do or don't.'

'Darling!'

'It's not. Stop poking your stick in my ear. Anyway, he's a married man.'

Puzzled, Mary said, 'He can't be, dear. Not now.'

'That's all you know,' the girl replied. 'It makes things a bit difficult. I'll go and look for that net.'

When Peter arrived home that evening he found Mary to be somewhat uninterested in Cairns but very much concerned about the baby. Moira had rung up again to say that she was sending a mosquito net, but it would clearly be some time before it could arrive. As a makeshift Mary had secured a long length of butter muslin and had draped this round the pram on the veranda, but she had not done it very well and the liaison officer spent some time on his first evening at home in fashioning a close fitting cover to

99

the pram hood from the muslin. 'I do hope she'll be able to breathe,' his wife said anxiously. 'Peter, are you sure she'll get enough air through that?'

He did what he could to reassure her, but three times in the night she left his side to go out to the veranda to make sure that the baby was still alive.

The social side of *Scorpion* was more interesting to her than the technical achievements of the ship. 'Are you going to ask Commander Towers down again?' she inquired.

'I really hadn't thought about it,' he replied. 'Would you like to have him down?'

'I quite liked him,' she said. 'Moira liked him a lot. So funny for her, because he's such a quiet man. But you never can tell.'

'He took her out before we went away,' he said. 'Showed her the ship and took her out. I bet she leads him a dance.'

'She rang up three times while you were away to ask if we had any news,' his wife said. 'I don't believe that was because of you.'

'She was probably just bored,' he remarked.

He had to go up to town next day for a meeting at the Navy Department with John Osborne and the principal scientific officer. The meeting ended at about noon; as they were going out of the office the scientist said, 'By the way, I've got a parcel for you.' He produced a brown paper packet tied with string. 'Mosquito net. Moira asked me to give it to you.'

'Oh – thanks. Mary wanted that badly.'

'What are you doing for lunch?'

'I hadn't thought.'

'Come along to the Pastoral Club.'

The young naval officer opened his eyes; this was

somewhat up-stage and rather expensive. 'Are you a member there?'

John Osborne nodded. 'I always intended to be one before I died. It was now or never.'

They took a tram up to the club at the other end of the town. Peter Holmes had been inside it once or twice before, and had been suitably impressed. It was an ancient building for Australia, over a hundred years old, built in the spacious days in the manner of one of the best London clubs of the time. It had retained its old manners and traditions in a changing era; more English than the English, it had carried the standards of food and service practically unaltered from the middle of the nineteenth century to the middle of the twentieth. Before the war it had probably been the best club in the Commonwealth. Now it certainly was.

They parked their hats in the hall, washed their hands in the old fashioned washroom, and moved out into the garden cloister for a drink. Here they found a number of members, mostly past middle age, discussing the affairs of the day. Among them Peter Holmes noticed several State and Federal ministers. An elderly gentleman waved to them from a group upon the lawn and started towards them.

John Osborne said quietly, 'It's my great-uncle – Douglas Froude. Lieutenant-General – you know.'

Peter nodded. Sir Douglas Froude had commanded the army before he was born and had retired soon after that event, fading from great affairs into the obscurity of a small property near Macedon, where he had raised sheep and tried to write his memoirs. Twenty years later he was still trying, though he was gradually abandoning the struggle. For some time his chief interest had lain in his garden and in the study of Australian wild birds;

his weekly visit into town to lunch at the Pastoral Club was his one remaining social activity. He was still erect in figure though white-haired and red of face. He greeted his great-nephew cheerfully.

'Ha, John,' he said. 'I heard last night that you were back again. Had a good trip?'

John Osborne introduced the naval officer. 'Quite good,' he said. 'I don't know that we found out very much, and one of the ship's company developed measles. Still, that's all in the day's work.'

'Measles, eh? Well, that's better than this cholera thing. I hope none of you got that. Come and have a drink – I'm in the book.'

They crossed to the table with him. John said, 'Thank you, uncle. I didn't expect to see you here today. I thought your day was Friday.'

They helped themselves to pink gins. 'Oh no, no. It *used* to be Friday. Three years ago my doctor told me that if I didn't stop drinking the club port he couldn't guarantee my life for longer than a year. But everything's changed now, of course.' He raised his glass of sherry. 'Well, here's thanks for your safe home-coming. I suppose one ought to pour it on the ground as a libation or something, but the situation is too serious for that. Do you know we've got over three thousand bottles of vintage port still left in the cellars of this club, and only about six months left to go, if what you scientists say is right?'

John Osborne was suitably impressed. 'Fit to drink?'

'In first-class condition, absolutely first-class. Some of the Fonseca may be just a trifle young, a year or two maybe, but the Gould Campbell is in its prime. I blame the Wine Committee very much, very much indeed. They should have seen this coming.'

Peter Holmes repressed a smile. 'It's a bit difficult to

blame anyone,' he said mildly. 'I don't know that anybody really saw this coming.'

'Stuff and nonsense. *I* saw this coming twenty years ago. Still, it's no good blaming anybody now. The only thing to do is to make the best of it.'

John Osborne asked, 'What are you doing about the port?'

'There's only one thing to do,' the old man said.

'What's that?'

'Drink it, my boy, drink it – every drop. No good leaving it for the next comer, with the cobalt half-life over five years. I come in now three days a week and take a bottle home with me.' He took another drink of his sherry. 'If I'm to die, as I most certainly am, I'd rather die of drinking port than of this cholera thing. You say none of you got that upon your cruise?'

Peter Holmes shook his head. 'We took precautions. We were submerged and under water most of the time.'

'Ah, that makes a good protection.' He glanced at them. 'There's nobody alive up in North Queensland, is there?'

'Not at Cairns, sir. I don't know about Townsville.'

The old man shook his head. 'There's been no communication with Townsville since last Thursday, and now Bowen has it. Somebody was saying that they've had some cases in Mackay.'

John Osborne grinned. 'Have to hurry up with that port, uncle.'

'I know that. It's a very terrible situation.' The sun shone down on them out of a cloudless sky, warm and comforting; the big chestnut in the garden cast dappled shadows on the lawn. 'Still, we're doing our best. The secretary tells me that we put away over three hundred bottles last month.'

He turned to Peter. 'How do you like serving in an American ship?'

'I like it very much, sir. It's a bit different from our navy, of course, and I've never served in a submarine before. But they're quite a nice party to be with.'

'Not too gloomy? Not too many widowers?'

He shook his head. 'They're all pretty young, except the captain. I don't think many of them were married. The captain was, of course, and some of the petty officers. But most of the officers and the enlisted men are in their early twenties. A lot of them seem to have got themselves girls here in Australia.' He paused. 'It's not a gloomy ship.'

The old man nodded. 'Of course, it's been some time, now.' He drank again, and then he said, 'The captain – is he a Commander Towers?'

'That's right, sir. Do you know him?'

'He's been in here once or twice, and I've been introduced to him. I have an idea that he's an honorary member. Bill Davidson was telling me that Moira knows him.'

'She does, sir. They met at my house.'

'Well, I hope she doesn't get him into mischief.'

At that moment she was ringing up the Commander in the aircraft carrier, doing her best to do so. 'This is Moira, Dwight,' she said. 'What's this I hear about your ship all getting measles?'

His heart lightened at the sound of her voice. 'You're very right,' he said. 'But that's classified information.'

'What does that mean?'

'Secret. If a ship in the US Navy gets put out of action for a while we just don't tell the world about it.'

'All that machinery put out of action by a little thing like measles. It sounds like bad management to me. Do you think *Scorpion*'s got the right captain?'

'I'm darned sure she hasn't,' he said comfortably. 'Let's you and me get together some place and talk over a replacement. I'm just not satisfied myself.'

'Are you going down to Peter Holmes this weekend?'

'He hasn't asked me.'

'Would you go if you were asked? Or have you had him keelhauled for insubordination since we met?'

'He never caught a seagull,' he said. 'I guess that's all I've got against him. I never logged him for it.'

'Did you expect him to catch seagulls?'

'Sure. I rated him chief seagull catcher, but he fell down on the job. The Prime Minister, your Mr Ritchie, he'll be mighty sore with me about no seagull. A ship's captain, though, he's just so good as his officers and no better.'

She asked, 'Have you been drinking, Dwight?'

'I'll say I have. Coca-Cola.'

'Ah, that's what's wrong. You need a double brandy — no, whisky. Can I speak to Peter Holmes?'

'Not here, you can't. He's lunching with John Osborne some place, I believe. Could be the Pastoral Club.'

'Worse and worse,' she said. 'If he happens to ask you down, will you come? I'd like to see if you can sail that dinghy any better this time. I've got a padlock for my bra.'

He laughed. 'I'll be glad to come. Even on those terms.'

'He may not ask you,' she pointed out. 'I don't like the sound of this seagull business at all. It seems to me that there's bad trouble in your ship.'

'Let's talk it over.'

'Certainly,' she replied. 'I'll hear what you've got to say.'

She rang off, and succeeded in catching Peter on the telephone as he was about to leave the club. She came directly to the point. 'Peter, will you ask Dwight Towers down to your place for the weekend? I'll ask myself.'

He temporized. 'I'll get hell from Mary if he gives Jennifer measles.'

'I'll tell her she caught it from you. Will you ask him?'

'If you like. I don't suppose he'll come.'

'He will.'

She met him at Falmouth station in her buggy, as she had before. As he passed through the ticket barrier he greeted her with, 'Say, what happened to the red outfit?'

She was dressed in khaki, khaki slacks and khaki shirt, practical and workmanlike. 'I wasn't sure about wearing it, meeting you,' she said. 'I didn't want to get it all messed up.'

He laughed. 'You've got quite an opinion of me!'

'A girl can't be too careful,' she said primly. 'Not with all this hay about.'

They walked down to where her horse and buggy stood tied to the rail. 'I suppose we'd better settle up this seagull business before meeting Mary,' she said. 'I mean, it's not a thing one wants to talk about in mixed company. What about the Pier Hotel?'

'Okay with me,' he said. They got up into the jinker and drove through the empty streets to the hotel. She tied the reins to the same bumper of the same car, and they went into the Ladies' Lounge.

He bought her a double brandy, and bought a single whisky for himself. 'Now, what's all this about the seagull?' she demanded. 'You'd better come clean, Dwight, however discreditable it is.'

'I saw the Prime Minister before we went off on this cruise,' he told her. 'The First Naval Member, he took me over. He told us this and that, and among other things he wanted us to find out all we could about the bird life in the radioactive area.'

'All right. Well, did you find out anything for him?'

'Nothing at all,' he replied comfortably. 'Nothing about the birds, nothing about the fish, and not much about anything else.'

'Didn't you catch any fish?'

He grinned at her. 'If anyone can tell me how to catch a fish out of a submarine that's submerged, or a seagull when nobody can go on deck, I'd like to know. It could probably be done with specially designed equipment. Everything's possible. But this was at the final briefing, half an hour before we sailed.'

'So you didn't bring back a seagull?'

'No.'

'Was the Prime Minister very much annoyed?'

'I wouldn't know. I wouldn't dare go see him.'

'I'm not surprised.' She paused and took a drink from her glass; and then more seriously she said, 'Tell me. There's nobody alive up there, is there?'

He shook his head. 'I don't think so. It's difficult to say for certain unless one was prepared to put a man on shore, in a protective suit. Looking back, I think that's what we should have done in some of those places. But we weren't briefed for that this time, and no equipment on board. The decontamination is a problem, when he comes back in the ship.'

'"This time",' she quoted. 'Are you going again?'

He nodded. 'I think so. We've had no orders, but I've got a hunch they'll send us over to the States.'

She opened her eyes. 'Can you go there?'

He nodded. 'It's quite a way, and it'd be a very long time under water. Pretty hard on the crew. But yet – it could be done. *Swordfish* took a cruise like that, and so could we.'

He told her about *Swordfish* and her cruise around the North Atlantic. 'The trouble is, you see so very little through the periscope. We've got the captain's report on the *Swordfish* cruise, and, when you sum it all up, they really learned very little. Not much more than you'd know if you sat down to think it out. You can only see the waterfront, and that from a height of about twenty feet. You can see if there's been bomb damage in a city or a port, but that's about all you *can* see. It was the same with us. We found out very little on this cruise. Just stayed there calling on the loud hailer for a while, and when nobody came down to look at us or answer, we assumed they were all dead.' He paused. 'It's all you can assume.'

She nodded. 'Somebody was saying that they've got it in Mackay. Do you think that's true?'

'I think it is true,' he said. 'It's coming south very steadily, just like the scientists said it would.'

'If it goes on at this rate, how long will it be before it gets here?'

'I'd say around September. Could be a bit before.'

She got restlessly to her feet. 'Get me another drink, Dwight.' And when he brought it she said, 'I want to go somewhere – do something – *dance*!'

'Anything you say, honey.'

'We can't just sit here mooning and moaning about what's coming to us!'

'You're right,' he said. 'But what do you want to do, more'n you're doing now?'

'Don't be sensible,' she said fretfully. 'I just can't bear it.'

'Okay,' he said equably. 'Drink up and let's go up and meet the Holmeses, and then go sail that boat.'

They found at the flat that Peter and Mary Holmes had

arranged a beach picnic supper for the evening's entertainment. Not only was it cheaper than a party and more pleasant in the heat of summer, but in Mary's somewhat muddled view the more the men were kept out of the house the less likely they were to give the baby measles. That afternoon Moira and Dwight went down to the sailing club after a quick lunch to rig the boat and sail her in the race, while Peter and Mary followed with the baby in the bicycle trailer in the middle of the afternoon.

The race went reasonably well that time. They bumped the buoy at the start, and engaged in a luffing match on the second round which ended in a minor collision because neither party knew the rules, but in that club such incidents were not infrequent, and protests very few. They finished the race in sixth place, an improvement on the time before, and in much better order. They sailed in to the beach at the conclusion of the race, parked the vessel on a convenient sandbank, and waded on shore to drink a cup of tea and eat small cakes with Peter and Mary.

They bathed in leisurely fashion in the evening sun; in bathing costumes they unrigged the boat, put away the sails, and got her up to her resting place upon the dry sand of the beach. The sun dropped down to the horizon and they changed into their clothes, took drinks from the hamper, and walked out to the jetty's end to see the sunset while Peter and Mary got busy with the supper.

Sitting with him perched upon a rail, watching the rosy lights reflected in the calm sea, savouring the benison of the warm evening and the comfort of her drink, she asked him, 'Dwight, tell me about the cruise that *Swordfish* made. Did you say she went to the United States?'

'That's right.' He paused, and then he said, 'She went everywhere she could along the eastern seaboard, but all it amounted to was just a few of the small ports and harbours,

Delaware Bay, the Hudson River, and, of course, New London. They took a big chance going in to look at New York City.'

She was puzzled. 'Was that dangerous?'

He nodded. 'Minefields – our own mines. Every major port or river entrance on the eastern seaboard was protected by a series of minefields. At any rate, that's what we think. The west coast, too.' He paused for a moment in thought. 'They should have been put down before the war. Whether they got them down before, or whether they were put down after, or whether they were never laid at all – we just don't know. All we know is that there should be minefields there, and unless you have the plan of them to show the passage through – you can't go in.'

'You mean, if you hit one it'd sink you?'

'It most certainly would. Unless you have the key chart you just daren't go near.'

'Did they have the key chart when they went in to New York?'

He shook his head. 'They had one that was eight years old, with NOT TO BE USED stamped all over it. Those things are pretty secret; they don't issue them unless a ship needs to go in there. They only had this old one. They must have wanted to go in very much. They got to figuring what alterations could have been made, retaining the main leading marks to show the safe channels in. They got it figured out that not much alteration to the plan they'd got would have been possible save on one leg. They chanced it, and went in, and got away with it. Maybe there were never any mines there at all.'

'Did they find out much that was of value when they got in to the harbour?'

He shook his head. 'Nothing but what they knew

already. It's how it seems to be, exploring places in this way. You can't find out a lot.'

'There was nobody alive there?'

'Oh no, honey. The whole geography was altered. It was very radioactive, too.'

They sat in silence for a time, watching the sunset glow, smoking over their drinks. 'What was the other place you say she went to?' the girl asked at last. 'New London?'

'That's right,' he said.

'Where is that?'

'In Connecticut, in the eastern part of the state,' he told her. 'At the mouth of the Thames River.'

'Did they run much risk in going there?'

He shook his head. 'It was their home port. They had the key chart for the minefields there, right up to date.' He paused. 'It's the main US Navy submarine base on the east coast,' he said quietly. 'Most of them lived there, I guess, or in the general area. Like I did.'

'You lived there?'

He nodded.

'Was it just the same as all the other places?'

'So it seems,' he said heavily. 'They didn't say much in the report, just the readings of the radioactivity. They were pretty bad. They got right up to the base, to their own dock that they left from. It must have been kind of funny going back like that, but there was nothing much about it in the report. Most of the officers and the enlisted men, they must have been very near their homes. There was nothing they could do, of course. They just stayed there a while, and then went out and went on with their mission. The captain said in his report they had some kind of a religious service in the ship. It must have been painful.'

In the warm, rosy glow of the sunset there was still

beauty in the world. 'I wonder they went in there,' she observed.

'I wondered about that, just at first,' he said. 'I'd have passed it by, myself, I think. Although . . . well, I don't know. But thinking it over, I'd say they had to go in there. It was the only place they had the key chart for – that, and Delaware Bay. They were the only two places that they could get in to safely. They just had to take advantage of the knowledge of the minefields that they had.'

She nodded. 'You lived there?'

'Not in New London itself,' he said quietly. 'The base is on the other side of the river, the east side. I've got a home about fifteen miles away, up the coast from the river entrance. Little place called West Mystic.'

She said, 'Don't talk about it if you'd rather not.'

He glanced at her. 'I don't mind talking, not to some people. But I wouldn't want to bore you.' He smiled gently. 'Nor to start crying, because I'd seen the baby.'

She flushed a little. 'When you let me use your cabin to change in,' she said, 'I saw your photographs. Are those your family?'

He nodded. 'That's my wife and our two kids,' he said a little proudly. 'Sharon. Dwight goes to Grade School, and Helen, she'll be going next fall. She goes to a little kindergarten right now, just up the street.'

She had known for some time that his wife and family were very real to him, more real by far than the half-life in a far corner of the world that had been forced upon him since the war. The devastation of the northern hemisphere was not real to him, as it was not real to her. He had seen nothing of the destruction of the war, as she had not; in thinking of his wife and of his home it was impossible for him to visualize them in any other circumstances than those in which he had left them. He had little imagination, and that formed a solid core for his contentment in Australia.

She knew that she was treading upon very dangerous ground. She wanted to be kind to him, and she had to say something. She asked a little timidly, 'What's Dwight going to be when he grows up?'

'I'd like him to go to the Academy,' he said. 'The Naval Academy. Go into the Navy, like I did. It's a good life for a boy – I don't know any better. Whether he can make the grade or not, well, that's another thing. His mathematics aren't so hot, but it's too early yet to say. He won't be ten years old till next July. But I'd like to see him get into the Academy. I think he wants it, too.'

'Is he keen on the sea?' she asked.

He nodded. 'We live right near the shore. He's on the water, swimming and running the outboard motor, most of the summer.' He paused thoughtfully. 'They get so *brown*,' he said. 'All kids seem to be the same. I sometimes think that kids get browner than we do, with the same amount of exposure.'

'They get very brown here,' she remarked. 'You haven't started him sailing yet?'

'Not yet,' he said. 'I'm going to get a sail boat when I'm home on my next leave.'

He raised himself from the rail that they had been sitting on, and stood for a moment looking at the sunset glow.

'I guess that'll be next September,' he said quietly. 'Kind of late in the season to start sailing, up at Mystic.'

She was silent, not knowing what to say.

He turned to her. 'I suppose you think I'm nuts,' he said heavily. 'But that's the way I see it, and I can't seem to think about it any other way. At any rate, I don't cry over babies.'

She rose and turned to walk with him down the jetty.

'I don't think you're nuts,' she said.

They walked together in silence to the beach.

4

Next morning, Sunday, everyone in the Holmeses' house-
hold got up in pretty good shape, unlike the previous
Sunday that Commander Towers had spent with them.
They had gone to bed after a reasonable evening, unexcited
by a party. At breakfast Mary asked her guest if he wanted
to go to church, thinking that the more she got him out of
the house the less likely he was to give Jennifer measles.

'I'd like to go,' he said, 'if that's convenient.'

'Of course it is,' she said. 'Just do whatever you like. I
thought we might take tea down to the club this afternoon,
unless you've got anything else you'd like to do.'

He shook his head. 'I could use another swim. But I'll
have to get back to the ship tonight some time, after
supper, maybe.'

'Can't you stay over till tomorrow morning?'

He shook his head, knowing her concern about the
measles. 'I'll have to get back tonight.'

He went out into the garden directly the meal was over
to smoke a cigarette, thinking to ease Mary's mind. Moira
found him there when she came out from helping with
the dishes, sitting in a deck chair looking out over the
bay. She sat down beside him. 'Are you really going to
church?' she asked.

'That's right,' he said.

'Can I come too?'

He turned his head, and looked at her in surprise. 'Why, certainly. Do you go regularly?'

She smiled. 'Not once in a blue moon,' she admitted. 'It might be better if I did. Maybe I wouldn't drink so much.'

He pondered that one for a moment. 'Could be,' he said uncertainly. 'I don't know that that's got a lot to do with it.'

'You're sure you wouldn't rather go alone?'

'Why, no,' he said. 'I'd like your company.'

As they left to walk down to the church Peter Holmes was getting out the garden hose to do some watering before the sun grew hot. His wife came out of the house presently. 'Where's Moira?' she asked.

'Gone to church with the captain.'

'Moira? Gone to church?'

He grinned. 'Believe it or not, that's where she's gone.'

She stood in silence for a minute. 'I hope it's going to be all right,' she said at last.

'Why shouldn't it?' he asked. 'He's dinkum, and she's not a bad sort when you get to know her. They might even get married.'

She shook her head. 'There's something funny about it. I hope it's going to be all right,' she repeated.

'It's no concern of ours, anyway,' he said. 'Lots of things are going a bit weird these days.'

She nodded, and started pottering about the garden while he watered. Presently she said, 'I've been thinking, Peter. Could we take out those two trees, do you think?'

He came and looked at them with her. 'I'd have to ask the landlord,' he said. 'What do you want to take them out for?'

'We've got so little space for growing vegetables,' she said. 'They *are* so expensive in the shops. If we could take those trees out and cut back the wattle we could make a kitchen garden here, from *here* to *here*.' She indicated with her hands. 'I'm sure we could save nearly a pound a week by growing our own stuff. And it'd be fun, too.'

He went to survey the trees. 'I could get them down all right,' he said, 'and there's a nice bit of firewood in them. It'd be green, of course, too green to burn this winter. We'd have to stack it for a year. The only thing is, getting out the stumps. It's quite a big job, that.'

'There are only two of them,' she said. 'I could help – keep on nibbling at them while you're away. If we could get them out this winter and dig the ground over, I could plant it in the spring and we'd have vegetables all next summer.' She paused. 'Peas and beans,' she said. 'And a vegetable marrow. I'd make marrow jam.'

'Good idea,' he said. He looked the trees up and down. 'They're not very big,' he said. 'It'd be better for the pine if they came out.'

'Another thing I want to do,' she said, 'is to put in a flowering gum tree, *here*. I think that'd look lovely in the summer.'

'Takes about five years to come into bloom,' he said.

'Never mind. A gum tree there would be just lovely, up against the blue of the sea. We could see it from our bedroom window.'

He paused, considering the brilliance of the scarlet flowers all over the big tree against the deep blue sea, in the brilliant sunlight. 'It'd certainly be quite a sensation when it was in bloom,' he said. 'Where would you put it? Here?'

'A bit more over this way, here,' she said. 'When it got big we could take down this holly thing and have a seat in the shade, here.' She paused. 'I went to Wilson's nurseries while you were away,' she said. 'He's got some lovely little flowering gum trees there, only ten and sixpence each. Do you think we could put in one of those this autumn?'

'They're a bit delicate,' he said. 'I think the thing to do would be to put in two fairly close to each other, so that you'd have one if the other died. Then take out one of them in a couple of years' time.'

'The trouble is, one never does it,' she observed.

They went on happily planning their garden for the next ten years, and the morning passed very quickly. When Moira and Dwight came back from church they were still at it. They were called into consultation on the layout of the kitchen garden. Presently Peter and Mary went into the house, the former to get drinks and the latter to get the lunch.

The girl glanced at the American. 'Someone's crazy,' she said quietly. 'Is it me or them?'

'Why do you say that?'

'They won't be *here* in six months' time. I won't be here. You won't be here. They won't *want* any vegetables next year.'

Dwight stood in silence for a moment, looking out at the blue sea, the long curve of the shore. 'So what?' he said at last. 'Maybe they don't believe it. Maybe they think that they can take it all with them and have it where they're going to, some place. I wouldn't know.' He paused. 'The thing is, they just kind of like to plan a garden. Don't you go and spoil it for them, telling them they're crazy.'

'I wouldn't do that.' She stood in silence for a minute. 'None of us really believe it's ever going to happen – not to us,' she said at last. 'Everybody's crazy on that point, one way or another.'

'You're very right,' he said emphatically.

Drinks came, and put a closure on the conversation, and then lunch. After lunch Mary turned the men out into the garden, thinking them to be infectious, while she washed the dishes with Moira. Seated in deck chairs with a cup of coffee, Peter asked his captain, 'Have you heard anything about our next job, sir?'

The American cocked his eye at him. 'Not a thing. Have you?'

'Not really. Something was said at that conference with PSO that made me wonder if anything was in the wind.'

'What was it that was said?'

'Something about fitting us with new directional wireless of some kind. Have you heard anything?'

Dwight shook his head. 'We've got plenty of radio.'

'This is for taking a bearing – accurately. Perhaps when we're submerged to periscope depth. We can't do that, can we?'

'Not with our existing equipment. What do they want us to do that for?'

'I don't know. It wasn't on the agenda. It was just one of the backroom boys speaking out of turn.'

'They want us to track down radio signals?'

'Honestly, I don't know, sir. How it came up was that they asked if the radiation detector could be moved to the forward periscope so that this thing could be put on the aft periscope. John Osborne said he was pretty sure it could, but he'd take it up with you.'

'That's right. It can go on the forward periscope. I thought they wanted to fit two.'

'I don't think so, sir. I think they want to fit this other gadget in its place on the aft one.'

The American stared at the smoke rising from his cigarette. Then he said, 'Seattle.'

'What's that, sir?'

'Seattle. There were radio signals coming from some place near Seattle. Do you know if they're still coming through?'

Peter shook his head, amazed. 'I didn't know anything about that. Do you mean that somebody's still operating a transmitter?'

The captain shrugged his shoulders. 'Could be. If so, it's somebody that doesn't know how to send. Sometimes they make a group, sometimes a word in clear. Most times it's just a jumble, like a child might make, playing at radio stations.'

'Does this go on all the time?'

Dwight shook his head. 'I don't think so. It comes on the air irregularly, now and then. I know they're monitoring that frequency most of the time. At least, they were till Christmas. I haven't heard since.'

The liaison officer said, 'But that must mean there's somebody alive up there.'

'It's just a possibility. You can't have radio without power, and that means starting up some kind of a motor. A big motor, to run a big station with global range. But – I don't know. You'd think a guy who could start up an outfit of that size and run it – you'd think he'd know Morse code. Even if he had to spell it out two words a minute with the book in front of him.'

'Do you think we're going there?'

'Could be. It was one of the points they wanted information on, way back last October. They wanted all the information on the US radio stations that we had.'

'Did you have anything that helped?'

Dwight shook his head. 'Only the US Navy stations. Very little on the Air Force or the Army stations. Practically nothing on the civil stations. There's more radio on the West Coast than you could shake a stick at.'

That afternoon they strolled down to the beach and bathed, leaving Mary with the baby at the house. Lying on the warm sand with the two men, Moira asked, 'Dwight, where is *Swordfish* now? Is she coming here?'

'I haven't heard it,' he replied. 'The last I heard she was in Montevideo.'

'She could turn up here, any time,' said Peter Holmes. 'She's got the range.'

The American nodded. 'That's so. Maybe they'll send her over here one day with mail or passengers. Diplomats, or something.'

'Where is Montevideo?' asked the girl. 'I ought to know that, but I don't.'

Dwight said, 'It's in Uruguay, on the east side of South America. Way down towards the bottom.'

'I thought you said she was at Rio de Janeiro. Isn't that in Brazil?'

He nodded. 'That was when she made her cruise up in the North Atlantic. She was based on Rio then. But after that they moved down into Uruguay.'

'Was that because of radiation?'

'Uh-huh.'

Peter said, 'I don't know that it's got there yet. It may have done. They've not said anything upon the radio. It's just about on the tropic, isn't it?'

'That's right,' said Dwight. 'Like Rockhampton.'

The girl asked, 'Have they got it in Rockhampton?'

'I haven't heard that they have,' said Peter. 'It said on the wireless this morning that they've got it at Salisbury, in Southern Rhodesia. I think that's a bit further north.'

'I think it is,' said the captain. 'It's in the middle of a land mass, too, and that might make a difference. These other places that we're talking about – they're all on a coast.'

'Isn't Alice Springs just about on the tropic?'

'It might be. I wouldn't know. That's in the middle of a land mass, too, of course.'

The girl asked, 'Does it go quicker down a coast than in the middle?'

Dwight shook his head. 'I wouldn't know. I don't think they've got any evidence on that, one way or the other.'

Peter laughed. 'They'll know by the time it gets here. Then they can etch it on the glass.'

The girl wrinkled her brows. 'Etch it on the glass?'

'Hadn't you heard about that one?'

She shook her head.

'John Osborne told me about it, yesterday,' he said. 'It seems that somebody in CSIRO is getting busy with a history, about what's happened to us. They do it on glass bricks. They etch it on the glass and then they fuse another brick down on the top of it in some way, so that the writing's in the middle.'

Dwight turned upon his elbow, interested. 'I hadn't heard of that. What are they going to do with them?'

'Put them up on top of Mount Kosciusko,' Peter said. 'It's the highest peak in Australia. If ever the world gets inhabited again they must go there some time. And it's not so high as to be inaccessible.'

'Well, what do you know! They're really doing that, are they?'

'So John says. They've got a sort of concrete cellar made up there. Like in the Pyramids.'

The girl asked, 'But how long is this history?'

'I don't know. I don't think it can be very long. They're doing it with pages out of books, though, too. Sealing them in between sheets of thick glass.'

'But these people who come after,' the girl said. 'They

won't know how to read our stuff. They may be . . . animals.'

'I believe they've gone to a lot of trouble about that. First steps in reading. Picture of a cat, and then C A T and all that sort of thing. John said that was about all that they'd got finished so far.' He paused. 'I suppose it's something to do,' he said. 'Keeps the wise men out of mischief.'

'A picture of a cat won't do them much good,' Moira remarked. 'There won't be any cats. They won't know what a cat is.'

'A picture of a fish might be better,' said Dwight. 'F I S H. Or – say – a picture of a seagull.'

'You're getting into awful spelling difficulties.'

The girl turned to Peter curiously. 'What sort of books are they preserving? All about how to make the cobalt bomb?'

'God forbid.' They laughed. 'I don't know what they're doing. I should think a copy of the Encyclopaedia Britannica would make a good kick-off, but there's an awful lot of it. I really don't know what they're doing. John Osborne might know – or he could find out.'

'Just idle curiosity,' she said. 'It won't affect you or me.' She stared at him in mock consternation. 'Don't tell me they're preserving any of the newspapers. I just couldn't bear it.'

'I shouldn't think so,' he replied. 'They're not as crazy as that.'

Dwight sat up on the sand. 'All this beautiful warm water going to waste,' he remarked. 'I think we ought to use it.'

Moira stood up. 'Make the most of it,' she agreed. 'There's not much of it left.'

Peter yawned. 'You two go and use the water. I'll use the sun.'

They left him lying on the beach and went into the sea together. As they swam out she said, 'You're pretty fast in the water, aren't you?'

He paused, treading water beside her. 'I used to swim quite a lot when I was younger. I swam for the Academy against West Point one time.'

She nodded. 'I thought you were something like that. Do you swim much now?'

He shook his head. 'Not in races. That's a thing you have to give up pretty soon, unless you've got the time to do a lot of it, and keep in training.' He laughed. 'I think the water's colder now than when I was a boy. Not here, of course. I mean, in Mystic.'

'Were you born in Mystic?' she asked.

He shook his head. 'I was born on Long Island Sound, but not at Mystic. A place called Westport. My Dad's a doctor there. He was a Navy surgeon in the First World War, and then he got this practice in Westport.'

'Is that on the sea?'

He nodded. 'Swimming and sailing and fishing. That's the way it was when I was a boy.'

'How old are you, Dwight?'

'I'm thirty-three. How old are you?'

'What a rude question! I'm twenty-four.' She paused. 'Does Sharon come from Westport, too?'

'In a way,' he said. 'Her Dad's a lawyer in New York City, lives in an apartment on West 84th Street, near the park. They have a summer home at Westport.'

'So you met her there.'

He nodded. 'Boy meets girl.'

'You must have married quite young.'

'Just after graduation,' he replied. 'I was twenty-two, an ensign on the *Franklin*. Sharon was nineteen; she never finished college. We'd made our minds up more than a year before. Our folks got together when they saw that we weren't going to change, and they decided that they'd better stake us for a while.' He paused. 'Her Dad was mighty nice about it,' he said quietly. 'We could have gone on until we got some money somehow, but they thought it wasn't doing either of us any good. So they let us get married.'

'They gave you an allowance.'

'That's right. We only needed it three or four years, and then an aunt died and I got promoted, and we were all set.'

They swam to the end of the jetty, got out, and sat basking in the sun. Presently they walked back to Peter on the beach, sat with him while they smoked a cigarette, and then went to change. They re-assembled on the beach carrying their shoes, drying their feet in leisurely manner in the sun and brushing off the sand. Presently Dwight started to put on his socks.

The girl said, 'Fancy going round in socks like that!'

The Commander glanced at them. 'It's only in the toe,' he said. 'It doesn't show.'

'It's not only in the toe.' She leaned across and picked up his foot. 'I thought I saw another one. The heel's all holes across the bottom!'

'It still doesn't show,' he said. 'Not when I've got a shoe on.'

'Doesn't anybody mend them for you?'

'They've paid off a lot of the ship's company in *Sydney* recently,' he said. 'I still get my bed made up, but he's too busy now to bother about mending. It never did work very well aboard that ship, anyway. I do them myself, sometimes. Most times I just throw them away and get another pair.'

'You've got a button off your shirt, too.'

'That doesn't show, either,' he said equably. 'It's way down at the bottom, goes underneath my belt.'

'I think you're a perfect disgrace,' she remarked. 'I know what the Admiral would say, if he saw you going round like that. He'd say *Scorpion* needs another captain.'

'He wouldn't see it,' he replied. 'Not unless he made me take off my pants.'

'This conversation's taking an unprofitable line,' she said. 'How many pairs of socks have you got in that condition?'

'I wouldn't know. It's quite a while since I went through the drawer.'

'If you give them to me I'll take them home and mend them for you.'

He glanced at her. 'That's mighty nice of you, to offer to do that. But you don't have to. It's time I got more, anyway. These are just about done.'

'*Can* you get more socks?' she asked. 'Daddy can't. He says they're going off the market, with a lot of other things. He can't get any new handkerchiefs, either.'

Peter said, 'That's right. I couldn't get socks to fit me, the last time I tried. The ones I got were about two inches too long.'

Moira pressed the point. 'Have you tried to buy any more recently?'

'Well – no. The last lot I bought was some time back in the winter.'

Peter yawned. 'Better let her mend them for you, sir. You'll have a job getting any more.'

'If that's the way it is,' Dwight said, 'I'd be very grateful.' He turned to the girl. 'But you don't have to do it. I can do them for myself.' He grinned. 'I can, you know. I can do them quite well.'

She sniffed audibly. 'About as well as I can run your submarine. You'd better make up a parcel of everything you've got that needs mending, and let me have it. That shirt included. Have you got the button?'

'I think I lost that.'

'You should be more careful. When a button comes off, you don't just chuck it away.'

'If you talk to me like that,' he said grimly, 'I really will give you everything I've got that needs mending. I'll bury you in the stuff.'

'Now we're getting somewhere,' she remarked. 'I thought you'd been concealing things. You'd better put it all into a cabin trunk, or two cabin trunks, and let me have them.'

'There's quite a lot,' he said.

'I knew it. If there's too much I'll shove some of it off on to Mummy and she'll probably distribute it all round the district. The First Naval Member lives quite near us; Mummy'll probably give Lady Hartman your underpants to mend.'

He looked at her in mock alarm. 'Say, *Scorpion* certainly would need another captain then.'

She said, 'This conversation's going round in circles. You let me have everything that you've got that needs mending, anyway, and I'll see if I can't get you dressed up like a naval officer.'

'Okay,' he said. 'Where shall I bring the stuff to?'

She thought for a moment. 'You're on leave, aren't you?'

'On and off,' he said. 'We're giving leave over ten days, but I don't get that much. The captain has to stick around, or thinks he has.'

'Probably do the ship a world of good if he didn't,' she said. 'You'd better bring them down to me at

Berwick, and stay a couple of nights. Can you drive a bullock?'

'I've never driven one,' he said. 'I could try.'

She eyed him speculatively. 'I suppose you'd be all right. If you can command a submarine you probably can't do much harm to one of our bullocks. Daddy's got a cart horse now called Prince, but I don't suppose he'd let you touch that. He'd probably let you drive one of the bullocks.'

'That's all right with me,' he said meekly. 'What am I supposed to do with the bullock?'

'Spread the dung,' she said. 'The cowpats. It has a harness that pulls a chain harrow over the grass. You walk beside it, leading it with a halter. You have a stick to tap it with as well. It's a very restful occupation. Good for the nerves.'

'I'm sure it is,' he said. 'What's it for? I mean, why do you do it?'

'It makes a good pasture,' she said. 'If you just leave the droppings where they are the grass comes up in rank tufts and the animals won't eat it. Then the pasture isn't half as good next year as if you'd harrowed it. Daddy's very particular about harrowing each pasture after the beasts come out. We used to do it with a tractor. Now we do it with a bullock.'

'This is all so that he'd get a better pasture next year?'

'Yes, it is,' she said firmly. 'All right, you needn't say it. It's good farming to harrow the paddocks, and Daddy's a good farmer.'

'I wasn't going to say it. How many acres does he farm?'

'About five hundred. We do Angus beef cattle and sheep.'

'You shear the sheep for the wool?'

'That's right.'

'When do you do that?' he asked. 'I've never seen a shearing.'

'Usually we shear in October,' she said. 'Daddy's a bit worried that if we leave it till October this year it won't get done. He's talking of putting it forward and shearing in August.'

'That makes sense,' he observed gravely. He bent forward to put on his shoes. 'It's a long time since I was on a farm,' he said. 'I'd like to come and spend a day or two, if you can put up with me. I expect I can make myself useful, one way or another.'

'Don't worry about that,' she said. 'Daddy'll see you make yourself useful. It's going to be a godsend to him, having another man on the place.'

He smiled. 'And you'd really like me to bring all the mending with me?'

'I'll never forgive you if you just turn up with a couple of pairs of socks and say that your pyjamas are all right. Besides, Lady Hartman's looking forward to doing your pants. She doesn't know it, but she is.'

'I'll take your word for it.'

She drove him down to the station that evening in the Abbott buggy. As he got down from the vehicle she said, 'I'll expect you on Tuesday, at Berwick station, in the afternoon. Give me a ring about the time of your train if you can. Otherwise I'll be there at about four o'clock, and wait.'

He nodded. 'I'll call you. You really mean that about bringing all the mending?'

'I'll never forgive you if you don't.'

'Okay.' He hesitated. 'It'll be dark by the time you get home,' he said. 'Look after yourself.'

She smiled at him. 'I'll be all right. See you on Tuesday. Goodnight, Dwight.'

'Goodnight,' he said a little thickly. She drove off. He stood watching her until the buggy turned a corner and was out of sight.

It was ten o'clock at night when she drove into the yard outside the homestead. Her father heard the horse and came out in the darkness to help her unharness and put the buggy in the shed. In the dim light as they eased the vehicle back under cover, she said, 'I asked Dwight Towers down here for a couple of days. He's coming on Tuesday.'

'Coming here?' he asked, surprised.

'Yes. They've got leave before they go off on some other trip. You don't mind, do you?'

'Of course not. I hope it's not going to be dull for him, though. What are you going to do with him all day?'

'I told him he could drive the bullock round the paddocks. He's very practical.'

'I could do with somebody to help feed out the silage,' her father said.

'Well, I expect he could do that. After all, if he commands a nuclear powered submarine he ought to be able to learn to shovel silage.'

They went into the house. Later that night he told her mother about their visitor. She was properly impressed. 'Do you think there's anything in it?'

'I don't know,' he said. 'She must like him all right.'

'She hasn't had a man to stay since that Forrest boy, before the war.'

He nodded. 'I remember. Never thought much of him. I'm glad that came to an end.'

'It was his Austin-Healey,' her mother remarked. 'I don't think she ever cared for him, not really.'

'This one's got a submarine,' her father said helpfully. 'It's probably the same thing.'

'He can't take her down the road in that at ninety miles an hour.' She paused, and then she said, 'Of course, he must be a widower now.'

He nodded. 'Everybody says that he's a very decent sort of chap.'

Her mother said, 'I do hope something comes of it. I would like to see her settled down, and happily married with some children.'

'She'll have to be quick about it, if you're going to see that,' remarked her father.

'Oh dear, I keep forgetting. But you know what I mean.'

He came to her on Tuesday afternoon; she met him with the horse and buggy. He got out of the train and looked around, sniffing the warm country air. 'Say,' he said, 'you've got some pretty nice country round here. Which way is your place?'

She pointed to the north. 'Over there, about three miles.'

'Up on that range of hills?'

'Not right up,' she said. 'Just a bit of the way up.'

He was carrying a suitcase, and swung it up into the buggy, pushing it under the seat. 'Is that all you've got?' she demanded.

'That's right. It's full of mending.'

'It doesn't look much. I'm sure you must have more than that.'

'I haven't. I brought everything there was. Honest.'

'I hope you're telling me the truth.' They got up into the driving seat and started off towards the village. Almost immediately he said, 'That's a beech tree! There's another!'

She glanced at him curiously. 'They grow round here. I suppose it's cooler on the hills.'

He looked at the avenue, entranced. 'That's an oak tree, but it's a mighty big one. I don't know that I ever saw an oak tree grow so big. And there's some maples!' He turned to her. 'Say, this is just like an avenue in a small town in the States!'

'Is it?' she asked. 'Is it like this in the States?'

'It certainly is,' he said. 'You've got all the trees here from the northern hemisphere. Parts of Australia I've seen up till now, they've only had gum trees and wattles.'

'They don't make you feel bad?' she asked.

'Why, no. I just love to see these northern trees again.'

'There are plenty of them round the farm,' she said. They drove through the village, across the deserted bitumen road, and out upon the road to Harkaway. Presently the road trended uphill; the horse slowed to a walk and began to slog against the collar. The girl said, 'This is where we get out and walk.'

He got down with her from the buggy, and they walked together up the hill, leading the horse. After the stuffiness of the dockyard and the heat of the steel ships the woodland air seemed fresh and cool to him. He took off his jacket and laid it in the buggy, and loosened the collar of his shirt. They walked on up the hill, and now a panorama started to unfold behind them, a wide view over the flat plain to the sea at Port Phillip Bay ten miles away. They went on, riding on the flats and walking on the steeper parts, for half an hour. Gradually they entered a country of gracious farms on undulating hilly slopes, a place where well kept paddocks were interspersed with coppices and many trees. He said, 'You're mighty lucky to have a home in country like this.'

She glanced at him. 'We like it all right. Of course, it's frightfully dull living out here.'

He stopped, and stood in the road, looking around him at the smiling countryside, the wide unfettered views. 'I don't know that I ever saw a place that was more beautiful,' he said.

'It *is* beautiful?' she asked. 'I mean, is it as beautiful as places in America or England?'

'Why, sure,' he said. 'I don't know England so well. I'm told that parts of that are just a fairyland. There's plenty of lovely scenery in the United States, but I don't know of any place that's just like this. No, this is beautiful all right, by any standard in the world.'

'I'm glad to hear you say that,' she replied. 'I mean, I like it here, but then I've never seen anything else. One sort of thinks that everything in England or America must be much better. That this is all right for Australia, but that's not saying much.'

He shook his head. 'It's not like that at all, honey. This is good by any standard that you'd like to name.'

They came to a flat and, driving in the buggy, the girl turned in to an entrance gate. A short drive led between an avenue of pine trees to a single-storey wooden house, a fairly large house painted white that merged with farm buildings towards the back. A wide veranda ran along the front and down one side, partially glazed in. The girl drove past the house and into the farm yard. 'Sorry about taking you in by the back door,' she said. 'But the mare won't stand, not when she's so near the stable.'

A farm hand called Lou, the only employee on the place, came to help her with the horse, and her father came out to meet them. She introduced Dwight all round, and they left the horse and buggy to Lou and went into the house to meet her mother. Later they gathered on the veranda to sit in the warm evening sun over short drinks before the evening meal. From the veranda there was a pastoral view over undulating pastures and coppices, with a distant view of the plain down below the trees. Again Dwight commented upon the beauty of the countryside.

'Yes, it's nice up here,' said Mrs Davidson. 'But it can't compare with England. England's beautiful.'

The American asked, 'Were you born in England?'

'Me? No. I was born Australian. My grandfather came out to Sydney in the very early days, but he wasn't a convict. Then he took up land in the Riverina. Some of the family are there still.' She paused. 'I've only been home once,' she said. 'We made a trip to England and the Continent in 1948, after the Second War. We thought England was quite beautiful. But I suppose it's changed a lot now.'

She left the veranda presently with Moira to see about the tea, and Dwight was left on the veranda with her father. He said, 'Let me give you another whisky.'

'Why, thanks. I'd like one.'

They sat in warm comfort in the mellow evening sun over their drinks. After a time the grazier said, 'Moira was telling us about the cruise that you just made up to the north.'

The captain nodded. 'We didn't find out much.'

'So she said.'

'There's not much that you *can* see, from the water's edge and through the periscope,' he told his host. 'It's not as if there was any bomb damage, or anything like that. It all looks just the same as it always did. It's just that people don't live there any more.'

'It was very radioactive, was it?'

Dwight nodded. 'It gets worse the further north you go, of course. At Cairns, when we were there, a person might have lived for a few days. At Port Darwin nobody could live so long as that.'

'When were you at Cairns?'

'About a fortnight ago.'

'I suppose the intensity at Cairns would be worse by now.'

'Probably so. I'd say it gets worse steadily as time goes on. Finally, of course, it'll get to the same level all around the world.'

'They're still saying that it's going to get here in September.'

'I would say that's right. It's coming very evenly, all round the world. All places in the same latitude seem to be getting it just about the same time.'

'They were saying on the wireless they've got it in Rockhampton.'

The captain nodded. 'I heard that, too. And at Alice Springs. It's coming very evenly along the latitudes.'

His host smiled, a little grimly. 'No good agonizing about it. Have another whisky.'

'I don't believe I will, not now. Thank you.'

Mr Davidson poured himself another small one. 'Anyway,' he said, 'it comes to us last of all.'

'That seems to be so,' said Dwight. 'If it goes on the way it's going now, Cape Town will go out a little before Sydney, about the same time as Montevideo. There'll be nothing left then in Africa and South America. Melbourne is the most southerly major city in the world, so we'll be near to the last.' He paused for a moment in thought. 'New Zealand, most of it, may last a little longer, and, of course, Tasmania. A fortnight or three weeks, perhaps. I don't know if there's anybody in Antarctica. If so, they might go on for quite a while.'

'But Melbourne is the last big city?'

'That's what it looks like, at the moment.'

They sat in silence for a little while. 'What will you do,' the grazier asked at last. 'Will you move your ship?'

'I haven't decided that,' the captain said slowly. 'Maybe I won't have to decide it. I've got a senior officer, Captain Shaw, in Brisbane. I don't suppose he'll move because his ship can't move. Maybe he'll send me orders. I don't know.'

'*Would* you move, if it was at your own discretion?'

'I haven't decided that,' the captain said again. 'I can't see that there's a great deal to be gained. Nearly forty per cent of my ship's company have got themselves tied up with girls in Melbourne – married, some of them. Say I was to move to Hobart. I can't take them along, and they can't get there any other way, and if they could there's nowhere there for them to live. It seems kind of rough on the men to separate them from their women in the last few days, unless there was some compelling reason in the interest of the naval service.' He glanced up, grinning. 'Anyway, I don't suppose they'd come. Most of them would probably jump ship.'

'I suppose they would. I think they'd probably decide to put the women first.'

The American nodded. 'It's reasonable. And there's no sense in giving orders that you know won't be obeyed.'

'Could you take your ship to sea without them?'

'Why, yes – just for a short run. Hobart would be a short trip, six or seven hours. We could take her there with just a dozen men, or even less. We wouldn't submerge if we were as short-handed as that, and we couldn't cruise for any length of time. But if we got her there, or even to New Zealand – say to Christchurch; without a full crew we could never be effective, operationally.' He paused. 'We'd be just refugees.'

They sat in silence for a time. 'One of the things that's been surprising me,' the grazier said, 'is that there have been so few refugees. So few people coming down from the north. From Cairns and Townsville, and from places like that.'

'Is that so?' the captain asked. 'It's just about impossible to get a bed in Melbourne – anywhere.'

'I know there have been some. But not the numbers that I should have expected.'

'That's the radio, I suppose,' Dwight said. 'These talks that the Prime Minister's been giving have been kind of steadying. The ABC's been doing a good job in telling people just the way things are. After all, there's not much comfort in leaving home and coming down here to live in a tent or in a car, and have the same thing happen to you a month or two later.'

'Maybe,' the grazier said. 'I've heard of people going back to Queensland after a few weeks of that. But I'm not sure that that's the whole story. I believe it is that nobody really thinks it's going to happen, not to them, until they start to feel ill. And by that time, well, it's less effort to stay at home and take it. You don't recover from this once it starts, do you?'

'I don't think that's true. I think you *can* recover, if you get out of the radioactive area into a hospital where you get proper treatment. They've got a lot of cases from the north in the Melbourne hospitals right now.'

'I didn't know that.'

'No. They don't say anything about that over the radio. After all, what's the use? They're only going to get it over again next September.'

'Nice outlook,' said the grazier. 'Will you have another whisky now?'

'Thank you, I believe I will.' He stood up and poured

himself a drink. 'You know,' he said, 'now that I've got used to the idea I think I'd rather have it this way. We've all got to die one day, some sooner and some later. The trouble always has been that you're never ready, because you don't know when it's coming. Well, now we do know, and there's nothing to be done about it. I kind of like that. I kind of like the thought that I'll be fit and well up till the end of August and then – home. I'd rather have it that way than go on as a sick man from when I'm seventy to when I'm ninety.'

'You're a regular naval officer,' the grazier said. 'You're probably more accustomed to this sort of thing than I would be.'

'Will you evacuate?' the captain asked. 'Go some place else when it gets near? Tasmania?'

'Me? Leave this place?' the grazier said. 'No, I shan't go. When it comes, I'll have it here, on this veranda, in this chair, with a drink in my hand. Or else in my own bed. I wouldn't leave this place.'

'I'd say that's the way most folks think about it, now that they've got used to the idea.'

They sat on the veranda in the setting sun till Moira came to tell them that tea was ready. 'Drink up,' she said, 'and come in for the blotting paper, if you can still walk.'

Her father said, 'That's not the way to talk to our guest.'

'You don't know our guest as well as I do, Daddy. I tell you, you just can't get him past a pub. Any pub.'

'More likely he can't get you past one.' They went into the house.

There followed a very restful two days for Dwight Towers. He handed over a great bundle of mending to the two women, who took it away from him, sorted it, and busied themselves over it. In the hours of daylight he was occupied with Mr Davidson upon the farm from dawn till dusk. He was initiated into the arts of crutching sheep and of shovelling silage up into a cart and distributing it in the paddocks; he spent long hours walking by the bullock on the sunlit pastures. The change did him good after his confined life in the submarine and in the mother ship; each night he went to bed early and slept heavily, and awoke refreshed for the next day.

On the last morning of his stay, after breakfast, Moira found him standing at the door of a small outside room beside the laundry, now used as a repository for luggage, ironing boards, gum boots, and junk of every description. He was standing at the open door smoking a cigarette, looking at the assortment of articles inside. She said, 'That's where we put things when we tidy up the house and say we'll send it to the jumble sale. Then we never do.'

He smiled. 'We've got one of those, only it's not so full as this. Maybe that's because we haven't lived there so long.' He stood looking in upon the mass with interest. 'Say, whose tricycle was that?'

'Mine,' she said.

'You must have been quite small when you rode around on that.'

She glanced at it. 'It does look small now, doesn't it? I should think I was four or five years old.'

'There's a Pogo stick!' He reached in and pulled it out; it squeaked rustily. 'It's years and years since I saw a Pogo stick. There was quite a craze for them at one time, back home.'

'They went out for a time, and then they came back into fashion,' she said. 'Quite a lot of kids about here have Pogo sticks now.'

'How old would you have been when you had that?'

139

She thought for a moment. 'It came after the tricycle, after the scooter, and before the bicycle. I should think I was about seven.'

He held it in his hands thoughtfully. 'I'd say that's about the right age for a Pogo stick. You can buy them in the shops here, now?'

'I should think so. The kids use them.'

He laid it down. 'It's years since I saw one of those in the United States. They go in fashions, as you say.' He glanced around. 'Who owned the stilts?'

'My brother had them first, and then I had them. I broke that one.'

'He was older than you, wasn't he?'

She nodded. 'Two years older – two and a half.'

'Is he in Australia now?'

'No. He's in England.'

He nodded; there was nothing useful to be said about that. 'Those stilts are quite high off the ground,' he remarked. 'I'd say you were older then.'

She nodded. 'I must have been ten or eleven.'

'Skis.' He measured the length of them with his eye. 'You must have been older still.'

'I didn't go skiing till I was about sixteen. But I used those up till just before the war. They were getting a bit small for me by then, though. That other pair were Donald's.'

He ran his eye around the jumbled contents of the little room. 'Say,' he said, 'there's a pair of water-skis!'

She nodded. 'We still use those – or we did up till the war.' She paused. 'We used to go for summer holidays at Barwon Heads. Mummy used to rent the same house every year . . .' She stood in silence for a moment, thinking of the sunny little house by the golf links, the warm sands, the cool air rushing past as she flew behind the motor boat in a flurry of warm spray. 'There's the wooden spade I used to build sand castles with when I was very little . . .'

He smiled at her. 'It's kind of fun, looking at other people's toys and trying to think what they must have looked like at that age. I can just imagine you at seven, jumping around on that Pogo stick.'

'And flying into a temper every other minute,' she said. She stood for a moment looking in at the door thoughtfully. 'I never would let Mummy give any of my toys away,' she said quietly. 'I said that I was going to keep them for my children to play with. Now there aren't going to be any.'

'Too bad,' he said. 'Still, that's the way it is.' He pulled the door to and closed it on so many sentimental hopes. 'I think I'll have to get back to the ship this afternoon and see if she's sunk at her moorings. Do you know what time there'd be a train?'

'I don't, but we can ring the station and find out. You don't think you could stay another day?'

'I'd like to, honey, but I don't think I'd better. There'll be a pile of paper on my desk that needs attention.'

'I'll find out about the train. What are you going to do this morning?'

'I told your father that I'd finish harrowing the hill paddock.'

'I've got an hour or so to do around the house. I'll probably come out and walk around with you after that.'

'I'd like that. Your bullock's a good worker, but he doesn't make a lot of conversation.'

They gave him his newly mended clothes after lunch. He expressed his thanks for all that they had done for him, packed his bag, and Moira drove him down to the station. There was an exhibition of Australian religious paintings at the National Gallery; they arranged to go and see that together before it came off; he would give her a ring. Then he was in the train for Melbourne, on his way back to his work.

He got back to the aircraft carrier at about six o'clock. As he had supposed, there was a pile of paper on his desk, including a sealed envelope with a security label gummed on the outside. He slit it open and found that it contained a draft operation order, with a personal note attached to it from the First Naval Member asking him to ring up for an appointment and come and see him about it.

He glanced the order through. It was very much as he had thought that it would be. It was within the capacity of his ship to execute, assuming that there were no mines at all laid on the west coast of the United States, which seemed to him to be a bold assumption.

He rang up Peter Holmes that evening at his home near Falmouth. 'Say,' he said, 'I've got a draft operation order lying on my desk. There's a covering letter from the First Naval Member, wants me to go and see him. I'd like it if you could come on board tomorrow and look it over. Then I'd say you'd better come along when I go to see the Admiral.'

'I'll be on board tomorrow morning, early,' said the liaison officer.

'Well, that's fine. I hate to pull you back off leave, but this needs action.'

'That's all right, sir. I was only going to take down a tree.'

He was in the aircraft carrier by half past nine next morning, seated with Commander Towers in his little office cabin, reading through the order. 'It's more or less what you thought it was going to be, sir, isn't it?' he asked.

'More or less,' the captain agreed. He turned to the side

table. 'This is all we've got on the minefields. This radio station that they want investigated. They've pinpointed that in the Seattle area. Well, we're all right for that.' He raised a chart from the table. 'This is the key minefield chart of the Juan de Fuca and Puget Sound. We should be safe to go right up to Bremerton naval yard. We're all right for Pearl Harbor, but they don't ask us to go there. The Gulf of Panama, San Diego, and San Francisco – we've got nothing on those at all.'

Peter nodded. 'We'll have to explain that to the Admiral. As a matter of fact, I think he knows it. I know that he's quite open to a general discussion of this thing.'

'Dutch Harbor,' said the captain. 'We've got nothing on that.'

'Would we meet any ice up there?'

'I'd say we would. And fog, a lot of fog. It's not so good to go there at this time of year, with no watch on deck. We'll have to be careful up around those parts.'

'I wonder why they want us to go there.'

'I wouldn't know. Maybe he'll tell us.'

They pored over the charts together for a time. 'How would you go?' the liaison officer asked at last.

'On the surface along Latitude Thirty, north of New Zealand, south of Pitcairn, till we pick up Longitude One-twenty. Then straight up the longitude. That brings us to the States in California, around Santa Barbara. Coming home from Dutch Harbor we'd do the same. Straight south down One-six-five past Hawaii. I guess we'd take a look in at Pearl Harbor while we're there. Then right on south till we can surface near the Friendly Islands, or maybe a bit south of that.'

'How long would that mean that we should be submerged?'

The captain turned and took a paper from the desk. 'I

was trying to figure that out last night. I don't suppose that we'd stay very long in any place, like the last time. I make the distance around two hundred degrees, twelve thousand miles submerged. Say six hundred hours cruising – twenty-five days. Add a couple of days for investigations and delays. Say twenty-seven days.'

'Quite a long time under water.'

'*Swordfish* went longer. She went thirty-two days. The thing is to take it easy, and relax.'

The liaison officer studied the chart of the Pacific. He laid his finger on the mass of reefs and island groups south of Hawaii. 'There's not going to be much relaxing when we come to navigate through all this stuff, submerged. And that comes at the end of the trip.'

'I know it.' He stared at the chart. 'Maybe we'll move away towards the west a trifle, and come down on Fiji from the north.' He paused. 'I'm more concerned about Dutch Harbor than I am of the run home,' he said.

They stood studying the charts with the operation order for half an hour. Finally the Australian said, 'Well, it's going to be quite a cruise.' He grinned. 'Something to tell our grandchildren about.'

The captain glanced at him quickly, and then broke into a smile. 'You're *very* right.'

The liaison officer waited in the cabin while the captain rang the Admiral's secretary in the Navy Department. An appointment was made for ten o'clock the following morning. There was nothing then for Peter Holmes to stay for; he arranged to meet his captain next morning in the secretary's office before the appointment, and he took the next train back to his home at Falmouth.

He got there before lunch and rode his bicycle up from the station. He was hot when he got home, and glad to get out of uniform and take a shower before the cold meal. He found Mary to be very much concerned about the baby's prowess in crawling. 'I left her in the lounge,' she told him, 'on the hearth rug, and I went into the kitchen to peel the potatoes. The next thing I knew, she was in the passage, just outside the kitchen door. She's a little devil. She can get about now at a tremendous pace.'

They sat down to their lunch. 'We'll have to get some kind of a play pen,' he said. 'One of those wooden things, that fold up.'

She nodded. 'I was thinking about that. One with a few rows of beads on part of it, like an abacus.'

'I suppose you can get play pens still,' he said. 'Do we know anyone who's stopped having babies – might have one they didn't want?'

She shook her head. 'I don't. All our friends seem to be having baby after baby.'

'I'll scout around a bit and see what I can find,' he said.

It was not until lunch was nearly over that she was able to detach her mind from the baby. Then she asked, 'Oh, Peter, what happened with Commander Towers?'

'He'd got a draft operation order,' he told her. 'I suppose it's confidential, so don't talk about it. They want us to make a fairly long cruise in the Pacific. Panama, San Diego, San Francisco, Seattle, Dutch Harbor, and home, probably by way of Hawaii. It's all a bit vague just at present.'

She was uncertain of her geography. 'That's an awfully long way, isn't it?'

'It's quite a way,' he said. 'I don't think we shall do it all. Dwight's very much against going into the Gulf of Panama because he hasn't got a clue about the minefields, and if we don't go there that cuts off thousands of miles. But even so, it's quite a way.'

'How long would it take?' she asked.

'I haven't worked it out exactly. Probably about two months. You see,' he explained, 'you can't set a direct course, say for San Diego. He wants to keep the underwater time down to a minimum. That means we set course east on a safe latitude, steaming on the surface till we're two-thirds of the way across the South Pacific, and then go straight north till we come to California. It makes a dog-leg of it, but it means less time submerged.'

'How long would you be submerged, Peter?'

'Twenty-seven days, he reckons.'

'That's an awfully long time, isn't it?'

'It's quite long. It's not a record, or anywhere near it. Still, it's quite a time to be without fresh air. Nearly a month.'

'When would you be starting?'

'Well, I don't know that. The original idea was that we'd get away about the middle of next month, but now we've got this bloody measles in the ship. We can't go until we're clear of that.'

'Have there been any more cases?'

'One more – the day before yesterday. The surgeon seems to think that's probably the last. If he's right we might be cleared to go about the end of the month. If not – if there's another one – it'll be some time in March.'

'That means that you'd be back here some time in June?'

'I should think so. We'll be clear of measles by the tenth of March whatever happens. That means we'd be back here by the tenth of June.'

The mention of measles had aroused anxiety in her again. 'I do hope Jennifer doesn't get it.'

They spent a domestic afternoon in their own garden. Peter started on the job of taking down the tree. It was not a very large tree, and he had little difficulty in sawing it half through and pulling it over with a rope so that it fell along the lawn and not on to the house. By tea time he had lopped its branches and stacked them away to be burned in the winter, and he had got well on with sawing the green wood up into logs. Mary came with the baby, newly wakened from her afternoon sleep, and laid a rug out on the lawn and put the baby on it. She went back into the house to fetch a tray of tea things; when she returned the baby was ten feet from the rug trying to eat a bit of bark. She scolded her husband and set him to watch his child while she went in for the kettle.

'It's no good,' she said. 'We'll have to have that play pen.'

He nodded. 'I'm going up to town tomorrow morning,' he said. 'We've got a date at the Navy Department, but after that I should be free. I'll go to Myers and see if they've still got them there.'

'I do hope they have. I don't know what we'll do if we can't get one.'

'We could put a belt round her waist and tether her to a peg stuck in the ground.'

'We couldn't, Peter!' she said indignantly. 'She'd wind it round her neck and strangle herself!'

He mollified her, accustomed to the charge of being a heartless father. They spent the next hour playing with their baby on the grass in the warm sun, encouraging it to crawl about the lawn. Finally Mary took it indoors to bath it and give it its supper, while Peter went on sawing up the logs.

He met his captain next morning in the Navy Department, and together they were shown into the office of the First Naval Member, who had a captain from the Operations Division with him. He greeted them cordially, and made them sit down. 'Well now,' he said. 'You've had a look at the draft operation order that we sent you down?'

'I made a very careful study of it, sir,' said the captain.

'What's your general reaction?'

'Minefields,' Dwight said. 'Some of the objectives that you name would almost certainly be mined.' The Admiral nodded. 'We have full information on Pearl Harbor and on the approaches to Seattle. We have nothing on any of the others.'

They discussed the order in some detail for a time. Finally the Admiral leaned back in his chair. 'Well, that gives me the general picture. That's what I wanted.' He paused. 'Now, you'd better know what this is all about.

'Wishful thinking,' he observed. 'There's a school of thought among the scientists, a section of them, who consider that this atmospheric radioactivity may be dissipating – decreasing in intensity, fairly quickly. The general argument is that the precipitation during this last winter in the northern hemisphere, the rain and snow, may have washed the air, so to speak.' The American nodded. 'According to that theory, the radioactive elements in the atmosphere will be falling to the ground, or to the sea, more quickly than we had anticipated. In that case the ground masses of the northern hemisphere would continue to be uninhabitable for many centuries, but the transfer of radioactivity to us would be progressively decreased. In that case life – human life – might continue to go on down here, or at any rate in Antarctica. Professor Jorgensen holds that view very strongly.'

He paused. 'Well, that's the bare bones of the theory. Most of the scientists disagree, and think that Jorgensen is optimistic. Because of the majority opinion nothing has

148

been said about this on the wireless broadcasting, and we've been spared the Press. It's no good raising people's hopes without foundation. But clearly it's a matter that must be investigated.'

'I see that, sir,' Dwight said. 'It's very important. That's really the main object of this cruise?'

The Admiral nodded. 'That's right. If Jorgensen is correct, as you go north from the equator the atmospheric radioactivity should be steady for a time and then begin to decrease. I don't say at once, but at some point a decrease should be evident. That's why we want you to go as far north in the Pacific as you can, to Kodiak and to Dutch Harbor. If Jorgensen is right there should be much less radioactivity up there. It might even be near normal. In that case, you might be able to go out on deck.' He paused. 'On shore, of course, ground radioactivity would still be intense. But out at sea, life might be possible.'

Peter asked, 'Is there any experimental support for this yet, sir?'

The Admiral shook his head. 'Not much. The Air Force sent out a machine the other day. Did you hear about that?'

'No, sir.'

'Well, they sent out a Victor bomber with a full load of fuel. It flew from Perth due north and got as far as the China Sea, about Latitude Thirty North, somewhere south of Shanghai, before it had to turn back. That's not far enough for the scientists, but it was as far as the machine could go. The evidence they got was inconclusive. Atmospheric radioactivity was still increasing, but towards the northern end of the flight it was increasing slowly.' He smiled. 'I understand the backroom boys are still arguing about it. Jorgensen, of course, claims it as his victory. He says there'll be a positive reduction by the time you get to Latitude Fifty or Sixty.'

'Sixty,' the captain said. 'We can make that close inshore in the Gulf of Alaska. The only thing up there is that we'd have to watch the ice.'

They discussed the technicalities of the operation again for a time. It was decided that protective clothing should be carried in the submarine to permit one or two men to go on deck in moderate conditions, and that decontamination sprays should be arranged in one of the escape chambers. An inflatable rubber dinghy would be carried in the superstructure, and the new directional aerial would be mounted on the aft periscope.

Finally the Admiral said, 'Well, that clears the decks so far as we are concerned. I think the next step is that I call a conference with CSIRO and anybody else who may be concerned. I'll arrange that for next week. In the meantime, Commander, you might see the Third Naval Member or one of his officers about this dockyard work. I'd like to see you get away by the end of next month.'

Dwight said, 'I think that should be possible, sir. There's not a lot of work in this. The only thing might hold us up would be the measles.'

The Admiral laughed shortly. 'The fate of human life upon the world at stake, and we're stuck with the measles! All right, Captain – I know you'll do your best.'

When they left the office Dwight and Peter separated, Dwight to call at the Third Naval Member's office, and Peter to go to find John Osborne in his office in Albert Street. He told the scientist what he had learned that morning. 'I know all about Jorgensen,' Mr Osborne said impatiently. 'The old man's crackers. It's just wishful thinking.'

'You don't think much of what the aeroplane found out

– the reduced rate of increase of the radioactivity as you go north?'

'I don't dispute the evidence. The Jorgensen effect may well exist. Probably it does. But nobody but Jorgensen thinks that it's significant.'

Peter got to his feet. 'I'll leave the wise to wrangle,' he quoted sardonically. 'I've got to go and buy a play pen for my eldest unmarried daughter.'

'Where are you going to for that?'

'Myers.'

The scientist got up from his chair. 'I'll come with you. I've got something in Elizabeth Street I'd like to show you.'

He would not tell the naval officer what it was. They walked together down the centre of the traffic-free streets to the motor car district of the town, turned up a side street, and then into a mews. John Osborne produced a key from his pocket, unlocked the double doors of a building, and pushed them open.

It had been the garage of a motor dealer. Silent cars stood ranged in rows along the walls, some of them unregistered, all covered in dust and dirt with flat tyres sagging on the floor. In the middle of the floor stood a racing car. It was a single-seater, painted red. It was a very low-built car, a very small car, with a bonnet sloping forward to an aperture that lay close to the ground. The tyres were inflated and it had been washed and polished with loving care; it shone in the light from the door. It looked venomously fast.

'My goodness!' Peter said. 'What's that?'

'It's a Ferrari,' said John Osborne. 'It's the one that Donezetti raced the year before the war. The one he won the Grand Prix of Syracuse on.'

'How did it get out here?'

'Johnny Bowles bought it and had it shipped out. Then the war came and he never raced it.'

'Who owns it now?'

'I do.'

'You?'

The scientist nodded. 'I've been keen on motor racing all my life. It's what I've always wanted to do, but there's never been any money. Then I heard of this Ferrari. Bowles was caught in England. I went to his widow and offered her a hundred quid for it. She thought I was mad, of course, but she was glad to sell it.'

Peter walked round the little car with the large wheels, inspecting it. 'I agree with her. What on earth are you going to do with it?'

'I don't know yet. I only know that I'm the owner of what's probably the fastest car in the world.'

It fascinated the naval officer. 'Can I sit in it?'

'Go ahead.'

He squeezed down into the little seat behind the plastic windscreen. 'What will she do, all out?'

'I don't really know. Two hundred, anyway.'

Peter sat fingering the wheel, feeling the controls. The single-seater felt delightfully a part of him. 'Have you had her on the road?'

'Not yet.'

He got out of the seat reluctantly. 'What are you going to use for petrol?'

The scientist grinned. 'She doesn't drink it.'

'Doesn't use petrol?'

'She runs on a special ether-alcohol mixture. It's no good in an ordinary car. I've got eight barrels of it in my mother's back garden.' He grinned. 'I made sure that I'd got that before I bought the car.'

He lifted the bonnet and they spent some time examining

the engine. John Osborne had spent all his leisure hours since they returned from their first cruise in polishing and servicing the racing car; he hoped to try her out upon the road in a couple of days' time. 'One thing,' he said, grinning in delight, 'there's not a lot of traffic to worry about.'

They left the car reluctantly, and locked the garage doors. In the quiet mews they stood for a few moments. 'If we get away upon this cruise by the end of next month,' Peter said, 'we should be back about the beginning of June. I'm thinking about Mary and the kid. Think they'll be all right till we get back?'

'You mean – the radioactivity?'

The naval officer nodded.

The scientist stood in thought. 'Anybody's guess is as good as mine,' he said at last. 'It may come quicker or it may come slower. So far it's been coming very steadily all round the world, and moving southwards at just about the rate that you'd expect. It's south of Rockhampton now. If it goes on like this it should be south of Brisbane by the beginning of June – just south. Say about eight hundred miles north of us. But, as I say, it may come quicker or it may come slower. That's all I can tell you.'

Peter bit his lip. 'It's a bit worrying. One doesn't want to start a flap at home. But all the same, I'd be happier if they knew what to do if I'm not there.'

'You may not be there anyway,' John Osborne said. 'There seem to be quite a few natural hazards on this course – apart from radiation. Minefields, ice – all sorts of things. I don't know what happens to us if we hit an iceberg at full cruising speed, submerged.'

'I do,' said Peter.

The scientist laughed. 'Well, let's keep our fingers crossed and hope we don't. I want to get back here and race that thing.' He nodded at the car behind the door.

'It's all a bit worrying,' Peter repeated. They turned towards the street. 'I think I'll have to do something about it before we go.'

They walked in silence into the main thoroughfare. John Osborne turned towards his office. 'You going my way?'

Peter shook his head. 'I've got to see if I can buy a play pen for the baby. Mary says we've got to have it or she'll kill herself.'

They turned in different directions and the scientist walked on, thankful that he wasn't married.

Peter went shopping for a play pen, and succeeded in buying one at the second shop he tried. A folded play pen is an awkward thing to carry through a crowd; he battled with it to the tram and got it to Flinders Street station. He got to Falmouth with it at about four o'clock in the afternoon. He put it in the cloak-room till he could come and fetch it with his bicycle trailer, took his bicycle, and rode slowly into the shopping street. He went to the chemist that they dealt with, whose proprietor he knew, and who knew him. At the counter he asked the girl if he could see Mr Goldie.

The chemist came to him in a white coat. Peter asked, 'Could I have a word with you in private?'

'Why, yes, Commander.' He led the way into the dispensary.

Peter said. 'I wanted to have a talk with you about this radiation disease.' The chemist's face was quite expressionless. 'I've got to go away. I'm sailing in the *Scorpion*, the American submarine. We're going a long way. We shan't be back till the beginning of June, at the earliest.' The chemist nodded slowly. 'It's not a very easy trip,' the naval officer said. 'There's just the possibility that we might not come back at all.'

They stood in silence for a moment. 'Are you thinking about Mrs Holmes and Jennifer?' the chemist asked.

Peter nodded. 'I'll have to make sure Mrs Holmes understands about things before I go.' He paused. 'Tell me, just what does happen to you?'

'Nausea,' the chemist said. 'That's the first symptom. Then vomiting, and diarrhoea. Bloody stools. All the symptoms increase in intensity. There may be slight recovery, but if so it would be very temporary. Finally death occurs from sheer exhaustion.' He paused. 'In the very end, infection or leukaemia may be the actual cause of death. The blood-forming tissues are destroyed, you see, by the loss of body salts in the fluids. It might go one way or the other.'

'Somebody was saying it's like cholera.'

'That's right,' the chemist said. 'It *is* rather like cholera.'

'You've got some stuff for it, haven't you?'

'Not to cure it, I'm afraid.'

'I don't mean that. To end it.'

'We can't release that yet, Commander. About a week before it reaches any district, details will be given on the wireless. After that we may distribute it to those who ask for it.' He paused. 'There must be terrible complications over the religious side,' he said. 'I suppose then it's a matter for the individual.'

'I've got to see that my wife understands about it,' Peter said. 'She'll have to see to the baby . . . And I may not be here. I've got to see this all squared up before I go.'

'I could explain it all to Mrs Holmes, when the time comes.'

'I'd rather do it myself. She'll be a bit upset.'

'Of course . . .' He stood for a moment, and then said, 'Come into the stockroom.'

He went through into a back room through a locked door. There was a packing case in one corner, the lid part lifted. He wrenched it back. The case was full of little red boxes, of two sizes.

The chemist took out one of each and went back into the dispensary. He undid the smaller of the two; it contained a little plastic vial with two white tablets in it. He opened it, took out the tablets, put them carefully away, and substituted two tablets of aspirin. He put the vial back in the red box and closed it. He handed it to Peter. 'That is for anybody who will take a pill,' he said. 'You can take that and show it to Mrs Holmes. One causes death, almost immediately. The other is a spare. When the time comes, we shall be distributing these at the counter.'

'Thanks a lot,' he said. 'What does one do about the baby?'

The chemist took the other box. 'The baby, or a pet animal – a dog or a cat,' he said. 'It's just a little more complicated.' He opened the second box and took out a small syringe. 'I've got a used one I can put in for you, here. You follow these instructions on the box. Just give the hypodermic injection under the skin. She'll fall asleep quite soon.'

He packed the dummy back into the box, and gave it to Peter with the other.

The naval officer took them gratefully. 'That's very kind of you,' he said. 'She'll be able to get these at the counter when the time comes?'

'That's right.'

'Will there be anything to pay?'

'No charge,' the chemist said. 'They're on the free list.'

5

Of the three presents which Peter Holmes took back to his wife that night, the play pen was the most appreciated.

It was a brand new play pen, painted in a pastel green, with brightly coloured beads upon the abacus. He set it up upon the lawn before he went into the house, and then called Mary out to see it. She came and examined it critically, testing it for stability to make sure the baby couldn't pull it over on top of her. 'I do hope the paint won't come off,' she said. 'She sucks everything, you know. Green paint's awfully dangerous. It's got verdigris in it.'

'I asked about that in the shop,' he said. 'It's not oil paint – it's Duco. She'd have to have acetone in her saliva to get that off.'

'She can get the paint off most things . . .' She stood back and looked at it. 'It's an awfully pretty colour,' she said. 'It'll go beautifully with the curtains in the nursery.'

'I thought it might,' he said. 'They had a blue one, but I thought you'd like this better.'

'Oh, I do!' She put her arms round him and kissed him. 'It's a lovely present. You must have had a fearful job with it on the tram. Thank you so much.'

'That's all right,' he said. He kissed her back. 'I'm so glad you like it.'

She went and fetched the baby from the house and put her in the pen. Then they got short drinks for themselves and sat on the lawn, the bars between them and the baby, smoking cigarettes and watching her reaction to the new environment. They watched her as she grasped one of the bars in a tiny fist.

'You don't think she'll get up on her feet too soon, with that to hold on to?' her mother asked, worried. 'I mean, she wouldn't learn to walk without it for a long time. If they walk too soon they grow up bandy-legged.'

'I shouldn't think so,' Peter said. 'I mean, everyone has play pens. I had one when I was a kid, and I didn't grow up bandy-legged.'

'I suppose if she didn't pull herself up on this she'd be pulling herself up on something else. A chair, or something.'

When Mary took the baby away to give her her bath and make her ready for bed, Peter took the play pen indoors and set it up in the nursery. Then he laid the table for the evening meal. Then he went and stood on the veranda, fingering the red boxes in his pocket, wondering how on earth he was to give his other presents to his wife.

Presently he went and got himself a whisky.

He did it that evening, shortly before she went to take the baby up before they went to bed. He said awkwardly, 'There's one thing I want to have a talk about before I go off on this cruise.'

She looked up. 'What's that?'

'About this radiation sickness people get. There's one or two things that you ought to know.'

She said impatiently, 'Oh, *that*. It's not until September. I don't want to talk about it.'

'I'm afraid we'll have to talk about it,' he said.

'I don't see why. You can tell me all about it nearer the time. When we know it's coming. Mrs Hildred says her husband heard from somebody that it isn't coming here after all. It's slowing down or something. It's not going to get here.'

'I don't know who Mrs Hildred's husband has been talking to. But I can tell you that there's not a word of truth in it. It's coming here, all right. It may come in September, or it may come sooner.'

She stared at him. 'You mean that we're all going to get it?'

'Yes,' he said. 'We're all going to get it. We're all going to die of it. That's why I want to tell you just a bit about it.'

'Can't you tell me about it nearer the time? When we know it's really going to happen?'

He shook his head. 'I'd rather tell you now. You see, I might not be here when it happens. It might come quicker than we think, while I'm away. Or I might get run over by a bus – *anything*.'

'There aren't any buses,' she said quietly. 'What you mean is the submarine.'

'Have it your own way,' he said. 'I'd be much happier while I'm away in the submarine if I knew you knew about things more than you do now.'

'All right,' she said reluctantly. She lit a cigarette. 'Go on and tell me.'

He thought for a minute. 'We've all got to die one day,' he said at last. 'I don't know that dying this way is much worse than any other. What happens is that you get ill. You start feeling sick, and then you *are* sick. Apparently you go on being sick – you can't keep anything down. And then, you've got to go. Diarrhoea. And that gets worse and worse, too. You may recover for a little while,

159

but it comes back again. And finally you get so weak that you just – die.'

She blew a long cloud of smoke. 'How long does all this take?'

'I didn't ask about that. I think it varies with the individual. It may take two or three days. I suppose if you recover it might take two or three weeks.'

There was a short silence. 'It's messy,' she said at last. 'I suppose if everybody gets it all at once, there's nobody to help you. No doctors, and no hospitals?'

'I shouldn't think so. I think this is a thing you've got to battle through with on your own.'

'But you'll be here, Peter?'

'I'll be here,' he comforted her. 'I'm just telling you to cover the thousand to one chance.'

'But if I'm all alone, who's going to look after Jennifer?'

'Leave Jennifer out of it for the moment,' he said. 'We'll come to her later.' He leaned towards her. 'The thing is this, dear. There's no recovery. But you don't have to die in a mess. You can die decently, when things begin to get too bad.' He drew the smaller of the two red boxes from his pocket.

She stared at it, fascinated. 'What's that?' she whispered.

He undid the little carton and took out the vial. 'This is a dummy,' he said. 'These aren't real. Goldie gave it me to show you what to do. You just take one of them with a drink – any kind of drink. Whatever you like best. And then you just lie back, and that's the end.'

'You mean, you die?' The cigarette was dead between her fingers.

He nodded. 'When it gets too bad – it's the way out.'

'What's the other pill for?' she whispered.

'That's a spare,' he said. 'I suppose they give it you in case you lose one of them, or funk it.'

She sat in silence, her eyes fixed on the red box.

'When the time comes,' he said, 'they'll tell you all about this on the wireless. Then you just go to Goldie's and ask the girl for it, over the counter, so that you can have it in the house. She'll give it to you. Everybody will be given it who wants it.'

She reached out, dropping the dead cigarette, and took the box from him. She read the instructions printed on it in black. At last she said, 'But, Peter, however ill I was, I couldn't do that. Who would look after Jennifer?'

'We're all going to get it,' he said. 'Every living thing. Dogs and cats and babies – everyone. I'm going to get it. You're going to get it. Jennifer's going to get it, too.'

She stared at him. 'Jennifer's going to get this sort of – cholera?'

'I'm afraid so, dear,' he said. 'We're all going to get it.'

She dropped her eyes. 'That's beastly,' she said vehemently. 'I don't mind for myself so much. But that's . . . it's simply vile.'

He tried to comfort her. 'It's the end of everything for all of us,' he said. 'We're going to lose most of the years of life that we've looked forward to, and Jennifer's going to lose all of them. But it doesn't have to be too painful for her. When things are hopeless, you can make it easy for her. It's going to take a bit of courage on your part, but you've got that. This is what you'll have to do if I'm not here.'

He drew the other red box from his pocket and began to explain the process to her. She watched him with growing hostility. 'Let me get this straight,' she said, and now there was an edge in her voice. 'Are you trying to tell me what I've got to do to kill Jennifer?'

He knew that there was trouble coming, but he had to face it. 'That's right,' he said. 'If it becomes necessary you'll have to do it.'

She flared suddenly into anger. 'I think you're crazy,' she exclaimed. 'I'd never do a thing like that, however ill she was. I'd nurse her to the end. You must be absolutely mad. The trouble is that you don't love her. You never have loved her. She's always been a nuisance to you. Well, she's not a nuisance to me. It's you that's the nuisance. And now it's reached the stage that you're trying to tell me how to murder her.' She got to her feet, white with rage. 'If you say one more word I'll murder you!'

He had never seen her so angry before. He got to his feet. 'Have it your own way,' he said wearily. 'You don't have to use these things if you don't want to.'

She said furiously. 'There's a trick here, somewhere. You're trying to get me to murder Jennifer and kill myself. Then you'd be free to go off with some other woman.'

He had not thought that it would be so bad as this. 'Don't be a bloody fool,' he said sharply. 'If I'm here I'll have it myself. If I'm not here, if you've got to face things on your own, it'll be because I'm dead already. Just think of that, and try and get that into your fat head. I'll be dead.'

She stared at him in angry silence.

'There's another thing you'd better think about,' he said. 'Jennifer may live longer than you will.' He held up the first red box. 'You can chuck these in the dustbin,' he said. 'You can battle on as long as you can stand, until you die. But Jennifer may not be dead. She may live on for days, crying and vomiting all over herself in her cot and lying in her muck, with you dead on the floor beside her and nobody to help her. Finally, of course, she'll die. Do you want her to die like that? If you do, I don't.' He turned away. 'Just think about it, and don't be such a bloody fool.'

She stood in silence. For a moment he thought that she was going to fall, but he was too angry now himself to help her.

'This is a time when you've just got to show some guts and face up to things,' he said.

She turned and ran out of the room, and presently he heard her sobbing in the bedroom. He did not go to her. Instead he poured himself a whisky and soda and went out on to the veranda and sat down in a deck chair, looking out over the sea. These bloody women, sheltered from realities, living in a sentimental dream world of their own! If they'd face up to things they could help a man, help him enormously. While they clung to the dream world they were just a bloody millstone round his neck.

About midnight, after his third whisky, he went into the house and to their bedroom. She was in bed and the light was out; he undressed in the dark, fearing to wake her. She lay with her back to him; he turned from her and fell asleep, helped by the whisky. At about two in the morning he awoke, and heard her sobbing in the bed beside him. He stretched out a hand to comfort her.

She turned to him, still sobbing. 'Oh Peter, I'm sorry I've been such a fool.'

They said no more about the red boxes, but next morning he put them in the medicine cupboard in the bathroom, at the back, where they would not be obtrusive but where she could hardly fail to see them. In each box he left a little note explaining that it was a dummy, explaining what she had to do to get the real ones. He added to each note a few words of love, thinking that she might well read it after he was dead.

The pleasant summer weather lasted well on into March.

In *Scorpion* there were no more cases of measles, and the work upon the submarine progressed quickly in the hands of dockyard fitters who had little else to do. Peter Holmes took down the second tree, cut it up and stacked the logs to dry out so that they could be burned the following year, and started to dig out the stumps to make the kitchen garden.

John Osborne started up his Ferrari and drove it out upon the road. There was no positive prohibition upon motoring at that time. There was no petrol available to anybody because officially there was no petrol in the country; the stocks reserved for doctors and for hospitals had been used up. Yet very occasionally cars were still seen in motion on the roads. Each individual motorist had cans of petrol tucked away in his garage or in some private hiding place, provision that he had made when things were getting short, and these reserves were sometimes called upon in desperate emergency. John Osborne's Ferrari on the road did not call for any action by the police, even when his foot slipped upon the unfamiliar accelerator on his first drive and he touched eighty-five in second gear in Bourke Street, in the middle of the city. Unless he were to kill anybody, the police were not disposed to prosecute him for a trifle such as that.

He did not kill anybody, but he frightened himself very much. There was a private road racing-circuit in South Gippsland near a little place called Tooradin, owned and run by a club of enthusiasts. Here there was a three mile circuit of wide bitumen road, privately owned, leading nowhere, and closed to the public. The course had one long straight and a large number of sinuous turns and bends. Here races were still held, sparsely attended by the public for lack of road transport. Where the enthusiasts got their petrol from remained a closely guarded secret, or a number of secrets, because each seemed to have his own private hoard, as John Osborne hoarded his eight drums of special racing fuel in his mother's back garden.

John Osborne took his Ferrari down to this place several times, at first for practice and later to compete in races, short races for the sake of fuel economy. The car fulfilled a useful purpose in his life. His had been the life of a scientist, a man whose time was spent in theorizing in an office or, at best, in a laboratory. Not for him had been the life of action. He was not very well accustomed to taking personal risks, to endangering his life, and his life had been the poorer for it. When he had been drafted to the submarine for scientific duties he had been pleasurably excited by the break in his routine, but in secret he had been terrified each time that they submerged. He had managed to control himself and carry out his duties without much of his nervous tension showing during their week of underwater cruising in the north, but he had been acutely nervous of the prospect of nearly a month of it in the cruise that was coming.

The Ferrari altered that. Each time he drove it, it excited him. At first he did not drive it very well. After touching a hundred and fifty miles an hour or so upon the straight he failed to slow enough to take his corners safely. Each corner at first was a sort of dice with death, and twice he spun and ended up on the grass verge, white and trembling with shock and deeply ashamed that he had treated his car so. Each little race or practice run upon the circuit left him with the realization of mistakes that he must never make again, with the realization of death escaped by inches.

With these major excitements in the forefront of his mind, the coming cruise in *Scorpion* ceased to terrify. There was no danger in that comparable with the dangers that he courted in his racing car. The naval interlude became a somewhat boring chore to be lived through, a waste of time that now was growing precious, till he could get back to Melbourne and put in three months of road racing before the end.

Like every other racing motorist, he spent a lot of time endeavouring to track down further supplies of fuel.

Sir David Hartman held his conference as had been arranged. Dwight Towers went to it as captain of *Scorpion* and took his liaison officer with him. He also took the radio and electrical officer, a Lieutenant Sunderstrom, to the conference because matters connected with the Seattle radio were likely to arise. CSIRO were represented by the Director with John Osborne, the Third Naval Member was there with one of his officers, and the party was completed by one of the Prime Minister's secretaries.

At the commencement the First Naval Member outlined the difficulties of the operation. 'It is my desire,' he said, 'and it is the Prime Minister's instruction, that *Scorpion* should not be exposed to any extreme danger in the course of this cruise. In the first place, we want the results of the scientific observations we are sending her to make. With the low height of her radio aerial and the necessity that she remains submerged for much of the time, we cannot expect free radio communication with her. For that reason alone she must return safely or the whole value of the operation will be lost. Apart from that, she is the only long range vessel left at our disposal for communication with South America and with South Africa. With these considerations in mind I have made fairly drastic alterations to the cruise that we discussed at our last meeting. The investigation of the Panama Canal has been struck out. San Diego and San Francisco also have been struck out. All these are on account of minefields. Commander

Towers, will you tell us shortly how you stand in regard to minefields.'

Dwight gave the conference a short dissertation on the mines and on his lack of knowledge. 'Seattle is open to us, and the whole of Puget Sound,' he said. 'Also Pearl Harbor. I'd say there wouldn't be much danger from mines up around the Gulf of Alaska on account of the ice movements. The ice constitutes a problem in those latitudes, and the *Scorpion's* no icebreaker. Still, in my opinion we can feel our way up there without unduly hazarding the ship. If we just can't make it all the way to Latitude Sixty, well, we'll have done our best. I'd say we probably can do most of what you want.'

They turned to a discussion of the radio signals still coming from somewhere in the vicinity of Seattle. Sir Phillip Goodall, the Director of CSIRO, produced a synopsis of the messages monitored since the war. 'These signals are mostly incomprehensible,' he said. 'They occur at random intervals, more frequently in the winter than the summer. The frequency is 4.92 megacycles.' The radio officer made a note upon the paper in front of him. 'One hundred and sixty-nine transmissions have been monitored. Of these, three contained recognizable code groups, seven groups in all. Two contained words in clear, in English, one word in each. The groups were undecipherable; I have them here if anyone wants to see them. The words were WATERS and CONNECT.'

Sir David Hartman asked, 'How many hours transmission, in all, were monitored?'

'About a hundred and six hours.'

'And in that time only two words have come through in clear? The rest is gibberish?'

'That is correct.'

The Admiral said, 'I don't think the words can be

significant. It's probably a fortuitous transmission. After all, if an infinite number of monkeys start playing with an infinite number of typewriters, one of them will write a play of Shakespeare. The real point to be investigated is this – how are these transmissions taking place at all? It seems certain that there is electrical power available there still. There may be human agency behind that power. It's not very likely, but it could be so.'

Lieutenant Sunderstrom leaned towards his captain and spoke in a low tone. Dwight said aloud, 'Mr Sunderstrom knows the radio installations in that district.'

The Lieutenant said diffidently, 'I wouldn't say that I know all of them. I attended a short course on Naval Communications at Santa Maria Island about five years back. One of the frequencies that was used there was 4.92 megacycles.'

The Admiral asked, 'Where is Santa Maria Island?'

'That one is just near Bremerton in Puget Sound, sir. There's several others on the Coast. This one is the main Navy communications school for that area.'

Commander Towers unrolled a chart, and pointed to the island with his finger. 'Here it is, sir. It connects with the mainland by a bridge to this place Manchester right next to Clam Bay.'

The Admiral asked, 'What would be the range of the station on Santa Maria Island?'

The Lieutenant said, 'I wouldn't know for certain, but I guess it's global.'

'Does it look like a global station? Very high aerials?'

'Oh, yes, sir. The antennas there are quite a sight. I think it's a part of the regular communication system covering the Pacific area, but I don't know that for sure. I only attended the communications school.'

'You never communicated with the station direct, from any ship that you were serving in?'

'No, sir. We operated on a different set of frequencies.'

They discussed the techniques of radio for a time. 'If it turns out to be Santa Maria,' Dwight said at last, 'I'd say we can investigate it without difficulty.' He glanced at the chart that he had studied before, to confirm his studies. 'There's forty feet of water right close up to it,' he said. 'Maybe we could even lie alongside a wharf. In any case, we've got the rubber boat. If the radiation level is anywhere near reasonable we can put an officer on shore for a while, in the protective suit, of course.'

The Lieutenant said, 'I'd be glad to volunteer for that. I guess I know the way around that installation pretty well.'

They left it so, and turned to a consideration of the Jorgensen effect, and the scientific observations that were needed to prove or disprove it.

Dwight met Moira Davidson for lunch after the conference. She had picked a small restaurant in the city for their meeting and he was there before her. She came to him bearing an attaché case.

He greeted her and offered her a drink before lunch. She elected for a brandy and soda, and he ordered it. 'Double?' he inquired, as the waiter stood by.

'Single,' she said. He nodded to the waiter without comment. He glanced at the attaché case. 'Been shopping?'

'Shopping!' she said indignantly. 'Me – full of virtue!'

'I'm sorry,' he replied. 'You're going some place?'

'No,' she said, enjoying his curiosity. 'I'll give you three guesses what's in it.'

'Brandy,' he suggested.

'No. I carry that inside me.'

He thought for a moment. 'A carving knife. You're

going to cut one of those religious pictures out of the frame and take it away to hang in the bathroom.'

'No. One more.'

'Your knitting.'

'I don't knit. I don't do anything restful. You ought to know that by now.'

The drinks came. 'Okay,' he said, 'you win. What's in it?'

She lifted the lid of the case. It contained a reporter's notebook, a pencil, and a manual of shorthand.

He stared at these three items. 'Say,' he exclaimed, 'you aren't studying that stuff?'

'What's wrong with that? You said I ought to, once.'

He remembered vaguely what he had once said in an idle moment. 'You taking a course, or something?'

'Every morning,' she said. 'I've got to be in Russell Street at half past nine. Half past *nine* – for me. I have to get up before seven!'

He grinned. 'Say, that's bad. What are you doing it for?'

'Something to do. I got fed up with harrowing the dung.'

'How long have you been doing this?'

'Three days. I'm getting awfully good at it. I can make a squiggle now with anyone.'

'Do you know what it means when you've made it?'

'Not yet,' she admitted. She took a drink of brandy. 'That's rather advanced work.'

'Are you taking typing, too?'

She nodded. 'And book-keeping. All the lot.'

He glanced at her in wonder. 'You'll be quite a secretary by the time you're through.'

'Next year,' she said. 'I'll be able to get a good job next year.'

'Are many other people doing it?' he asked. 'You go to a school, or something?'

She nodded. 'There are more there than I'd thought there'd be. I think it's about half the usual number. There were hardly any pupils just after the war and they sacked most of the teachers. Now the numbers are going up and they've had to take them on again.'

'More people are doing it now?'

'Mostly teenagers,' she told him. 'I feel like a grandmother among them. I think their people got tired of having them at home and made them go to work.' She paused. 'It's the same at the University,' she said. 'There are many more enrolments now than there were a few months ago.'

'I'd never have thought it would work out that way,' he remarked.

'It's dull just living at home,' she said. 'They meet all their friends at the Shop.'

He offered her another drink but she refused it, and they went in to lunch. 'Have you heard about John Osborne and his car?' she asked.

He laughed. 'I sure have. He showed it to me. I'd say he's showing it to everybody that will come and look at it. It's a mighty nice car.'

'He's absolutely mad,' she said. 'He'll kill himself on it.'

He sipped his cold consommé. 'So what? So long as he doesn't kill himself before we start off on this cruise. He's having lots of fun.'

'When *are* you starting off on the cruise?' she asked.

'I suppose we'll be starting about a week from now.'

'Is it going to be very dangerous?' she asked quietly.

There was a momentary pause. 'Why, no,' he said. 'What made you think that?'

'I spoke to Mary Holmes over the telephone yesterday. She seemed a bit worried over something Peter told her.'

'About this cruise?'

'Not directly,' she replied. 'At least, I don't think so. More like making his will, or something.'

'That's always a good thing to do,' he observed. 'Everybody ought to make a will, every married man, that is.'

The grilled steaks came. 'Tell me, *is* it dangerous?' she asked again.

He shook his head. 'It's quite a long cruise. We shall be away nearly two months, and nearly half of that submerged. But it's not more dangerous than any other operation would be up in northern waters.' He paused. 'It's always tricky to go nosing round in waters where there may have been a nuclear explosion,' he said. 'Especially submerged. You never really know what you may run into. Big changes in the sea bed. You may tangle with a sunken ship you didn't know was there. You've got to go in carefully and watch your step. But no, I wouldn't say it's dangerous.'

'Come back safely, Dwight,' she said softly.

He grinned. 'Sure, we'll come back safely. We've been ordered to. The Admiral wants his submarine back.'

She sat back and laughed. 'You're impossible! As soon as I get sentimental you just – you just prick it like a toy balloon.'

'I guess I'm not the sentimental type,' he said. 'That's what Sharon says.'

'Does she?'

'Sure. She gets quite cross with me.'

'I can't say that I'm surprised,' she observed. 'I'm very sorry for her.'

They finished lunch, left the restaurant, and walked to the National Gallery to see the current exhibition of religious pictures. They were all oil paintings, mostly in a modernistic style. They walked around the gallery set aside for the forty paintings in the exhibition, the girl interested, the naval officer frankly uncomprehending. Neither of them had much to say about the green Crucifixions or the pink Nativities; the five or six paintings dealing with religious aspects of the war stirred them to controversy. They paused before the prizewinner, the sorrowing Christ on a background of the destruction of a great city. 'I think that one's got something,' she said. 'For once I believe that I'd agree with the judges.'

He said, 'I hate it like hell.'

'What don't you like about it?'

He stared at it. 'Everything. To me it's just phoney. No pilot in his senses would be flying as low as that with thermonuclear bombs going off all round. He'd get burned up.'

She said, 'It's got good composition and good colouring.'

'Oh, sure,' he replied. 'But the subject's phoney.'

'In what way?'

'If that's meant to be the RCA building, he's put Brooklyn Bridge on the New Jersey side and the Empire State in the middle of Central Park.'

She glanced at the catalogue. 'It doesn't say that it's New York.'

'Wherever it's meant to be, it's phoney,' he replied. 'It couldn't have looked like that.' He paused. 'Too dramatic.' He turned away, and looked around him with distaste. 'I don't like any part of it,' he said.

'Don't you see anything of the religious angle here?' she asked. It was funny to her, because he went to church a lot and she had thought this exhibition would appeal to him.

He took her arm. 'I'm not a religious man,' he said. 'That's my fault, not the artists'. They see things differently than me.'

They turned from the exhibition. 'Are you interested in paintings?' she asked. 'Or are they just a bore?'

'They're not a bore,' he said. 'I like them when they're full of colour and don't try to teach you anything. There's a painter called Renoir, isn't there?'

She nodded. 'They've got some Renoirs here. Would you like to see them?'

They went and found the French art, and he stood for some time before a painting of a river and a tree-shaded street beside it, with white houses and shops, very French and very colourful. 'That's the kind of picture I like,' he said. 'I've got a lot of time for that.'

They strolled around the galleries for a time, chatting and looking at the pictures. Then she had to go; her mother was unwell and she had promised to be home in time to get the tea. He took her to the station on the tram.

In the rush of people at the entrance she turned to him. 'Thanks for the lunch,' she said, 'and for the afternoon. I hope the other pictures made up for the religious ones.'

He laughed. 'They certainly did. I'd like to go back there again and see more of them. But as for religion, that's just not my line.'

'You go to church regularly,' she said.

'Oh well, that's different,' he replied.

She could not argue it with him, nor would she have attempted to in that crowd. She said, 'Will we be able to meet again before you go?'

'I'll be busy in the daytime, most days,' he said. 'We might take in a movie one evening, but we'd have to make it soon. We'll be sailing as soon as the work gets completed, and it's going well right now.'

They arranged to meet for dinner on the following Tuesday, and she waved goodbye to him and vanished in the crowd. There was nothing of urgency to take him back to the dockyard, and there was still an hour left before the shops shut. He went out into the streets again and walked along the pavements looking at the shop windows. Presently he came to a sports store, hesitated for a moment, and went in.

In the fishing department he said to the assistant, 'I want a spinning outfit, a rod and a reel and a nylon line.'

'Certainly, sir,' said the assistant. 'For yourself?'

The American shook his head. 'This is a present for a boy ten years old,' he said. 'His first rod. I'd like something good quality, but pretty small and light. You got anything in Fibreglas?'

The assistant shook his head. 'I'm afraid we're right out of those at the moment.' He reached down a rod from the rack. 'This is a very good little rod in steel.'

'How would that stand up in sea water, for rusting? He lives by the sea, and you know what kids are.'

'They stand up all right,' the assistant said. 'We sell a lot of these for sea fishing.' He reached for reels while Dwight examined the rod and tested it in his hand. 'We have these plastic reels for sea fishing, or I can give you a multiplying reel in stainless steel. They're the better job, of course, but they come out a good deal more expensive.'

Dwight examined them. 'I think I'll take the multiplier.'

He chose the line, and the assistant wrapped the three articles together in a parcel. 'Makes a nice present for a boy,' he observed.

'Sure,' said Dwight. 'He'll have a lot of fun with that.'

He paid and took the parcel, and went through into that portion of the store that sold children's bicycles and scooters. He said to the girl, 'Have you got a Pogo stick?'

'A Pogo stick? I don't think so. I'll ask the manager.'

The manager came to him. 'I'm afraid we're right out of Pogo sticks. There hasn't been a great deal of demand for them recently, and we sold the last only a few days ago.'

'Will you be getting any more in?'

'I put through an order for a dozen. I don't know when they'll arrive. Things are getting just a bit disorganized, you know. It was for a present, I suppose?'

The Commander nodded. 'I wanted it for a little girl of six.'

'We have these scooters. They make a nice present for a little girl that age.'

He shook his head. 'She's got a scooter.'

'We have these children's bicycles, too.'

Too bulky and too awkward, but he did not say so. 'No, it's a Pogo stick I really want. I think I'll shop around, and maybe come back if I can't get one.'

'You might try McPhails,' said the man helpfully. 'They might have one left.'

He went out and tried McPhails, but they, too, were out of Pogo sticks. He tried another shop with similar results; Pogo sticks, it seemed, were off the market. The more frustration he encountered the more it seemed to him that a Pogo stick was what he really wanted, and that nothing else would do. He wandered into Collins Street looking for another toy shop, but here he was out of the toy shop district and in a region of more expensive merchandise.

In the last of the shopping hour he paused before a jeweller's window. It was a shop of good quality; he stood for a time looking in at the windows. Emeralds and diamonds would be best. Emeralds went magnificently with her dark hair.

He went into the shop. 'I was thinking of a bracelet,' he said to the young man in the black morning coat. 'Emeralds and diamonds, perhaps. Emeralds, anyway. The lady's dark, and she likes to wear green. You got anything like that?'

The man went to the safe, and came back with three bracelets which he laid on a black velvet pad. 'We have these, sir,' he said. 'What sort of price had you in mind?'

'I wouldn't know,' said the Commander. 'I want a nice bracelet.'

The assistant picked one up. 'We have this, which is forty guineas, or this one which is sixty-five guineas. They are very attractive, I think.'

'What's that one, there?'

The man picked it up. 'That is much more expensive, sir. It's a very beautiful piece.' He examined the tiny tag. 'That one is two hundred and twenty-five guineas.'

It glowed on the black velvet. Dwight picked it up and examined it. The man had spoken the truth when he said it was a lovely piece. She had nothing like it in her jewel box. He knew that she would love it.

'Would that be English or Australian work?' he asked.

The man shook his head. 'This came originally from Cartier's, in Paris. It came to us from the estate of a lady in Toorak. It's in quite new condition, as you see. Usually we find that the clasp needs attention, but this didn't even need that. It is in quite perfect order.'

He could picture her delight in it. 'I'll take that,' he said. 'I'll have to pay you with a cheque. I'll call in and pick it up tomorrow or the next day.'

He wrote the cheque and took his receipt. Turning away, he stopped, and turned back to the man. 'One thing,' he said. 'You wouldn't happen to know where I could buy a Pogo stick, a present for a little girl? Seems they're kind of scarce around here just at present.'

'I'm afraid I can't, sir,' said the man. 'I think the only thing to do would be to try all the toy shops in turn.'

The shops were closing and there was no time that night to do any more. He took his parcel back with him to Williamstown, and when he reached the carrier he went down into the submarine and laid it along the back of his berth, where it was inconspicuous. Two days later, when he got his bracelet, he took that down into the submarine also and locked it away in the steel cupboard that housed the confidential books.

That day a Mrs Hector Fraser took a broken silver cream jug to the jeweller's to have the handle silver-soldered. Walking down the street that afternoon she encountered Moira Davidson, whom she had known from a child. She stopped and asked after her mother. Then she said, 'My dear, you know Commander Towers, the American, don't you?'

The girl said, 'Yes. I know him quite well. He spent a weekend out with us the other day.'

'Do you think he's crazy? Perhaps all Americans are crazy. I don't know.'

The girl smiled. 'No crazier than all the rest of us, these days. What's he been up to?'

'He's been trying to buy a Pogo stick in Simmonds'.'

Moira was suddenly alert. 'A Pogo stick?'

'My dear, in Simmonds' of all places. As if they'd sell Pogo sticks there! It seems he went in and bought the most beautiful bracelet and paid some fabulous price for it. That wouldn't be for you by any chance?'

'I haven't heard about it. It sounds very unlike him.'

'Ah well, you never know with these men. Perhaps he'll spring it on you one day as a surprise.'

'But what about the Pogo stick?'

'Well, then when he'd bought the bracelet he asked Mr Thompson, the fair haired one, the nice young man – he asked him if he knew where he could buy a Pogo stick. He said he wanted it for a present for a little girl.'

'What's wrong with that?' Miss Davidson asked quietly. 'It would make a very good present for a little girl of the right age.'

'I suppose it would. But it seems such a funny thing for the captain of a submarine to want to buy. In Simmonds' of all places.'

The girl said, 'He's probably courting a rich widow with a little girl. The bracelet for the mother and the Pogo stick for the daughter. What's wrong with that?'

'Nothing,' said Mrs Fraser, 'only we all thought that he was courting you.'

'That's just where you've been wrong,' the girl said equably. 'It's me that's been courting him.' She turned away. 'I must get along. It's been so nice seeing you. I'll tell Mummy.'

She walked on down the street, but the matter of the Pogo stick stayed in her mind. She went so far that afternoon as to inquire into the condition of the Pogo stick market, and found it to be depressed. If Dwight wanted a Pogo stick, he was evidently going to have some difficulty in getting one.

Everyone was going a bit mad these days, of course – Peter and Mary Holmes with their garden, her father with his farm programme, John Osborne with his racing motor car, Sir Douglas Froude with the club port, and now Dwight Towers with his Pogo stick. Herself also, possibly, with Dwight Towers. All with an eccentricity that verged on madness, born of the times they lived in.

She wanted to help him, wanted to help him very much indeed, and yet she knew she must approach this very cautiously. When she got home that evening she went to the lumber room and pulled out her old Pogo stick and rubbed the dirt off it with a duster. The wooden handle might be sandpapered and revarnished by a skilled craftsman and possibly it might appear as new, though wet had made dark stains in the wood. Rust had eaten deeply into the metal parts, however, and at one point the metal step was rusted through. No amount of paint could ever make that part of it look new, and her own childhood was still close enough to raise in her distaste at the thought of a second-hand toy. That wasn't the answer.

She met him on Tuesday evening for the movie, as they had arranged. Over dinner she asked him how the submarine was getting on. 'Not too badly,' he told her. 'They're giving us a second electrolytic oxygen regeneration outfit to work in parallel with the one we've got. I'd say that work might be finished by tomorrow night, and then we'll run a test on Thursday. We might get away from here by the end of the week.'

'Is that very important?'

He smiled. 'We shall have to run submerged for quite a while. I wouldn't like to run out of air, and have to surface in the radioactive area or suffocate.'

'Is this a sort of spare set, then?'

He nodded. 'We were lucky to get it. They had it over in the naval stores, in Fremantle.'

He was absent-minded that evening. He was pleasant and courteous to her, but she felt all the time that he was thinking of other things. She tried several times during dinner to secure his interest, but failed. It was the same in the movie theatre; he went through all the motions of enjoying it and giving her a good time, but there was no life in the performance. She told herself that she could hardly expect it to be otherwise, with a cruise like that ahead of him.

After the show they walked down the empty streets towards the station. As they neared it she stopped at the dark entrance to an arcade, where they could talk quietly. 'Stop here a minute, Dwight,' she said. 'I want to ask you something.'

'Sure,' he said kindly. 'Go ahead.'

'You're worried over something, aren't you?'

'Not really. I'm afraid I've been bad company tonight.'

'Is it about the submarine?'

'Why, no, honey. I told you, there's nothing dangerous in that. It's just another job.'

'It's not about a Pogo stick, is it?'

He stared at her in amazement in the semi-darkness. 'Say, how did you get to hear about that?'

She laughed gently. 'I have my spies. What did you get for Junior?'

'A fishing rod.' There was a pause, and then he said, 'I suppose you think I'm nuts.'

She shook her head. 'I don't. Did you get a Pogo stick?'

'No. Seems like they're completely out of stock.'

'I know.' They stood in silence for a moment. 'I had a look at mine,' she said. 'You can have that if it's any good to you. But it's awfully old, and the metal parts are rusted through. It works still, but I don't think it could ever be made into a very nice present.'

He nodded. 'I noticed that. I think we'll have to let it go, honey. If I get time before we sail I'll come up here and shop around for something else.'

She said, 'I'm quite sure it must be possible to get a Pogo stick. They must have been made somewhere here in Melbourne. In Australia, anyway. The trouble is to get one in the time.'

'Leave it,' he said. 'It was just a crazy idea I had. It's not important.'

'It *is* important,' she said. 'It's important to me.' She raised her head. 'I can get one for you by the time you come back,' she said. 'I'll do that, even if I have to get it made. I know that isn't quite what you want. But would that do?'

'That's mighty kind of you,' he said huskily. 'I could tell her you were bringing it along with you.'

'I could do that,' she said. 'But anyway, I'll have it with me when we meet again.'

'You might have to bring it a long way,' he said.

'Don't worry, Dwight. I'll have it with me when we meet.'

In the dark alcove he took her in his arms and kissed her. 'That's for the promise,' he said softly, 'and for everything else. Sharon wouldn't mind me doing this. It's from us both.'

6

Twenty-five days later, USS *Scorpion* was approaching
the first objective of her cruise. It was ten days since
she had submerged thirty degrees south of the equator.
She had made her landfall at San Nicolas Island off Los
Angeles and had given the city a wide berth, troubled
about unknown minefields. She had set a course outside
Santa Rosa and had closed the coast to the west of Santa
Barbara; from there she had followed it northwards,
cruising at periscope depth about two miles off shore.
She had ventured cautiously into Monterey Bay and
she had inspected the fishing port, seeing no sign of
life on shore and learning very little. Radioactivity was
uniformly high, so that they judged it prudent to keep
the hull submerged.

They inspected San Francisco from five miles outside
the Golden Gate. All they learned was that the bridge was
down. The supporting tower at the south end seemed to
have been overthrown. The houses visible from the sea
around the Golden Gate Park had suffered much from fire
and blast; it did not look as if any of them were habitable.
They saw no evidence of any human life, and the radiation
level made it seem improbable that life could still exist in
that vicinity.

They stayed there for some hours, taking photographs

through the periscope and making such a survey as was possible. They went back southwards as far as Half Moon Bay and closed the coast to within half a mile, surfacing for a time and calling through the loud hailer. The houses here did not appear to be much damaged, but there was no sign of any life on shore. They stayed in the vicinity till dusk, and then set course towards the north, rounding Point Reyes and going on three or four miles off shore, following the coast.

Since crossing the equator it had been their habit to surface once in every watch to get the maximum antenna height, and to listen for the radio transmission from Seattle. They had heard it once, in Latitude Five North; it had gone on for about forty minutes, a random, meaningless transmission, and then had stopped. They had not heard it since. That night, somewhere off Fort Bragg, they surfaced in a stiff north-westerly wind and a rising sea, and directly they switched on the direction finder they heard it again. This time they were able to pinpoint it fairly accurately.

Dwight bent over the navigation table with Lieutenant Sunderstrom as he plotted the bearing. 'Santa Maria,' he said. 'Looks like you were right.'

They stood listening to the meaningless jumble coming out of the speaker. 'It's fortuitous,' the Lieutenant said at last. 'That's not someone keying, even somebody that doesn't know about radio. That's something that's just happening.'

'Sounds like it.' He stood listening. 'There's power there,' he said. 'Where there's power there's people.'

'It's not absolutely necessary,' the Lieutenant said.

'Hydro-electric,' Dwight said. 'I know it. But hell, those turbines won't run two years without maintenance.'

'You wouldn't think so. Some of them are mighty good machinery.'

Dwight grunted, and turned back to the charts. 'I'll aim to be off Cape Flattery at dawn. We'll go on as we're going now and get a fix around midday, and adjust speed then. If it looks all right from there I'll take her in, periscope depth, so we can blow tanks if we hit anything that shouldn't be there. Maybe we'll be able to go right up to Santa Maria. Maybe we won't. You ready to go on shore if we do?'

'Sure,' said the Lieutenant. 'I'd kind of like to get out of the ship for a while.'

Dwight smiled. They had been submerged now for eleven days, and though health was still good they were all suffering from nervous tension. 'Let's keep our fingers crossed,' he said, 'and hope we can make it.'

'You know something?' said the Lieutenant. 'If we can't get through the strait, maybe I could make it overland.' He pulled out a chart. 'If we got in to Grays Harbor I could get on shore at Hoquiam or Aberdeen. This road runs right through to Bremerton and Santa Maria.'

'It's a hundred miles.'

'I could probably pick up a car, and gas.'

The captain shook his head. Two hundred miles in a light radiation suit, driving a hot car with hot gas over hot country, was not practical. 'You've only got a two hours' air supply,' he said. 'I know you could take extra cylinders. But it's not practical. We'd lose you, one way or another. It's not that important, anyway.'

They submerged again, and carried on upon the course. When they surfaced four hours later the transmissions had stopped.

They carried on towards the north all the next day, most of the time at periscope depth. The morale of his crew was now becoming important to the captain. The close confinement was telling on them; no broadcast entertainment had been available for a long time, and the recordings they could play over the speakers had long grown stale. To stimulate their minds and give them something to talk about he gave free access to the periscope to anyone who cared to use it, though there was little to look at. This rocky and somewhat uninteresting coast was their home country, and the sight of a café with a Buick parked outside it was enough to set them talking and revive starved minds.

At midnight they surfaced according to their routine, off the mouth of the Columbia River. Lieutenant Benson was coming to relieve Lieutenant-Commander Farrell. The Lieutenant-Commander raised the periscope from the well and put his face to it, swinging it around. Then he turned quickly to the other officer. 'Say, go and call the captain. Lights on shore, thirty to forty degrees on the starboard bow.'

In a minute or two they were all looking through the periscope in turn and studying the chart, Peter Holmes and John Osborne with them. Dwight bent over the chart with his executive officer. 'On the Washington side of the entrance,' he said. 'They'll be around these places Long Beach and Ilwaco. There's nothing in the state of Oregon.'

From behind him Lieutenant Sunderstrom said, 'Hydro-electric.'

'I guess so. If there's lights it would explain a lot.' He turned to the scientist. 'What's the outside radiation level, Mr Osborne?'

'Thirty in the red, sir.'

The captain nodded. Much too high for life to be maintained, though not immediately lethal; there had been little change in the last five or six days. He went to the periscope himself and stood there for a long time. He did not care to take his vessel closer to the shore, at night. 'Okay,' he said at last. 'We'll carry on the way we're going now. Log it, Mr Benson.'

He went back to bed. Tomorrow would be an anxious, trying day; he must get his sleep. In the privacy of his little curtained cabin he unlocked the safe that held the confidential books and took out the bracelet; it glowed in the synthetic light. She would love it. He put it carefully in the breast pocket of his uniform suit. Then he went to bed again, his hand upon the fishing rod, and slept.

They surfaced again at four in the morning just before dawn, a little to the north of Grays Harbor. No lights were visible on shore, but as there were no towns and few roads in the district, that evidence was inconclusive. They went down to periscope depth and carried on. When Dwight came to the control-room at six o'clock the day was bright through the periscope and the crew off duty were taking turns to look at the desolate shore. He went to breakfast and then stood smoking at the chart table, studying the minefield chart that he already knew so well, and the well-remembered entrance to the Juan de Fuca Strait.

At seven-forty-five his executive officer reported that Cape Flattery was abeam. The captain stubbed out his cigarette. 'Okay,' he said. 'Take her in, Commander. Course is zero-seven-five. Fifteen knots.'

The hum of the motors dropped to a lower note for the first time in three weeks; within the hull the relative silence was almost oppressive. All morning they made their way south-eastwards down the strait between Canada and the United States, taking continuous bearings through the periscope, keeping a running plot at the chart table and altering course many times. They saw little change on shore, except in one place on Vancouver Island near Jordan River, where a huge area on the southern slopes of Mount Valentine seemed to have been burned and blasted. They judged this area to be no less than seven miles long and five miles wide; in it no vegetation seemed to grow although the surface of the ground seemed undisturbed.

'I'd say that's an air burst,' the captain said, turning from the periscope. 'Perhaps a guided missile got one there.'

As they approached more populous districts there were always one or two men waiting to look through the periscope as soon as the officers relinquished it. Soon after midday they were off Port Townsend and turning southwards into Puget Sound. They went on, leaving Whidbey Island on the port hand, and in the early afternoon they came to the mainland at the little town of Edmonds, fifteen miles north of the centre of Seattle. They were well past the mine defences by that time. From the sea the place seemed quite undamaged, but the radiation level was still high.

The captain stood studying it through the periscope. If the Geiger counter was correct, no life could exist there for more than a few days, and yet it all looked so normal in the spring sunlight that he felt there *must* be people there. There did not seem to be glass broken in the windows, even, save for a pane here and there. He turned from the periscope. 'Left ten, seven knots,' he said. 'We'll close the shore here, and lie off the jetty, and hail for a while.'

He relinquished the command to his executive, and ordered the loud hailer to be tested and made ready. Lieutenant-Commander Farrell brought the vessel to the surface and took her in, and they lay-to a hundred yards from the boat jetty, watching the shore.

The Chief of the Boat touched the executive officer on

the shoulder. 'Be all right for Swain to have a look, sir?' he inquired. 'This is his home town.' Yeoman First Class Ralph Swain was a radar operator.

'Oh, sure.'

He stepped aside, and the Yeoman went to the periscope. He stood there for a long while, and then raised his head. 'Ken Puglia's got his drug store open,' he said. 'The door's open and the shades are up. But he's left his neon sign on. It's not like Ken to leave that burning in the daytime.'

The Chief asked, 'See anybody moving around, Ralph?'

The radar operator bent to the eyepieces again. 'No. There's a window broken in Mrs Sullivan's house, up at the top.'

He stood looking for three or four long minutes, till the executive officer touched him on the shoulder and took the periscope. He stood back in the control room.

The Chief said, 'See your own house, Ralphie?'

'No. You just can't see that from the sea. It's up Rainier Avenue, past the Safeway.' He fidgeted irritably. 'I don't see anything different,' he said. 'It all looks just the same.'

Lieutenant Benson took the microphone and began hailing the shore. He said, 'This is US Submarine *Scorpion* calling Edmonds. US Submarine *Scorpion* calling Edmonds. If anybody is listening, will you please come to the waterfront, to the jetty at the end of Main street. US Submarine calling Edmonds.'

The Yeoman left the control room and went forward. Dwight Towers came to the periscope, detached another sailor from it, and stood looking at the shore. The town sloped upwards from the waterfront giving a good view of the street and the houses. He stood back after a while. 'There doesn't seem to be much wrong on shore,' he said. 'You'd think with Boeing as the target all this area would have been well plastered.'

Farrell said, 'The defences here were mighty strong. All the guided missiles in the book.'

'That's so. But they got through to San Francisco.'

'It doesn't look as though they ever got through here.' He paused. 'There was that air burst, way back in the strait.'

Dwight nodded. 'See that neon sign that's still alight, over the drug store?' He paused. 'We'll go on calling here for quite a while – say half an hour.'

'Okay, sir.'

The captain stood back from the periscope and the executive officer took it, and issued a couple of orders to keep the ship in position. At the microphone the Lieutenant went on calling; Dwight lit a cigarette and leaned back on the chart table. Presently he stubbed out the cigarette and glanced at the clock.

From forward there was the clang of a steel hatch; he started and looked round. It was followed a moment later by another, and then footsteps on the deck above them. There were steps running down the alley, and Lieutenant Hirsch appeared in the control-room. 'Swain got out through the escape hatch, sir,' he said. 'He's out on deck now!'

Dwight bit his lip. 'Escape hatch closed?'

'Yes, sir. I checked that.'

The captain turned to the Chief of the Boat. 'Station a guard on the escape hatches forward and aft.'

There was a splash in the water beside the hull as Mortimer ran off. Dwight said to Farrell, 'See if you can see what he's doing.'

The executive dropped the periscope down and put it to maximum depression, sweeping around. The captain said to Hirsch, 'Why didn't somebody stop him?'

'I guess he did it too quick. He came from aft and sat

down, kind of biting his nails. Nobody paid him much attention. I was in the forward torpedo flat, so I didn't see. First they knew, he was in the escape trunk with the door shut, and the outer hatch open to the air. Nobody cared to chase out there after him.'

Dwight nodded. 'Sure. Get the trunk blown through and then go in and see the outer hatch is properly secure.'

From the periscope Farrell said, 'I can see him now. He's swimming for the jetty.'

Dwight stooped almost to the deck and saw the swimmer. He stood up and spoke to Lieutenant Benson at the microphone. The Lieutenant touched the volume control and said, 'Yeoman Swain, hear this.' The swimmer paused and trod water. 'The captain's orders are that you return immediately to the ship. If you come back at once he will take you on board again and take a chance on the contamination. You are to come back on board right now.'

From the speaker above the navigation table they all heard the reply, 'You go and get stuffed!'

A faint smile flickered on the captain's face. He bent again to the periscope and watched the man swim to the shore, watched him clamber up the ladder at the jetty. Presently he stood erect. 'Well, that's it,' he remarked. He turned to John Osborne by his side. 'How long would you say he'll last?'

'He'll feel nothing for a time,' said the scientist. 'He'll probably be vomiting tomorrow night. After that – well, it's just anybody's guess, sir. It depends upon the constitution of the individual.'

'Three days? A week?'

'I should think so. I shouldn't think it could be longer, at this radiation level.'

'And we'd be safe to take him back – till when?'

'I've got no experience. But after a few hours everything that he evacuates would be contaminated. We couldn't guarantee the safety of the ship's company if he should be seriously ill on board.'

Dwight raised the periscope and put his eyes to it. The man was still visible walking up the street in his wet clothes. They saw him pause at the door of the drug store and look in; then he turned a corner and was lost to sight. The captain said, 'Well, he doesn't seem to have any intention of coming back.' He turned over the periscope to his executive. 'Secure that loud hailer. The course is for Santa Maria, in the middle of the channel. Ten knots.'

There was dead silence in the submarine, broken only by the helm orders, the low murmur of the turbines, and the intermittent whizzing of the steering engine. Dwight Towers went heavily to his cabin, and Peter Holmes followed him. He said, 'You're not going to try to get him back, sir? I could go on shore in a radiation suit.'

Dwight glanced at his liaison officer. 'That's a nice offer, Commander, but I won't accept it. I thought of that myself. Say we put an officer on shore with a couple of men to go fetch him. First we've got to find him. Maybe we'd be stuck off here four or five hours, and then not know if we'd be risking everybody in the ship by taking him back in with us. Maybe he'll have eaten contaminated food, or drunk contaminated water . . .' He paused. 'There's another thing. On this mission we shall be submerged and living on tinned air for twenty-seven days, maybe twenty-eight. Some of us will be in pretty bad shape by then. You tell me on the last day if you'd like it to be four or five hours longer because we wasted that much time on Yeoman Swain.'

Peter said, 'Very good, sir. I just thought I'd like to make the offer.'

'Sure. I appreciate that. We'll be coming back past here tonight or else maybe soon after dawn tomorrow. We'll stop a little while and hail him then.'

The captain went back to the control-room and stood by the executive officer, taking alternate glances through the periscope with him. They went close to the entrance to the Lake Washington Canal, scanning the shore, rounded Fort Lawton, and stood in to the naval dock and the commercial docks in Elliott Bay, in the heart of the city.

The city was undamaged. A minesweeper lay at the Naval Receiving Station, and five or six freighters lay in the commercial docks. Most of the window glass was still in place in the high buildings at the centre of the city. They did not go very close in, fearing underwater obstructions, but so far as they could see conditions through the periscope there seemed to be nothing wrong with the city at all, except that there were no people there. Many electric lights and neon signs were burning still.

At the periscope Lieutenant-Commander Farrell said to his captain, 'It was a good defensive proposition, sir – better than San Francisco. The land in the Olympic Peninsula reaches way out to the west, over a hundred miles.'

'I know it,' said the captain. 'They had a lot of guided missiles out there, like a screen.'

There was nothing there to stay for, and they went out of the bay and turned south-west for Santa Maria Island; already they could see the great antenna towers. Dwight called Lieutenant Sunderstrom to his cabin. 'You all set to go?' he asked.

'Everything's all ready,' said the radio officer. 'I just got to jump into the suit.'

'Okay. Your job's half done before you start, because we know now that there's still electric power. And we're pretty darned near certain there's no life, although we don't know that for sure. It's sixty-four thousand dollars to a sausage you'll find a reason for the radio that's just an accident of some sort. If it was just to find out what kind of an accident makes those signals, I wouldn't risk the ship and I wouldn't risk *you*. Got that?'

'I got that, sir.'

'Well now, hear this. You've got air for two hours in the cylinders. I want you back decontaminated and in the hull in an hour and a half. You won't have a watch. I'll keep the time for you from here. I'll sound the siren every quarter of an hour. One blast when you've been gone a quarter of an hour, two blasts half an hour, and so on. When you hear four blasts you start winding up whatever you may be doing. At five blasts you drop everything, whatever it may be, and come right back. Before six blasts you must be back and decontaminating in the escape trunk. Is that all clear?'

'Quite clear, sir.'

'Okay. I don't want this mission completed particularly now. I want you back on board safe. For two bits I wouldn't send you at all, because we know now most all of what you'll find, but I told the Admiral we'd put somebody on shore to investigate. I don't want you to go taking undue risks. I'd rather have you back on board, even if we don't find out the whole story of what makes these signals. The only thing would justify you taking any risk would be if you find any signs of life on shore.'

'I get that, sir.'

'No souvenirs from shore. The only thing to come back in the hull is you, stark naked.'

'Okay, sir.'

The captain went back into the control-room, and the radio officer went forward. The submarine nosed her way forward with the hull just awash, feeling her way to Santa Maria at a slow speed in the bright sunlight of the spring afternoon, ready to stop engines immediately and blow tanks if she hit any obstruction. They went very cautiously, and it was about five o'clock in the afternoon when she finally lay-to off the jetty of the island, in six fathoms of water.

Dwight went forward, and found Lieutenant Sunderstrom sitting in the radiation suit complete but for the helmet and the pack of oxygen bottles, smoking a cigarette. 'Okay, fella,' he said. 'Off you go.'

The young man stubbed out his cigarette and stood while a couple of men adjusted the helmet and the harness of the pack. He tested the air, glanced at the pressure gauge, elevated one thumb, and climbed into the escape trunk, closing the door behind him.

Out on deck he stretched and breathed deeply, relishing the sunlight and the escape from the hull. Then he raised a hatch of the superstructure and pulled out the dinghy pack, stripped off the plastic sealing strips, unfolded the dinghy, and pressed the lever of the air bottle that inflated it. He tied the painter and lowered the rubber boat into the water, took the paddle and led the boat aft to the steps beside the conning tower. He clambered down into it, and pushed off from the submarine.

The boat was awkward to manoeuvre with the single paddle, and it took him ten minutes to reach the jetty. He made it fast and clambered up the ladder; as he began to walk towards the shore he heard one blast from the siren of the submarine. He turned and waved, and walked on.

He came to a group of grey painted buildings, stores of some kind. There was a weatherproof electric switch upon an outside wall; he went to it and turned it, and a lamp above his head lit up. He turned it off again, and went on.

He came to a latrine. He paused, then crossed the road, and looked in. A body in khaki gabardine lay half in and half out of one of the compartments, much decomposed. It was no more than he had expected to see, but the sight was sobering. He left it, and went on up the road.

The Communication School lay over on the right, in buildings by itself. This was the part of the installation that he knew, but that was not what he had come to see. The Coding Office lay to the left, and near the Coding Office the main transmitting office would almost certainly be located.

He entered the brick building that was the Coding Office, and stood in the hallway trying the doors. Every door was locked except for two that led into the toilets. He did not go in there.

He went out and looked around. A transformer station with a complex of wires and insulators attracted his attention, and he followed the wiring to another two-storey, wooden office building. As he approached he heard the hum of an electrical machine running, and at the same moment the siren of the submarine sounded two blasts.

When they had died away he heard the hum again, and followed it to a power house. The converter that was running was not very large; he judged it to be about fifty kilowatts. On the switchboard the needles of the instruments stood steady, but one indicating temperature stood in a red sector of the dial. The machine itself was running with a faint grating noise beneath the quiet hum. He thought it would not last very much longer.

He left the power house and went into the office building. Here all the doors were unlocked, some of them open. The rooms on the ground floor appeared to be executive offices; here papers and signals lay strewn about the floor like dead leaves, blown by the wind. In one room a casement window was entirely missing and there was much water damage. He crossed this room and looked out of the window; the casement window frame lay on the ground below, blown from its hinges.

He went upstairs, and found the main transmitting room. There were two transmitting desks, each with a towering metal frame of grey radio equipment in front of it. One of these sets was dead and silent, the instruments all at zero.

The other set stood by the window, and here the casement had been blown from its hinges and lay across the desk. One end of the window frame projected outside the building and teetered gently in the light breeze. One of the upper corners rested on an overturned Coke bottle on the desk. The transmitting key lay underneath the frame that rested unstably above it, teetering a little in the wind.

He reached out and touched it with his gloved hand. The frame rocked on the transmitting key, and the needle of a milliammeter upon the set flipped upwards. He released the frame, and the needle fell back. There was one of the USS *Scorpion*'s missions completed, something that they had come ten thousand miles to see, that had absorbed so much effort and attention in Australia, on the other side of the world.

He lifted the window frame from the transmitting desk and set it down carefully on the floor; the woodwork was not damaged and it could be repaired and put back in its place quite easily. Then he sat down at the desk and with gloved hand upon the key began transmitting in English and in clear.

He sent, 'Santa Maria sending. USS *Scorpion* reporting. No life here. Closing down.' He went on repeating this message over and over again, and while he was doing so the siren blew three blasts.

197

As he sat there, his mind only half occupied with the mechanical repetition of the signal that he knew was almost certainly being monitored in Australia, his eyes roamed around the transmitting office. There was a carton of American cigarettes with only two packs removed that he longed for, but the captain's orders had been very definite. There were one or two bottles of Coke. On a window-sill there was a pile of copies of the *Saturday Evening Post*.

He finished transmitting when he judged he had been at it for twenty minutes. In the three final repetitions he added the words, 'Lieutenant Sunderstrom sending. All well on board. Proceeding northwards to Alaska.' Finally he sent, 'Closing down the station now, and switching off.'

He took his hand from the key and leaned back in the chair. Gee, these tubes and chokes, this milliammeter and that rotary converter down below – they'd done a mighty job. Nearly two years without any maintenance or replacement, and still functioning as well as ever! He stood up, inspected the set, and turned off three switches. Then he walked round to the back and opened a panel and looked for the name of the manufacturer on the tubes; he would have liked to send them a testimonial.

He glanced again at the carton of Lucky Strikes, but the captain was right, of course; they would be hot and it might well be death to smoke them. He left them with regret, and went downstairs. He went to the power house where the converter was running, inspected the switchboard carefully and tripped two switches. The note of the machine sank progressively in a diminuendo; he stood watching it till finally it came to rest. It had done a swell job and it would be good as ever when the bearings had been overhauled.

He could not have borne to leave it running till it cracked up.

The siren blew four blasts while he was there, and his work now was over. He had still a quarter of an hour. There was everything here to be explored and nothing to be gained by doing so. In the living quarters he knew he would find bodies like the one that he had found in the latrine; he did not want to see them. In the coding room, if he broke down a door, there might be papers that would interest historians in Australia, but he could not know which they would be, and anyway the captain had forbidden him to take anything on board.

He went back and up the stairs into the transmitting office. He had a few minutes left for his own use, and he went straight to the pile of copies of the *Saturday Evening Post*. As he had suspected, there were three numbers issued after *Scorpion* had left Pearl Harbor before the outbreak of the war, that he had not seen and that no one in the ship had seen. He leafed them through avidly. They contained the three concluding instalments of the serial, *The Lady and the Lumberjack*. He sat down to read.

The siren blew five blasts and roused him before he was halfway through the first instalment. He must go. He hesitated for a moment, and then rolled up the three magazines and tucked them under his arm. The dinghy and his radiation suit would be hot and must be left in the locker on the outer casing of the submarine to be washed by the sea water; he could roll up these hot magazines in the deflated dinghy and perhaps they would survive, perhaps they could be decontaminated and dried out and read when they got back to the safe southern latitudes. He left the office, closing the door carefully behind him, and made his way towards the jetty.

The Officers' Mess stood facing the Sound, a little way

from the jetty. He had not noticed it particularly on landing, but now something about it attracted his attention and he deviated fifty yards towards it. The building had a deep veranda, facing the view. He saw now that there was a party going on there. Five men in khaki gabardine sat with two women in easy chairs around a table; in the light breeze he saw the flutter of a summer frock. On the table there were highball and old fashioned glasses.

For a moment he was deceived, and went quickly closer. Then he stopped in horror, for the party had been going on for over a year. He broke away, and turned, and went back to the jetty, only anxious now to get back into the close confinement and the warmth of fellowship and the security of the submarine.

On deck he deflated and stowed the dinghy, wrapping up his magazines in the folds. Then he stripped quickly, put the helmet and the clothing into the locker, slammed the hatch down and secured it, and got down into the escape trunk, turning on the shower. Five minutes later he emerged into the humid stuffiness of the submarine.

John Osborne was waiting at the entrance to the trunk to run a Geiger counter over him and pass him as clean, and a minute later he was standing with a towel round his waist making his report to Dwight Towers in his cabin, the executive officer and the liaison officer beside him. 'We got your signals on the radio here,' the captain said. 'I don't just know if they'll have got them in Australia – it's daylight all the way. It's around eleven in the morning there. What would you say?'

'I'd say they'd have got them,' the radio officer replied. 'It's autumn there, and not too many electric storms.'

The captain dismissed him to get dressed, and turned to his executive. 'We'll stay right here tonight,' he said. 'It's seven o'clock, and dark before we reach the minefields.'

With no lights he could depend upon he did not dare to risk the navigation through the minefields of the Juan de Fuca Strait during the hours of darkness. 'We're out of the tide here. Sunrise is around zero-four-fifteen – that's twelve noon, Greenwich. We'll get under way then.'

They stayed that night in the calm waters of the harbour just off Santa Maria Island, watching the shore lights through the periscope. At dawn they got under way on a reverse course, and immediately ran aground upon a mudbank. The tide was ebbing and within a couple of hours of low water; even so there should have been a fathom of water underneath their keel according to the chart. They blew tanks to surface, and got off with ears tingling from the pressure reduction in the hull, reviling the Survey, and tried again to get away, twice, with the same result. Finally they settled down to wait irritably for the tide, and at about nine o'clock in the morning they got out into the main channel and set course northwards for the open sea.

At twenty minutes past ten Lieutenant Hirsch at the periscope said suddenly, 'Boat ahead, under way.' The executive jumped to the eyepieces, looked for a moment, and said, 'Go call the captain.' When Dwight came he said, 'Outboard motor boat ahead, sir. About three miles. One person in it.'

'Alive?'

'I guess so. The boat's under way.'

Dwight took the periscope and stood looking for a long time. Then he stood back from it. 'I'd say that's Yeoman Swain,' he said quietly. 'Whoever it is, he's fishing. I'd say he's got an outboard motor boat, and gas for it, and he's gone fishing.'

The executive stared at him. 'Well, what do you know!'

The captain stood in thought for a moment. 'Go on and close the boat, and lie close up,' he said. 'I'll have a talk with him.'

There was silence in the submarine, broken only by the orders from the executive. Presently he stopped engines and reported that the boat was close aboard. Dwight took the long lead of the microphone and went to the periscope. He said, 'This is the captain speaking. Good morning, Ralphie. How are you doing?'

From the speaker they all heard the response. 'I'm doing fine, Cap.'

'Got any fish yet?'

In the boat the Yeoman held up a salmon to the periscope. 'I got one.' And then he said, 'Hold on a minute, Cap – you're getting across my line.' In the submarine Dwight grinned, and said, 'He's reeling in.'

Lieutenant-Commander Farrell asked, 'Shall I give her a touch ahead?'

'No – hold everything. He's getting it clear now.'

They waited while the fisherman secured his tackle. Then he said, 'Say, Cap, I guess you think me a heel, jumping ship like that.'

Dwight said, 'That's all right, fella. I know how it was. I'm not going to take you on board again, though. I've got the rest of the ship's company to think about.'

'Sure, Cap, I know that. I'm hot and getting hotter every minute, I suppose.'

'How do you feel right now?'

'Okay so far. Would you ask Mr Osborne for me how long I'll go on that way?'

'He thinks you'll go for a day or so, and then you'll get sick.'

From the boat the fisherman said, 'Well, it's a mighty

nice day to have for the last one. Wouldn't it be hell if it was raining?'

Dwight laughed. 'That's the way to take it. Tell me, what are things like on shore?'

'Everybody's dead here, Cap – but I guess you know that. I went home. Dad and Mom were dead in bed – I'd say they took something. I went round to see the girl, and she was dead. It was a mistake, going there. No dogs or cats or birds, or anything alive – I guess they're all dead, too. Apart from that, everything is pretty much the way it always was. I'm sorry about jumping ship, Cap, but I'm glad to be home.' He paused. 'I got my own car and gas for it, and I got my own boat and my own outboard motor and my own fishing gear. And it's a fine, sunny day. I'd rather have it this way, in my own home town, than have it in September in Australia.'

'Sure, fella. I know how you feel. Is there anything you want right now, that we can put out on the deck for you? We're on our way, and we shan't be coming back.'

'You got any of those knockout pills on board, that you take when it gets bad? The cyanide?'

'I haven't got those, Ralphie. I'll put an automatic out on deck if you want it.'

The fisherman shook his head. 'I got my own gun. I'll take a look around the pharmacy when I get on shore – maybe there's something there. But I guess the gun would be the best.'

'Is there anything else you want?'

'Thanks, Cap, but I got everything I want on shore. Without a dime to pay, either. Just tell the boys on board hullo for me.'

'I'll do that, fella. We'll be going on now. Good fishing.'

'Thanks, Cap. It's been pretty good under you, and I'm sorry I jumped ship.'

'Okay. Now just watch the suck of the propellers as I go ahead.'

He turned to the executive. 'Take the con, Commander. Go ahead, and then on course, ten knots.'

That evening Mary Holmes rang Moira at her home. It was a pouring wet evening in late autumn, the wind whistling around the house at Harkaway. 'Darling,' she said, 'there's been a wireless signal from them. They're all well.'

The girl gasped, for this was totally unexpected. 'However did they get a signal through?'

'Commander Peterson just rang me up. It came through on the mystery station that they went to find out about. Lieutenant Sunderstrom was sending and he said they were all well. Isn't it splendid?'

The relief was so intense that for a moment the girl felt faint. 'It's marvellous,' she whispered. 'Tell me, can they get a message back to them?'

'I don't think so. Sunderstrom said that he was closing down the station, and there wasn't anyone alive there.'

'Oh . . .' The girl was silent. 'Well, I suppose we'll just have to be patient.'

'Was there something you particularly wanted to send?'

'Not really. Just something I wanted to tell Dwight. But it'll have to wait.'

'Darling! You don't mean . . .'

'No, I don't.'

'Are you feeling all right, dear?'

'I'm feeling much better than I was five minutes ago.' She paused. 'How are you getting on, and how's Jennifer?'

'She's fine. We're all right, except it's raining all the

time. Can't you come over some time? It's an age since we met.'

The girl said, 'I could come down one evening after work, and go up again next day.'

'Darling! That would be wonderful!'

She arrived at Falmouth station two nights later, and set herself to walk two miles up the hill in a misty drizzle. In the little flat Mary was waiting to welcome her with a bright fire in the lounge. She changed her shoes, helped Mary bath the baby and put her down, and then they got the supper. Later they sat together on the floor before the fire.

The girl asked, 'When do you think they'll be back?'

'Peter said that they'd be back about the fourteenth of June.' She reached out for a calendar upon the desk behind her. 'Three more weeks – just over. I've been crossing off the days.'

'Do you think they're up to time at this place – wherever they sent the wireless signal from?'

'I don't know. I ought to have asked Commander Peterson that. I wonder if it would be all right to ring him up tomorrow and ask?'

'I shouldn't think he'd mind.'

'I think I'll do that. Peter says this is his last job for the Navy, he'll be unemployed after they come back. I was wondering if we couldn't get away in June or July and have a holiday. It's so piggy here in the winter – nothing but rain and gales.'

The girl lit a cigarette. 'Where would you go to?'

'Somewhere where it's warm. Queensland or somewhere. It's such an awful bore not having a car. We'd have to take Jennifer by train, I suppose.'

Moira blew a long cloud of smoke. 'I shouldn't think Queensland would be very easy.'

'Because of the sickness? It's so far away.'

'They've got it at Maryborough,' the girl said. 'That's only just north of Brisbane.'

'But there are plenty of warm places to go to without going right up there, aren't there?'

'I should think there would be. But it's coming down south pretty steadily.'

Mary twisted round and glanced at her. 'Tell me, do you really think it's going to come here?'

'I think I do.'

'You mean, we're all going to die of it? Like the men say?'

'I suppose so.'

Mary twisted round and pulled a catalogue of garden flowers down from a muddle of papers on the settee. 'I went to Wilson's today and bought a hundred daffodils,' she said. 'Bulbs. King Alfreds – these ones.' She showed the picture. 'I'm going to put them in that corner by the wall, where Peter took out the tree. It's sheltered there. But I suppose if we're all going to die that's silly.'

'No sillier than me starting in to learn shorthand and typing,' the girl said drily. 'I think we're all going a bit mad, if you ask me. When do daffodils come up?'

'They should be flowering by the end of August,' Mary said. 'Of course, they won't be much this year, but they should be lovely next year and the year after. They sort of multiply, you know.'

'Well, of course it's sensible to put them in. You'll see them anyway, and you'll sort of feel you've done something.'

Mary looked at her gratefully. 'Well, that's what I think. I mean, I couldn't bear to – to just stop doing things and do nothing. You might as well die now and get it over.'

Moira nodded. 'If what they say is right, we're none of

us going to have time to do all that we planned to do. But we can keep on doing it as long as we can.'

They sat on the hearthrug, Mary playing with the poker and the wood fire. Presently she said, 'I forgot to ask you if you'd like a brandy or something. There's a bottle in the cupboard, and I think there's some soda.'

The girl shook her head. 'Not for me. I'm quite happy.'

'Really?'

'Really.'

'Have you reformed, or something?'

'Or something,' said the girl. 'I never tip it up at home. Only when I'm out at parties, or with men. With men particularly. Matter of fact, I'm even getting tired of that, now.'

'It's not men, is it, dear? Not now. It's Dwight Towers.'

'Yes,' the girl said. 'It's Dwight Towers.'

'Don't you ever want to get married? I mean, even if we *are* all dying next September.'

The girl stared into the fire. 'I wanted to get married,' she said quietly. 'I wanted to have everything you've got. But I shan't have it now.'

'Couldn't you marry Dwight?'

The girl shook her head. 'I don't think so.'

'I'm sure he likes you.'

'Yes,' she said. 'He likes me all right.'

'Has he ever kissed you?'

'Yes,' she said again. 'He kissed me once.'

'I'm sure he'd marry you.'

The girl shook her head again. 'He wouldn't ever do that. You see, he's married already. He's got a wife and two children in America.'

Mary stared at her. 'Darling, he *can't* have. They must be dead.'

'He doesn't think so,' she said wearily. 'He thinks he's going home to meet them, next September. In his own home town, at Mystic.' She paused. 'We're all going a bit mad in our own way,' she said. 'That's his way.'

'You mean, he really thinks his wife is still alive?'

'I don't know if he thinks that or not. No, I don't think he does. He thinks he's going to be dead next September, but he thinks he's going home to them, to Sharon and Dwight junior and Helen. He's been buying presents for them.'

Mary sat trying to understand. 'But if he thinks like that, why did he kiss you?'

'Because I said I'd help him with the presents.'

Mary got to her feet. 'I'm going to have a drink,' she said firmly. 'I think you'd better have one, too.' And when that was adjusted and they were sitting with glasses in their hands, she asked curiously, 'It must be funny, being jealous of someone that's dead?'

The girl took a drink from her glass and sat staring at the fire. 'I'm not jealous of her,' she said at last. 'I don't think so. Her name is Sharon, like in the Bible. I want to meet her. She must be a very wonderful person, I think. You see, he's such a *practical* man.'

'Don't you want to marry him?'

The girl sat for a long time in silence. 'I don't know,' she said at last. 'I don't know if I do or not. If it wasn't for all this . . . I'd play every dirty trick in the book to get him away from her. I don't think I'll ever be happy with anyone else. But then, there's not much time left now to be happy with anyone.'

'There's three or four months, anyway,' said Mary. 'I saw a motto once, one of those things you hang on the wall to inspire you. It said, "Don't worry – it may never happen."'

'I think this is going to happen all right,' Moira remarked. She picked up the poker and began playing with it. 'If it was for a lifetime it'd be different,' she said. 'It'd be worth doing her dirt if it meant having Dwight for good, and children, and a home, and a full life. I'd go through anything if I could see a chance of that. But to do her dirt just for three months' pleasure and nothing at the end of it – well, that's another thing. I may be a loose woman, but I don't know that I'm all that loose.' She looked up, smiling. 'Anyway, I don't believe that I could do it in the time. I think he'd take a lot of prising away from her.'

'Oh dear,' said Mary. 'Things *are* difficult, aren't they!'

'Couldn't be worse,' Moira agreed. 'I think I'll probably die an old maid.'

'It doesn't make sense. But nothing does seem to make sense, these days. Peter . . .' She stopped.

'What about Peter?' the girl asked curiously.

'I don't know. It was just horrible, and crazy.' She shifted restlessly.

'What was? Tell me.'

'Did you ever murder anybody?'

'Me? Not yet. I've often wanted to. Country telephone girls, mostly.'

'This was serious. It's a frightful sin to murder anybody, isn't it? I mean, you'd go to Hell.'

'I don't know. I suppose you would. Who do you want to murder?'

The mother said dully, 'Peter told me I might have to murder Jennifer.' A tear formed and trickled down her cheek.

The girl leaned forward impulsively and touched her hand. 'Darling, that can't be right! You must have got it wrong.'

She shook her head. 'It's not wrong,' she sobbed. 'It's right enough. He told me I might have to do it, and he showed me how.' She burst into a torrent of tears.

Moira took her in her arms and soothed her, and gradually the story came out. At first the girl could not believe the words she heard, but later she was not so sure. Finally they went together to the bathroom and looked at the red boxes in the cabinet. 'I've heard something about all this,' she said seriously. 'I never knew that it had got so far . . .' One craziness was piled on to another.

'I couldn't do it alone,' the mother whispered. 'However bad she was, I couldn't do it. If Peter isn't here . . . if anything happens to *Scorpion* . . . will you come and help me, Moira? Please?'

'Of course I will,' the girl said gently. 'Of course I'll come and help. But Peter *will* be here. They're coming back all right. Dwight's that kind of a man.' She produced a little screwed up ball of handkerchief, and gave it to Mary. 'Dry up, and let's make a cup of tea. I'll go and put the kettle on.'

They had a cup of tea before the dying fire.

Eighteen days later USS *Scorpion* surfaced in clean air in Latitude Thirty-one degrees South, near Norfolk Island. At the entrance to the Tasman Sea in winter the weather was bleak and the sea rough, the low deck swept by every wave. It was only possible to allow the crew up to the bridge deck eight at a time; they crept up, white faced and trembling, to huddle in oilskins in the driving rain and spray. Dwight kept the submarine hove-to head into wind for most of the day till everyone had had his allotted half hour in the fresh air, but few of the men stayed on the bridge so long.

Their resistance to the cold and wet conditions on the

bridge was low, but at least he had brought them all back alive, with the exception of Yeoman Swain. All were white faced and anaemic after thirty-one days' confinement within the hull, and he had three cases of intense depression rendering those men unreliable for duty. He had had one bad fright when Lieutenant Brody had developed all the symptoms of acute appendicitis; with John Osborne helping him he had read up all the procedure for the operation and prepared to do it on the wardroom table. However, the symptoms had subsided and the patient was now resting comfortably in his berth; Peter Holmes had taken over all his duties and the captain now hoped that he might last out until they docked at Williamstown in five days' time. Peter Holmes was as normal as anyone on board. John Osborne was nervous and irritable, though still efficient; he talked incessantly of his Ferrari.

They had disproved the Jorgensen effect. They had ventured slowly into the Gulf of Alaska, using their underwater mine detector as a defence against floating icebergs, till they had reached Latitude Fifty-eight North in the vicinity of Kodiak. The ice was thicker near the land and they had not approached it; up there the radiation level was still lethal and little different from that they had experienced in the Seattle district. There seemed to be no point in risking the vessel in those waters any longer than was necessary; they took their readings and set course a little to the east of south till they found warmer water and less chance of ice, and then south-west towards Hawaii and Pearl Harbor.

At Pearl Harbor they had learned practically nothing. They had cruised right into the harbour and up to the dock that they had sailed from before the outbreak of the war. Psychologically this was relatively easy for them, because Dwight had ascertained before the cruise commenced that none of the ship's company had had their homes in Honolulu or had any close ties with the islands. He could have put an officer on shore in a radiation suit as he had done at Santa Maria, and he debated for some days with Peter Holmes before he reached the islands whether he should do so, but they could think of nothing to be gained by such an expedition. When Lieutenant Sunderstrom had had time on his hands at Santa Maria all that he had found to do had been to read the *Saturday Evening Post*, and they could think of little more useful that an officer on shore could do at Pearl Harbor. The radiation level was much as it had been at Seattle; they noted and listed the many ships in the harbour, the considerable destruction on the shore, and left.

That day, hove-to at the entrance to the Tasman Sea, they were within easy radio communication with Australia. They raised the radio mast and made a signal reporting their position and their estimated time of arrival back at Williamstown. They got a signal in reply asking for their state of health, and Dwight answered in a fairly lengthy message that he worded with some difficulty in regard to Yeoman Swain. A few routine messages came through then, dealing with weather forecasts, fuelling requirements, and engineering work required when they docked, and in the middle of the morning came a more important one.

It bore a dateline three days previous. It read,

FROM: *Commanding Officer, US Naval Forces, Brisbane.*

TO: *Commander Dwight L. Towers, USS Scorpion.*

SUBJECT: *Assumption of additional duties.*

1. On the retirement of the present Commanding Officer US Naval Forces at this date you will immediately and henceforth assume the duty of Commanding Officer US Naval Forces in all areas. You will use your discretion as to the disposition of these Forces, and you will terminate or continue their employment under Australian command as you think fit.

2. Guess this makes you an admiral if you want to be one. Goodbye and good luck. JERRY SHAW.

3. *Copy to First Naval Member, Royal Australian Navy*.

Dwight read this in his cabin with an expressionless face. Then, since a copy had already gone to the Australians, he sent for his liaison officer. When Peter came he handed him the signal without a word.

The Lieutenant-Commander read it. 'Congratulations, sir,' he said quietly.

'I suppose so . . .' said the captain. And then he said, 'I suppose this means that Brisbane's out now.'

Brisbane was two hundred and fifty miles in latitude to the north of their position then. Peter nodded, his mind on the radiation figures. 'It was pretty bad still yesterday afternoon.'

'I thought he might have left his ship and come down south,' the captain said.

'They couldn't move at all?'

'No fuel oil,' Dwight said. 'They had to stop all services in the ships. The tanks were bone dry.'

'*I* should have thought that he'd have come to Melbourne. After all, the Supreme Commander of the US Navy . . .'

Dwight smiled, a little wryly. 'That doesn't mean a

thing, not now. No, the real point is that he was captain of his ship and the ship couldn't move. He wouldn't want to run out on his ship's company.'

There was no more to be said, and he dismissed his liaison officer. He drafted a short signal in acknowledgement and gave it to the signals officer for transmission via Melbourne, with a copy for the First Naval Member. Presently the yeoman came to him and laid a signal on his desk.

Your 12/05663.
Regret no communications are now possible with Brisbane.

The captain nodded. 'Okay,' he said. 'Let it go.'

7

Peter Holmes reported to the Second Naval Member the day after they returned to Williamstown. The Admiral motioned to him to sit down. 'I met Commander Towers for a few minutes last night, Lieutenant-Commander,' he said. 'You seem to have got on well with him.'

'I'm glad to hear that, sir.'

'Yes. Now I suppose you want to know about a continuation of your appointment.'

Peter said diffidently, 'In a way. I take it that the general situation is the same? I mean, there's only two or three months left to go?'

The Admiral nodded. 'That seems to be correct. You told me when I saw you last that you would prefer to be on shore in these last months.'

'I should.' He hesitated. 'I've got to think a bit about my wife.'

'Of course.' He offered the young man a cigarette, and lit one himself. '*Scorpion* is going into dry dock for hull reconditioning,' he said. 'I suppose you know that.'

'Yes, sir. The captain was anxious to have that done. I saw the Third Naval Member's office about it this morning.'

'Normally that might take about three weeks. It may take longer under present conditions. Would you like to stay on with her as liaison officer while that work is going on?' He paused. 'Commander Towers has asked for you to continue in the appointment for the time being.'

'Could I live at home, down at Falmouth? It takes me about an hour and three quarters to get to the dockyard.'

'You'd better take that up with Commander Towers. I don't suppose you'll find that he has any objection. It's not as if the ship was in commission. I understand he's giving leave to most of the ship's company. I don't suppose your duties would be very arduous, but you would be a help to him in dealing with the dockyard.'

'I'd like to carry on with him, sir, subject to living at home. But if the ship is programmed for another cruise, I'd like you to replace me. I don't think I could undertake another seagoing appointment.' He hesitated. 'I don't like saying that.'

The Admiral smiled. 'That's all right, Lieutenant-Commander. I'll keep that in mind. Come back and see me if you want to be relieved.' He rose to his feet, terminating the interview. 'Everything all right at home?'

'Quite all right. Housekeeping seems to be more difficult than when I went away, and it's all becoming a bit of a battle for my wife, with the baby to look after.'

'I know it is. And I'm afraid it's not going to get any easier.'

That morning Moira Davidson rang up Dwight Towers in the aircraft carrier at lunch time. 'Morning, Dwight,' she said. 'They tell me that I've got to congratulate you.'

'Who told you that?' he asked.

'Mary Holmes.'

'You can congratulate me if you like,' he said a little heavily. 'But I'd just as soon you didn't.'

'All right,' she said, 'I won't. Dwight, how are you? Yourself?'

'I'm okay,' he said. 'Got a bit of a let-down today, but I'm okay.' In fact, everything that he had done since they had come back to the aircraft carrier had been an effort; he had slept badly and was infinitely tired.

'Are you very busy?'

'I should be,' he said. 'But I don't know – nothing seems to get done and the more nothing gets done the more there is to do.'

This was a different Dwight from the one that she had grown accustomed to. 'You sound as if you're getting ill,' she said severely.

'I'm not getting ill, honey,' he said a little irritably. 'It's just that there's some things to do and everybody off on leave. We've been away so long at sea we've just forgotten what work is.'

'I think you ought to take some leave yourself,' she said. 'Could you come out to Harkaway for a bit?'

He thought for a moment. 'That's mighty nice of you. I couldn't do that for a while. We're putting *Scorpion* into the dry dock tomorrow.'

'Let Peter Holmes do that for you.'

'I couldn't do that, honey. Uncle Sam wouldn't like it.'

She forbore to say that Uncle Sam would never know. 'After you've done that, the ship'll be in dockyard hands, won't she?'

'Say, you know a lot about the navy.'

'I know I do. I'm a beautiful spy, Mata Hari, *femme fatale*, worming secrets out of innocent naval officers over a double brandy. She will be in dockyard hands, won't she?'

'You're very right.'

'Well then, you can chuck everything else on Peter Holmes and get away on leave. What time are you putting her in dock?'

'Ten o'clock tomorrow morning. We'll probably be through by midday.'

'Come out and spend a little time at Harkaway with us, tomorrow afternoon. It's perishing cold up there. The wind just whistles round the house. It rains most of the time, and you can't go out without gum boots. Walking beside the bullock and the pasture harrows is the coldest job known to man – to woman, anyway. Come out and try it. After a few days with us you'll be just longing to get back and fug it in your submarine.'

He laughed. 'Say, you're making it sound really attractive.'

'I know I am. Will you come out tomorrow afternoon?'

It would be a relief to relax, to forget his burdens for a day or two. 'I think I could,' he said. 'I'll have to shuffle things around a little, but I think I could.'

She arranged to meet him the next afternoon at four o'clock in the Australia Hotel. When she did so she was concerned at his appearance; he greeted her cheerfully and seemed glad to see her, but he had gone a yellowish colour beneath his tan, and in unguarded moments he was depressed. She frowned at the sight of him. 'You're looking like something that the cat brought in and didn't want,' she told him. 'Are you all right?' She took his hand and felt it. 'You're hot. You've got a temperature!'

He withdrew his hand. 'I'm okay,' he said. 'What'll you have to drink?'

'You'll have a double whisky and about twenty grains of quinine,' she said. 'A double whisky, anyway. I'll see about the quinine when we get home. You ought to be in bed!'

It was pleasant to be fussed over, and relax. 'Double brandy for you?' he asked.

'Small one for me, double for you,' she said. 'You ought to be ashamed of yourself, going about like this. You're probably spreading germs all over the place. Have you seen a doctor?'

He ordered the drinks. 'There's no doctor in the dockyard now. *Scorpion* is the only ship that's operational, and she's in dockyard hands. They took the last naval surgeon away while we were on the cruise.'

'You *have* got a temperature, haven't you?'

'I might have just a little one,' he said, 'perhaps I might have a cold coming on.'

'I'd say perhaps you might. Drink up that whisky while I telephone Daddy.'

'What for?'

'To meet us with the buggy at the station. I told them we'd walk up the hill, but I'm not going to have you doing that. You might die on my hands, and then I'd have a job explaining to the coroner. It might even make a diplomatic incident.'

'Who with, honey?'

'The United States. It's not so good to kill the Supreme Commander of the US Naval Forces.'

He said wearily, 'I guess the United States is me, right now. I'm thinking of running for President.'

'Well, think about it while I go and telephone Mummy.'

In the little telephone booth, she said, 'I think he's got 'flu, Mummy. He's frightfully tired, for one thing. He'll have to go to bed directly we get home. Could you light a fire in his room, and put a hot water bag in the bed? And, Mummy, ring up Dr Fletcher and ask if he could possibly come round this evening. I shouldn't think it's anything but 'flu, but he *has* been in the radioactive area for over a month, and he hasn't seen a doctor since he got back. Tell Dr Fletcher who he is. He's rather an important person now, you know.'

'What train will you be catching, dear?'

She glanced at her wrist. 'We'll catch the four-forty. Look, Mummy, it's going to be perishing cold in the buggy. Ask Daddy to bring down a couple of rugs.'

She went back to the bar. 'Drink up and come along,' she said. 'We've got to catch the four-forty.'

He went with her obediently. A couple of hours later he was in a bedroom with a blazing log fire, creeping into a warm bed as he shook with a light fever. He lay there infinitely grateful while the shakes subsided, glad to relax and lie staring at the ceiling, listening to the patter of the rain outside. Presently his grazier host brought him a hot whisky and lemon and asked what he wanted to eat, which was nothing.

At about eight o'clock there was the sound of a horse outside, and voices in the rain. Presently the doctor came to him; he had discarded his wet coat, but his jodhpurs and riding boots were dark with rain and steamed a little as he stood by the fire. He was a man of about thirty-five or forty, cheerful and competent.

'Say, Doctor,' said the patient, 'I'm really sorry they brought you out here on a night like this. There's not a thing wrong with me that a day or two in bed won't cure.'

The doctor smiled. 'I'm glad to come out to meet you,' he said. He took the American's wrist and felt the pulse. 'I understand you've been up in the radioactive area.'

'Why, yes. But we didn't get exposed.'

'You were inside the hull of the submarine all the time?'

'All the time. We had a guy from the CSIRO poking Geiger counters at us every day. It's not that. Doctor.'

'Have you had any vomiting, or diarrhoea?'

'None at all. Nor did any of the ship's company.'

The doctor put a thermometer into his mouth, and stood feeling his pulse. Presently he withdrew the thermometer. 'A hundred and two,' he said. 'You'd better stay in bed for a bit. How long were you at sea?'

'Fifty-three days.'

'And how long submerged?'

'More than half of it.'

'Are you very tired?'

The captain thought for a moment. 'I might be,' he admitted.

'I should say you might. You'd better stay in bed till that temperature goes down, and one full day after that. I'll look in and see you again in a couple of days' time. I think you've only got a dose of 'flu – there's quite a lot of it about. You'd better not go back to work for at least a week after you get up, and then you ought to take some leave. Can you do that?'

'I'll have to think about it.'

They talked a little of the cruise and of conditions at Seattle and in Queensland. Finally the doctor said, 'I'll probably look in tomorrow afternoon with one or two things you'd better take. I've got to go to Dandenong; my partner's operating at the hospital and I'm giving the anaesthetic for him. I'll pick up the stuff there and look in on my way home.'

'Is it a serious operation?'

'Not too bad. Woman with a growth upon the stomach. She'll be better with it out. Give her a few more years of useful life, anyway.'

He went away, and outside the window Dwight heard

the backing and curvetting of the horse as the rider got into the saddle, and heard the doctor swear. Then he listened to the diminuendo of the hoofs as they trotted away down the drive in the rain. Presently his door opened, and the girl came in.

'Well,' she said, 'you've got to stay in bed tomorrow, anyway.' She moved to the fire and threw a couple of logs on. 'He's nice, isn't he?'

'He's nuts,' said the Commander.

'Why? Because he's making you stay in bed?'

'Not that. He's operating on a woman at the hospital tomorrow so that she'll have some years of useful life ahead of her.'

She laughed. 'He would. I've never met anyone so conscientious.' She paused. 'Daddy's going to make another dam next summer. He's been talking about it for some time, but now he says he's really going to do it. He rang up a chap who has a bulldozer today and booked him to come in as soon as the ground gets hard.'

'When will that be?'

'About Christmas time. It really hurts him to see all this rain running away to waste. This place gets pretty dry in the summer.'

She took his empty glass from the table by his bed. 'Like another hot drink?'

He shook his head. 'Not now, honey. I'm fine.'

'Like anything to eat?'

He shook his head.

'Like another hot water bag?'

He shook his head. 'I'm fine.'

She went away, but in a few minutes she was back again, and this time she carried a long paper parcel in her hand, a parcel with a bulge at the bottom. 'I'll leave this with you, and you can look at it all night.'

She put it in a corner of the room, but he raised himself on one elbow. 'What's that?' he asked.

She laughed. 'I'll give you three guesses and you can see which one's right in the morning.'

'I want to see now.'

'Tomorrow.'

'No – now.'

She took the parcel and brought it to him in the bed, and stood watching as he tore off the paper. The Supreme Commander of the US Naval Forces was really just a little boy, she thought.

The Pogo stick lay on the bedclothes in his hands, shining and new. The wooden handle was brightly varnished, the metal step gleaming in red enamel. On the wooden handle was painted in neat red lettering the words HELEN TOWERS.

'Say,' he said huskily, 'that's a dandy. I never saw one with the name on it and all. She's going to love that.' He raised his eyes. 'Where did you get it honey?'

'I found the place that makes them, out at Elsternwick,' she said. 'They aren't making any more, but they made one for me.'

'I don't know what to say,' he muttered. 'Now I've got something for everyone.'

She gathered up the torn brown paper. 'That's all right,' she said casually. 'It was fun finding it. Shall I put it in the corner?'

He shook his head. 'Leave it right here.'

She nodded, and moved towards the door. 'I'll turn this top light out. Don't stay up too long. Sure you've got everything you want?'

'Sure, honey,' he said. 'I've got everything now.'

'Goodnight,' she said.

She closed the door behind her. He lay for some time

in the firelight thinking of Sharon and of Helen, of bright summer days and tall ships at Mystic, of Helen leaping on the Pogo stick on the swept sidewalk with the piles of snow on either hand, of this girl and her kindness. Presently he drifted into sleep, one hand upon the Pogo stick beside him.

Peter Holmes lunched with John Osborne at the United Services Club next day. 'I rang the ship this morning,' said the scientist. 'I wanted to get hold of Dwight to show him the draft report before I get it typed. They told me that he's staying out at Harkaway with Moira's people.'

Peter nodded. 'He's got 'flu. Moira rang me up last night to tell me that I wouldn't see him for a week, or longer if she'd got anything to do with it.'

The scientist was concerned. 'I can't hold it so long as that. Jorgensen's got wind of our findings already, and he's saying that we can't have done our job properly. I'll have to get it to the typist by tomorrow at the latest.'

'I'll look it over if you like, and we might be able to get hold of the Exec., though he's away on leave. But Dwight ought to see it before it goes out. Why don't you give Moira a ring and take it out to him at Harkaway?'

'Would she be there? I thought she was in Melbourne every day, doing shorthand and typing.'

'Don't be so daft. Of course she's there.'

The scientist brightened. 'I might run it out to him this afternoon in the Ferrari.'

'Your juice won't last out if you're going to use it for trips like that. There's a perfectly good train.'

'This is official business, naval business,' said John Osborne. 'One's entitled to draw on naval stores.' He bent towards Peter and lowered his voice. 'You know that aircraft carrier, the *Sydney*? She's got about three thousand gallons of my ether-alcohol mixture in one of her tanks.

They used it for getting reluctant piston-engined aircraft off the deck at full boost.'

'You can't touch that!' said Peter, shocked.

'Can't I? This is naval business, and there's going to be a whole lot more.'

'Well, don't tell *me* about it. Would a Morris Minor run on it?'

'You'd have to experiment a bit with the carburettion, and you'd have to raise the compression. Take the gasket out and fit a bit of thin sheet copper, with cement. It's worth trying.'

'Can you run that thing of yours upon the road, safely?'

'Oh, yes,' said the scientist. 'There's not much else upon the road to hit, except a tram. And people, of course. I always carry a spare set of plugs because she oils up if you run her under about three thousand.'

'What's she doing at three thousand revs?'

'Oh well, you wouldn't put her in top gear. She'd be doing about a hundred, or a bit more than that. She does about forty-five in first at those revs. She gets away with a bit of a rush, of course; you want a couple of hundred yards of empty road ahead of you. I generally push her out of the mews into Elizabeth Street and wait till there's a gap between the trams.'

He did so that afternoon directly after lunch, with Peter Holmes helping him to push. He wedged the attaché case containing the draft report down beside the seat and climbed in, fastened the safety belt and adjusted his crash helmet before an admiring crowd. Peter said quietly, 'For God's sake don't go and kill anybody.'

'They're all going to be dead in a couple of months' time anyway,' said the scientist. 'So am I, and so are you. I'm going to have a bit of fun with this thing first.'

A tram passed and he tried the cold engine with the self starter, but it failed to catch. Another tram came by; when that was gone a dozen willing helpers pushed the racing car until the engine caught and she shot out of their hands like a rocket with an ear-splitting crash from the exhaust, a screech of tyres, a smell of burnt rubber, and a cloud of smoke. The Ferrari had no horn and no need for one because she could be heard coming a couple of miles away; more important to John Osborne was the fact that she had no lights at all, and it was dark by five o'clock. If he was to get out to Harkaway, do his business, and be back in daylight he must step on it.

He weaved around the tram at fifty, skidded round into Lonsdale Street, and settled in his seat as he shot through the city at about seventy miles an hour. Cars on the road at that time were a rarity and he had little trouble in the city streets but for the trams; the crowds parted to let him through. In the suburbs it was different; children had grown accustomed to playing in the empty roads and had no notion of getting out of the way; he had to brake hard on a number of occasions and go by with engine roaring as he slipped the clutch, agonizing over the possibility of damage, consoling himself with the thought that the clutch was built to take it in a race.

He got to Harkaway in twenty-three minutes, having averaged seventy-two miles an hour over the course without once getting into top. He drew up at the homestead in a roaring skid around the flowerbeds and killed the motor; the grazier with his wife and daughter came out suddenly and watched him as he unbuttoned his crash hat and got out stiffly. 'I came to see Dwight Towers,' he said. 'They told me he was here.'

'He's trying to get some sleep,' Moira said severely. 'That's a loathsome car, John. What does she do?'

'About two hundred, I think. I want to see him – on business. I've got a thing here that he's got to look over before it gets typed. It's got to be typed tomorrow, at the latest.'

'Oh well, I don't suppose he's sleeping now.'

She led the way into the spare bedroom. Dwight was awake and sitting up in bed. 'I guessed it must be you,' he said. 'Killed anybody yet?'

'Not yet,' said the scientist. 'I'm hoping to be the first. I'd hate to spend the last days of my life in prison. I've had enough of that in the last two months.' He undid his attaché case and explained his errand.

Dwight took the report and read it through, asking a question now and then. 'I kind of wish we'd left that radio station operational, the way it was,' he said once. 'Maybe we'd have heard a little more from Yeoman Swain.'

'It was a good long way away from him.'

'He had his outboard motor boat. He might have stopped off one day when he was tired of fishing, and sent a message.'

'I don't think he'd have lasted long enough for that, sir. I'd have given him three days, at the very outside.'

The captain nodded. 'I don't suppose he'd have wanted to be bothered with it, anyway. I wouldn't, if the fish were taking well, and it was my last day.' He read on, asking a question now and then. At the end he said, 'That's okay. You'd better take out that last paragraph, about me and the ship.'

'I'd prefer to leave it in, sir.'

'And I'd prefer you take it out. I don't like things like that said about what was just a normal operation in the line of duty.'

The scientist put his pencil through it. 'As you like.'

'You got that Ferrari here?'

227

'I came out in it.'

'Sure. I heard you. Can I see it from the window?'

'Yes. It's just outside.'

The captain got out of bed and stood in his pyjamas at the window. 'That's the hell of a car,' he said. 'What are you going to do with it?'

'Race it. There's not much time left, so they're starting the racing season earlier than usual. They don't usually begin before about October, because of the wet roads. They're having little races all the winter, though. As a matter of fact I raced it twice before I went away.'

The captain got back into bed. 'So you said. I never raced a car like that. I never even drove one. What's it like in a race?'

'You get scared stiff. Then directly it's over you want to go on and do it again.'

'Have you ever done this before?'

The scientist shook his head. 'I've never had the money, or the time. It's what I've wanted to do all my life.'

'Is that the way you're going to make it, in the end?'

There was a pause. 'It's what I'd like to do,' John Osborne said. 'Rather than die in a sick muck, or take those pills. The only thing is, I'd hate to smash up the Ferrari. She's such a lovely bit of work. I don't think I could bring myself to do that, willingly.'

Dwight grinned. 'Maybe you won't have to do it willingly, not if you go racing at two hundred per on wet roads.'

'Well, that's what I've been thinking, too. I don't know that I'd mind that happening, any time from now on.'

The captain nodded. Then he said, 'There's no chance now of it slowing up and giving us a break, is there?'

John Osborne shook his head. 'Absolutely none. There's not the slightest indication – if anything it seems to be coming a little faster. That's probably associated with the reduced area of the earth's surface as it moves down from the equator; it seems to be accelerating a little now in terms of latitude. The end of August seems to be the time.'

The captain nodded. 'Well, it's nice to know. It can't be too soon for me.'

'Will you be taking *Scorpion* to sea again?'

'I've got no orders. She'll be operational again at the beginning of July. I'm planning to keep her under the Australian command up till the end. Whether I'll have a crew to make her operational – well, that's another thing again. Most of the boys have got girl friends in Melbourne here, about a quarter of them married. Whether they'll feel allergic to another cruise is anybody's guess. I'd say they will.'

There was a pause. 'I kind of envy you having that Ferrari,' he said quietly. 'I'll be worrying and working right up till the end.'

'I don't see that there's any need for you to do that,' the scientist said. 'You ought to take some leave. See a bit of Australia.'

The American grinned. 'There's not much left of it to see.'

'That's true. There's the mountain parts, of course. They're all skiing like mad up at Mount Buller and at Hotham. Do you ski?'

'I used to, but not for ten years or so. I wouldn't like to break a leg and get stuck in bed up till the end.' He paused. 'Say,' he said. 'Don't people go trout fishing up in those mountains?'

John Osborne nodded. 'The fishing's quite good.'

'Do they have a season, or can you fish all year round?'

'You can fish for perch in Eildon Weir all year round.

229

They take a spinner, trolling from a boat. But there's good trout fishing in all the little rivers up there.' He smiled faintly. 'There's a close season for trout. It doesn't open till September the First.'

There was a momentary pause. 'That's running it kind of fine,' Dwight said at last. 'I certainly would like a day or two trout fishing, but from what you say we might be busy just around that time.'

'I shouldn't think it would make any odds if you went up a fortnight early, this year.'

'I wouldn't like to do a thing like that,' the American said seriously. 'In the States – yes. But when you're in a foreign country, I think a fellow should stick by the rules.'

Time was going on, John Osborne had no lights on the Ferrari and no capacity to go much slower than fifty miles an hour. He gathered his papers together and put them in the attaché case, said goodbye to Dwight Towers, and left him, to get upon the road back to the city. In the lounge he met Moira. 'How did you think he was?' she asked.

'He's all right,' the scientist said. 'Only a bat or two flying round the belfry.'

She frowned a little; this wasn't the Pogo stick? 'What about?'

'He wants a couple of days trout fishing before we all go home,' her cousin said. 'But he won't go before the season opens, and that's not until September the First.'

She stood in silence for a moment. 'Well, what of it? He's keeping the law, anyway. More than you are, with that disgusting car. Where do you get the petrol for it?'

'It doesn't run on petrol,' he replied. 'It runs on something out of a test tube.'

'Smells like it,' she said. She watched him as he levered himself down into the seat and adjusted his crash helmet, as the engine crackled spitefully into life, he shot off down the drive leaving great wheel ruts on a flower bed.

A fortnight later, in the Pastoral Club, Mr Alan Sykes walked into the little smoking-room for a drink at twenty minutes past twelve. Lunch was not served till one o'clock, so he was the first in the room; he helped himself to a gin and stood alone, considering his problem. Mr Sykes was the Director of the State Fisheries and Game Department, a man who liked to run his business upon sound lines regardless of political expediency. The perplexities of the time had now invaded his routine, and he was a troubled man.

Sir Douglas Froude came into the room. Mr Sykes, watching him, thought that he was walking very badly and that his red face was redder than ever. He said, 'Good morning, Douglas. I'm in the book.'

'Oh, thank you, thank you,' said the old man. 'I'll take a Spanish sherry with you.' He poured it with a trembling hand. 'You know,' he said, 'I think the Wine Committee must be absolutely crazy. We've got over four hundred bottles of magnificent dry sherry, Ruy de Lopez, 1947, and they seemed to be prepared to let it stay there in the cellars. They said the members wouldn't drink it because of the price. I told them, I said: "Give it away, if you can't sell it. But don't just leave it there." So now it's the same price as the Australian.' He paused. 'Let me pour you a glass, Alan. It's in the most beautiful condition.'

'I'll have one later. Tell me, didn't I hear you say once that Bill Davidson was a relation of yours?'

The old man nodded shakily. 'Relation, or connection. Connection, I think. His mother married my . . . married my . . . No, I forget. I don't seem to remember things like I used to.'

'Do you know his daughter Moira?'

'A nice girl, but she drinks too much. Still, she does it on brandy they tell me, so that makes a difference.'

'She's been making some trouble for me.'

'Eh?'

'She's been to the Minister, and he sent her to me with a note. She wants us to open the trout season early this year, or nobody will get any trout fishing. The Minister thinks it would be a good thing to do. I suppose he's looking to the next election.'

'Open the trout season early? You mean, before September the First?'

'That's the suggestion.'

'A very bad suggestion, if I may say so. The fish won't have finished spawning, and if they have they'll be in very poor condition. You could ruin the fishing for years, doing a thing like that. When does he want to open the season?'

'He suggests August 10th.' He paused. 'It's that girl, that relation of yours, who's at the bottom of this thing. I don't believe it would ever have entered his head but for her.'

'I think it's a terrible proposal. Quite irresponsible. I'm sure I don't know what the world's coming to . . .'

As member after member came into the room the debate continued and more joined in the discussion. Mr Sykes found that the general opinion was in favour of the change in date. 'After all,' said one, 'they'll go and fish in August if they can get there and the weather's fine, whether you like it or not. And you can't fine them or send them to gaol because there won't be time to bring the case on. May as well give a reasonable date, and make a virtue of necessity. Of course,' he added conscientiously, 'it'd be for this year only.'

A leading eye surgeon remarked, 'I think it's a very

good idea. If the fish are poor we don't have to take them; we can always put them back. Unless the season should be very early they won't take a fly; we'll have to use a spinner. But I'm in favour of it, all the same. When I go, I'd like it to be on a sunny day on the bank of the Delatite with a rod in my hand.'

Somebody said, 'Like the man they lost from the American submarine.'

'Yes, just like that. I think that fellow had the right idea.'

Mr Sykes, having taken a cross section of the most influential opinion of the city, went back to his office with an easier mind, rang up his Minister, and that afternoon drafted an announcement to be broadcast on the radio that would constitute one of those swift changes of policy to meet the needs of the time, easy to make in a small, highly educated country and very characteristic of Australia. Dwight Towers heard it that evening in the echoing, empty wardroom of HMAS *Sydney*, and marvelled, not connecting it in the least with his own conversation with the scientist a few days before. Immediately he began making plans to try out Junior's rod. Transport was going to be the difficulty, but difficulties were there to be overcome by the Supreme Commander of the US Naval Forces.

In what was left of Australia that year a relief of tension came soon after mid-winter. By the beginning of July, when Broken Hill and Perth went out, few people in Melbourne were doing any more work than they wanted to. The electricity supply continued uninterrupted, as did the supply of the essential foodstuffs, but fuel for fires and little luxuries now had to be schemed and sought for by a people who had little else to do. As the weeks went by, the population became noticeably more sober; there were still riotous parties, still drunks sleeping in the gutter, but far fewer than there had been earlier. And, like harbingers of the coming spring, one by one motor cars started to appear on the deserted roads.

It was difficult at first to say where they came from or where they got the petrol, for each case on investigation proved to be exceptional. Peter Holmes' landlord turned up in a Holden one day to remove firewood from the trees that had been felled, explaining awkwardly that he had retained a little of the precious fluid for cleaning clothes. A cousin in the Royal Australian Air Force came to visit them from Laverton aerodrome driving an MG, explaining that he had saved the petrol but there didn't seem to be much sense in saving it any longer; this was clearly nonsense, because Bill never saved anything. An engineer who worked at the Shell refinery at Corio said that he had managed to buy a little petrol on the black market in Fitzroy, but very properly refused to name the scoundrel who had sold it. Like a sponge squeezed by the pressure of circumstances, Australia began to drip a little petrol, and as the weeks went on towards August the drip became a trickle.

Peter Holmes took a can with him to Melbourne one day and visited John Osborne. That evening heard the engine of his Morris Minor for the first time in two years, clouds of black smoke emerging from the exhaust till he stopped the engine and took out the jets and hammered them a little smaller. Then he drove her out upon the road, with Mary, delighted, at his side and Jennifer upon her knee. 'It's just like having one's first car all over again!' she exclaimed. 'Peter, it's wonderful! Can you get any more, do you think?'

'We saved this petrol,' he told her. 'We saved it up. We've got a few more tins buried in the garden, but we're not telling anybody how much.'

'Not even Moira?'

'Lord, no. Her last of all.' He paused. 'Tyres are the snag now. I don't know what we're going to do about those.'

Next day he drove to Williamstown, in at the dockyard gates, and parked the Morris on the quayside by the practically deserted aircraft carrier. In the evening he drove home again.

His duties at the dockyard were now merely nominal. Work upon the submarine was going very slowly, and his presence was required upon the job no more than two days in each week, which fitted in well with the requirements of his little car. Dwight Towers was there most days in the morning, but he, too, had become mobile. The First Naval Member had sent for him one morning and, with poker face, had declared that it was only fitting that the Supreme Commander of the US Naval Forces should have transport at his disposal, and Dwight had found himself presented with a grey-painted Chevrolet with Leading Seaman Edgar as the driver. He used it principally for going to the club for lunch or driving out to Harkaway to walk beside the bullock as they spread the dung, while the Leading Seaman shovelled silage.

The last part of July was a very pleasant time for most people. The weather was seasonably bad with high winds and plenty of rain and a temperature down in the low forties, but men and women cast off the restraints that long had galled them. The weekly wage packet became of little value or importance; if you went into the works on Friday you would probably get it whether you had worked or not, and when you had it there was little you could do with it. In the butcher's shop the cash desk would accept money thrust at them, but didn't grieve much if it wasn't, and if the meat was there you took it. If it wasn't, you just went and looked for somewhere where there was some. There was all day to do it in.

On the high mountains the skiers skied weekdays and weekends alike. In their little garden, Mary and Peter Holmes laid out the new beds and built a fence around the vegetable garden, planting a passion fruit vine to climb all over it. They had never had so much time for gardening before, or made such progress. 'It's going to be beautiful,' she said contentedly. 'It's going to be the prettiest garden of its size in Falmouth.'

In the city mews John Osborne worked on the Ferrari with a small team of enthusiasts to help him. The Australian Grand Prix at that time was the premier motor race of the southern hemisphere, and it had been decided to advance the date of the race that year from November to August the 17th. On previous occasions the race had been held at Melbourne in the Albert Park, roughly corresponding to Central Park in New York or Hyde Park in London. The organizing club would have liked to race for the last time in Albert Park but the difficulties proved to be insuperable. It was clear from the outset that there would be a shortage of marshals and a shortage of labour to provide the most elementary safety precautions for the crowd of a hundred and fifty thousand people who might well be expected to attend. Nobody worried very much about the prospect of a car spinning off the course and killing a few spectators, or the prospect of permission to use the park for racing in future years being withheld. It seemed unlikely, however, that there would be sufficient marshals ever to get the crowds off the road and away from the path of the oncoming cars, and, unusual though the times might be, few of the drivers were prepared to drive straight into a crowd of onlookers at a hundred and twenty miles an hour. Racing motor cars are frail at those speeds, and a collision even with one person would put the car out of the race. It was decided regretfully that it was impracticable to run the Australian Grand Prix in Albert Park, and that the race would have to take place at the track at Tooradin.

The race in this way became a race for racing drivers only; in the prevailing difficulties of transport not very many spectators could be expected to drive forty miles out of the city to see it. Rather unexpectedly, it attracted an enormous entry of drivers. Everybody in Victoria and southern New South Wales who owned a fast car, new or old, seemed to have entered for the last Australian Grand Prix, and the total of entries came to about two hundred and eighty cars. So many cars could not be raced together with any justice to the faster cars, and for two weekends previous to the great day eliminating heats were held in the various classes. These heats were drawn by ballot, so that John Osborne found himself competing with a three-litre Maserati piloted by Jerry Collins, a couple of Jaguars, a Thunderbird, two Bugattis, three vintage Bentleys, and a terrifying concoction of a Lotus chassis powered by a blown Gipsy Queen aero engine of about three hundred horsepower and little forward view, built and raced by a young air mechanic called Sam Bailey and reputed to be very fast.

In view of the distance from the city there was only a small crowd of people disposed around the three mile course. Dwight Towers drove down in the official Chevrolet, picking up Moira Davidson and Peter and Mary Holmes upon the way. On that day there were five classes of heats, commencing with the smallest cars, each race being of fifty miles. Before the first race was over the organizers had put in a hurried call to Melbourne for two more ambulances, the two already allocated to the meeting being busy.

237

For one thing, the track was wet with rain, although it was not actually raining at the time of the first race. Six Lotuses competed with eight Coopers and five MGs, one of which was piloted by a girl, Miss Fay Gordon. The track was about three miles in length. A long straight with the pits in the middle led with a slight sinuosity to a left-hand turn of wide radius but 180 degrees in extent enclosing a sheet of water; this was called Lake Bend. Next came Haystack Corner, a right-hand turn of about 120 degrees, fairly sharp, and this led to The Safety Pin, a sharp left-hand hairpin with rather a blind turn on top of a little mound, so that you went up and came down again. The back straight was sinuous and fast with a left-hand bend at the end of it leading down a steep hill to a very sharp right-hand corner, called The Slide. From there a long, fast left-hand bend led back to the finishing straight.

From the start of the first heat it was evident that the racing was to be unusual. The race started with a scream that indicated that the drivers intended to show no mercy to their engines, their competitors, or themselves. Miraculously the cars all came round on the first lap, but after that the troubles started. An MG spun on Haystack Corner, left the road and found itself careering through the low scrub on the rough ground away from the circuit. The driver trod on it and swung his car round without stopping and regained the road. A Cooper coming up behind swerved to avoid collision with the MG, spun on the wet road, and was hit fair and square amid-ships by another Cooper coming up behind. The first driver was killed instantaneously and both cars piled up into a heap by the roadside, the second driver being flung clear with a broken collar bone and internal injuries. The MG driver, passing on the next time round, wondered quickly as he took the corner what had happened to cause that crash.

On the fifth lap a Lotus overtook Fay Gordon at the end of the finishing straight and spun on the wet road of Lake Bend, thirty yards in front of her. Another Lotus was passing on her right; the only escape for her was to go left. She left the track at ninety-five miles an hour, crossed the short strip of land before the lake in a desperate effort to turn right and so back to the track, broadsided in the scrub, and rolled over into the water. When the great cloud of spray subsided, her MG was upside-down ten yards from shore, the bottom of the rear wheels just above the surface. It was half an hour before the wading helpers managed to right the little car and get the body out.

On the thirteenth lap three cars tangled at The Slide and burned. Two of the drivers were only slightly injured and managed to extract the third with both legs broken before the fire took hold. Of nineteen starters, seven finished the race, the first two qualifying to run in the Grand Prix.

As the chequered flag fell for the winner, John Osborne lit a cigarette. 'Fun and games,' he said. His race was the last of the day.

Peter said thoughtfully, 'They're certainly racing to win . . .'

'Well, of course,' said the scientist. 'It's racing as it ought to be. If you buy it, you've got nothing to lose.'

'Except to smash up the Ferrari.'

John Osborne nodded. 'I'd be very sorry to do that.'

A little rain began to fall on them, wetting the track again. Dwight Towers stood a little way apart with Moira. 'Get into the car, honey,' he said. 'You'll get wet.'

She did not move. 'They can't go on in this rain, can they?' she asked. 'Not after all these accidents?'

'I wouldn't know,' he said. 'I'd say they might. After all, it's the same for everybody. They don't *have* to go so

239

fast they spin. And if they wait for a dry day this time of year they might wait, well, longer than they've got.'

'But it's awful,' she objected. 'Two people killed in the first race and about seven injured. They *can't* go on. It's like the Roman gladiators, or something.'

He stood in silence for a moment in the rain. 'Not quite like that,' he said at last. 'There isn't any audience. They don't have to do it.' He looked around. 'Apart from the drivers and their crews, I don't suppose there's five hundred people here. They haven't taken any money at a gate. They're doing it because they like to do it, honey.'

'I don't believe they do.'

He smiled. 'You go up to John Osborne and suggest he scratch his Ferrari and go home.' She was silent. 'Come on in the car and I'll pour you a brandy and soda.'

'A very little one, Dwight,' she said. 'If I'm going to watch this, I'll watch it sober.'

The next two heats produced nine crashes, four ambulance cases, but only one death, the driver of the bottom Austin-Healey in a pile up of four cars at The Safety Pin. The rain had eased to a fine, misty drizzle that did nothing to damp the spirits of the competitors. John Osborne had left his friends before the last race, and he was now in the paddock sitting in the Ferrari and warming it up, his pit crew around him. Presently he was satisfied and got out of the car, and stood talking and smoking with some of the other drivers. Don Harrison, the driver of a Jaguar, had a glass of whisky in his hand and a couple of bottles with more glasses on an upturned box beside him; he offered John a drink, but he refused it.

'I've got nothing to give away on you muggers,' he said, grinning. Although he had what was probably the fastest car on the circuit, he had almost the least experience of any of the drivers. He still raced the Ferrari with the three broad bands of tape across the back that indicated a novice driver; he was still very conscious that he did not know by instinct when he was about to spin. A spin always caught him unawares and came as a surprise. If he had known it, all the drivers were alike on these wet roads; none of them had much experience of driving under such conditions and his consciousness of inexperience was perhaps a better protection than their confidence.

When his crew pushed the Ferrari out on to the grid he found himself placed on the second line, in front of him the Maserati, the two Jaguars, and the Gipsy-Lotus, beside him the Thunderbird. He settled himself into his seat, revving his engine to warm up, fastening his safety belt, making his crash helmet and his goggles comfortable upon his head. In his mind was the thought: 'This is where I get killed.' Better than vomiting to death in a sick misery in less than a month's time. Better to drive like hell and go out doing what he wanted to. The big steering wheel was a delight to handle, the crack of the Ferrari's exhaust music to his ears. He turned and grinned at his pit crew in unalloyed pleasure, and then fixed his eyes upon the starter.

When the flag dropped he made a good start and got away well, weaving ahead of the Gipsy-Lotus as he changed up into third, and outdistancing the Thunderbird. He went into Lake Bend hard on the heels of the two Jaguars, but driving cautiously on the wet road with seventeen laps to go. Time enough to take chances in the last five laps. He stayed with the Jaguars past Haystack Corner, past The Safety Pin, and cautiously put his foot down on the sinuous back straight. Not hard enough, apparently, for with a roar and a crackle the Gipsy-Lotus passed him on the right, showering him with water, Sam Bailey driving like a madman.

He slowed a little while he wiped his goggles and followed on behind. The Gipsy-Lotus was wandering all over the road, harnessed only by the immensely quick reaction time of its young driver. John Osborne, watching, sensed disaster round it like an aura; better follow on at a safe distance for a while and see what happened. He shot a quick glance at the mirror; the Thunderbird was fifty yards behind, with the Maserati overtaking it. There was time to take it easy down The Slide, but after that he must step on it.

On entering the straight at the end of the first lap he saw that the Gipsy-Lotus had taken one of the Jaguars. He passed the pits at about a hundred and sixty miles an hour, making up upon the second Jaguar; with a car between him and the Gipsy-Lotus he felt safer. A glance in the mirror as he braked before Lake Bend showed that he had drawn well away from the two cars behind; if he could do that he could hold the fourth position for a lap or two and still go carefully upon the corners.

He did so till the sixth lap. By that time the Gipsy-Lotus was in the lead and the first four cars had lapped one of the Bentleys. As he accelerated away from The Slide he glanced in his mirror and in a momentary glimpse saw what appeared to be a most colossal mix-up at the corner. The Maserati and the Bentley seemed to be tangled broadside-on across the road, and the Thunderbird was flying through the air. He could not look again. Ahead of him, in the lead, the Gipsy-Lotus was trying to lap one of the Bugattis by synchronizing its desperate swerves at a hundred and forty miles an hour with the manoeuvre necessary for passing, and failing to do so. The two Jaguars were holding back at a discreet distance.

When he came round again to The Slide he saw that the shambles at the corner had involved two cars only;

the Thunderbird lay inverted fifty yards from the track and the Bentley stood with its rear end crushed and a great pool of petrol on the road. The Maserati was apparently still racing. He passed on, and as he entered his eighth lap it began to rain quite heavily. It was time to step on it.

So thought the leaders, for on that lap the Gipsy-Lotus was passed by one of the Jaguars, taking advantage of Sam Bailey's evident nervousness of his unstable car upon a corner. Both leaders now lapped a Bugatti, and a Bentley immediately after. The second Jaguar went to pass them on Haystack Corner with John Osborne close behind. What happened then was very, very swift. The Bugatti spun upon the corner and was hit by the Bentley, which was deflected into the path of the oncoming Jaguar, which rolled over twice and finished right-side up by the roadside without a driver. John Osborne had no time to stop and little to avoid; the Ferrari hit the Bugatti a glancing blow at about seventy miles an hour and came to a standstill by the roadside with a buckled near-side front wheel.

John Osborne was shaken, but unhurt. Don Harrison, the driver of the Jaguar who had offered him a drink before the race, was dying of multiple injuries in the scrub; he had been thrown from his car as it rolled and had then been run over by the Bentley. The scientist hesitated for a moment but there were people about; he tried the Ferrari. The engine started and the car moved forward, but the buckled wheel scrooped against the frame. He was out of the race, and out of the Grand Prix, and with a sick heart he waited till the Gipsy-Lotus weaved by and then crossed the track to see if he could help the dying driver.

While he was standing there, helpless, the Gipsy-Lotus passed again.

He stood there in the steady rain for several seconds before it struck him that there had been no other cars between the two transits of the Gipsy-Lotus. When it did so, he made a dash for the Ferrari. If in fact there was only one car left in the race he still had a chance for the Grand Prix; if he could struggle round the track to the pits he might yet change the wheel and get the second place. He toured on slowly, wrestling with the steering, while the rain ran down his neck and the Gipsy-Lotus passed a third time. The tyre burst at The Slide, where about six cars seemed to be tangled in a heap, and he went on on the rim, and reached the pits as the Lotus passed again.

The wheel change took his pit crew about thirty seconds, and a quick inspection showed little damage apart from panelling. He was off again several laps behind, and now one of the Bugattis detached itself from the chaos around The Slide and joined in. It was never a threat, however, and John Osborne toured around the course discreetly to win second place in the heat and a start in the Grand Prix. Of the eleven starters in the heat, eight had failed to complete the course and three drivers had been killed.

He swung his Ferrari into the paddock and stopped the engine, while his pit crew and his friends crowded round to congratulate him. He hardly heard them; his fingers were trembling with shock and the release of strain. He had only one thought in his mind, to get the Ferrari back to Melbourne and take down the front end; all was not well with the steering, though he had managed to complete the course. Something was strained or broken; she had pulled heavily towards the left in the concluding stages of the race.

Between the friends crowding round he saw the

upturned box where Don Harrison had parked his Jaguar, the glasses, the two whisky bottles. 'God,' he said to no one in particular, 'I'll have that drink with Don now.' He got out of the car and walked unsteadily to the box; one of the bottles was still nearly full. He poured a generous measure with a very little water, and then he saw Sam Bailey standing by the Gipsy-Lotus. He poured another drink and took it over to the winner, pushing through the crowd. 'I'm having this on Don,' he said. 'You'd better have one, too.'

The young man took it, nodded, and drank. 'How did you come off?' he asked. 'I saw you'd tangled.'

'Got round for a wheel change,' said the scientist thickly. 'She's steering like a drunken pig. Like a bloody Gipsy-Lotus.'

'My car steers all right,' the other said nonchalantly. 'Trouble is, she won't stay steered. You driving back to town?'

'If she'll make it.'

'I'd pinch Don's transporter. He's not going to need it.'

The scientist stared at him. 'That's an idea . . .' The dead driver had brought his Jaguar to the race on an old truck to avoid destroying tune by running on the road. The truck was standing not far from them in the paddock, unattended.

'I should nip in quick, before someone else gets it.'

John Osborne downed his whisky, shot back to his car, and galvanized his pit crew of enthusiasts with the new idea. Together they mustered willing hands to help and pushed the Ferrari up the steel ramps on to the tray body, lashing her down with ropes. Then he looked round uncertainly. A marshal passed and he stopped him. 'Are there any of Don Harrison's crew about?'

'I think they're all over with the crash. I know his wife's down there.'

He had been minded to drive off in the transporter with the Ferrari because Don would never need it again, nor would his Jaguar. To leave his pit crew and his wife without transport back to town, however, was another thing.

He left the paddock and started to walk down the track towards the Haystack, with Eddie Brooks, one of his pit crew, beside him. He saw a little group standing by the wreckage of the cars in the rain, one of them a woman. He had intended to talk to Don's pit crew, but when he saw the wife was dry-eyed he changed his mind, and went to speak to her.

'I was the driver of the Ferrari,' he said. 'I'm very sorry that this happened, Mrs Harrison.'

She inclined her head. 'You come up and bumped into them right at the end,' she said. 'It wasn't anything to do with you.'

'I know. But I'm very sorry.'

'Nothing for you to be sorry about,' she said heavily. 'He got it the way he wanted it to be. None of this being sick and all the rest of it. Maybe if he hadn't had that whisky . . . I dunno. He got it the way he wanted it to be. You one of his cobbers?'

'Not really. He offered me a drink before the race, but I didn't take it. I've just had it now.'

'You have? Well, good on you. That's the way Don would have wanted it. Is there any left?'

He hesitated. 'There was when I left the paddock. Sam Bailey had a go at it, and I did. Maybe the boys have finished up the bottles.'

She looked up at him. 'Say, what do you want? His car? They say it isn't any good.'

He glanced at the wrecked Jaguar. 'I shouldn't think

it is. No, what I wanted to do was to put my car on his transporter and get it back to town. The steering's had it, but I'll get her right for the Grand Prix.'

'You got a place, didn't you? Well, it's Don's transporter, but he'd rather have it work with cars that go than work with wrecks. All right, chum, you take it.'

He was a little taken aback. 'Where shall I return it to?'

'I won't be using it. You take it.'

He thought of offering money but rejected the idea; the time was past for that. 'That's very kind of you,' he said. 'It's going to make a big difference to me, having the use of that transporter.'

'Fine,' she said. 'You go right ahead and win that Grand Prix. Any parts you need from *that*' – she indicated the wrecked Jaguar – 'you take them, too.'

'How are you getting back to town?' he asked.

'Me? I'll wait and go with Don in the ambulance. But they say there's another load of hospital cases for each car to go first, so it'll probably be around midnight before we get away.'

There seemed to be nothing more that he could do for her. 'Can I take some of the pit crew back?'

She nodded, and spoke to a fat, balding man of fifty. He detached two youngsters to go back with John. 'Alfie here, he'll stay with me and see this all squared up,' she said dully. 'You go right ahead, mister, and win that Grand Prix.'

He went a little way aside and talked to Eddie Brooks, standing in the rain. 'Tyres are the same size as ours. Wheels are different, but if we took the hubs as well . . . That Maserati's crashed up by The Slide. We might have a look at that one, too. I believe that's got a lot of the same front-end parts as we have . . .'

247

They walked back to their newly acquired transporter and drove it back in the half light to Haystack Corner, and commenced the somewhat ghoulish task of stripping the dead bodies of the wrecked cars of anything that might be serviceable to the Ferrari. It was dark before they finished and they drove back to Melbourne in the rain.

8

In Mary Holmes' garden the first narcissi bloomed on the first day of August, the day the radio announced, with studied objectivity, cases of radiation sickness in Adelaide and Sydney. The news did not trouble her particularly; all news was bad, like wage demands, strikes, or war, and the wise person paid no attention to it. What *was* important was that it was a bright, sunny day; her first narcissi were in bloom, and the daffodils behind them were already showing flower buds. 'They're going to be a picture,' she said happily to Peter. 'There are so many of them. Do you think some of the bulbs can have sent up two shoots?'

'I shouldn't think so,' he replied. 'I don't think they do that. They split in two and make another bulb, or something.'

She nodded. 'We'll have to dig them up in the autumn, after they die down, and separate them. Then we'll get a lot more and put them along *here*. They're going to look marvellous in a year or two.' She paused in thought. 'We'll be able to pick some then, and have them in the house.'

One thing troubled her upon that perfect day, that Jennifer was cutting her first tooth, and was hot and fractious. Mary had a book called *Baby's First Year* which told her that this was normal, and nothing to worry about, but she was troubled all the same. 'I mean,' she said, 'they don't know everything, the people who write these books. And all babies aren't the same, anyway. She oughtn't to keep crying like this, ought she? Do you think we ought to get in Dr Halloran?'

'I shouldn't think so,' Peter said. 'She's chewing her rusk all right.'

'She's so *hot*, the poor little lamb.' She picked up the baby from her cot and started patting it on the back across her shoulder; the baby had intended that, and stopped yelling. Peter felt that he could almost hear the silence. 'I think she's probably all right,' he said. 'Just wants a bit of company.' He felt he couldn't stand much more of it, after a restless night with the child crying all the time and Mary getting in and out of bed to soothe it. 'Look, dear,' he said. 'I'm terribly sorry, but I've got to go up to the Navy Department. I've got a date in the Third Naval Member's office at eleven forty-five.'

'What about the doctor, though? Don't you think he ought to see her?'

'I wouldn't worry him. The book says she may be upset for a couple of days. Well, she's been going on for thirty-six hours now.' By God, she has, he thought.

'It might be something different — not teeth at all. Cancer, or something. After all, she can't tell us where the pain is . . .'

'Leave it till I get back,' he said. 'I should be back here around four o'clock, or five at the latest. Let's see how she is then.'

'All right,' she said reluctantly.

He took the petrol cans and put them in the car, and drove out on the road, glad to be out of it. He had no appointment in the Navy Department that morning but there would be no harm in looking in on them, if, indeed, there was anybody in the office. *Scorpion* was out of dry dock and back alongside the aircraft carrier, waiting for orders that might never come; he could go and have a look at her and, as a minor issue, fill up his petrol tank and cans.

On that fine morning there was no one in the Third Naval Member's office save for one Wren writer, prim, spectacled, and conscientious. She said that she was expecting Commander Mason on board any minute now. Peter said he might look in again, and went down to his car, and drove to Williamstown. He parked beside the aircraft carrier and walked up the gangway with his cans in hand, accepting the salute of the officer of the day. 'Morning,' he said. 'Is Commander Towers about?'

'I think he's down in *Scorpion*, sir.'

'And I want some juice.'

'Very good, sir. If you leave the cans here . . . Fill the tank as well?'

'If you would.' He went on through the cold, echoing, empty ship and down the gangplank to the submarine. Dwight Towers came up to the bridge deck as he stepped on board. Peter saluted him formally. 'Morning, sir,' he said. 'I came over to see what's doing, and to get some juice.'

'Plenty of juice,' said the American. 'Not much doing. I wouldn't say there would be now, not ever again. You haven't any news for me?'

Peter shook his head. 'I looked in at the Navy Department just now. There didn't seem to be anyone there, except one Wren.'

'I had better luck than you. I found a lieutenant there yesterday . . . Kind of running down.'

'There's not so long to run now, anyway.' They leaned

on the bridge rail; he glanced at the captain. 'You heard about Adelaide and Sydney?'

Dwight nodded. 'Sure. First it was months, and then it got to be weeks, and now I'd say it's getting down to days. How long are they figuring on now?'

'I haven't heard. I wanted to get in touch with John Osborne today and get the latest gen.'

'You won't find him in the office. He'll be working on that car. Say, that was quite a race.'

Peter nodded. 'Are you going down to see the next one – the Grand Prix itself? That's the last race ever, as I understand it. It's really going to be something.'

'Well, I don't know. Moira didn't like the last one so much. I think women look at things differently. Like boxing or wrestling.' He paused. 'You driving back to Melbourne now?'

'I was – unless you want me for anything, sir?'

'I don't want you. There's nothing to do here. I'll thumb a ride to town with you, if I may. My Leading Seaman Edgar hasn't shown up with the car today; I suppose he's running down, too. If you can wait ten minutes while I change this uniform I'll be with you.'

Forty minutes later they were talking to John Osborne in the garage in the mews. The Ferrari hung with its nose lifted high on chain blocks to the roof, its front end and steering dismantled. John was in an overall working on it with one mechanic; he had got it all so spotlessly clean that his hands were hardly dirty. 'It's very lucky we got those parts off the Maserati,' he said seriously. 'One of these wishbones was bent all to hell. But the forgings are the same; we've had to bore out a bit and fit new bushes. I wouldn't have liked to race her if we'd had to heat the old one and bend it straight. I mean, you never know what's going to happen after a repair like that.'

'I'd say you don't know what's going to happen anyway in this kind of racing,' said Dwight. 'When is the Grand Prix to be?'

'I'm having a bit of a row with them over that,' said the scientist. 'They've got it down for Saturday fortnight, the 17th, but I think that's too late. I think we ought to run it on Saturday week, the 10th.'

'Getting kind of close, is it?'

'Well, I think so. After all, they've got definite cases in Canberra now.'

'I hadn't heard of that. The radio said Adelaide and Sydney.'

'The radio's always about three days late. They don't want to create alarm and despondency until they've got to. But there's a suspect case in Albury today.'

'In Albury? That's only about two hundred miles north.'

'I know. I think Saturday fortnight is going to be too late.'

Peter asked, 'How long do you think we've got then, John?'

The scientist glanced at him. 'I've got it now. You've got it, we've all got it. This door, this spanner – everything's getting touched with radioactive dust. The air we breathe, the water that we drink, the lettuce in the salad, even the bacon and eggs. It's getting down now to the tolerance of the individual. Some people with less tolerance than others could quite easily be showing symptoms in a fortnight's time. Maybe sooner.' He paused. 'I think it's crazy to put off an important race like the Grand Prix till Saturday fortnight. We're having a meeting of the Committee this afternoon and I'm going to tell them so. We can't have a decent race if half the drivers have got diarrhoea and vomiting. It just means that the Grand Prix might be won

253

by the chap with the best tolerance to radioactivity. Well, that's not what we're racing for!'

'I suppose that's so,' said Dwight. He left them in the garage, for he had a date to lunch with Moira Davidson. John Osborne suggested lunch at the Pastoral Club, and presently he wiped his hands on a clean piece of rag, took off his overall, locked the garage, and they drove up through the city to the club.

As they went, Peter asked, 'How's your uncle getting on?'

'He's made a big hole in the port, him and his cobbers,' the scientist said. 'He's not quite so good, of course. We'll probably see him at lunch; he comes in most days now. Of course, it's made a difference to him now that he can come in in his car.'

'Where does he get his petrol from?'

'God knows. The Army, probably. Where does anybody get his petrol from, these days?' He paused. 'I *think* he'll stay the course, but I wouldn't bank on it. The port'll probably give him longer than most of us.'

'The port?'

The other nodded. 'Alcohol, taken internally, seems to increase the tolerance to radioactivity. Didn't you know that?'

'You mean, if you get pickled you last longer?'

'A few days. With Uncle Douglas it's a toss-up which'll kill him first. Last week I thought the port was winning, but when I saw him yesterday he looked pretty good.'

They parked the car and went into the club. They found Sir Douglas Froude sitting in the garden-room, for the wind was cold. A glass of sherry was on the table by him and he was talking to two old friends. He made an effort to get to his feet when he saw them, but abandoned it at John's request. 'Don't get about so well as I used to, once,' he said. 'Come, pull a chair up, and have some of this sherry. We're down to about fifty bottles now of the Amontillado. Push that bell.'

John Osborne did so, and they drew up chairs. 'How are you feeling now, sir?'

'So-so. So-so. That doctor was probably right. He said that if I went back to my old habits I shouldn't last longer than a few months, and I shan't. But nor will he, and nor will you.' He chuckled. 'I hear you won that motor race that you were going in for.'

'I didn't win it – I was second. It means I've got a place in the Grand Prix.'

'Well, don't go and kill yourself. Although, I'm sure, it doesn't seem to matter very much if you do. Tell me, somebody was saying that they've got it in Cape Town. Do you think that's true?'

His nephew nodded. 'That's true enough. They've had it for some days. We're still in radio communication, though.'

'So they've got it before us?'

'That's true.'

'That means that all of Africa is out, or will be out, before we get it here?'

John Osborne grinned. 'It's going to be a pretty near thing. It looks as though all Africa might be gone in a week or so.' He paused. 'It seems to go quite quickly at the end, so far as we can ascertain. It's a bit difficult, because when more than half the people in a place are dead the communications usually go out, and then you don't quite know what's happening. All services are usually stopped by then, and food supplies. The last half seem to go quite quickly . . . But, as I say, we don't really know what does happen, in the end.'

'Well, I think that's a good thing,' the General said

255

robustly. 'We'll find out soon enough.' He paused. 'So all of Africa is out. I've had some good times there, back in the days before the First War, when I was a subaltern. But I never did like that apartheid . . . Does that mean that we're going to be the last?'

'Not quite,' his nephew said. 'We're going to be the last major city. They've got cases now in Buenos Aires and Montevideo, and they've got a case or two in Auckland. After we're gone Tasmania may last another fortnight, and the South Island of New Zealand. The last of all to die will be the Indians in Tierra del Fuego.'

'The Antarctic?'

The scientist shook his head. 'There's nobody there now, so far as we know.' He smiled. 'Of course, that's not the end of life upon the earth. You mustn't think that. There'll be life here in Melbourne long after we've gone.'

They stared at him. 'What life?' Peter asked.

He grinned broadly. 'The rabbit. That's the most resistant animal we know about.'

The General pushed himself upright in his chair, his face suffused with anger. 'You mean to say the rabbit's going to live longer than we do?'

'That's right. About a year longer. It's got about twice the resistance that we've got. There'll be rabbits running about Australia and eating all the feed next year.'

'You're telling me the bloody rabbit's going to put it across us, after all? They'll be alive and kicking when we're all dead?'

John Osborne nodded. 'Dogs will outlive us. Mice will last a lot longer, but not so long as rabbits. So far as we can see, the rabbit has them all licked – he'll be the last.' He paused. 'They'll all go in the end, of course. There'll be nothing left alive here by the end of the next year.'

The General sank back in his chair. 'The rabbit! After all we've done, and all we've spent in fighting him – to know he's going to win out in the end!' He turned to Peter. 'Just press that bell beside you. I'm going to have a brandy and soda before going in to lunch. We'd all better have a brandy and soda after that.'

In the restaurant Moira Davidson and Dwight settled at a table in a corner, and ordered lunch. Then she said, 'What's troubling you, Dwight?'

He took up a fork and played with it. 'Not very much.'

'Tell me.'

He raised his head. 'I've got another ship in my command – USS *Swordfish* at Montevideo. It's getting hot around those parts right now. I radioed the captain three days ago, asking him if he thought it practical to leave and sail his vessel over here.'

'What did he say?'

'He said it wasn't. Shore associations, he called them. What he meant was girls, same as *Scorpion*. Said he'd try and come if there was a compelling reason, but he'd be leaving half his crew behind.' He raised his head. 'There'd be no point in coming that way,' he told her. 'He wouldn't be operational.'

'Did you tell him to stay there?'

He hesitated. 'Yes,' he said at last. 'I ordered him to take *Swordfish* out beyond the twelve mile limit and sink her on the high seas, in deep water.' He stared at the prongs of the fork. 'I dunno if I did the right thing or not,' he said. 'I thought that was what the Navy Department would want me to do – not to leave a ship like that, full of classified gear, kicking around in another country. Even if there wasn't anybody there.' He glanced at her. 'So now the US

Navy's been reduced again,' he said. 'From two ships down to one.'

They sat in silence for a minute. 'Is that what you're going to do with *Scorpion*?' she asked at last.

'I think so. I'd have liked to take her back to the United States, but it wouldn't be practical. Too many shore associations, like he said.'

Their lunch came. 'Dwight,' she said when the waiter had departed. 'I had an idea.'

'What's that, honey?'

'They're opening the trout fishing early this year, on Saturday week. I was wondering if you'd like to take me up into the mountains for the weekend.' She smiled faintly. 'For the fishing, Dwight – fishing to fish. Not for anything else. It's lovely up by Jamieson.'

He hesitated for a moment. 'That's the day that John Osborne thinks they'll be running the Grand Prix.'

She nodded. 'So I thought. Would you rather see that?'

He shook his head. 'Would you?'

'No. I don't want to see any more people get killed. We're going to see enough of that in a week or two.'

'I feel that way about it, too. I don't want to see that race, and maybe see John get killed. I'd rather go fishing.' He glanced at her and met her eyes. 'There's just one thing, honey. I wouldn't want to go if it was going to mean that you'd get hurt.'

'I shan't get hurt,' she said. 'Not in the way you mean.'

He stared across the crowded restaurant. 'I'm going home quite soon,' he said. 'I've been away a long time, but it's nearly over now. You know the way it is. I've got a wife at home I love, and I've played straight with her the two years that I've been away. I wouldn't want to spoil that now, these few last days.'

'I know,' she said. 'I've known that all the time.' She was silent for a minute, and then she said, 'You've been very good for me, Dwight. I don't know what would have happened if you hadn't come along. I suppose half a loaf is better than no bread, when you're starving.'

He wrinkled his brows. 'I didn't get that, honey.'

'It doesn't matter. I wouldn't want to start a smutty love affair when I'm dying in a week or ten days' time. I've got some standards too – now, anyway.'

He smiled at her. 'We could try out Junior's rod . . .'

'That's what I thought you'd want to do. I've got a little fly rod I could bring but I'm no good.'

'Go any flies and leaders?'

'We call them casts. I'm not quite sure. I'll have to look around and see what I can find at home.'

'We'd go by car, would we? How far is it?'

'I think we'd want petrol for about five hundred miles. But you don't have to worry about that. I asked Daddy if I might borrow the Customline. He's got it out and running, and he's got nearly a hundred gallons of petrol tucked away in the hayshed behind the hay.'

He smiled again. 'You think of everything. Say, where would we stay?'

'I think at the hotel,' she said. 'It's only a small, country place, but I think it's the best bet. I could borrow a cottage, but it wouldn't have been slept in for two years, and we'd spend all our time in housekeeping. I'll ring up and make a booking at the hotel. For two rooms,' she said.

'Okay. I'll have to chase that Leading Seaman Edgar and see if I can use my car without taking him along. I'm not just sure if I'm allowed to drive myself.'

'That's not terribly important now, is it? I mean, you could just take it and drive it.'

He shook his head. 'I wouldn't want to do that.'

'But, Dwight, why not? I mean, it doesn't matter – we can go in the Customline. But if that car's been put at your disposal, you can use it, surely. We're all going to be dead in a fortnight's time. Then nobody will be using it.'

'I know . . .' he said. 'It's just that I'd like to do things right, up till the end. If there's an order I'll obey it. That's the way I was trained, honey, and I'm not changing now. If it's against the rules for an officer to take a service car and drive it up into the mountains for a weekend with a girl, then I'll not do it. There'll be no alcoholic liquor on board *Scorpion*, not even in the last five minutes.' He smiled. 'That's the way it is, so let me buy you another drink.'

'I can see that it will have to be the Customline. You're a very difficult man – I'm glad I'm not a sailor serving under you. No, I won't have a drink, thanks, Dwight. I've got my first test this afternoon.'

'Your first test?'

She nodded. 'I've got to try and take dictation at fifty words a minute. You've got to be able to do that and type it out without more than three mistakes in shorthand and three in typing. It's very difficult.'

'I'd say it might be. You're getting to be quite a short-hand typist.'

She smiled faintly. 'Not at fifty words a minute. You have to be able to do a hundred and twenty if you're ever going to be any good.' She raised her head. 'I'd like to come and see you in America one day,' she said. 'I want to meet Sharon – if she'd want to meet me.'

'She'll want to meet you,' he said. 'I'd say she's kind of grateful to you now, already.'

She smiled faintly. 'I don't know. Women are funny about men . . . If I came to Mystic, would there be a shorthand typing school where I could finish off my course?'

He thought for a minute. 'Not in Mystic itself,' he said. 'There's plenty of good business colleges in New London. That's only about fifteen miles away.'

'I'll just come for an afternoon,' she said thoughtfully. 'I want to see Helen jumping round upon that Pogo stick. But after that, I think I'd better come back here.'

'Sharon would be very disappointed if you did that, honey. She'd want you to stay.'

'That's what *you* think. I shall want a bit of convincing on that point.'

He said, 'I think things may be kind of different by that time.'

She nodded slowly. 'Possibly. I'd like to think they would be. Anyway, we'll find out pretty soon.' She glanced at her wrist watch. 'I must go, Dwight, or I'll be late for my test.' She gathered up her gloves and her bag. 'Look, I'll tell Daddy that we'd like to take the Customline and about thirty gallons of petrol.'

He hesitated. 'I'll find out about my car. I don't like taking your father's car away for all that time, with all that gas.'

'He won't be using it,' she said. 'He's had it on the road for a fortnight, but I think he's only used it twice. There's so much that he wants to see done on the farm while there's still time.'

'What's he working on now?'

'The fence along the wood – the one in the forty acre. He's digging post-holes to put up a new one. It's about twenty chains long. That's going to mean nearly a hundred holes.'

'There's not so much to do at Williamstown. I could come out and lend a hand, if he'd like that.'

She nodded. 'I'll tell him. Give you a ring tonight, at about eight o'clock?'

'Fine,' he said. He escorted her to the door. 'Good luck with the test.'

He had no engagement for that afternoon. He stood in the street outside the restaurant after she had left him, completely at a loose end. Inactivity was unusual for him, and irksome. At Williamstown there was absolutely nothing for him to do; the aircraft carrier was dead and his ship all but dead. Although he had received no orders, he knew that now she would never cruise again; for one thing, with South America and South Africa out there was now nowhere much for them to cruise to, unless it were New Zealand. He had given half of his ship's company leave, each half alternating a week at a time; of the other half he kept only about ten men on duty for maintenance and cleaning in the submarine, permitting the rest daily leave on shore. No signals now arrived for him to deal with; once a week he signed a few stores requisitions as a matter of form, though the stores they needed were supplied from dockyard sources with a disregard of paper work. He would not admit it, but he knew that his ship's working life was over, as his own was. He had nothing to replace it.

He thought of going to the Pastoral Club, and abandoned the idea; there would be no occupation for him there. He turned and walked towards the motor district of the town, where he would find John Osborne working on his car; there might be work there of the sort that interested him. He must be back at Williamstown in time to receive Moira's call at about eight o'clock; that was his next appointment. He would go out next day and help her father with that fence, and he looked forward to the labour and the occupation.

On his way down town he stopped at a sports shop and asked for flies and casts. 'I'm sorry, sir,' the man said. 'Not a cast in the place, and not a fly. I've got a few hooks left, if you can tie your own. Sold clean out of everything the last few days, on account of the season opening, and there won't be any more coming in now, either. Well, as I said to the wife, it's kind of satisfactory. Get the stock down to a minimum before the end. It's how the accountants would like to see it, though I don't suppose they'll take much interest in it now. It's a queer turn-out.'

He walked on through the city. In the motor district there were still cars in the windows, still motor mowers, but the windows were dirty and the stores closed, the stock inside covered in dust and dirt. The streets were dirty now and littered with paper and spoilt vegetables; it was evidently some days since the street cleaners had operated. The trams still ran, but the whole city was becoming foul and beginning to smell; it reminded the American of an oriental city in the making. It was raining a little and the skies were grey; in one or two places the street drains were choked, and great pools stood across the road.

He came to the mews and to the open garage door. John Osborne was working with two others, and Peter Holmes was there, his uniform coat off, washing strange, nameless parts of the Ferrari in a bath of kerosene, more valuable at that time than mercury. There was an atmosphere of cheerful activity in the garage that warmed his heart.

'I thought we might see you,' said the scientist. 'Come for a job?'

'Sure,' said Dwight. 'This city gives me a pain. You got anything I can do?'

'Yes. Help Bill Adams fit new tyres on every wheel you can find.' He indicated a stack of brand new racing tyres; there seemed to be wire wheels everywhere.

Dwight took his coat off thankfully. 'You've got a lot of wheels.'

'Eleven, I think. We got the ones off the Maserati – they're the same as ours. I want a new tyre on every wheel we've got. Bill works for Goodyear and he knows the way they go, but he needs somebody to help.'

The American, rolling up his sleeves, turned to Peter. 'He got you working, too.'

The naval officer nodded. 'I'll have to go before very long. Jennifer's teething, and been crying for two bloody days. I told Mary I was sorry I'd got to go on board today, but I'd be back by five.'

Dwight smiled. 'Left her to hold the baby.'

Peter nodded. 'I got her a garden rake and a bottle of dillwater. But I must be back by five.'

He left half an hour later, and got into his little car, and drove off down the road to Falmouth. He got back to his flat on time, and found Mary in the lounge, the house miraculously quiet. 'How's Jennifer?' he asked.

She put her finger to her lips. 'She's sleeping,' she whispered. 'She went off after dinner, and she hasn't woken up since.'

He went towards the bedroom, and she followed him. 'Don't wake her,' she whispered.

'Not on your life,' he whispered back. He stood looking down at the child, sleeping quietly. 'I don't think she's got cancer,' he remarked.

They went back into the lounge, closing the door quietly behind them, and he gave her his presents. 'I've got dillwater,' she said, 'masses of it, and anyway she doesn't have it now. You're about three months out of date. The rake's lovely. It's just what we want for getting all the leaves and twigs up off the lawn. I was trying to pick them up by hand yesterday, but it breaks your back.'

They got short drinks, and presently she said, 'Peter, now that we've got petrol, couldn't we have a motor mower?'

'They cost quite a bit,' he objected, almost automatically.

'That doesn't matter so much now, does it? And with the summer coming on, it *would* be a help. I know we've not got very much lawn to mow, but it's an awful chore with the hand mower, and you may be away at sea again. If we had a very *little* motor mower that I could start myself. Or an electric one. Doris Haynes has an electric one, and it's no trouble to start at all.'

'She's cut its cord in two at least three times, and each time she does that she darn nearly electrocutes herself.'

'You don't have to do that if you're careful. I think it would be a lovely thing to have.'

She lived in the dream world of unreality, or else she would not admit reality; he did not know. In any case, he loved her as she was. It might never be used, but it would give her pleasure to have it. 'I'll see if I can find one next time I go up to town,' he said. 'I know there are plenty of motor mowers, but I'm not just sure about an electric one.' He thought for a moment. 'I'm afraid the electric ones may all be gone. People would have bought them when there wasn't any petrol.'

She said, 'A little motor one would do, Peter. I mean, you could show me how to start it.'

He nodded. 'They're not much trouble, really.'

'Another thing we ought to have,' she said, 'is a garden seat. You know – one that you can leave outside all winter, and sit on whenever it's a nice fine day. I was thinking, how nice it would be if we had a garden seat in that sheltered corner just by the arbutus. I think we'd use it an awful lot next summer. Probably use it all the year round, too.'

He nodded. 'Not a bad idea.' It would never be used next summer, but let that go. Transport would be a difficulty; the only way he could transport a garden seat with the Morris Minor would be by putting it on the roof, and that might scratch the enamel unless he padded it very well. 'We'll get the motor mower first, and then see what the bank looks like.'

He drove her up to Melbourne the next day to look for a motor mower; they went with Jennifer in her carrying basket on the back seat. It was some weeks since she had been in the city, and its aspect startled and distressed her. 'Peter,' she said, 'what's the matter with everything? It's all so dirty, and it smells horrid.'

'I suppose the street cleaners have stopped working,' he observed.

'But why should they do that? Why aren't they working? Is there a strike, or something?'

'Everything's just slowing down,' he said. 'After all, I'm not working.'

'That's different,' she said. 'You're in the Navy.' He laughed. 'No, what I mean is, you go to sea for months and months, and then you go on leave. Street cleaners don't do that. They go on all the time. At least, they ought to.'

He could not elucidate it any further for her, and they drove on to the big hardware store. It had only a few customers, and very few assistants. They left the baby in the car and went through to the gardening department, and searched some time for an assistant. 'Motor mowers?' he said. 'You'll find a few in the next hall, through that archway. Look them over and see if what you want is there.'

They did so, and picked a little twelve-inch mower. Peter looked at the price tag, picked up the mower, and went to find the assistant. 'I'll take this one,' he said.

'Okay,' said the man. 'Good little mower, that.' He grinned sardonically. 'Last you a lifetime.'

'Forty-seven pounds ten,' said Peter. 'Can I pay by cheque?'

'Pay by orange peel for all I care,' the man said. 'We're closing down tonight.'

The naval officer went over to a table and wrote his cheque; Mary was left talking to the salesman. 'Why are you closing down?' she asked. 'Aren't people buying things?'

He laughed shortly. 'Oh – they come in and they buy. Not much to sell them now. But I'm not going on right up till the end, same with all the staff. We had a meeting yesterday, and then we told the management. After all, there's only about a fortnight left to go. They're closing down tonight.'

Peter came back and handed his cheque to the salesman. 'Okey-doke,' the man said. 'I don't know if they'll ever pay it in without a staff up in the office. Maybe I'd better give you a receipt in case they get on to your tail next year . . .' He scribbled a receipt and turned to another customer.

Mary shivered. 'Peter, let's get out of this and go home. It's horrid here, and everything smells.'

'Don't you want to stay up here for lunch?' He had thought she would enjoy the little outing.

She shook her head. 'I'd rather go home now, and have lunch there.'

They drove in silence out of the city and down to the bright little seaside town that was their home. Back in their apartment on the hill she regained a little of her poise; here were the familiar things she was accustomed to, the cleanness that was her pride, the carefully tended little garden, the clean wide view out over the bay. Here was security.

After lunch, smoking before they did the washing up, she said, 'I don't think I want to go to Melbourne again, Peter.'

He smiled. 'Getting a bit piggy, isn't it?'

'It's horrible,' she said vehemently. 'Everything shut up, and dirty, and stinking. It's as if the end of the world had come already.'

'It's pretty close, you know,' he said.

She was silent for a moment. 'I know; that's what you've been telling me all along.' She raised her eyes to his. 'How far off is it, Peter?'

'About a fortnight,' he said. 'It doesn't happen with a click, you know. People start getting ill, but not all on the same day. Some people are more resistant than others.'

'But everybody gets it, don't they?' she asked in a low tone. 'I mean, in the end.'

He nodded. 'Everybody gets it, in the end.'

'How much difference is there in people? I mean, when they get it?'

He shook his head. 'I don't really know. I think everybody would have got it in three weeks.'

'Three weeks from now, or three weeks after the first case?'

'Three weeks after the first case, I mean,' he said. 'But I don't really know.' He paused. 'It's possible to get it slightly and get over it,' he said. 'But then you get it again ten days or a fortnight later.'

She said, 'There's no guarantee, then, that you and I would get it at the same time? Or Jennifer? We might any of us get it, any time?'

He nodded. 'That's the way it is. We've just got to take it as it comes. After all, it's what we've always had to face,

268

only we've never faced it, because we're young. Jennifer might always have died first, of the three of us, or I might have died before you. There's nothing much that's new about it.'

'I suppose not,' she said. 'I did hope it all might happen on one day.'

He took her hand. 'It may quite well do so,' he said. 'But – we'd be lucky.' He kissed her. 'Let's do the washing up.' His eye fell on the lawn mower. 'We can mow the lawn this afternoon.'

'The grass is all wet,' she said sadly. 'It'll make it rusty.'

'Then we'll dry it in front of the fire in the lounge,' he promised her. 'I won't let it get rusty.'

Dwight Towers spent the weekend with the Davidsons at Harkaway, working from dawn till dusk each day on the construction of the fences. The hard physical work was a relief from all his tensions, but he found his host to be a worried man. Someone had told him about the resistance of the rabbit to radioactive infection. The rabbit did not worry him a great deal, for Harkaway had always been remarkably free from rabbits, but the relative immunity of the furred animals raised questions in regard to his beef cattle, and to these he had found no answer.

He unburdened himself one evening to the American. 'I never thought of it,' he said. 'I mean, I assumed the Aberdeen Angus, they'd die at the same time as us. But now it looks as though they'll last a good while longer. How much longer they'll last – that I can't find out. Apparently there's been no research done on it. But as it is, of course, I'm feeding out both hay and silage, and up here we go on feeding out until the end of September in an average year – about half a bale of hay a beast each day. I find you have to do that if you're going to keep them prime.

Well, I can't see how to do it if there's going to be no one here. It really is a problem.'

'What would happen if you opened the haybarn to them, and let them take it as they want it?'

'I thought of that, but they'd never get the bales undone. If they did, they'd trample most of it underfoot and spoil it.' He paused. 'I've been puzzling to think out if there isn't some way we could do it with a time clock and an electric fence . . . But any way you look at it, it means putting out a month's supply of hay into the open paddock, in the rain. I don't know what to do . . .'

He got up. 'Let me get you a whisky.'

'Thank you – a small one.' The American reverted to the problem of the hay. 'It certainly is difficult. You can't even write to the papers and find out what anybody else is doing.'

He stayed with the Davidsons until the Tuesday morning, and then went back to Williamstown. At the dockyard his command was beginning to disintegrate, in spite of everything that the executive and the Chief of the Boat had been able to do. Two men had not returned from leave and one was reported to have been killed in a street brawl at Geelong, but there was no confirmation. There were eleven cases of men drunk on return from leave waiting for his jurisdiction and he found these very difficult to deal with. Restriction of leave when there was no work to do aboard and only about a fortnight left to go did not seem to be the answer. He left the culprits confined in the brig of the aircraft carrier while they sobered up and while he thought about it; then he had them lined up before him on the quarterdeck.

'You men can't have it both ways,' he told them. 'We've none of us got long to go now, you or me. As of today, you're members of the ship's company of USS *Scorpion*, and that's the last ship of the US Navy in commission. You can stay as part of the ship's company, or you can get a dishonourable discharge.'

He paused. 'Any man coming aboard drunk or late from leave, from this time on, will get discharged next day. And when I say discharged, I mean dishonourable discharge, and I mean it quick. I'll strip the uniform off you right there and then and put you outside the dockyard gates as a civilian in your shorts, and you can freeze and rot in Williamstown for all the US Navy cares. Hear that, and think it over. Dismissed.'

He got one case next day, and turned the man outside the dockyard gates in shirt and underpants to fend for himself. He had no more trouble of that sort.

He left the dockyard early on the Friday morning in the Chevrolet driven by his Leading Seaman, and went to the garage in the mews off Elizabeth Street in the city. He found John Osborne working on the Ferrari, as he had expected; the car stood roadworthy and gleaming, to all appearances ready to race there and then. Dwight said, 'Say, I just called in as I was passing by to say I'm sorry that I won't be there to see you win tomorrow. I've got another date up in the mountains, going fishing.'

The scientist nodded. 'Moira told me. Catch a lot of fish. I don't think there'll be many people there this time except competitors and doctors.'

'I'd have thought there would be, for the Grand Prix.'

'It may be the last weekend in full health for a lot of people. They've got other things they want to do.'

'Peter Holmes – he'll be there?'

John Osborne shook his head. 'He's going to spend it gardening.' He hesitated. 'I oughtn't to be going really.'

'You don't have a garden.'

The scientist smiled wryly. 'No, but I've got an old

mother, and she's got a Pekinese. She's just woken up to the fact that little Ming's going to outlive her by several months, and now she's worried stiff what's going to happen to him . . .' He paused. 'It's the hell of a time, this. I'll be glad when it's all over.'

'End of the month, still?'

'Sooner than that for most of us.' He said something in a low tone, and added, 'Keep that under your hat. It's going to be tomorrow afternoon for me.'

'I hope that's not true,' said the American. 'I kind of want to see you get that cup.'

The scientist glanced lovingly at the car. 'She's fast enough,' he said. 'She'd win it if she had a decent driver. But it's me that's the weak link.'

'I'll keep my fingers crossed for you.'

'Okay. Bring me back a fish.'

The American left the mews and went back to his car, wondering if he would see the scientist again. He said to his Leading Seaman, 'Now drive out to Mr Davidson's farm at Harkaway, near Berwick. Where you've taken me once before.'

He sat in the back seat of the car fingering the little rod as they drove out into the suburbs, looking at the streets and houses that they passed in the grey light of the winter day. Very soon, perhaps in a month's time, there would be no one here, no living creatures but the cats and dogs that had been granted a short reprieve. Soon they too would be gone; summers and winters would pass by and these houses and these streets would know them. Presently, as time passed, the radio-activity would pass also; with a cobalt half-life of about five years these streets and houses would be habitable again in twenty years at the latest, and probably much sooner than that. The human race was to be wiped out and the world made clean again for wiser occupants without undue delay. Well, probably that made sense.

He got to Harkaway in the middle of the morning; the Ford was in the yard, the boot full of petrol cans. Moira was ready for him, a little suitcase stowed on the back seat with a good deal of fishing gear. 'I thought we'd get away before lunch and have sandwiches on the road,' she said. 'The days are pretty short.'

'Suits me,' he said. 'You got sandwiches?'

She nodded. 'And beer.'

'Say, you think of everything.' He turned to the grazier. 'I feel kind of mean taking your car like this,' he said. 'I could take the Chev, if you'd rather.'

Mr Davidson shook his head. 'We went into Melbourne yesterday. I don't think we'll be going again. It's too depressing.'

The American nodded. 'Getting kind of dirty.'

'Yes. No, you take the Ford. There's a lot of petrol might as well be used up, and I don't suppose that I'll be needing it again. There's too much to do here.'

Dwight transferred his gear into the Ford and sent his Leading Seaman back to the dockyard with the Chev. 'I don't suppose he'll go there,' he said reflectively as the car moved off. 'Still, we go through the motions.'

They got into the Ford. Moira said, 'You drive.'

'No,' he replied. 'You'd better drive. I don't know the way, and maybe I'd go hitting something on the wrong side of the road.'

'It's two years since I drove,' she said. 'But it's your neck.' They got in and she found first gear after a little exploration, and they moved off down the drive.

It pleased her to be driving again, pleased her very much indeed. The acceleration of the car gave her a sense of freedom, of escape from the restraints of her daily life. They went by side roads through the Dandenong mountains spattered with guest houses and residences, and stopped for lunch not far from Lilydale beside a rippling stream. The day had cleared up and it was now sunny, with white clouds against a bright blue sky.

They eyed the stream professionally as they ate their sandwiches. 'It's muddy kind of water,' said Dwight. 'I suppose that's because it's early in the year.'

'I think so,' the girl said. 'Daddy said it would be too muddy for fly fishing. He said you might do all right with a spinner, but he advised me to kick about upon the bank until I found a worm and dab about with that.'

The American laughed. 'I'd say there's some sense in that, if the aim is to catch fish. I'll stick to spinner for a time, at any rate, because I want to see that this rod handles right.'

'I'd like to catch *one* fish,' the girl said a little wistfully. 'Even if it's such a dud one that we put it back. I think I'll try with worm unless the water's a lot clearer up at Jamieson.'

'It might be clearer high up in the mountains, with the melting snow.'

She turned to him. 'Do fish live longer than we're going to? Like dogs?'

He shook his head. 'I wouldn't know, honey.'

They drove on to Warburton and took the long, winding road up through the forests to the heights. They emerged a couple of hours later on the high ground at Matlock; here there was snow upon the road and on the wooded mountains all around; the world looked cold and bleak. They dropped down into a valley to the little town of Woods Point and then up over another watershed. From there a twenty mile run through the undulating, pleasant valley of the Goulburn brought them to the Jamieson hotel just before dusk.

The American found the hotel to be a straggling collection of somewhat tumbledown single-storey wooden buildings, some of which dated from the earliest settlement of the State. It was well that they had booked rooms, for the place was crowded with fishermen. More cars were parked outside it than ever in the palmiest days of peace time; inside, the bar was doing a roaring trade. They found the landlady with some difficulty, her face aglow with excitement. As she showed them their rooms, small and inconvenient and badly furnished, she said, 'Isn't this lovely, having all you fishermen here again? You can't think what it's been like the last two years, with practically no one coming here except on pack horse trips. But this is just like old times. Have you got a towel of your own? Oh well, I'll see if I can find one for you. But we're so *full*.' She dashed off in a flurry of pleasure.

The American looked after her. 'Well,' he said, 'she's having a good time, anyway. Come on, honey, and I'll buy you a drink.'

They went to the crowded bar-room, with a boarded, sagging ceiling, a huge fire of logs in the grate, a number of chromium-plated chairs and tables, and a seething mass of people.

'What'll I get you, honey?'

'Brandy,' she shouted above the din. 'There's only one thing to do here tonight, Dwight.'

He grinned, and forced his way through the crowd towards the bar. He came back in a few minutes, struggling, with a brandy and a whisky. They looked around for chairs, and found two at a table where two earnest men in shirt sleeves were sorting tackle. They looked up and nodded as Dwight and Moira joined them. 'Fish for breakfast,' said one.

'Getting up early?' asked Dwight.

The other glanced at him. 'Going to bed late. The season opens at midnight.'

He was interested. 'You're going out then?'

'If it's not actually snowing. Best time to fish.' He held up a huge white fly tied on a small hook. 'That's what I use. That's what gets them. Put a shot or two on it, and sink it down, and then cast well across. Never fails.'

'It does with me,' his companion said. 'I like a little frog. You get alongside a pool you know about two in the morning with a little frog, and put the hook just through the skin on his back and cast him across and let him swim about . . . That's what I do. You going out tonight?'

Dwight glanced at the girl, and smiled. 'I guess not,' he said. 'We just fish around in daylight – we're not in your class. We don't catch much.'

The other nodded. 'I used to be like that. Look at the birds and the river and the sun upon the ripples, and not care much what you caught. I do that sometimes. But then I got to this night fishing, and that's really something.' He glanced at the American. 'There's a ruddy great monster of a fish in a pool down just below the bend that I've been trying to get for the last two years. I had him on a frog the year before last, and he took out most of my line and then broke me. And then I had him on again last year, on a sort of doodlebug in the late evening, and he broke me again – brand new, o.x. nylon.. He's twelve pounds if he's an ounce. I'm going to get him this time if I've got to stay up all of every night until the end.'

The American leaned back to talk to Moira. 'You want to go out at two in the morning?'

She laughed. 'I'll want to go to bed. You go if you'd like to.'

He shook his head. 'I'm not that kind of fisherman.'

'Just the drinking kind,' she said. 'I'll toss you who goes and battles for the next drink.'

'I'll get you another,' he said.

She shook her head. 'Just stay where you are and learn something about fishing. I'll get you one.'

She struggled through the crowd to the bar carrying the glasses, and came back presently to the table by the fireside. Dwight got up to meet her, and as he did so his sports jacket fell open. She handed him the glass and said accusingly, 'You've got a button off your pullover!'

He glanced down. 'I know. It came off on the way up here.'

'Have you got the button?'

He nodded. 'I found it on the floor of the car.'

You'd better give it to me with the pullover tonight, and I'll sew it on for you.'

'It doesn't matter,' he said.

'Of course it matters.' She smiled softly. 'I can't send you back to Sharon looking like that.'

'She wouldn't mind, honey . . .'

'No, but I should. Give it me tonight, and I'll give it back to you in the morning.'

He gave it to her at the door of her bedroom at about eleven o'clock at night. They had spent most of the evening smoking and drinking with the crowd, keenly anticipating the next day's sport, discussing whether to fish the lake or the streams. They had decided to try it on the Jamieson River, having no boat. The girl took the garment from him and said, 'Thanks for bringing me up here, Dwight. It's been a lovely evening, and it's going to be a lovely day tomorrow.'

He stood uncertain. 'You really mean that, honey? You're not going to be hurt?'

She laughed. 'I'm not going to be hurt, Dwight. I know you're a married man. Go to bed. I'll have this for you in the morning.'

'Okay.' He turned and listened to the noise and snatches of songs still coming from the bar. 'They're having themselves a real good time,' he said. 'I still can't realize it's never going to happen again, not after this weekend.'

'It may do, somehow,' she said. 'On another plane, or something. Anyway, let's have fun and catch fish tomorrow. They say it's going to be a fine day.'

He grinned. 'Think it ever rains, on that other plane?'

'I don't know,' she said. 'We'll find out soon enough.'

'Got to get some water in the rivers, somehow,' he said thoughtfully. 'Otherwise there wouldn't be much fishing . . .' He turned away. 'Goodnight, Moira. Let's have a swell time tomorrow, anyway.'

She closed her door, and stood for a few moments holding the pullover to her. Dwight was as he was, a married man whose heart was in Connecticut with his wife and children; it would never be with her. If she had had more time things might have been different, but it would have taken many years. Five years, at least, she thought, until the memories of Sharon and of Junior and of Helen had begun to fade; then he would have turned to her, and she could have given him another family, and made him happy again. Five years were not granted to her; it would be five days, more likely. A tear trickled down beside her nose and she wiped it away irritably; self-pity was a stupid thing, or was it the brandy? The light from the one fifteen-watt bulb high in the ceiling of her dark little bedroom was too dim for sewing buttons on. She threw off her clothes, put on her pyjamas, and

278

went to bed, the pullover on the pillow by her head. In the end she slept.

They went out next day after breakfast to fish the Jamieson not far from the hotel. The river was high and the water clouded; she dabbled her flies amateurishly in the quick water and did no good, but Dwight caught a two-pounder with the spinning tackle in the middle of the morning and she helped him to land it with the net. She wanted him to go on and catch another, but having proved the rod and tackle he was now more interested in helping her to catch something. About noon one of the fishermen that they had sat with at the bar came walking down the bank, studying the water and not fishing. He stopped to speak to them.

'Nice fish,' he said, looking at Dwight's catch. 'Get him on the fly?'

The American shook his head. 'On the spinner. We're trying with the fly now. Did you do any good last night?'

'I got five,' the man said. 'Biggest about six pounds. I got sleepy about three in the morning and turned it in. Only just got out of bed. You won't do much good with fly, not in this water.' He produced a plastic box and poked about in it with his forefinger. 'Look, try this.'

He gave them a tiny fly spoon, a little bit of plated metal about the size of a sixpence ornamented with one hook. 'Try that in the pool where the quick water runs out. They should come for that, on a day like this.'

They thanked him, and Dwight tied it on the cast for her. At first she could not get it out; it felt like a ton of lead on the end of her rod and fell in the water at her feet. Presently she got the knack of it, and managed to put it into the fast water at the head of the pool. On the fifth or sixth successful cast there was a sudden pluck at the line, the rod bent, and the reel sang as the line ran out. She gasped, 'I believe I've got one, Dwight.'

'Sure, you've got one,' he said. 'Keep the rod upright, honey. Move down a bit this way.' The fish broke surface in a leap. 'Nice fish,' he said. 'Keep a tight line, but let him run if he really wants to go. Take it easy, and he's all yours.'

Five minutes later she got the exhausted fish in to the bank at her feet, and he netted it for her. He killed it with a quick blow on a stone, and they admired her catch. 'Pound and a half,' he said. 'Maybe a little bigger.' He extracted the little spoon carefully from its mouth. 'Now catch another one.'

'It's not so big as yours,' she said, but she was bursting with pride.

'The next one will be. Have another go at it.' But it was close to lunch time, and she decided to wait till the afternoon. They walked back to the hotel proudly carrying their spoils and had a glass of beer before lunch, talking over their catch with the other anglers.

They went out again in the middle of the afternoon to the same stretch of river and again she caught a fish, a two-pounder this time, while Dwight caught two smaller fish, one of which he put back. Towards evening they rested before going back to the hotel, pleasantly tired and content with the day's work, the fish laid out beside them. They sat against a boulder by the river, enjoying the last of the sunlight before it sank behind the hill, smoking cigarettes. It was growing chilly, but they were reluctant to leave the murmur of the river.

A sudden thought struck her. 'Dwight,' she said. 'That motor race must be over by this time.'

He stared at her. 'Holy smoke! I meant to listen to it on the radio. I forgot all about it.'

'So did I,' she said. There was a pause, and then she said, 'I wish we'd listened. I'm feeling a bit selfish.'

'We couldn't have done anything, honey.'

'I know. But – I don't know. I do hope John's all right.'

'The news comes on at seven,' he said. 'We could listen then.'

'I'd like to know,' she said. She looked around her at the calm, rippling water, the long shadows, the golden evening light. 'This is such a lovely place,' she said. 'Can you believe – really believe – that we shan't see it again?'

'I'm going home,' he said quietly. 'This is a grand country, and I've liked it here. But it's not my country, and now I'm going back to my own place, to my own folks. I like it in Australia well enough, but all the same I'm glad to be going home at last, home to Connecticut.' He turned to her. 'I shan't see this again, because I'm going home.'

'Will you tell Sharon about me?' she asked.

'Sure,' he said. 'Maybe she knows already.'

She stared down at the pebbles at her feet. 'What will you tell her?'

'Lots of things,' he said quietly. 'I'll tell her that you turned what might have been a bad time for me into a good time. I'll tell her that you did that although you knew, right from the start, that there was nothing in it for you. I'll tell her it's because of you I've come back to her like I used to be, and not a drunken bum. I'll tell her that you've made it easy for me to stay faithful to her, and what it cost you.'

She got up from the stone. 'Let's go back to the hotel,' she said. 'You'll be lucky if she believes a quarter of all that.'

He got up with her. 'I don't think so,' he said. 'I think she'll believe it all, because it's true.'

They walked back to the hotel carrying their fish. When they had cleaned up they met again in the hotel bar for a drink before tea; they ate quickly in order to be back at the radio before the news. It came on presently, mostly concerned with sport; as they sat tense the announcer said:

'The Australian Grand Prix was run today at Tooradin and was won by Mr John Osborne, driving a Ferrari. The second place . . .'

The girl exclaimed, 'Oh Dwight, he did it!' They sat forward to listen.

'The race was marred by the large number of accidents and casualties. Of the eighteen starters only three finished the race of eighty laps, six of the drivers being killed outright in accidents and many more removed to hospital with more or less severe injuries. The winner, Mr John Osborne, drove cautiously for the first half of the race and at the fortieth lap was three laps behind the leading car, driven by Mr Sam Bailey. Shortly afterwards Mr Bailey crashed at the corner known as The Slide, and from that point onwards the Ferrari put on speed. At the sixtieth lap the Ferrari was in the lead, the field by that time being reduced to five cars, and thereafter Mr Osborne was never seriously challenged. On the sixty-fifth lap he put up a record for the course, lapping at 97.83 miles an hour, a remarkable achievement for this circuit. Thereafter Mr Osborne reduced speed in response to signals from his pit, and finished the race at an average speed of 89.61 miles an hour. Mr Osborne is an official of the CSIRO; he has no connection with the motor industry and races as an amateur.'

Later they stood on the veranda of the hotel for a few minutes before bed, looking out at the black line of the hills, the starry night. 'I'm glad John got what he wanted,' the girl said. 'I mean, he wanted it so much. It must kind of round things off for him.'

The American beside her nodded. 'I'd say things are rounding off for all of us right now.'

'I know. There's not much time. Dwight, I think I'd like to go home tomorrow. We've had a lovely day up here and caught some fish. But there's so much to do, and now so little time to do it in.'

'Sure, honey,' he said. 'I was thinking that myself. You glad we came, though?'

She nodded. 'I've been very happy, Dwight, all day. I don't know why – not just catching fish. I feel like John must feel – as if I've won a victory over something. But I don't know what.'

He smiled. 'Don't try and analyse it,' he said. 'Just take it, and be thankful. I've been happy, too. But I'd agree with you, we should get home tomorrow. Things will be happening down there.'

'Bad things?' she asked.

He nodded in the darkness by her side. 'I didn't want to spoil the trip for you,' he said. 'But John Osborne told me yesterday before we came away they got several cases of this radiation sickness in Melbourne, as of Thursday night. I'd say there'd be a good many more by now.'

9

On the Tuesday morning Peter Holmes went to Melbourne in his little car. Dwight Towers had telephoned to him to meet him at ten forty-five in the ante-room to the office of the First Naval Member. The radio that morning announced for the first time the incidence of radiation sickness in the city, and Mary Holmes had been concerned about his going there. 'Do be careful, Peter,' she said. 'I mean, about all this infection. Do you think you ought to go?'

He could not bring himself to tell her again that the infection was there around them, in their pleasant little flat; either she did not or she would not understand. 'I'll have to go,' he said. 'I won't stay longer than I've absolutely got to.'

'Don't stay up to lunch,' she said. 'I'm sure it's healthier down here.'

'I'll come straight home,' he said.

A thought struck her. 'I know,' she said. 'Take those formalin lozenges with you that got for my cough, and suck one now and then. They're awfully good for all kinds of infection. They're so antiseptic.'

It would set her mind at ease if he did so. 'That's not a bad idea,' he said.

He drove up to the city deep in thought. It was no longer

a matter of days now; it was coming down to hours. He did not know what this conference with the First Naval Member was to be about, but it was very evident that it would be one of the last naval duties of his career. When he drove back again that afternoon his service life would probably be over, as his physical life soon would be.

He parked his car and went into the Navy Department. There was practically no one in the building; he walked up to the ante-room and there he found Dwight Towers in uniform, and alone. His captain said cheerfully, 'Hi, fella.'

Peter said, 'Good morning, sir.' He glanced around; the secretary's desk was locked, the room empty. 'Hasn't Lieutenant-Commander Torrens shown up?'

'Not that I know of. I'd say he's taking the day off.'

The door into the Admiral's office opened, and Sir David Hartman stood there. The smiling, rubicund face was more serious and drawn than Peter had remembered. He said, 'Come in, gentlemen. My secretary isn't here today.'

They went in, and were given seats before the desk. The American said, 'I don't know if what I have to say concerns Lieutenant-Commander Holmes or not. It may involve a few liaison duties with the dockyard. Would you prefer he wait outside, sir?'

'I shouldn't think so,' said the Admiral. 'If it will shorten our business, let him stay. What is it you want, Commander?'

Dwight hesitated for a moment, choosing his words. 'It seems that I'm the senior executive officer of the US Navy now,' he said. 'I never thought I'd rise so high as that, but that's the way it is. You'll excuse me if I don't put this in the right form or language, sir. But I have to tell you that I'm taking my ship out of your command.'

The Admiral nodded slowly. 'Very good, Commander.

Do you wish to leave Australian territorial waters, or to stay here as our guest?'

'I'll be taking my ship outside territorial waters,' the Commander said. 'I can't just say when I'll be leaving, but probably before the weekend.'

The Admiral nodded. He turned to Peter. 'Give any necessary instructions in regard to victualling and towage to the dockyard,' he said. 'Commander Towers is to be given every facility.'

'Very good, sir.'

The American said, 'I don't just know what to suggest about payments, sir. You must forgive me, but I have no training in these matters.'

The Admiral smiled thinly. 'I don't know that it would do us much good if you had, Commander. I think we can leave those to the usual routine. All countersigned indents and requisitions are costed here and are presented to the Naval Attaché at your Embassy in Canberra, and forwarded by him to Washington for eventual settlement. I don't think you need worry over that side of it.'

Dwight said, 'I can just cast off and go?'

'That's right. Do you expect to be returning to Australian waters?'

The American shook his head. 'No, sir. I'm taking my ship out in Bass Strait to sink her.'

Peter had expected that, but the imminence and the practical negotiation of the matter came with a shock; somehow this was the sort of thing that did not happen. He wanted for a moment to ask if Dwight required a tug to go out with the submarine to bring back the crew, and then abandoned the question. If the Americans wanted a tug to give them a day or two more life they would ask for it, but he did not think they would. Better the sea than death by sickness and diarrhoea, homeless in a strange land.

The Admiral said, 'I should probably do the same, in your shoes . . . Well, it only remains to thank you for your co-operation, Commander. And to wish you luck. If there's anything you need before you go don't hesitate to ask for it – or just take it.' A sudden spasm of pain twisted his face and he gripped a pencil on the desk before him. Then he relaxed a little, and got up from the desk. 'Excuse me,' he said. 'I'll have to leave you for a minute.'

He left them hurriedly, and the door closed behind him. The captain and the liaison officer had stood up at his sudden departure; they remained standing, and glanced at each other. 'This is it,' said the American.

Peter said in a low tone, 'Do you suppose that's what's happened to the secretary?'

'I'd think so.'

They stood in silence for a minute or two, staring out of the window. 'Victualling,' Peter said at last. 'There's nothing much in *Scorpion*. Is the exec getting out a list of what you'll need, sir?'

Dwight shook his head. 'We shan't need anything,' he said. 'I'm only taking her down the bay and just outside the territorial limit.'

The liaison officer asked the question that he had wanted to ask before. 'Shall I lay on a tug to sail with you and bring the crew back?'

Dwight said, 'That won't be necessary.'

They stood in silence for another ten minutes. Finally the Admiral reappeared, grey faced. 'Very good of you to wait,' he said. 'I've been a bit unwell . . .' He did not resume his seat, but remained standing by the desk. 'This is the end of a long association, Captain,' he said. 'We British have always enjoyed working with Americans, especially upon the sea. We've had cause to be grateful to you very many times, and in return I think we've taught you something out of our experience. This is the end of it.' He stood in thought for a minute, and then he held out his hand, smiling. 'All I can do now is to say goodbye.'

Dwight took his hand. 'It certainly has been good, working under you, sir,' he said. 'I'm speaking for the whole ship's company when I say that, as well as for myself.'

They left the office and walked down through the desolate, empty building to the courtyard. Peter said, 'Well, what happens now, sir? Would you like me to come down to the dockyard?'

The captain shook his head. 'I'd say that you can consider yourself to be relieved of duty,' he said. 'I won't need you any more down there.'

'If there's anything that I can do, I'll come very gladly.'

'No. If I should find I need anything from you, I'll ring your home. But that's where your place is now, fellow.'

This, then, was the end of their fellowship. 'When will you be sailing?' Peter asked.

'I wouldn't know exactly,' the American said. 'I've got seven cases in the crew, as of this morning. I guess we'll stick around a day or two, and sail maybe on Saturday.'

'Are many going with you?'

'Ten. Eleven, with myself.'

Peter glanced at him. 'Are you all right, so far?'

Dwight smiled. 'I thought I was, but now I don't just know. I won't be taking any lunch today.' He paused. 'How are you feeling?'

'I'm all right. So is Mary – I think.'

Dwight turned towards the cars. 'You get back to her, right now. There's nothing now for you to stay here for.'

'Will I see you again, sir?'

'I don't think you will,' said the captain. 'I'm going home now, home to Mystic in Connecticut, and glad to go.'

There was nothing more for them to say or do. They shook hands, got into their cars, and drove off on their separate ways.

In the old fashioned, two-storey brick house in Malvern, John Osborne stood by his mother's bed. He was not unwell, but the old lady had fallen sick upon the Sunday morning, the day after he had won the Grand Prix. He had managed to get a doctor for her on Monday, but there was nothing he could do and he had not come again. The daily maid had not turned up, and the scientist was now doing everything for his sick mother.

She opened her eyes for the first time in a quarter of an hour. 'John,' she said. 'This is what they said would happen, isn't it?'

'I think so, Mum,' he said gently. 'It's going to happen to me, too.'

'Did Dr Hamilton say that was what it was? I can't remember.'

'That's what he told me, Mum. I don't think he'll be coming here again. He said he was getting it himself.'

There was a long silence. 'How long will it take me to die, John?'

'I don't know,' he said. 'It might be a week.'

'How absurd,' said the old lady. 'Much too long.'

She closed her eyes again. He took a basin to the bathroom, washed it out, and brought it back into the bedroom. She opened her eyes again. 'Where is Ming?' she asked.

'I put him out in the garden,' he said. 'He seemed to want to go.'

'I am so terribly sorry about him,' she muttered. 'He'll be so dreadfully lonely, without any of us here.'

'He'll be all right, Mum,' her son said, though without much confidence. 'There'll be all the other dogs for him to play with.'

She did not pursue the subject, but she said, 'I'll be quite all right now, dear. You go on and do whatever you have to do.'

He hesitated. 'I think I ought to look in at the office,' he said. 'I'll be back before lunch. What would you like for lunch?'

She closed her eyes again. 'Is there any milk?'

'There's a pint in the fridge,' he said. 'I'll see if I can get some more. It's not too easy, though. There wasn't any yesterday.'

'Ming ought to have a little,' she said. 'It's so good for him. There should be three tins of rabbit in the larder. Open one of those for his dinner, and put the rest in the fridge. He's so fond of rabbit. Don't bother about lunch for me till you come back. If I'm feeling like it I might have a cup of cornflour.'

'Sure you'll be all right if I go out?' he asked.

'Quite sure,' she said. She held out her arms. 'Give me a kiss before you go.'

He kissed the limp old cheeks, and she lay back in bed, smiling at him.

He left the house and went down to the office. There was nobody there, but on his desk there was the daily report of radioactive infection. Attached to it was a note from his secretary. She said that she was feeling very unwell, and probably would not be coming to the office again. She thanked him for his kindness to her, congratulated him upon the motor race, and said how much she had enjoyed working for him.

He laid the note aside and took up the report. It said that in Melbourne about fifty per cent of the population appeared to be affected. Seven cases were reported from Hobart in Tasmania, and three from Christchurch in New Zealand. The report, probably the last that he would see, was much shorter than usual.

He walked through the empty offices, picking up a paper here and there and glancing at them. This phase of his life was coming to an end, with all the others. He did not stay very long, for the thought of his mother was heavy on him. He went out and made his way towards his home by one of the occasional, crowded trams still running in the streets. It had a driver, but no conductor; the days of paying fares were over. He spoke to the driver. The man said, 'I'll go on driving this here bloody tram till I get sick, cock. Then I'll drive it to the Kew depot and go home. That's where I live, see? I been driving trams for thirty-seven years, rain or shine, and I'm not stopping now.'

In Malvern he got off the tram and commenced his search for milk. He found it to be hopeless; what there was had been reserved for babies by the dairy. He went home empty handed to his mother.

He entered the house and released the Pekinese from the garden, thinking that his mother would like to see him. He went upstairs to her bedroom, the dog hopping up the stairs before him.

In the bedroom he found his mother lying on her back with her eyes closed, the bed very neat and tidy. He moved a little closer and touched her hand, but she was dead. On the table by her side was a glass of water, a pencilled note, and one of the little red cartons, open, with the empty vial beside it. He had not known that she had that.

He picked up the note. It read,

My dear son,

It's quite absurd that I should spoil the last days of your life by hanging on to mine, since it is such a burden to me now. Don't bother about any funeral. Just close the door and leave me in my own bed, in my own room, with my own things all round me. I shall be quite all right.

Do whatever you think best for little Ming. I am so very, very sorry for him, but I can do nothing.

I am so very glad you won your race.

My very dearest love.
MOTHER.

A few tears trickled down his cheeks, but only a few. Mum had always been right, all his life, and now she was right again. He left the room and went down to the drawing-room, thinking deeply. He was not yet ill himself, but now it could only be a matter of hours. The dog followed him; he sat down and took it on his lap, caressing the silky ears.

Presently he got up, put the little dog in the garden, and went out to the chemist at the corner. There was a girl behind the counter still, surprisingly; she gave him one of the red cartons. 'Everybody's after these,' she said, smiling. 'We're doing quite a lot of business in them.'

He smiled back at her. 'I like mine chocolate coated.'

'So do I,' she said. 'But I don't think they make them like that. I'm going to take mine with an ice-cream soda.'

He smiled again, and left her at the counter. He went back to the house, released the Pekinese from the garden, and began to prepare a dinner for him in the kitchen. He opened one of the tins of rabbit and warmed it a little in the oven, and mixed with it four capsules of Nembutal. Then he put it down before the little dog, who attacked it greedily, and made his basket comfortable for him before the stove.

He went out to the telephone in the hall and rang up the club, and booked a bedroom for a week. Then he went to his own room and began to pack a suitcase.

Half an hour later he came down to the kitchen; the Pekinese was in his basket, very drowsy. The scientist read the directions on the carton carefully and gave him the injection; he hardly felt the prick.

When he was satisfied that the little dog was dead he carried him upstairs in the basket and laid it on the floor beside his mother's bed.

Then he left the house.

Tuesday night was a disturbed night for the Holmeses. The baby began crying at about two in the morning, and it cried almost incessantly till dawn. There was little sleep for the young father or mother. At about seven o'clock it vomited.

Outside it was raining and cold. They faced each other in the grey light, weary and unwell themselves. Mary said, 'Peter – you don't think this is it, do you?'

'I don't know,' he replied. 'But I should think it might be. Everybody seems to be getting it.'

She passed a hand across her brow, wearily. 'I thought we'd be all right, out here in the country.'

He did not know what he could say to comfort her, and so he said, 'If I put the kettle on, would you like a cup of tea?'

She crossed to the cot again, and looked down at the baby; she was quiet for the moment. He said again, 'What about a cup of tea?'

It would be good for him, she thought; he had been up for most of the night. She forced a smile. 'That'd be lovely.'

He went through to the kitchen to put the kettle on. She was feeling terrible, and now she wanted to be sick. It was being up all night, of course, and the worry over Jennifer. Peter was busy in the kitchen; she could go quietly to the bathroom without his knowing. She was often sick, but this time he might think it was something else, and get worried.

In the kitchen there was a stale smell, or seemed to be. Peter Holmes filled the kettle at the tap, and plugged it in; he switched on and saw with some relief the indicator light come on that showed the current was flowing. One of these days the juice would fail, and then they would be in real trouble.

The kitchen was intolerably stuffy; he threw open the window. He was hot, and then suddenly cold again, and then he knew that he was going to be sick. He went quietly to the bathroom, but the door was locked; Mary must be in there. No point in alarming her; he went out of the back door in the rain and vomited in a secluded corner behind the garage.

He stayed there for some time. When he came back he was white and shaken, but feeling more normal. The kettle was boiling and he made the tea, and put two cups on a tray, and took it to their bedroom. Mary was there, bending over the cot. He said, 'I've got the tea.'

She did not turn, afraid her face might betray her. She said, 'Oh, thanks. Pour it out; I'll be there in a minute.' She did not feel that she could touch a cup of tea, but it would do him good.

He poured out the two cups and sat on the edge of the bed, sipping his; the hot liquid seemed to calm his stomach. He said presently, 'Come on and have your tea, dear. It's getting cold.'

She came a little reluctantly; perhaps she could manage it. She glanced at him, and his dressing gown was soaking wet with rain. She exclaimed, 'Peter, you're all wet! Have you been outside?'

He glanced at his sleeve; he had forgotten that. 'I had to go outside,' he said.

'Whatever for?'

He could not keep up a dissimulation; 'I've just been sick,' he said. 'I don't suppose it's anything.'

'Oh, Peter! So have I.'

They stared at each other in silence for a minute. Then she said dully, 'It must be those meat pies we had for supper. Did you notice anything about them?'

He shook his head. 'Tasted all right to me. Besides, Jennifer didn't have any meat pie.'

She said, 'Peter. Do you think this is it?'

He took her hand. 'It's what everybody else is getting,' he said. 'We wouldn't be immune.'

'No,' she said thoughtfully. 'No. I suppose we wouldn't.' She raised her eyes to his. 'This is the end of it, is it? I mean, we just go on now getting sicker till we die?'

'I think that's the form,' he said. He smiled at her. 'I've never done it before, but they say that's what happens.'

She left him and went through to the lounge; he hesitated for a moment and then followed her. He found her standing by the french window looking out into the garden that she loved so much, now grey and wintry and windswept. 'I'm so sorry that we never got that garden seat,' she said irrelevantly. 'It would have been lovely just there, just beside that bit of wall.'

'I could have a stab at getting one today,' he said.

She turned to him, 'Not if you're ill.'

'I'll see how I'm feeling later on,' he said. 'Better to be doing something than sit still and think how miserable you are.'

She smiled. 'I'm feeling better now, I think. Could you eat any breakfast?'

'Well, I don't know,' he said. 'I don't know that I'm feeling quite so good as all that. What have you got?'

'We've got three pints of milk,' she said. 'Can we get any more?'

'I think so. I could take the car for it.'

'What about some cornflakes, then? It says they're full of glucose on the packet. That's good for when you're being sick, isn't it?'

He nodded. 'I think I'll have a shower,' he said. 'I might feel better after that.'

He did so; when he came out to their bedroom she was in the kitchen busy with the breakfast. To his amazement, he heard her singing, singing a cheerful little song that inquired who'd been polishing the sun. He stepped into the kitchen. 'You sound cheerful,' he remarked.

She came to him. 'It's such a relief,' she said, and now he saw she had been crying a little as she sang. He wiped her tears away, puzzled, as he held her in his arms.

'I've been so terribly worried,' she sobbed. 'But now it's going to be all right.'

Nothing was further from right, he thought, but he did not say so. 'What's been worrying you?' he asked gently.

'People get this thing at different times,' she said. 'That's what they say. Some people can get it as much as a fortnight later than others. I might have got it first and had to leave you, or Jennifer, or you might have got it and left us alone. It's been such a nightmare . . .'

She raised her eyes to his, smiling through her tears.

'But now we've got it all together, on the same day. Aren't we lucky?'

On Friday Peter Holmes drove up to Melbourne in his little car, ostensibly to try and find a garden seat. He went quickly because he could not be away from home too long. He wanted to find John Osborne and to find him without delay; he tried the garage in the mews first, but that was locked; then he tried the CSIRO offices. Finally, he found him in his bedroom at the Pastoral Club; he was looking weak and ill.

Peter said, 'John, I'm sorry to worry you. How are you feeling?'

'I've got it,' said the scientist. 'I've had it two days. Haven't you?'

'That's what I wanted to see you about,' Peter said. 'Our doctor's dead, I think – at any rate, he isn't functioning. Look, John, Mary and I both started giving at both ends on Tuesday. She's pretty bad. But on Thursday, yesterday, I began picking up. I didn't tell her, but I'm feeling as fit as a flea now, and bloody hungry. I stopped at a café on the way up and had breakfast – bacon and fried eggs and all the trimmings, and I'm still hungry. I believe I'm getting well. Look – can that happen?'

The scientist shook his head. 'Not permanently. You can recover for a bit, but then you get it again.'

'How long is a bit?'

'You might get ten days. Then you'll get it again. I don't think there's a second recovery. Tell me, is Mary very bad?'

'She's not too good. I'll have to get back to her pretty soon.'

'She's in bed, is she?'

297

Peter shook his head. 'She came down to Falmouth with me this morning to buy mothballs.'

'To buy *what*?'

'Mothballs. Naphthalene – you know.' He hesitated. 'It's what she wanted,' he said. 'I left her putting all our clothes away to keep the moths out of them. She can do that in between the spasms, and she wants to do it.' He reverted to the subject he had come for. 'Look, John. I take it that I get a week or ten days' health, but there's no chance for me at all after that?'

'Not a hope, old boy,' the scientist said. 'Nobody survives this thing. It makes a clean sweep.'

'Well, that's nice to know,' said Peter. 'No good hanging on to any illusions. Tell me, is there anything that I can do for you? I'll have to beat it back to Mary in a minute.'

The scientist shook his head. 'I'm just about through. I've got one or two things that I've got to do today, but then I think I'll finish it.'

Peter knew he had responsibilities at home. 'How's your mother?'

'She's dead,' the scientist said briefly. 'I'm living here now.'

Peter nodded, but the thought of Mary filled his mind. I'll have to go,' he said. 'Good luck, old man.'

The scientist smiled weakly. 'Be seeing you,' he replied.

When the naval officer had gone he got up from the bed and went along the passage. He returned half an hour later a good deal weaker, his lip curling with disgust at his vile body. Whatever he had to do must be done today; tomorrow he would be incapable.

He dressed carefully, and went downstairs. He looked into the garden-room; there was a fire burning in the grate and his uncle sitting there alone, a glass of sherry by his side. He glanced up, and said, 'Good morning, John. How did you sleep?'

The scientist said briefly, 'Very badly. I'm getting pretty sick.'

The old man raised his flushed, rubicund face in concern. 'My dear boy, I'm sorry to hear that. Everybody seems to be sick now. Do you know, I had to go down to the kitchen and cook my breakfast for myself? Imagine that, in a club like this!'

He had been living there for three days, since the death of the sister who had kept house for him at Macedon. 'However, Collins the hall porter has come in now, and he's going to cook us some lunch. You'll be lunching here today?'

John Osborne knew that he would not be lunching anywhere. 'I'm sorry I can't today, uncle. I've got to go out.'

'Oh, what a pity. I was hoping that you'd be here to help us out with the port. We're on the last bin now – I think about fifty bottles. It should just see us through.'

'How are you feeling yourself, uncle?'

'Never better, my boy, never better. I felt a little unsteady after dinner last night, but really, I think that was the Burgundy. I don't think Burgundy mixes very well with other wines. In France, in the old days, if you drank Burgundy you drank it from a pint pot or the French equivalent, and you drank nothing else all evening. But I came in here and had a quiet brandy and soda with a little ice in it, and by the time I went upstairs I was quite myself again. No, I had a very good night.'

The scientist wondered how long the immunity from radioactive disease conferred by alcohol would last. So far as he was aware no research had yet been done upon that subject; here was an opportunity, but there was now nobody to do it. 'I'm sorry I can't stay to lunch,' he said. 'But I'll see you tonight, perhaps.'

'I shall be here, my boy, I shall be here. Tom Fotherington was in last night for dinner, and he said that he'd be coming in this morning, but he hasn't shown up. I hope he isn't ill.'

John Osborne left the club and walked down the tree-lined street in a dream. The Ferrari was urgently in need of his attention and he must go there; after that he could relax. He passed the open door of a chemist's shop and hesitated for a moment; then he went in. The shop was unattended and deserted. In the middle of the floor was an open packing case full of the little red cartons, and a heap of these had been piled untidily upon the counter between the cough medicines and the lipsticks. He picked up one and put it in his pocket, and went on his way.

When he pushed back the sliding doors of the mews garage the Ferrari stood facing him in the middle of the floor, just as he had left it, ready for instant use. It had come through the Grand Prix unscratched, in bandbox condition. It was a glorious possession to him still, the more so since the race. He was now feeling too ill to drive it and he might never drive it again, but he felt that he would never be too ill to touch it and to handle it and work on it. He hung his jacket on a nail, and started.

First of all, the wheels must be jacked up and bricks arranged under the wishbones to bring the tyres clear of the floor. The effort of manoeuvring the heavy jack and working it and carrying the bricks upset him again. There was no toilet in the garage but there was a dirty yard behind, littered with the black, oily junk of ancient and forgotten motor cars. He retired there and presently

300

came back to work, weaker than ever now, more resolute to finish the jobs that day.

He finished jacking up the wheels before the next attack struck him. He opened a cock to drain the water from the cooling system, and then he had to go out to the yard again. Never mind, the work was easy now. He detached the terminals from the battery and greased the connections. Then he took out each of the six sparking plugs and filled the cylinders with oil, and screwed the plugs back finger tight.

He rested then against the car; she would be all right now. The spasm shook him, and again he had to go out to the yard. When he came back evening was drawing near and the light was fading. There was no more to be done to preserve the car he loved so well, but he stayed by it, reluctant to leave it and afraid that another spasm might strike him before he reached the club.

For the last time he would sit in the driving seat and handle the controls. His crash helmet and goggles were in the seat; he put the helmet on and snugged it down upon his head, and hung the goggles round his neck beneath his chin. Then he climbed into the seat and settled down behind the wheel.

It was comfortable there, far more so than the club would be. The wheel beneath his hands was comforting, the three small dials grouped around the huge rev counter were familiar friends. This car had won for him the race that was the climax of his life. Why trouble to go further?

He took the red carton from his pocket, took the tablets from the vial, and threw the carton on the ground beside him. No point in going on; this was the way he'd like to have it.

He took the tablets in his mouth, and swallowed them with an effort.

Peter Holmes left the club and drove down to the hardware store in Elizabeth Street where he had bought the motor mower. It was untenanted and empty of people, but somebody had broken in a door and it had been partially looted in that anyone who wanted anything had just walked in to take it. It was dim inside, for all the electricity had been turned off at the main. The garden department was on the second floor; he climbed the stairs and found the garden seats he had remembered. He selected a fairly light one with a brightly coloured detachable cushion that he thought would please Mary and would also serve to pad the roof of his car. With great effort he dragged the seat down two flights of stairs to the pavement outside the shop, and went back for the cushion and some rope. He found a hank of clothes line on a counter. Outside he heaved the seat up on to the roof of the Morris Minor and lashed it in place with many ties of rope attached to all parts of the car. Then he set off for home.

He was still ravenously hungry, and feeling very well. He had not told Mary anything of his recovery, and he did not intend to do so now; it would only upset her, confident as she now was that they were all going together. He stopped on the way home at the same café that he had breakfast at, kept by a beery couple who appeared to be enjoying remarkably good health. They were serving hot roast beef for lunch; he had two platefuls of that and followed it up with a considerable portion of hot jam roly-poly. Then as an afterthought he got them to make him an enormous parcel of beef sandwiches; he could leave those in the boot of the car where Mary would not know about them, so that he could go out in the evening and have a quiet little meal unknown to her.

He got back to his little flat in the early afternoon; he left the garden seat on top of the car and went into the house. He found Mary lying on the bed, half dressed, with an eiderdown over her; the house seemed cold and damp. He sat down on the bed beside her. 'How are you feeling now?' he asked.

'Awful,' she said. 'Peter, I'm so worried about Jennifer. I can't get her to take anything at all, and she's messing all the time.' She added some details.

He crossed the room and looked at the baby in the cot. It looked thin and weak, as did Mary herself. It seemed to him that both were very ill.

She asked, 'Peter – how are you feeling yourself?'

'Not too good,' he said. 'I was sick twice on the way up and once on the way down. As for the other end, I've just been running all the time.'

She laid her hand upon his arm. 'You oughtn't to have gone . . .'

He smiled down at her. 'I got you a garden seat, anyway.'

Her face lightened a little. 'You did? Where is it?'

'On the car,' he said. 'You lie down and keep warm. I'm going to light the fire and make the house cosy. After that I'll get the seat down off the car and you can see it.'

'I can't lie down,' she said wearily. 'Jennifer needs changing.'

'I'll see to that, first of all,' he said. He led her gently to the bed. 'Lie down and keep warm.'

An hour later he had a blazing fire in their sitting-room, and the garden seat was set up by the wall where she wanted it to be. She came to look at it from the french window, with the brightly coloured cushion on the seat.

'It's lovely,' she said. 'It's exactly what we needed for that corner. It's going to be awfully nice to sit there, on a summer evening . . .' The winter afternoon was drawing in, and a fine rain was falling. 'Peter, now that I've seen it, would you bring the cushion in and put it in the veranda? Or, better bring it in here till it's dry. I do want to keep it nice for the summer.'

He did so, and they brought the baby's cot into the warmer room. She said, 'Peter, do you want anything to eat? There's plenty of milk, if you could take that.'

He shook his head. 'I couldn't eat a thing,' he said. 'How about you?'

She shook her head.

'If I mixed you a hot brandy and lemon?' he suggested. 'Could you manage that?'

She thought for a moment. 'I could try.' She wrapped her dressing gown around her. 'I'm so cold . . .'

The fire was roaring in the grate. 'I'll go out and get some more wood,' he said. 'Then I'll get you a hot drink.' He went out to the woodpile in the gathering darkness, and took the opportunity to open the boot of the car and eat three beef sandwiches. He came back presently to the living-room with a basket of wood, and found her standing by the cot. 'You've been so long,' she said. 'Whatever were you doing?'

'I had a bit of trouble,' he told her. 'Must be the meat pies again.'

Her face softened. 'Poor old Peter. We're all of us in trouble . . .' She stooped over the cot, and stroked the baby's forehead; she lay inert now, too weak apparently to cry. 'Peter, I believe she's dying . . .'

He put his arm around her shoulder. 'So am I,' he said quietly, 'and so are you. We've none of us got very long to go. I've got the kettle here. Let's have that drink.'

He led her from the cot to the warmth of the huge fire that he had made. She sat down on the floor before it and he gave her the hot drink of brandy and water with a little lemon squeezed in it. She sat sipping it and staring into the fire, and it made her feel a little better. He mixed one for himself, and they sat in silence for a few minutes.

Presently she said, 'Peter, why did all this happen to us? Was it because Russia and China started fighting each other?'

He nodded. 'That's about the size of it,' he said. 'But there was more to it than that. America and England and Russia started bombing for destruction first. The whole thing started with Albania.'

'But we didn't have anything to do with it at all, did we – here in Australia?'

'We gave England moral support,' he told her. 'I don't think we had time to give her any other kind. The whole thing was over in a month.'

'Couldn't anyone have stopped it?'

'I don't know . . . Some kinds of silliness you just can't stop,' he said. 'I mean, if a couple of hundred million people all decide that their national honour requires them to drop cobalt bombs upon their neighbour, well, there's not much that you or I can do about it. The only possible hope would have been to educate them out of their silliness.'

'But how could you have done that, Peter? I mean, they'd all left school.'

'Newspapers,' he said. 'You could have done something with newspapers. We didn't do it. No nation did, because we were all too silly. We liked our newspapers with pictures of beach girls and headlines about cases of indecent assault, and no Government was wise enough to stop us having them that way. But something might have been done with newspapers, if we'd been wise enough.'

She did not fully comprehend his reasoning. 'I'm glad we haven't got newspapers now,' she said. 'It's been much nicer without them.'

A spasm shook her, and he helped her to the bathroom. While she was in there he came back to the sitting-room and stood looking at his baby. It was in a bad way, and there was nothing he could do to help it; he doubted now if it would live through the night. Mary was in a bad way, too, though not quite so bad as that. The only one of them who was healthy was himself, and that he must not show.

The thought of living on after Mary appalled him. He could not stay in the flat; in the few days that would be left to him he would have nowhere to go, nothing to do. The thought crossed his mind that if *Scorpion* were still in Williamstown he might go with Dwight Towers and have it at sea, the sea that had been his life's work. But why do that? He didn't want the extra time that some strange quirk of his metabolism had given to him. He wanted to stay with his family.

She called him from the bathroom, and he went to help her. He brought her back to the great fire that he had made; she was cold and trembling. He gave her another hot brandy and water, and covered her with the eiderdown around her shoulders. She sat holding the glass in both hands to still the tremors that were shaking her.

Presently she said, 'Peter, how is Jennifer?'

He got up and crossed to the cot, and then came back to her. 'She's quiet now,' he said. 'I think she's much the same.'

'How are you, yourself?' she asked.

'Awful,' he said. He stooped by her, and took her hand. 'I think you're worse than I am,' he told her, for she must know that. 'I think I may be a day or so behind you, but not more. Perhaps that's because I'm physically stronger.'

She nodded slowly. Then she said, 'There's no hope at all, is there? For any of us?'

He shook his head. 'Nobody gets over this one, dear.'

She said, 'I don't believe I'll be able to get to the bathroom tomorrow. Peter dear, I think I'd like to have it tonight, and take Jennifer with me. Would you think that beastly?'

He kissed her. 'I think it's sensible,' he said. 'I'll come too.'

She said weakly, 'You're not so ill as we are.'

'I shall be tomorrow,' he said. 'It's no good going on.'

She pressed his hand. 'What do we do, Peter?'

He thought for a moment. 'I'll go and fill the hot water bags and put them in the bed,' he said. 'Then you put on a clean nightie and go to bed and keep warm. I'll bring Jennifer in there. Then I'll shut up the house and bring you a hot drink, and we'll have it in bed together, with the pill.'

'Remember to turn off the electricity at the main,' she said. 'I mean, mice can chew through a cable and set the house on fire.'

'I'll do that,' he said.

She looked up at him with tears in her eyes. 'Will you do what has to be done for Jennifer?'

He stroked her hair. 'Don't worry,' he said gently. 'I'll do that.'

He filled the hot water bags and put them in the bed, tidying it and making it look fresh as he did so. Then he helped her into the bedroom. He went into the kitchen and put the kettle on for the last time, and while it boiled he read the directions on the three red cartons again very carefully.

He filled a thermos jug with the boiling water, and put it neatly on a tray with the two glasses, the brandy, and half a lemon, and took it into the bedroom. Then he wheeled the cot back and put it by the bedside. Mary was in bed looking clean and fresh; she sat up weakly as he wheeled the cot to her.

He said, 'Shall I pick her up?' He thought that she might like to hold the baby for a little.

She shook her head. 'She's too ill.' She sat looking down at the child for a minute, and then lay back wearily. 'I'd rather think about her like she was, when we were all well. Give her the thing, Peter, and let's get this all over.'

She was right, he thought; it was better to do things quickly and not agonize about them. He gave the baby the injection in the arm. Then he undressed himself and put on clean pyjamas, turned out all the lights in the flat except their bedside light, put up the fire screen in the sitting-room, and lit a candle that they kept in case of a blackout of the electricity. He put that on the table by their bed and turned off the current at the main.

He got into bed with Mary, mixed the drinks, and took the tablets out of the red cartons. 'I've had a lovely time since we got married,' she said quietly. 'Thank you for everything, Peter.'

He drew her to him and kissed her. 'I've had a grand time, too,' he said. 'Let's end on that.'

They put the tablets in their mouths, and drank.

That evening Dwight Towers rang up Moira Davidson at Harkaway. He doubted when he dialled if he would get through or, if he did, whether there would be an answer from the other end. But the automatic telephone was still functioning, and Moira answered him almost at once.

'Say,' he said, 'I wasn't sure I'd get an answer. How are things with you, honey?'

'Bad,' she said. 'I think Mummy and Daddy are just about through.'

'And you?'

'I'm just about through, too, Dwight. How are you?'

'I'd say I'm much the same,' he said. 'I rang to say goodbye for the time being, honey. We're taking *Scorpion* out tomorrow morning to sink her.'

'You won't be coming back?' she asked.

'No, honey. We shan't be coming back. We've just got this last job to do, and then we've finished.' He paused. 'I called to say thank you for the last six months,' he said. 'It's meant a lot to me, having you near.'

'It's meant a lot to me, too,' she said. 'Dwight, if I can make it, may I come and see you off?'

He hesitated for a moment. 'Sure,' he said. 'We can't wait, though. The men are pretty weak right now, and they'll be weaker by tomorrow.'

'What time are you leaving?'

'We're casting off at eight o'clock,' he said. 'As soon as it's full daylight.'

She said, 'I'll be there.'

He gave her messages for her father and her mother, and then rang off. She went through to their bedroom, where they were lying in their twin beds; both of them sicker than she was, and gave them the messages. She told them what she wanted to do. 'I'll be back by dinner time,' she said.

Her mother said, 'You must go and say goodbye to him, dearie. He's been such a good friend for you. But if we're not here when you come back, you must understand.'

She sat down on her mother's bed. 'As bad as that, Mummy?'

'I'm afraid so, dear. And Daddy's worse than me today. But we've got everything we need, in case it gets too bad.'

From his bed her father said weakly, 'Is it raining?'

'Not at the moment, Daddy.'

'Would you go out and open the stockyard gate into the lane, Moira? All the other gates are open, but they must be able to get at the hay.'

'I'll do that right away, Daddy. Is there anything else I can do?'

He closed his eyes. 'Give Dwight my regards. I wish he'd been able to marry you.'

'So do I,' she said. 'But he's the kind of man who doesn't switch so easily as that.'

She went out into the night and opened the gate and checked that all the other gates in the stockyard were open; the beasts were nowhere to be seen. She went back into the house and told her father what she had done; he seemed relieved. There was nothing that they wanted; she kissed them both goodnight and went to bed herself, setting her little alarm clock for five o'clock in case she slept.

She slept very little. In the course of the night she visited the bathroom four times, and drank half a bottle of brandy, the only thing she seemed to be able to keep down. She got up when the alarm went off and had a hot shower, which refreshed her, and dressed in the red shirt and slacks that she had worn when she had met Dwight first of all, so many months ago. She made her face up with some care and put on an overcoat. Then she opened the door of her parents' room quietly and looked in, shading the light of an electric torch between her fingers. Her father seemed to be asleep, but her mother smiled at her from the bed; they, too, had been up and down most of the night. She went in quietly and kissed her mother, and then went, closing the door softly behind her.

She took a fresh bottle of brandy from the larder and went out to the car, and started it, and drove off on the road to Melbourne. Near Oakleigh she stopped on the deserted road in the first grey light of dawn, and took a swig out of the bottle, and went on.

She drove through the deserted city and out along the drab, industrial road to Williamstown. She came to the dockyard at about a quarter past seven; there was no guard at the open gates and she drove straight in to the quay, beside which lay the aircraft carrier. There was no sentry on the gangway, no officer of the day to challenge her. She walked into the ship, trying to remember how she had gone when Dwight had showed her the submarine, and presently she ran into an American rating who directed her to the steel port in the ship's side from which the gangway led down to the submarine.

She stopped a man who was going down to the vessel. 'If you see Captain Towers, would you ask him if he could come up and have a word with me?' she said.

'Sure, lady,' he replied. 'I'll tell him right away,' and presently Dwight came in view, and came up the gangway to her.

He was looking very ill, she thought, as they all were. He took her hands regardless of the onlookers. 'It was nice of you to come to say goodbye,' he said. 'How are things at home, honey?'

'Very bad,' she said. 'Daddy and Mummy will be finishing quite soon, and I think I shall, too. This is the end of it for all of us, today.' She hesitated, and then said, 'Dwight, I want to ask something.'

'What's that, honey?'

'May I come with you, in the submarine?' She paused,

and then she said, 'I don't believe that I'll have anything at home to go back to. Daddy said I could just park the Customline in the street and leave it. He won't be using it again. May I come with you?'

He stood silent for so long that she knew the answer would be, no. 'I've been asked the same thing by four men this morning,' he said. 'I've refused them all, because Uncle Sam wouldn't like it. I've run this vessel in the Navy way right through, and I'm running her that way up till the end. I can't take you, honey. We'll each have to take this on our own.'

'That's all right,' she said dully. She looked up at him. 'You've got your presents with you?'

'Sure,' he said. 'I've got those, thanks to you.'

'Tell Sharon about me,' she said. 'We've nothing to conceal.'

He touched her arm. 'You're wearing the same outfit that you wore first time we met.'

She smiled faintly. 'Keep him occupied – don't give him time to think about things, or perhaps he'll start crying. Have I done my job right, Dwight?'

'Very right indeed,' he said. He took her in his arms and kissed her, and she clung to him for a minute.

Then she freed herself. 'Don't let's prolong the agony,' she said. 'We've said everything there is to say. What time are you leaving?'

'Very soon,' he said. 'We'll be casting off in about five minutes.'

'What time will you be sinking her?' she asked.

He thought for a moment. 'Thirty miles down the bay, and then twelve miles out. Forty-two sea miles. I shan't waste any time. Say two hours and ten minutes after we cast off from here.'

She nodded slowly. 'I'll be thinking of you.' And

then she said, 'Go now, Dwight. Maybe I'll see you in Connecticut one day.'

He drew her near to kiss her again, but she refused him. 'No – go on now.' In her mind she phrased the words, 'Or I'll be the one that starts crying'. He nodded slowly, and said, 'Thanks for everything,' and then he turned and went away down the gangway to the submarine.

There were two or three women now standing at the head of the gangway with her. There were apparently no men aboard the carrier to run the gangway in. She watched as Dwight appeared on the bridge from the interior of the submarine and took the con, watched as the lower end of the gangway was released, as the lines were singled up. She saw the stern line and the spring cast off, watched as Dwight spoke into the voice pipe, watched the water swirl beneath her stern as the propellers ran slow ahead and the stern swung out. It began to rain a little from the grey sky. The bow line and spring were cast off and men coiled them down and slammed the steel hatch of the superstructure shut as the submarine went slow astern in a great arc away from the carrier. Then they all vanished down below, and only Dwight with one other was left on the bridge. He lifted his hand in salutation to her, and she lifted hers to him, her eyes blurred with tears, and the low hull of the vessel swung away around Point Gellibrand and vanished in the murk.

With the other women, she turned away from the steel port. 'There's nothing now to go on living for,' she said.

One of the women replied, 'Well, you won't have to, ducks.'

She smiled faintly, and glanced at her watch. It showed three minutes past eight. At about ten minutes past ten Dwight would be going home, home to the Connecticut village that he loved so well. There was nothing now for her in her own home; if she went back to Harkaway she would find nothing there now but the cattle and sad memories. She could not go with Dwight because of naval discipline, and that she understood. Yet she could be very near him when he started home, only about twelve miles away. If then she turned up by his side with a grin on her face, perhaps he would take her with him, and she could see Helen hopping round upon the Pogo stick.

She hurried out through the dim, echoing caverns of the dead aircraft carrier, and found the gangway, and went down on to the quay to her big car. There was plenty of petrol in the tank; she had filled it up from the cans hidden behind the hay the previous day. She got into it and opened her bag; the red carton was still there. She uncorked the bottle of brandy and took a long swallow of the neat liquor; it was good, that stuff, because she hadn't had to go since she left home. Then she started the car and swung it round upon the quay, and drove out of the dockyard, and on through minor roads and suburbs till she found the highway to Geelong.

Once on the highway she trod on it, and went flying down the unobstructed road at seventy miles an hour in the direction of Geelong, a bare headed, white face girl in a bright crimson costume, slightly intoxicated, driving a big car at speed. She passed Laverton with its big aerodrome, Werribee with its experimental farm, and went flying southwards down the deserted road. Somewhere before Corio a spasm shook her suddenly, so that she had to stop and retire into the bushes; she came out a quarter of an hour later, white as a sheet, and took a long drink of her brandy.

Then she went on, as fast as ever. She passed the grammar school away on the left and came to shabby, industrial Corio, and so to Geelong, dominated by its cathedral. In the great tower the bells were ringing for some service. She slowed a little to pass through the city, but there was nothing on the road except deserted cars at the roadside. She saw only three people, all of them men.

Out of Geelong upon the fourteen miles of road to Barwon Heads and to the sea. As she passed the flooded common she felt her strength was leaving her, but there was now not far to go. A quarter of an hour later she swung right into the great avenue of macrocarpa that was the main street of the little town. At the end she turned left away from the golf links and the little house where so many happy hours of childhood had been spent, knowing now that she would never see it again. She turned right at the bridge at about twenty minutes to ten, and passed through the empty caravan park up on to the headland. The sea lay before her, grey and rough with great rollers coming in from the south on to the rocky beach below.

The ocean was empty and grey beneath the overcast sky, but away to the east there was a break in the clouds and a shaft of light striking down on to the waters. She parked across the road in full view of the sea, got out of her car, took another drink from her bottle, and scanned the horizon for the submarine. Then as she turned towards the lighthouse on Point Lonsdale and the entrance to Port Phillip Bay she saw the low grey shape appear, barely five miles away and heading southwards from the Heads.

She could not see detail but she knew that Dwight was there upon the bridge, taking his ship out on her last cruise. She knew he could not see her and he could not know that she was watching, but she waved to him. Then she got back into the car because the wind was raw and chilly from south polar regions, and she was feeling very ill, and she could watch him just as well when sitting down in shelter.

She sat there dumbly watching as the low grey shape went forward to the mist on the horizon, holding the bottle on her knee. This was the end of it, the very, very end.

Presently she could see the submarine no longer; it had vanished in the mist. She looked at her little wrist watch; it showed one minute past ten. Her childhood religion came back to her in those last minutes; one ought to do something about that, she thought. A little alcoholically she murmured the Lord's Prayer.

Then she took out the red carton from her bag, and opened the vial, and held the tablets in her hand. Another spasm shook her, and she smiled faintly. 'Foxed you this time,' she said.

She took the cork out of the bottle. It was ten past ten. She said earnestly, 'Dwight, if you're on your way already, wait for me.'

Then she put the tablets in her mouth and swallowed them down with a mouthful of brandy, sitting behind the wheel of her big car.

A TOWN LIKE ALICE

It was in occupied Malaya where Jean Paget became inured to
illness, cruelty and death. Yet it was there that she first heard of
Alice Springs and fell in love with the gentle Australian and his
strange tales. Then something so terrible occurred she knew she
would never see Joe Harman again – or so she believed . . .

One of the best-loved of Nevil Shute's novels, *A Town Like Alice*
is his masterpiece of love, enterprise and triumph over the
ravages of war.

'Nevil Shute is an accomplished storyteller . . . He has
contrived a gripping novel of an English girl's courage and
unflagging faith in humanity' *The Scotsman*

'A very well told tale, bound to hold the attention of everyone
who reads it. Mr Shute is a born narrator, a talent enjoyed by
very few indeed' *Tatler*

REQUIEM FOR A WREN

Some years after the war has ended Alan Duncan decides to
return to the family farm in Australia. But his homecoming is
upset by the shocking suicide of his parents' much-loved maid.

Disturbed and puzzled, Alan finds that a long night's vigil at the
fireside unleashes his memories of wartime Britain – the
breathless weeks before D-Day, the tragic death of his brother
Bill, and above all, the unknown fate of Janet Prentice, the
brave but sensitive Wren who had been Bill's fiancée.

'A fine example of the work of the "Prince of
Storytellers" ' *Glasgow Herald*

'What a magnificent storyteller . . . his best novel since *A Town
Like Alice*' *Observer*

A Selected List of Classics Available from Mandarin

While every effort is made to keep prices low, it is sometimes necessary to increase prices at short notice. Mandarin Paperbacks reserves the right to show new retail prices on covers which may differ from those previously advertised in the text or elsewhere.

The prices shown below were correct at the time of going to press.

☐ 7493 0325 5	**Cannery Row**	John Steinbeck	£3.50
☐ 7493 0326 3	**East of Eden**	John Steinbeck	£4.99
☐ 7493 0327 1	**Grapes of Wrath**	John Steinbeck	£3.50
☐ 7493 0328 X	**Long Valley**	John Steinbeck	£3.50
☐ 7493 0329 8	**Once There Was a War**	John Steinbeck	£3.99
☐ 7493 0330 1	**The Pearl**	John Steinbeck	£2.50
☐ 7493 0331 X	**To a God Unknown**	John Steinbeck	£3.50
☐ 7493 0332 8	**Tortilla Flat**	John Steinbeck	£3.50
☐ 7493 0333 6	**Travels with Charley**	John Steinbeck	£3.99
☐ 7493 0334 4	**Log from Sea of Cortez**	John Steinbeck	£4.99
☐ 7497 0194 3	**The Red Pony**	John Steinbeck	£2.50
☐ 7493 0371 9	**The English Teacher**	R. K. Narayan	£3.99
☐ 7493 0370 0	**The Financial Expert**	R. K. Narayan	£3.99
☐ 7493 0305 0	**The Bachelor of Arts**	R. K. Narayan	£3.99
☐ 7493 0304 2	**The Dark Room**	R. K. Narayan	£3.99
☐ 7493 0461 8	**The Balkan Trilogy**	Olivia Manning	£6.99
☐ 7493 0414 6	**A Town Like Alice**	Neville Shute	£3.99
☐ 7493 0408 1	**On the Beach**	Neville Shute	£3.99
☐ 7493 0341 7	**Requiem for a Wren**	Neville Shute	£3.99
☐ 7493 0413 8	**No Highway**	Neville Shute	£3.99
☐ 7493 0412 X	**Trustee from the Toolroom**	Neville Shute	£3.99
☐ 7493 0410 3	**Slide Rule**	Neville Shute	£3.99

All these books are available at your bookshop or newsagent, or can be ordered direct from the publisher. Just tick the titles you want and fill in the form below.

Mandarin Paperbacks, Cash Sales Department, PO Box 11, Falmouth, Cornwall TR10 9EN.

Please send cheque or postal order, no currency, for purchase price quoted and allow the following for postage and packing:

UK   80p for the first book, 20p for each additional book ordered to a maximum charge of £2.00.

BFPO   80p for the first book, 20p for each additional book.

Overseas including Eire   £1.50 for the first book, £1.00 for the second and 30p for each additional book thereafter.

NAME (Block letters) ....

ADDRESS ....

....

....